IF
ONLY
YOU
KNEW

A Novel

Mags Storey

Kregel
Publications

If Only You Knew: A Novel
© 2009 by Mags Storey

Published by Kregel Publications, a division of Kregel, Inc., P.O. Box 2607, Grand Rapids, MI 49501.

All rights reserved. No part of this book may be reproduced, stored in a retrieval system, or transmitted in any form or by any means—electronic, mechanical, photocopy, recording, or otherwise—without written permission of the publisher, except for brief quotations in printed reviews.

The persons and events portrayed in this work are the creations of the author, and any resemblance to persons living or dead is purely coincidental.

All Scripture quotations are from the Holy Bible, New International Version®. Copyright © 1973, 1978, 1984 by International Bible Society. Used by permission of Zondervan. All rights reserved.

ISBN 978-0-8254-3895-0

Printed in the United States of America
09 10 11 12 13 / 5 4 3 2 1

ACKNOWLEDGEMENTS

THANK YOU to all of you who helped, pushed, and encouraged me during the writing process. I hope you know who you are. Thank you especially to Jenn, Sophia, and Bethan for helping me keep my spirits up. Thank you to NJ for going above and beyond. Thank you to Les for taking a chance on me. Thank you to Steve, Miranda, and all the other wonderful people at Kregel who helped bring this story to life.

Thank you to those of you who were Kevin in my life. Thank you to those who were Jo and Kat; Lisa, Nate, and Patrick; and especially Sam—wherever in the world you ended up. You challenged me to grow when I didn't want to and bore the brunt of my insecurities and lapses into immaturity. You showed me unbelievable friendship and more love than I ever dreamed imaginable. You helped me find a God worth believing in. I am forever in your debt.

Thank you to Michael, for your love, your strength, your sacrifice, your heroism, and your unfailing support. I could not have written this without you. And I love you more than words can say. Happy 10th.

Thank you, God, for being real. You gave it all to me. And now I give it all back to you.

CHAPTER ONE

PERHAPS I should have read something into the fact that when I first laid eyes on Sam some girl was yelling at him, and when I first met Kevin he nearly killed me.

There I'd been, minding my own business, wandering aimlessly down Silverpoint beach letting the sun soak into my limbs when—

"I hate you, Sam! You hear me? I hate you! I HATE you!"

This shrieking, high-pitched voice took over the air, and all of a sudden, my day got a lot more interesting.

"You are so arrogant, Sam!"

A beach bag went flying past my nose.

"And you're completely insane!"

A beach umbrella followed.

"You are the most self-centered, egotistical, controlling, annoying, irritating, idiotic guy I have ever met . . ."

A bleached blonde in a lurid, pink sarong was having a rather spectacular fight with her boyfriend on the beach.

". . . and I'd rather eat rusty nails than go out with you ever again! We're over, Sam! You hear that? Over!"

Make that ex-boyfriend.

"Traci . . ." Sam started to say, then ducked as a half-empty can of diet cola went flying by his head. "Traci . . ." he started again. "Look, why don't we just—"

"No, Sam! NO! For once you're going to stand there and listen to what I have to say!"

Fair enough. But the problem was they were sort of blocking my path.

Sam was standing on the road, beside his car. And Traci was busy jumping, and screaming, and stomping around on the beach. I really couldn't keep going without walking right between them, and risk getting hit by whatever Traci decided to hurl next, or making a spectacle of myself by either traipsing through the water or out onto the road to get around them. So I did the next best thing. I sat down and watched.

Of course I didn't let them know I was watching. Fortunately there was this massive blue and rust pickup parked right next to me, and the tailgate was down, so I climbed up and perched myself on the very edge and pretended I was waiting for someone.

I'd been carrying around this big, clunky tote bag that I'd found in the back of my cousin Kat's closet, because I'd kind of told her that I'd try looking for a job and I needed something to carry my pathetic excuse for a résumé around in. I plunked it next to me on the back of the truck and it promptly tumbled over and fell off. Not my smoothest moment. It bounced a couple of times on the rough cement before half disappearing from view under the tailgate. I winced. Kat was not exactly convinced that I was all that reliable, and borrowing her leather tote without asking and returning it with a couple dozen scuff marks probably wasn't going to help change her mind on that.

Luckily, Traci was too busy spitting out short, overused swear words to notice I existed.

But the guy she was yelling at noticed. Man, did he notice.

Sam cut his eyes over in my direction and glanced up at me through a shock of sandy brown hair, and I could feel this weird blush-like tingling spreading up my arms so I quickly bent over and pretended I was really focused on retying the long, flimsy laces I had on my sandals. The sandals were a typical gift from my mother—hypothetically on the cutting edge of fashion somewhere in the world, but incredibly uncomfortable and pretty impossible to wear. Should have just stuck to flip-flops.

When I looked up, Sam wasn't looking my way anymore.

Not that I blamed him. Traci was the type that guys consider good looking, in a very obvious way. Fake blonde, fake tan, long fake bubblegum nails. My mother would have loved Traci. My mother would have tried to clone me into Traci. My mother would have taken Traci shopping and tried to convince everyone that they were sisters, and then she would have come home and droned on and on about why, oh why, her miserable daughter Jo couldn't just be more like pretty little Traci.

You see, I was the big, embarrassing disappointment in my mother's life. You'd think her five failed marriages and string of useless boyfriends she brought home all my life would have rated somewhere on her regrets list. But no, to hear her tell it, everything that was wrong in life culminated in the fact her one and only daughter was an uninspiring, ridiculously tall beanpole of a teen with an uncontrollable mass of mud-colored hair.

In other words, there was no reason why Sam would be looking at me when he could be looking at Traci. Especially considering she was screeching, swearing, and waving her arms out in front of her like she was trying to swat mosquitoes while summoning an angry rain god.

But it kind of looked a little like Sam was fighting the urge to laugh. He had a great mouth, wide and expressive and curling up just a little at the side, like he was trying not to smile at her, but couldn't help it. He glanced over my way and raised one eyebrow, like a guy caught in some crazy scene that wasn't really him. I blushed and ducked down again.

Somehow I doubted Sam and Traci would be making up any time soon. But you never can tell about other people's relationships. Maybe they did this every Saturday. Is it a sign that you've been single too long when you find yourself getting jealous of someone else's relationship, even as it's ending in public humiliation?

I didn't have too long to ponder why some people were lucky enough to have someone to scream abuse at, because, suddenly, I heard the truck's engine turn over. For about half a second I found it almost funny—I mean, trust me to pick the one vehicle that was going to drive off mid-fight. But then the vehicle gave a little lurch, like someone was shifting gears, and I sort of fell off the back of the truck, just as the driver started backing up.

It's amazing how quickly you can get scared—I mean, good and totally terrified. But I was down there on the ground, looking up at those big wheels coming toward me, and I suddenly realized the driver didn't know I was there, and was going to back right over me. I'd seen someone get run over by a car once, and all I could think of was that that was going to be me.

I scrambled over the curb, barely avoiding getting squashed into the pavement. *Thunk thunk.* Unfortunately Kat's bag wasn't so lucky.

The truck stopped moving. I stood up slowly, a tight pain in my chest like someone had just stamped on my heart. I felt angry. I felt foolish. I felt scared. I felt furious. I felt like I had so much adrenaline pumping through my veins I was ready to rip that idiotic driver's head off and stuff it in whatever remained of Kat's tote.

The driver's side door opened. A guy got out. My world froze.

He was gorgeous. I mean really mind-meltingly good looking. It's not like I believed in love at first sight, but I swear I wouldn't have been surprised if the Beatles had suddenly materialized on the beach beside me and started singing sappy love songs, while a bunch of cartoon hearts flew around my head.

"Did . . . uh, did I hit something?" he said, striding past me.

I opened my mouth, but no words came out.

He was tall—at least six three and seriously lanky, with this wicked stylized black angel design on his shirt and a silvery cross pendant on a thick chain around his neck. Definitely the best looking guy I'd ever seen. And he was seriously annoyed.

"Did I hit something?" he said again, not really looking at me. "I thought I heard something clunk." He bent down and looked under the truck. "Didn't I?"

"Well, yeah sort of, but not really."

"What do you mean 'sort of'?" he snapped, getting down on one knee, and checking to make sure the muffler was still in one piece. He was muttering something under his breath. Like a prayer.

I have to admit I was pretty indignant. I mean this stupid, reckless driver had nearly smashed into me and now here he was too busy making sure every bolt on his ugly rust-bucket was still in place to even make sure I wasn't hurt.

"Well, you did nearly hit me," I shot back.

"Oh really?" he said, not turning around, with an edge I took to be defensiveness cutting through his voice. "I didn't see you in my rearview mirror."

"Well that's because I was sitting on your tailgate."

Oh crud. I started regretting those words the second they flew out of my mouth. But needless to say, thinking before speaking had never really been one of my strong suits.

"Well," the guy said, his voice dripping heavily with sarcasm, "in that case I guess maybe I am the one who should apologize." He straightened up. "Because heaven knows . . ." He turned to face me. "I . . . uh . . . I should . . . um . . ." His words trailed off, as his eyes slid from my face, down to Kat's bag at my feet. He was even better looking up close.

His eyes met mine again. They were a spectacularly clear shade of blue and he had the slightest sunburn across the bridge of his nose. A small, teasing smile flickered out onto his face. And for a long second, neither of us said anything.

"I am sorry," he said, finally, wiping his hands on his jeans. "You're OK though . . . Right?"

"Oh, absolutely," I nodded enthusiastically. "You . . . umm . . . you did kind of bump my cousin's bag a little bit. But it's fine," I added quickly.

To be honest I hadn't really assessed the damage, but I held the tote up in what I hoped was a reassuring way. It was pretty badly scuffed. But I was almost certain Kat would forgive me.

"I'm Kevin," he said, reaching for my hand.

"Jo."

We shook hands, very slowly.

"I . . . I feel so bad about the bag," Kevin said. "Can . . . can I get you a new one or something?"

I shook my head. "No. It's OK. Don't worry about it."

Kevin still wasn't letting go of my hand. He just kept shaking it up and down and grinning at me. He was looking kind of sheepish now.

"I . . . I'm sorry for losing it back there a bit," he said, biting his lip.

"No, I'm sorry for sitting on your truck," I said.

"Aww, don't worry about it," Kevin shrugged. "If you need to sit on my truck feel free to just go ahead."

Excuse me?

"I . . . um . . . some friends of mine are having a concert on the pier and I've got to go . . . ah . . . pick someone up." Kevin slid his hand away from mine. "Look, why don't you come and maybe . . . maybe we can get together and do something after?"

What could I say? It's not like I got asked out by a guy that cute every day. OK, ever.

"Sure. Sounds great."

"Great," he said, "I'll see you then." And the next thing I knew I was standing there on the pavement like some love-struck kid as he backed his truck up, waved through the window at me, and drove away. Oh boy. I definitely did not see that coming.

By the time I turned around again Traci was gone, and Sam was busy shoving the demolished remains of his day at the beach into the trunk of his car. When Sam saw me there he opened his mouth like he was going to say something to me, but I kind of gave him this little shrug and kept walking past him down the beach. The last thing I wanted to do was encourage the wrong guy. And from where I was standing, it seemed pretty clear that if I ever had to choose between Kevin and Sam, Sam was going to be the absolutely wrong guy for me to even think about getting mixed up with.

Not that I was any kind of relationship expert. In fact, if there ever was some great cosmic quiz in that kind of stuff I'd be the one using all three of my lifelines in the first five minutes and still end up walking away with the conciliatory toaster.

You see my mother's second husband was a guy called Gary. I was almost eleven when mom first brought him home, and thirteen when he left, but even though he was only in my life for a short period of time he was definitely my favorite. Mom wasn't into religion, but Gary was. Albeit in a do-your-own-thing, make-it-up-as-you-go-along kind of way. But Gary told me that there was a God somewhere looking out for me, and that I could pray to him if I wanted. And that kind of made me feel good. "Everything happens for a reason, Jo," he used to tell me, "everything." Yeah, except maybe me.

I figured Gary would have taken it as some sort of omen that on the very first weekend of my "whole new life" plan, I managed to not only nearly get run over, but also come within a few steps of getting impaled by a beach umbrella in the middle of someone else's fight. "You've got to learn to look deeper, Jo," he'd tell me. "You've got to ask if God is trying to tell you something." But I'd long ago given up on the idea that there was anyone up there who had any great message they wanted to impart to me. Not that a heavenly hello wouldn't have been nice. But I figured, if there was a God, he wasn't really that interested in talking to me.

Which might explain why, while every other girl in my graduating class had left high school with college plans, and summer jobs, and boyfriends lavishing them with congratulatory roses, I'd sort of stumbled out the door with no idea what I was going to do next, which is how I ended up stuck in Silverpoint living with my cousin Kat.

Not that I was complaining! There were far worse places I could've gotten stuck. Kat was about eight years older than me, twenty-six, and really amazing. She'd left Ottawa and moved up to cottage country about three years earlier to chase little woodland animals for a living. She was a wildlife vet. And Silverpoint wasn't a bad town, especially for those two weeks a year when it was actually warm enough to swim in the lake. It was all trees, and rocks, and cute little touristy stores that sold ice cream, and beaded jewelry, and those plastic shoes canoeists wear. It even had a beach and a pier of sorts. So all in all, I was ecstatic when Kat showed up at my graduation—the only family member who bothered to —and invited me to come stay with her for a while.

The only hitch was, I didn't have a job, and I kind of needed one because I knew the meager savings I'd managed to scrape together in grade twelve weren't going to last too long and I wasn't planning on living off my cousin's generosity forever.

So while I waited to join Kevin down at the pier, I wandered around every little tourist store and restaurant until I was sure I was going to see smiling plastic fish and tacky seashell jewelry in my dreams. But as every single job—even the part time ones— seemed to have already been sewn up months ago by someone related to the owner who knew better than to wait until the beginning of July before trying to find a job, I finally gave up and decided to head back to the beach.

The music had already started when I got down to the pier. (Actually, the pier just looked like a big, long dock attached to the boardwalk that had a small stage and a couple of snack stands on it, and a few dozen boats moored at the sides. But what do I know, it's not like Ottawa is bursting with piers.)

I wandered up through the crowded beach and joined the even bigger crowd on the pier. Not a bad turnout considering the "band" was actually just a couple about my age. The music wasn't half-bad though. It was actually pretty good. Kind of an alternative folky rock with a good kick to it. They were "Nate & Lisa" according to the flyers someone had taped around, and by jumping up and down I could just barely make out the two figures.

Nate was presumably the guy on guitar—big, bald, and black, in a crumpled white dress shirt with the sleeves shoved up and cool dark sunglasses. He was very good looking, in a rugged, brooding way, and eerily familiar looking too. Lisa was tiny, I mean barely five foot if that. She was Chinese and her spiky elfin black hair was splashed with fantastic red highlights. She was playing the keyboard and bouncing on her heels like a little, perky, rubber ball made of pure energy. She practically had the word *cute* tattooed across her. So I kind of hoped Nate was the "friend" Kevin had gone to pick up.

I had no idea how I was going to find Kevin in this crowd, and I'd kind of been hoping for something a lot more subtle than just hanging around afterward until everyone else had gone. It's not exactly easy to carefully arrange bumping into someone at the best of times—and it kind of helps if you can find the person to begin with.

I tried squeezing through the crowd a bit and finally ended up pressed against the side of the pier. I leaned against the wooden railing, looked down through the gaps in the planks at the water whishing away underneath my feet, when it suddenly hit me—even I could use a height advantage.

I pressed against the railing with my fingers. It seemed sturdy enough. I set Kat's bag down at my feet, backed against the lowest rail, and clutched the top one with my hands. It felt OK. I stepped up one more railing, sat down on the top rail, and looped my fingers in tighter. Definitely not the world's steadiest seat, and the rail beneath my feet kept spinning, which was not exactly comforting. But a few other people on the pier were trying it too, and at least I could sort of see over the crowd.

That's when I saw Sam, standing a few feet away, lounging against the snack hut. I didn't see any sign of shrieking-Traci anywhere though. I had to admit, Sam was kind of cute, in a golden retriever puppy kind of way. If Sam's hair hadn't been so shaggy, and he wasn't way too short, and if I hadn't already met Kevin, and of course if it wasn't so obvious Sam had recently been with someone else, I might have even considered him dating potential . . . for an off-night.

The music stopped and I was clinging on too tightly to try clapping. But then someone walked across the stage and handed Nate a bass. It was Kevin. He glanced my way, and I thought he saw me too because he seemed a bit flustered and paused a little as he stepped offstage. I gave him a very quick little wave, and he waved back, and for a while we just kind of smiled at each other. Then the music started up again.

Kevin pointed down to his feet, and mouthed something, but I couldn't figure out what it was. I shrugged. He waved again, mouthed slower this time, then pointed down at his feet. I didn't know what he was trying to say, but my best guess was that he was asking me to meet him over there, or saying that he was going to come over to me. But to be honest, he could have just been telling me that he was leaving because he hated my sandals. Bad charades during music concerts is not exactly one of my strong points.

Kevin went through the whole wave, mouth words, point down thing again, slower and more exaggerated. I was beginning to be afraid that he'd think I was horribly rude for not joining in. So I let go of the bar, stood up a little bit, started to wave and . . . Uh oh . . .

Yeah, you can see where this is going. The rail spun. I slipped. Fell. Backward. Off the pier. Through the air. Into the water. Not my best moment.

The water was wet and way too cold for July. My jean shorts instantly became twenty pounds heavier and clung to my thighs like sticky burlap. My hair plastered over my eyes like a mass of seaweed. My favorite sunglasses were probably halfway to the bottom already. But the sinking feeling in the pit of my stomach was the worst. The very worst.

I ducked my head back under the water and tried to push my hair out of my eyes as I came back up again. I hoped Kevin wasn't looking. I hoped he was. Either way I was sunk.

The music stopped. Voices were yelling on the pier. Faces crowded around the side.

Yes, ladies and gentlemen, I am the world's biggest idiot. Yes, yes, I am destined to be alone for all of eternity . . .

"AHHHH AAHHH AAHHHH . . ."

Suddenly the air was full of a long, dramatic Tarzan yell. The kind of yell that is normally reserved for ten-year-old boys trying to scare their sisters, or for badly drawn cartoons.

I looked up. There was a wild flailing of arms and legs as someone catapulted off the pier and landed beside me in a dramatic splash. As if my day could have gotten more surreal. For a split second I entertained the fantasy that Kevin had sprinted through the crowd, shoving people aside, vaulting over the edge to my aid.

"Hey, how's it going?"

It was Sam. He'd surfaced, spluttering, a few feet away from me and was now treading water with an inane grin on his face.

"I . . . I don't need to be rescued."

"Good," he said, "because I didn't really want to drag you to shore. Even though they do say that adrenaline can make people do freaky things."

Sam turned toward the pier and waved both arms above his head. "Hey, hear that everybody? We're fine! Nobody needs to be rescued! We're going to swim to shore now! Go back to your concert!"

Slowly faces disappeared back over the railing and after a few moments the music started up again. Then he turned back to me. "Hi. I don't believe we've been formally introduced," he said.

"My name is Sam. Samuel James Underwood to be exact. And you are?"

"I'm Jo," I said. Then suspecting he was expecting something more added, "Uh . . . Joanna Mackenzie." For a moment I was tempted to swim closer and try to shake hands.

Sam grinned again. His shaggy hair was plastered down around his face like a soaked sheep dog. "Nice to meet you, Jo."

"Thanks."

This was a whole new level of weirdness. Or at least it should have been. Sam was just smiling away casually like he was standing at a party instead of floating in the lake, and there was something almost infectious about it.

"Did you know that according to psychologists most people's number one fear is public embarrassment?" Sam said lightly. "Death is only number two. So, maybe dying of embarrassment wouldn't be all that bad. In fact, research suggests that the main factor in whether horribly embarrassing situations cripple your psyche permanently is whether or not you have someone to share them with . . ."

So he was a little weird. OK, make that a lot weird. But at least he was in the water voluntarily.

"Look . . ." I started, "umm . . . thanks for uh . . . you know . . . trying to save my psyche."

"Any time," Sam said. "You were looking a bit lonely and I figured you could use the company. I would have joined you sooner but I thought I'd better kick my shoes off first." He dove down under water and came up a few feet closer. "As much fun as this is, do you mind if we swim to shore?"

Then without waiting for an answer, he rolled onto his side and started a slow crawl toward the beach. My feet had fallen out of my sandals, but the laces were still tangled tightly around my ankles. After several ungraceful kicking attempts I didn't have any luck at either getting them off or back onto my feet. So I curled my toes in a death grip and managed to propel myself forward in a cross between a frog kick and a wounded giraffe. It probably would be considered rude to drown yourself on a first date.

Sam talked the whole way back to shore. By the time I felt solid earth beneath my feet again I'd learned that Sam had also just finished high school and that he was going to college in Ashford in September. In the meantime he had his own little part-time business making Web sites for local companies, which he ran out of an apartment he shared with his sister. I have to admit I was kind of impressed. But I didn't let it show.

"Voila! Back on dry land!" Sam pronounced, throwing himself backward onto the beach.

Climbing up the sand beside him, things suddenly got awkward. I would have felt rude walking away and I kind of wanted to sit in the sun until I felt a little less soggy. But, the last thing I wanted was to encourage a guy who had a scary ex in the picture. Then again, as Gary used to say, everything happens for a reason . . .

"Sit! Sit and dry off a bit." Sam waved his hand at the patch of sand beside him like he'd been reading through my thoughts. "I'm not going to ask you out. I promise this was not some elaborate pick-up scheme. I have absolutely no intention of flirting with you and I would have jumped in the water after you even if you weren't good looking. I won't even ask for your phone number."

I could feel myself starting to blush. Fortunately I was wearing a black T-shirt so even though my jean shorts were clutching my legs for dear life, it wasn't as bad as it could have been. I tentatively pushed my fingers through my tangled mass of hair.

After a quick mental guesstimate of exactly how many millimeters of sand away from Sam was close enough to be friendly without being so close as to be more than friendly, I sat down next to him, stretched my legs out in front of me, and started trying to free my feet from my sandals.

"So come on, Jo, what's your story?" Sam said, lying back in the sand. He stretched his neck like a tired cat, put his hands behind his head, and closed his eyes. "What brought you to Silverpoint?"

Aha. See, I had kind of been hoping Sam wasn't going to ask that. Because here was this guy who seemed to have his entire life together—job, university, place to live, life goals—and what did I have? Nothing. I was crashed out at Kat's place with no clue what I was going to do next. I was so lost it was pathetic.

I mean, sure Sam's love life was in total shambles, but considering the fact I'd been on four first dates in the past year, and no second dates, it's not like I had anything to brag about.

"I just finished high school," I said, with a shrug. "My cousin lives here and we're kind of close, so I thought I'd move here and look for a job, or decide about school, or come up with a plan, or something . . ."

Man, it sounded even more pathetic out loud.

Sam nodded. "And you think you're going to find that here?"

My left sandal seemed to have melded itself onto my leg. I snapped the laces in half and threw it down the beach in disgust.

"Look," I said, "can we just skip the whole 'what are you going to do with the rest of your life' thing?"

"Sure," Sam rolled over onto his side and blinked up at me. "How about we play 'guess what's wrong with me' instead?" He grinned wickedly.

I laughed. So did he.

"I'll go first," Sam rolled onto his back again, and propped himself up on his elbows. "Just so happens I broke up with the love of my life this afternoon . . . and don't pretend you didn't notice." He shot me a sideways glance. "I definitely noticed you noticing."

Ignoring his gaze, I looked down at my feet and pretended I was really busy trying to untie the other sandal.

"The whole beach noticed," Sam went on, saving me from trying to deny it. "People on the moon noticed! Traci is not exactly the shy and quiet kind. But the relationship has been basically over for a long time, so I'm not exactly devastated over it."

Sam certainly wasn't acting like someone who had just been dumped, but still for all I knew he was deep in denial and still longing for Scary Girl. "How long had you and um . . . Traci been together?" I asked.

"Since we were almost fifteen. So three years and a bit, on and off . . ." Sam shrugged. "Very on and off."

"And . . . were you close?" I knew I sounded like a bad talk-show host. But I didn't know what I was supposed to be saying and I figured he might need to talk about it.

"Oh please!" Sam exclaimed, sitting up straight. "What's with the polite questions? Just say what you think! Just say something real like 'How on earth did you two ever get together in the first place?'"

"Yeah. OK."

A cloud moved over the sun. Sam stopped smiling. A cooler breeze cut through my damp T-shirt. I shivered.

"Well, fine," Sam said. "We met on this beach. I thought she was cute, and crazy, and strong, which I thought was awesome considering the useless fluffy-minded girls that went to my school. She had attitude and didn't let me get away with stuff. I liked that." He sounded defensive, almost angry. "We went to different schools which was how we lasted the first two years. And then we broke up. And then we got back together. And then we broke up again and I stupidly considered giving her yet another chance.

"And now it's over. Finally, 100 percent, no going back, point of no return—over. In fact," he stretched his arms up over his head, "I swear to God, if you are still up there and you still give a care what happens to me, then you have my permission to do whatever it takes to make sure I don't ever date that demented shrew again. And if I am ever even tempted to do so, I pray that whoever happens to be up there listening will send someone down here to knock some sense into me."

I just sat there, wanting to hug him, or pinch him, or do something to snap him back into the nice guy I was chatting with just a few seconds ago. I think Sam must have seen the look on my face, because he shook his head like he was getting water out of his ears. He smiled at me again, and this time it was a lot more real.

"So, who was the last guy to break your heart?" Sam asked.

I sighed. "I don't know. Dom I think. He was the artistic type." Sam nodded.

"We were sort of friends. Had some classes together. He was

always telling me he liked me and I didn't believe him. Then one night he had a party at his house and one thing led to another and, well we sort of got together."

"What happened?"

"I don't know. It was really great at first. But I think he was the kind of guy who basically just liked the chase, if you know what I mean. Anyway, we went out for a couple of weeks and then he said he wanted to date other people."

"Which meant he already was?" Sam said.

"Yeah."

"Sorry."

"Thanks."

"Traci is self-destructing," Sam said quietly. "She's into party-ing, big time. And Silverpoint is not exactly bursting with decent places to hang out on a Friday night. But I guess she figures if she gets drunk enough, fast enough, she won't notice."

I didn't know what to say. Sam's hand was sitting there, half buried in the sand beside me and something inside me just wanted to reach over and squeeze it, and to let him know that I even understood, in a way. In fact, I was beginning to wonder if I had misjudged him a bit, when Sam threw me a curve ball.

"So," he said, very casually, "tell me honestly, were you ter-ribly disappointed when you realized that I was the one jumping in after you, and not blond-tufty-God-boy?"

"You mean Kevin?" I said. Like I was going to answer that. "Do you know him?"

Sam shook his head. "No. Only that he apparently doesn't know how to use his rearview mirror."

"Look, don't joke about stuff like that!" I said, a little more indignantly than I'd intended. "Have you ever seen anyone get hit by a car? It's not something you laugh about!"

Sam's face turned serious for a second. "No, I haven't," he said soberly, "but my sister Mandy's a paramedic and I know she's seen some really rough stuff from accidents on the highway." He reached over and gave my arm a little, friendly squeeze. "Do you know anyone who's been in a car accident?"

I shook my head. "No, but I saw one once. It was last year,

when I was visiting my cousin. End of August. I think the guy died. It kind of messed me up for a bit."

Sam's eyes were on my face, and I was finding it hard to meet his gaze. "Maybe you can tell me about it sometime," he said finally.

"Maybe," I said quietly. "Anyway, you saw me talking to Kevin earlier?" I added quickly, more than ready to change the subject to something a little cheerier.

"Yeah, I saw your magical moment earlier," Sam said. He yawned as if the memory of Kevin was boring him into a coma. "I just hope my splashing heroics didn't permanently ruin your chance at eternal happiness."

"Kevin seemed really nice." I heard myself saying, sounding far more defensive than I intended to.

"Yeah, I'm sure he is nice," Sam said, emphasizing the word as though niceness was a fatal plague. "Most religious people are."

That one stumped me. "How do you know he's religious?"

"You didn't know?" Sam said, with a muffled laugh. "Nate and Lisa are a church group. 'Worship leaders' or whatever they call them. They're from a big church up on the hill. I think they do events in a restaurant-type place on the waterfront too. You know, sing a few songs, try to snag a few gullible ones. I take it you're not into church?"

"Uh . . . no," I nearly choked, "not at all."

"Do you believe in God?" Sam said.

"What? No." Not really. Well, sort of. But it's not like I ever really thought about it much.

"What about you?" I threw back at him quickly. "You into God?"

Sam shook his head. "Haven't found a God worth believing in."

"How about church?"

That seemed to knock him back one. "No," Sam said quietly. "I used to go to church. Every Sunday. But it didn't seem to work for me. My sister Mandy goes to church though. She's really into it and met her fiancé Brian there. They're getting married soon. So when I saw her church, Cornerstone, was having a concert I thought I'd wander over and check it out."

Nate and Lisa picked that very moment to end the concert with a rousing flourish. I think I must have glanced back at the pier longingly because the next thing I knew Sam was practically insisting I go back up there and talk to Kevin. My clothes were still damp, and I hated to think what my makeup must look like.

"Yeah right," I grabbed hold of Sam's wrist and let him pull me up. "Looking like this?" I asked. "Are you insane?"

Sam put his hands on my shoulders. He looked me up and down, shaking his head like he was a fashion designer, about to send me down the catwalk. "You don't look that bad. Honestly," he said. He pushed some of my hair down and then pulled it back up again. Then brushed his fingers hard against the side of my face. I wondered if this was how cats feel when they're being groomed by six-year-olds. "You definitely look like . . . you went swimming in your clothes," he said slowly, like he thought he was being helpful. "But, all things considered, I think it gives you a kind of wholesome, outdoorsy look."

I pulled away. "Forget it!" I said, with a little laugh, which didn't sound anywhere near as natural as I hoped it would.

"You are going to go over there and talk to him," Sam said firmly. "It's not every day you meet someone on the beach you think you could fall in love with."

I didn't know why Sam was suddenly so darn eager that I go talk with Kevin, but before I knew it he had his hand under my arm and was almost forcibly propelling me back toward the pier. "Believe me," he added, "this'll make you look like you're some interesting person with a fabulous sense of humor. Guys like that."

Did they? I wasn't convinced. But I figured that since Kevin had been undeniably adorable, and because Sam seemed in a hurry to get rid of me, I had nothing to lose by heading over to the pier and seeing if I could strike up a conversation with Kevin. I had to go back for Kat's tote anyway. I swept up the remains of my sandals into one hand, and let Sam lead me upstream through the crowd of people heading off the pier.

"Go on," Sam said. He gave me a little push on the back. "And don't worry, if it all ends in disaster, I'll be waiting on the beach."

So not exactly a huge vote of confidence.

There were a few people left mingling and the stage was being dismantled. I spotted Kevin almost right away. He was standing at the far end, talking to Nate, Lisa, and a couple of other guys.

I found Kat's bag where I'd left it, and I dumped my shoes inside. Then I leaned against the railing in what I hoped looked like a casual and carefree way, hoping Kevin would notice I was there and come over.

I didn't know what I was going to say, but I was usually better off shooting from the hip than trying to come up with something beforehand. Hopefully I'd come up with something kind of cute and funny and he'd ask me out. But if that didn't work I could say that Sam had put me up to it, and then try to swing a pity date.

It was kind of nice to be able to just stand there and watch Kevin without him noticing I was there. It gave me a chance to sort of see him in his natural habitat. Kevin and Nate were piling equipment onto a trolley. Nate made like he was going to pick Lisa up and pile her on top of the equipment. She giggled and pushed him away. Kevin rolled his eyes and flicked at them with a cable. Nate grinned.

The funny thing about Nate was that he looked so incredibly familiar.

While I would have hated to admit it to Sam, Kevin had a kind of "good boy" cuteness about him. Like a Boy Scout, or a Mountie. Maybe it was the short, blond hair, because even though he dressed a tiny bit like a bad boy (in a very good way), Sam's whole "God-boy" label still stuck to the way I saw Kevin somehow. I mean, it was just too easy to imagine him tipping an imaginary hat and saying, "Don't worry, ma'am, I'll find your lost kitty."

But Nate . . . Nate was hot in a totally different way. He was intimidatingly good looking. The kind that came from strength. I'll admit the bald head was part of it, but it was far more than that. It was the cut of his shoulders. It was the way he crossed his arms over his chest. I don't know what I expected church people to look like, but I had never imagined they could look anything like Nate. No, Nate looked like the kind of guy who should have been a movie action star, or a fierce business executive, or a three star general, or the bodyguard for someone really important. He just had that look. That look that said "you don't want to cross me."

And he looked very, very familiar. I was sure I'd seen him before. I just couldn't place it. But somehow, I knew it . . .

Nate looped a length of cable around his arm, and then started winding the rest of it up in a coil, whipping it around his arm so quickly that when Lisa accidentally stepped on it he nearly pulled her off her feet. Lisa squeaked, and Nate reached out and wrapped his free arm around her, pulling her into his side in an apologetic half hug. She nestled into his side, like a kitten cuddling against a wolf.

Kevin pushed a flatbed trolley of equipment toward them, pretending he was going to run them over. Kevin pulled up short, but the trolley slipped out of his hands and kept rolling. Nate let go of Lisa. Dropped the cable. Stepped forward with his arms out. Caught the weight of the trolley into his chest.

And then I knew. Like a cold chill spreading up my arms and across my body. I knew where I'd seen Nate before. And it was a bad memory. An extremely bad memory.

"Hey Jo?"

All of a sudden Sam was standing beside me. "Hey Jo, I was thinking that if you needed a wing-man we could go up and talk to Kevin together . . ."

Sam's voice trailed off, his eyes searching my face.

"You OK, Jo?" Sam asked softly, bending his head toward mine. "You look like you've seen a ghost."

I shook my head.

"You know I told you I saw someone get run over last summer?" I said, my voice catching in my throat.

Sam nodded.

"I don't think he's dead . . ."

Chapter Two

I DREADED to think what Sam must be thinking of me. Within a few hours of meeting him I'd already nearly gotten myself run over, fallen off the pier, and then announced that I'd once seen someone try and kill the very-much-alive worship leader at his sister's church. Not my most impressive day, I must admit.

At best Sam probably figured I was a total loon, but at least a slightly loopy distraction from his major fallout with Traci. And at worst? Well . . . let's just say I didn't want to know.

But Sam did drive me home. He had a decent car too. Silver and kind of sporty without being over the top. To be honest, I'm not sure how I would have made it back to Kat's if he hadn't caught me by the arm when I stumbled back off the pier and steered me toward his car.

Recognizing Nate like that was so unreal that it seemed to have temporarily wiped anything useful out of my mind. I was numb. Totally numb. I know I should have felt relieved, elated, mystified, stupefied, something, anything. But it was like my brain had gone searching madly through its database for "what to do when you realize that the guy who you saw get smashed into the pavement last summer is in fact alive, well, and friends with the hottie who just asked you out," and having come up with nothing, my brain decided to shut down entirely.

Kat lived over an empty store on a main shopping street. It was an amazing two-story apartment with a big, long living room on the main floor, three tiny bedrooms on the top floor, and a fenced-in garden out back. If you stood on the dining table and turned your head at just the right angle you could even sort of see the lake. So, it was kind of possible to pretend we lived in some funky, modern loft, instead of being sandwiched between a hairdresser and a travel agent.

I shoved the door open and was assailed almost immediately

by the smell of something hot and fudgey. Kat baked, I mean seriously baked. She didn't just throw eggs and flour and milk into a bowl and come up with chocolate chip cookies or banana loaf like everyone can. (Well, I couldn't, but I had it on good authority that every guy I've ever dated had an ex-girlfriend who could.) My cousin created things with chocolate. Amazing, gooey, nutty, good-enough-to-get-you-over-your-lousy-cheating-ex-boy-friend-type things.

Kat was curled up on the sofa with Buddy, her beagle puppy. I yanked an afghan off the back of one of her oversized chairs, wrapped it around myself, and then collapsed on the sofa beside her.

"There's chocolate caramel macadamia nut fudge in the kitchen," Kat told me, "and I bought a new cappuccino maker today, turned out pretty good for my first try." She lifted her mug in my direction. If there is a heaven, I hope they put Kat in charge of hospitality. If I had to sum up my cousin in one word it would be "distinctive." If you let me add a few more I'd throw in "warm," "colorful," and maybe "supersized" if I knew she'd never see the list.

"So, how was the beach?" Kat asked.

I shrugged. "It was OK. Fudge sounds great though."

Kat blew on her coffee. "In other words, you haven't found a job, but you have met a guy?"

Yeah, that's right, as if having a date-obsessed mother wasn't enough, now it seemed my cousin thought I couldn't take a simple walk on the beach without picking up a guy.

"Actually, I met two."

Kat smiled. "So, what are they like?"

"One's still hung up on his psychotic ex. The other is cuter and ran over your tote bag."

"Ran over my bag?" Kat jumped off the sofa, and her voice did this high-pitched squeaky thing. I quickly realized I should have thought half a second about how to tell her before just blurting it out.

So we went to assess the damage, and I said I was really, really sorry and Kat kind of sighed and said not to worry about it, and I said I'd replace it, and Kat said she never used it anyway. We went round and round in the same I'm-sorry-don't-worry-about-it loop a few dozen times, until Kat asked me why I looked like I'd just gone swimming in my clothes. So I tried to explain about doing sign-language calisthenics with Kevin and falling off the pier. By the time I got through trying to explain that Sam had only jumped in to save me from embarrassment and wasn't trying to either save my life or pick me up, Kat was laughing so hard I knew we really were OK.

Fortunately, the whole bag flattening fiasco had served to distract Kat from asking me about my job search, which was a good thing because I had no clue what I was going to tell her. The fact of the matter was I hadn't really been looking forward to spending my entire summer elbow deep in someone else's dirty dishes or learning how to fold little boutique sweaters into perfect rectangles. Not that I wanted to just sit around and do nothing indefinitely either. Well, part of me did, but only in a won-the-lottery manner, not a taking-advantage-of-your-cousin's-kindness kind of way.

I stuffed two pieces of fudge into my mouth and headed upstairs to the bathroom. My reflection in the mirror was truly terrifying—my mascara had streaked across my cheeks, my clothes were stretched and caked in dirt, my hair looked like it had just been through the washing machine on spin cycle. I made a mental note to never trust Sam again when he said I looked fine.

I peeled my clothes off, then climbed into the bathtub and sat there while it slowly filled with water. My cousin had the kind of bathroom you could soak in for hours—terracotta pots, blue glass beads, long green leafy things, bamboo screens, and a huge old-fashioned claw-foot tub. It was the perfect place to try and forget I had no job, no life, and that the first seriously cute guy to ask me out for ages had seen me fall off a pier.

Oh, and that I might just be going crazy.

I filled the tub so full that I couldn't move without sloshing water on the floor, then I laid back and thought about Nate.

I had never really told anyone that I'd seen someone get run over by a car. Kat knew, because she was there at the time. Kat was the one who calmed me down and helped me report everything to the police. But I'd never really talked about the accident with Kat much. I wasn't sure why, it just didn't seem like an easy thing to talk about.

I'd tried telling a couple of friends at school when I got back to Ottawa, but either their eyes would glaze over and they'd change the subject, or they'd ask stupid sensationalist questions about whether I thought it was done on purpose—I did—and whether there was a lot of blood—there wasn't.

But mostly I didn't talk about it. I especially never told my mother. Because no one seemed to get it. Seeing someone get hit by a car isn't a cool thing—it's a terrifying thing, a scary thing, a life-changing thing. And most of all a frustrating thing because it forces you to be a spectator in someone else's disaster and to know you can't do a single thing about it. Especially if you think the person died—which I did. So I never talked to anyone about it. Except maybe God.

I didn't know if God was listening. In my mind's eye I kind of saw God as this super busy business executive, like my mother's fourth husband, sitting behind his huge desk, absentmindedly clicking through his over-full e-mail inbox, with his six phones ringing at once, and a dozen angels hovering over his shoulder wanting to talk to him about very important things—like wars and diseases. And there was me, with my little squeaky voice, standing there in front of him, eclipsed by the important chaos of it all. In my imagination, this God never looked my way, or paid much attention to me, but somehow I hoped that maybe the fact I even tried to show up would count for something. Like maybe later, some very minor angel would note my name in the guest-book, and smile.

§ § §

"Hey Jo. Wake up! There's a guy here to see you!"

Yeah right, like that was going to work. It was Sunday morning and I was curled up in bed, with the duvet over my head. Kat and I had stayed up late the night before, eating popcorn and watching bad '80s movies and now I was planning to sleep in for at least another hour, maybe two if I was lucky. I'd tried to explain to Kat that just because she liked to bounce out of bed at the proverbial crack of dawn didn't mean she should expect me to make an appearance before noon, and all the freshly baked muffin smells in the world weren't going to change that. And now my daybreak-loving cousin seemed to think that if food wouldn't get me out of bed, something else would. Ha! Just because she wasn't above pretending there was some guy at the door to see me, didn't mean that I was about to budge from . . .

Then I heard a laugh—a distinctly male laugh—and then the sound of Buddy barking and the front door slamming shut. Oh drat.

I sprinted through a shower, flung on a T-shirt and my most comfortable jean shorts, and forced my unruly hair into a braid. Then I sauntered down the stairs in what I hoped looked like an air of carefree indifference, but to my disappointment the living room was empty.

I found Kat in the kitchen, alone. "Awake and alive at 10:38 AM, must be a new record." Kat took an overly long sip of her coffee, then added casually, "Sam's here. He's outside with Buddy."

I grabbed a muffin. "And since when do you let Buddy play with strangers?"

"Your friend has a trustworthy face or something," Kat said lightly, "but if you see an ear or a tail missing I suppose you'll let me know." She was enjoying this way too much. "Remind me, which one is Sam?"

"The one with the psychotic ex."

"So the one you're not interested in?"

"Right."

"Does he know that?"

I made a face at her.

I put my hand on the door to go outside, and then hesitated. "My mother hasn't called, has she?" I asked.

Kat looked down at the mug in her hands, and I knew the answer even before she opened her mouth. No, of course my mother hadn't called. I'd left her another message on her answering machine before I went to bed last night. My sixth so far. God only knows why I bothered.

"You've only been here a week," Kat said lamely. "She probably thinks you're so busy you don't want . . ."

I snorted and pushed past her outside. I'd been making excuses for my mother for so many years, I certainly didn't need her help doing it.

Kat had this wicked wooden patio with stairs leading down to the back garden. Technically, I guess, we must have shared the garden with the empty store below us, but Kat acted like she owned it. Sam was down in the grass on all fours, growling at Buddy. The seemingly intact puppy was barking back playfully and nipping at his fingers. I walked down to the garden and sat on the bottom step.

I could guess why Sam was there—he must want to talk to me about Nate's car accident. Not that I could blame him really. But that didn't mean I was looking forward to talking about it.

"Hello Sam."

Sam looked up and smiled this wide, lopsided grin. "Hey you," he said.

"Looks like you've made a friend."

"Buddy's cool," Sam said. He reached over and scratched Buddy's head. "My parents never let me have a dog. They're not really dog people . . . or even kid people for that matter. More look-at-how-much-money-I-can-make people."

Sam stood up and made a half-hearted attempt at brushing the grass off his jeans. He was wearing a rumpled yellow T-shirt with a moose pattern on it. Someone needed to teach this guy how to dress.

"Hope you don't mind my dropping by like this . . ." Sam started, sitting down next to me. I braced myself for what was coming next but instead he just said, "but I think I've found blond-tufty-God-boy for you."

"Kevin?" Is it pathetic to admit my heart leapt a bit when he said that?

"Yeah, his friends are playing a gig in town tonight and I was wondering if you and your cousin wanted to come with . . ."

OK, so that was not what I was expecting. Was Sam really some closet romantic or was he just buttering me up with something he thought I wanted in the hope I'd dish the dirt about seeing someone run over Nate? Don't get me wrong, I was definitely, definitely interested in seeing Kevin again, but still . . .

"I know you didn't end up hooking up with Kevin yesterday, but that could be a good thing, because this way you've got this air of mystery about you." Sam babbled on, "and even if things don't work out between the two of you, it still might be a fun night out and you could always meet someone else, or . . ."

"Is this about Nate?" I cut him off.

Sam sat back like I'd just punched him in the nose. "Nate? Nate the musician? I thought you liked Kevin."

OK, so if Sam kept on this way he really would end up getting punched in the nose.

"Is what about Nate?" Sam said again.

I sighed. "Is this about the fact I told you yesterday that I'd seen someone run over Nate with a car?"

Sam couldn't have looked more puzzled if he tried. "You saw someone run over Nate?"

"I told you I did!" I snapped, beginning to feel more than a little foolish. "Yesterday, when we were on the pier I told you that I'd seen someone run over Nate!"

"You told me you'd seen *someone* get run over by a car," Sam said defensively. "And I remember you said you thought he was dead, and then later said you thought he might not be dead—"

"Isn't dead!" I corrected him sharply.

"Fine. Isn't dead," Sam repeated back. "But you didn't give me a name, and you didn't want to talk about it, and I figured you wouldn't appreciate me pushing you about it."

That took me aback. Had I really not told him it was Nate? I pressed my palms up against my forehead.

"Do you *want* to talk about it?" Sam said, his voice still on edge.

"No! I don't!" I snapped.

Sam let out an exaggerated sigh. "Look, I was only trying to be a nice guy because I thought you might like to go out tonight. But if you don't—"

"No," I cut him off. "I mean, yeah, it sounds great. I'll talk to Kat and I'm sure we'll go."

I wasn't really sure what I was promising, but by that point I was so desperately eager to change the subject to something—anything—that I would have agreed to almost anything if it meant a new topic of conversation.

"OK then," Sam said, grinning a little. "Then maybe I'll see you there."

I managed a weak smile back. "Sure," I said, "sounds like fun."

"Great," Sam said happily. "I've got to warn you though, my sister Mandy and her fiancé Brian are coming too, and the concert is being run by Cornerstone Church, so there's always a chance it'll be pretty religious."

I could hardly wait.

Sam stood. "I've got to run. There's a new cell phone store opening up in town and I'm going to put some draft Web site ideas together for them, and maybe if I'm lucky they'll get me to do a site for them." I nodded.

"Well, maybe I'll see you later then," Sam continued. He started toward our back gate, then paused.

"Umm . . . Jo?"

"Yeah?"

"About what you said about Nate?"

"I don't want to talk about it. And I didn't see anything," I lied quickly. "So don't tell anyone I did."

Sam nodded his head slowly, his jaw moving like he was trying to swallow what I'd just said. "OK," he said. "I won't."

And, strangely, I believed him.

The good news was that Kat thought the event sounded like fun. The bad news is she asked me how the job search was going. So I told her things were going well—big lie—and that I expected to find a job very soon—bigger lie—and that I was going to spend the afternoon looking for a job—unfortunately true. I didn't like lying to Kat. In fact I felt downright guilty and wretched about it. I'd never liked lying, yet somehow I still ended up doing it way too often. Yet another reason why a guy like Kevin wouldn't want to go out with someone like me. But it's not like I thought I had any choice in the matter. I didn't want Kat to kick me out because I didn't want to go back to live with my mom, and I didn't think Kat would be willing to keep me around if I was going to stay useless.

It was Sunday, so it was pointless to pound the proverbial pavement looking for a job. Not that I'd had much luck doing it on Saturday either. I decided to polish my résumé, search the want ads, and maybe even send off a few applications. At least, that was the plan.

"Scouring the local newspaper" took five minutes flat. Did I want to be a part-time dry-cleaner? A part-time sandwich maker? Or maybe try a "challenging, hands on position" at the local cemetery? I moved on to my résumé, which was equally depressing. Actually more so, because I couldn't even pretend it was going to look any better tomorrow. I had spent a couple of months waitressing—but I hated it—and the few other things I had tried, like answering phones and selling magazine subscriptions, hadn't really worked for me either. To be totally honest, I kind of wanted to go to college and learn how to do something interesting and practical. I just didn't know what yet.

When Kat knocked at quarter to five, sixteen drafts of my résumé were flung across the room, along with the newspaper—which was still hopeless, no matter how many times I "just checked again"— and the entire contents of my wardrobe. I'd had the disastrous idea of trying to find the perfect outfit for the night that would make Kevin fall head over heels in love with me—or that would at least just cheer me up. I was sitting on the floor, in the middle of it all. I felt like crying.

"It's official, Kat," I said, "I'm hopeless. Completely hopeless."

"I'm sure you're not completely hopeless," Kat said. She handed me the shirt she was carrying. It was this gorgeous navy and white flowered tank top. Freshly washed. Newly ironed. In other words, it was Kat's. It was really tight on her, so of course totally loose fitting on me. But layered over the right strappy top with a pair of jean shorts and my favorite wedges it would be perfect for tonight.

"You were going to wear this, weren't you?" I said, pulling it on.

Kat shrugged. "I just got a call, I'm going to need to pop into the clinic later tonight. So I'm going to wear something else."

Now, if you knew Kat, you'd have known this was her way of trying to be nice, without making me feel guilty about it. I exaggerated a little when I said Kat chased woodland animals for a living. She did do field work but most of the time she worked out of an animal shelter, which took normal animals—like dogs and cats—but specialized in exotics—like squirrels and chipmunks. Sometimes Kat was on call, and occasionally she did work nights when there was some little animal in the shelter who needed to be watched. But Kat could have worn her shirt to work, if she'd wanted to. She was just a much nicer person than I was.

And she helped me clean up my room. And when I complained that I couldn't find a job, she told me all the right things like "don't worry, I'm sure something will come up." And she said nice soothing things about how I looked fine and that she was looking forward to getting to know "the new guy in your life," and just smiled knowingly when I tried to tell her that Kevin wasn't actually "in my life" yet. She even dug my brush out from under a pile of clothes and braided my hair into a French braid that almost went down to my waist.

And I wanted to yell at her, "If someone as great as you is still single, what hope is there for me?"

But instead I just vowed that I'd sort my life out tomorrow.

§ § §

The Ugly Pug looked more like a restaurant than a church building. According to Kat it used to be just a cool-looking place with bad tasting food until Cornerstone bought it and started using it for events and stuff. We could hear the music from the street, softer rock mingled with jazz.

Nate and Lisa were playing on a small curtained stage at the far end of the room. Ceiling-mounted spotlights cast a gentle glow on a bright mural of deserts and oceans. It was surreal.

About sixty people were gathered in the small room. Many

were sitting around tables. A few were mingling. But only one jumped to his feet and waved his arms at us like a broken windmill.

"Isn't this place awesome?" Sam said, pulling out chairs for both Kat and I before he sat down again. "The music only started fifteen minutes ago, so you haven't missed much." I gave Sam a slight, friendly hug, and he added in a mock-whisper, "I haven't seen Kevin yet."

Then Sam shook Kat's hand telling her, "It's excellent to see you again," and, "Why say 'nice' when I don't mean 'nice'?" Then he introduced us to his sister Mandy and his "almost-brother-in-law" Brian.

Brian was solid; friendly, but not much of a talker. Mandy was a little taller than Sam and she had long, auburn hair cascading around her shoulders. Her eyes were even a brighter shade of green than Sam's. There was something incredibly likeable about Mandy. It turned out she and Kat kind of knew each other, or at least they'd met through work—Mandy was a paramedic with Ashford Hospital and by the sounds of things one of the guys at Kat's work could be a bit accident-prone around animal traps. Kat asked Mandy something about wedding plans and the next thing I knew Mandy was off, talking about tulle and tulips at twenty miles an hour.

Sam pulled his chair up close to mine and leaned in toward me. "I'm glad you made it," he said in a low voice. "I don't think I could have taken one more second of wedding-planning mania." But I could tell by the way he smiled at his sister that he was only being half serious.

He waved a plate of cookies in my direction. "The nice· religious people have provided some pretty wicked food," he grinned. "Guess they're going to try to lure us in with the sweet stuff."

I shot a sideways glance at Mandy but she just smiled mildly and pretended she hadn't heard him.

Sam had chosen a table with a really great view of the stage. So every time I looked at Sam I could see Nate, right there, just behind him, over his shoulder. And whenever I looked at Nate I just got a really horrible sick feeling in the pit of my stomach. I mean there I'd gone, hoping to bump into this really cute guy and instead I was hit over the head by a totally ugly memory. Just seeing Nate there reminded me of a part of my life I didn't want to remember. Sure it was only a tiny part of my life—one night, a few minutes really. But it doesn't really take very long for something bad to happen that will stick with you for far longer than you would ever expect it to. And seeing Nate get hit by that car last year was like that for me.

I was certain that at some point soon someone there would tell me about it. Not realizing I had witnessed it, they'd say something like, "You know Nate was in a really bad car accident last year and for a while we didn't even know if he'd make it." And I'd have to decide whether to open my mouth and say, "Well, actually I saw it happen," or whether to just keep my mouth shut and nod like I knew nothing about it. And knowing me, I'd probably nod.

So needless to say, I wasn't really paying that much attention to what was going on around me. Fortunately Sam seemed quite content to carry on a conversation by himself. Apparently Traci had texted him sixteen times and he'd ignored them all. Traci had said she missed him and wanted him back, but Sam was holding firm that they were actually over this time—good boy. He was developing a Web site for some Bear Lake fishing lodge thing—sounded kind of boring. And he'd started ordering books for his college psychology course—actually more interesting than it sounded.

Lisa stepped away from the keyboard. She and Nate launched into a ballad about being lost and finding someone who loved you. It was sad, and hopeful, and slightly haunting. It was good, really good actually. I leaned back and let the music flow around me. Nate's deep voice rising and falling soulfully with the gentle strum of the guitar strings. Lisa's voice fluttering lightly above in harmony.

Nate's eyes skimmed over the crowd as he sang, and as his eyes flickered over our way something weird happened. This odd, almost uneasy look flashed across his eyes. Nate froze. He just stopped singing, his fingers frozen on the guitar strings.

Lisa didn't seem to notice. She just kept singing little *aa . . . ahh*

...ii ... *aahs*. I spun around and looked behind me. So did Sam. But there was no one there.

Well, that's not strictly true, there were a handful of people milling around: some women holding drinks, a couple with their arms around each other, two guys heading out the door. But no one that looked out of place.

Then it hit me—maybe Nate was looking at me. But that would be ridiculous. Nate had never met me. Nate had no way of knowing I'd been the one who'd anonymously called 911. Nate had no reason to even know I existed.

But something had spooked him. And that had me kind of spooked too.

"Hey Jo, you OK?" Sam whispered. "You look like you've seen a ghost."

"I . . . um . . . It's just . . . I just gotta . . ."

A bearded guy who looked about thirty stepped up to the microphone and introduced himself as Patrick. A couple of people stood and stretched, and I decided I needed to take a break too and get some air. I needed to clear my head. Splash some water on my face. Stop thinking about Nate for a minute. Long enough to get some perspective at least.

Sam started saying something about getting drinks, but brushing him off I started pushing through the crowd in what I hoped was the direction of the bathroom. But it seemed everyone else had gotten the same idea and I didn't really feel like lining up for half an hour, so I decided to take a shortcut around the back of the stage and maybe head them off.

There seemed to be a promising little space just around the back of the stage where someone had been stacking cables and equipment and stuff. So I started picking my way through—tripping over cables and dodging precariously stacked crates, when my foot snagged on something. I stumbled forward, tripping over a microphone cable. Then, I wobbled on my toes for a second, trying desperately to regain my balance, before careening headlong into a pile of folding chairs, leaving a destruction path of songbooks—stacked to fall in a domino effect—in my wake.

"Hey girl! Where do you think you're going?" an angry voice

barked. "That's some expensive equipment you're stepping on!" A form stepped out of the shadows in front of me and grabbed my arm. I almost screamed, but the sound caught in my throat. It was Kevin.

"Hey. It's you," Kevin said softly. His face melted into a smile. His hands relaxed their grip. I nearly fell into his chest. Kevin slid his fingers gently off my arms. "I was wondering when I was going to see you dry and on land again," he said teasingly. "I did try to warn you those railings are a little wonky but I guess you didn't see me waving to you."

Oh. But before I had to worry about coming up with something to say to that, he added, "So what on earth are you doing here?"

Kevin looked really happy to see me, but not quite sure what to do about it.

"A friend invited me," I said. Almost as abruptly as it started, my world stopped spinning and tipped back onto its axis. I took a deep breath and smiled apologetically. "I'm . . . I'm sorry. I didn't mean to step on your sound equipment."

Kevin shrugged. "Aw. It's no big deal," he said, grinning. "It's not that important, really."

I could feel my cheeks tingling.

"So, a friend invited you to our event," Kevin repeated, slowly. "Does she go to Cornerstone?"

Kevin's choice of words knocked me back one—was this some not-so-subtle attempt to figure out if I had a boyfriend? I could feel this silly grin slipping onto my face and I bit my lips to hold it in.

"Actually I'm here with a group of friends," I said.

"Hmm . . . a group of friends." Kevin nodded again.

What was I doing? Flirting?

I asked Kevin what he thought of Nate and Lisa's last song. But Kevin said he'd missed most of the performance—including the last song—because he'd been busy getting some stuff set up.

I think that was supposed to be my cue to head back to the table, but somehow Kevin and I just stood there talking.

"You live in town?" Kevin asked.

"Just moved here," I said.

He nodded. "You know anyone from Cornerstone Church?"

I shook my head. Then I told him I'd just met Mandy and Brian. Kevin said he didn't know them, but then again it was a pretty big church.

Kevin had a thin leather strap encircling his wrist, and he started to fiddle with it, twisting it hard one way and then the other. It was like he was testing to see whether it would snap. It definitely looked like the kind of tagging a girlfriend would leave and it made me wonder if we were still standing in a swamp of cables because someone on the floor would be looking for him. And I'd learned from experience there is no safe way to deal with that one, so instead I just plowed straight in and asked: "Do you have a girlfriend?"

Kevin made this sound that was halfway between a cough and a laugh. He looked down at the ground and didn't answer my question for the longest time. I could feel my heart begin to twist and turn inside my chest.

"OK, this is going to sound lame," he said, "but I've sort of been going through a single phase for a while." He raised his eyes and looked into mine. My heart flew back into my chest and crashed against my rib cage. Kevin took a step toward me. And I think that for a moment, just a moment, he thought about saying something more. But then he said, "I should really get you back to your friends before they wonder what happened to you," and brushed past me toward the main floor.

Nate was onstage, with a couple of other people, packing away the sound equipment. He was balancing the keyboard on his knee, trying to unstrap the board from the stand with one hand. Nate called Kevin to come over and give him a hand.

"Friend of yours?" I said.

"Yeah."

"Shouldn't you head over there?"

Kevin hesitated. "Yeah." He didn't move.

Nearly dropping the keyboard into its case Nate waved at Kevin as if to say, "Well, are you going to give me a hand here or not?" As Nate raised his arm, his shirt rode up a bit and for a second I saw a glimpse of a scar cutting along his side. Jagged and ugly and copper in the stage-lights.

I took a deep breath in and let it out slowly.

Kevin took a step toward Nate, then faltered. "It's OK," Kevin said firmly, "Nate'll be OK."

For some reason, I felt really uneasy when Kevin said that. I didn't know why, I just had the sense that there was something wrong about it somehow—but I couldn't put my finger on it.

So I pointed out to Kevin where Kat, Sam, and the rest were sitting. But before we'd gone six steps Patrick appeared behind us and clasped a hand on Kevin's shoulder.

"Hey Kevin. Who's your friend?"

I didn't even have a chance to be nervous, because just as Kevin was opening his mouth, music girl Lisa bounced over to join us too, and she monopolized the conversation all the way back to the table. Mandy and Brian facilitated the introductions. Kevin shook hands around the table. Patrick grabbed spare chairs from nearby.

 I slid back into my seat next to Sam, who glanced over at Kevin and raised one eyebrow theatrically. So I kicked him.

Then Kevin pulled up a chair—right in between me and Sam. He sat down and the two guys started grinning at each other. Kevin asked Sam how he'd enjoyed the music and Sam replied he was really glad we'd been able to come. They both had manic, overly cheerful smiles plastered on, but I couldn't shake the feeling the two guys were a little less than thrilled that the other was there.

Kat gave Kevin an almost imperceptible glance-over with her eyes, and then nodded at me ever so slightly. In other words, she thought he seemed OK but was reserving final judgment until she actually got to know him. Kat was a master at subtlety.

No big surprise but everyone started talking about wedding things again. It turned out that even though Mandy had grown up in Silverpoint, and Brian in Ashford, they had never met until they both went on a mission trip to Zimbabwe to help build a clinic. They were planning on going back there for five weeks for their honeymoon too. Kat asked Patrick if he was performing the ceremony, but he explained that he was only the junior pastor and Lisa's father, Pastor Wallace, would be doing it.

Lisa was even more chipper in person then she was on stage, and she kept smiling at me like she was certain we were going to become friends. It was kind of irritating, but also kind of nice. She popped off for a few minutes and came back with a pile of photocopied fliers for something called "the Gathering" Cornerstone held on Sunday nights. "It's right here at the Pug," Lisa enthused, "Nate and I do the music. You should really, really come," she told me. "It's really cool. It's like all young people too. There's like no one over the age of twenty-two—except for Patrick," she added. Then, obviously not realizing she'd just accidentally dismissed Mandy, Brian, and Kat as virtually octogenarian, Lisa bounced off to talk to someone else. I'd only known Lisa for twenty minutes and already I was exhausted trying to keep up with her.

Out of the corner of my eye I was vaguely aware of Nate's dark form as he stomped to the back of the room and started pulling the sound equipment apart. And he looked annoyed—really, really annoyed. Patrick shot a quick glance to Kevin that spoke volumes more than I was able to decipher.

Kevin leaned toward me and his arm accidentally brushed up against mine making me jump. "You should come out on a Sunday night," he said. "It's really good and not as churchy as you'd think."

"You too, Sam," he added like an afterthought.

"Sounds inspirational," Sam replied, forcing me to kick him under the table again—except I missed and my toe kind of caught Kevin instead, which then meant I had to fake a coughing fit so he wouldn't think I'd done it on purpose.

Then other conversations around the table seemed to die down into silence, like someone was fiddling with the volume control. I realized that Patrick had stopped talking, and was looking toward me with a peculiar look on his face. A weird hush started to creep around the table. It felt like one by one, everyone stopped talking and turned toward me. So I sort of self-consciously stopped coughing, in what I hoped was a normal sounding, petering out kind of way. I even thumped my chest twice for good measure. But they were still looking at me. Sam's face had gone totally serious, almost protective. *Come on*, I thought. *I'm not that bad at fake coughing.* Then Kat's eyes met mine and she gave a slight little nod over my shoulder.

I turned. Nate was standing behind us. He looked furious. His jaw was clenched. His arms folded tightly over his chest. He looked ready to pull someone's head off.

I was so startled I nearly jumped out of my seat. But I swear Kevin jumped even higher.

"Hi Nate. Join us." Patrick said evenly.

Nate seemed to melt a fraction. "Sorry Pat, I gotta get going," Nate said. "Packing up took longer than I expected."

Patrick stood. So did Kevin.

"Well just let me introduce you to a few people before you go." Patrick said calmly. Nate nodded and Patrick made introductions around the table, telling us all that Nate was his "right-hand man" who not only ran music for the Gathering, and was starting his second year of youth-work training in September, but also helped coordinate a program for at-risk youth.

"Silverpoint gets a lot of street kids in the summer," Nate said evenly. "A lot of them have petty crime problems, and most of them drink a lot, or are into some light drug use. The church did a study a couple years ago and found out a lot of them came from bigger towns like Ashford and migrated to Silverpoint beach when the weather was nicer."

"Then migrate again when the weather gets cold," Patrick added.

"Yeah," Nate nodded, "somewhere warmer. So in the summer we run a youth club on Friday nights and a Bible study on Tuesdays. It's a start."

Nate was almost smiling now—a slight smile really, but at least he didn't look ready to thump someone. I didn't know what to make of him. I mean, on the pier he seemed so laid-back and relaxed. Then tonight he was the opposite—all tense and on edge. And now here was Patrick describing him as some sort of social working saint. None of this seemed to explain why anyone would want to run him over.

"Are you ready to go Nate?" Kevin asked.

Nate's face tightened again. "If you're not too busy."

"I'm good." Kevin turned to us. "It was nice to meet you all," he said and his eyes flicked over my face again. "You really should come to the Gathering next Sunday. It's pretty amazing."

Nate headed toward the door, leaving Kevin to trail after him. I tried to watch them go without looking too obvious, but just as Kevin was walking out the door, he glanced back over his shoulder and his eyes caught mine again. And held them.

"So, what kind of stuff goes on at the Gathering?" Sam asked Patrick, dragging my attention back to the table.

"Nate and Lisa lead some music," Patrick said, "and then I bring up a topic like love, or commitment, or the future and look at how that relates to the Christian faith. Then we have a discussion if anyone has anything they want to ask or say. It's sort of a chance to examine the truth of Christianity in a no pressure setting."

"Really?" Sam leaned in. "Are we allowed to disagree? Debate? Challenge you?"

"Absolutely," Patrick said, smiling. "Bring all your questions and your arguments. And feel free to challenge me on anything you'd like."

"Very cool," Sam said with a grin. "I've always wanted a chance to put your religion though the wringer."

Patrick kind of chuckled at that, and then excused himself saying he had to go speak to some other people. Mandy and Brian wandered out soon afterward. Kat left for work and Sam offered to give me a ride home.

§ § §

I'm not sure how the "ride" home turned into a walk. Maybe Sam suggested it, but I could have sworn that neither of us did. We just passed his car and kept walking.

It was a muggy night. Lampposts dropped half-hearted pools of light in front of our feet. We walked down by the beach, watched the water slide back and forth over the sand, and neither of us spoke for a while.

"Your sister seems nice," I said after a while.

"She is nice. I'm going to miss living with her."

"Can I ask you a question?"

"Sure."

"Why did you stop going to church?"

Sam picked up a stone and sent it skidding along the beach.

"Do you want what my sister would say, or my answer?"

"What your sister would say."

Sam's mouth turned up at the corner. "I like you Jo, you're more interesting than I gave you credit for." I wasn't sure what to make of that.

"Mandy says there are two parts to faith," Sam went on without skipping a beat, "the head and the heart. She'd say that head-wise my brain was packed full of knowledge—heck, I could probably beat God-boy Kevin at a Bible quoting contest. But, she'd say I was never willing to take what she calls a 'leap of faith' and really give myself wholeheartedly to it."

"And what would you say?"

Sam shrugged. "That church was boring and irrelevant. Lots of kneeling. Lots of talking. And a complete and total disconnect with anything out here in the real world," he said. "My parents never went, but they made me go."

I must have looked puzzled because Sam quickly added, "Look you don't know my parents, but if you'd grown up around here you'd have heard of them, or at least their company. Underwood and Ogilvie. They run their own consulting company and tend to get their names on a bunch of stuff."

"I'm sorry," I said.

"Don't be. I like the fact you've never heard of them, because then you don't bother to be impressed. If it doesn't involve money they don't care about it—and that included Mandy and me. Though they had her on purpose which kind of put her at an advantage, I guess. Mandy bought her own place when she was twenty-five, and I was fifteen, and she invited me to move in with her. She's even offered to let me stay in her apartment and commute to college in Ashford.

"Of course my dad offered to pay for me to go to any college I wanted—as long as I majored in business. So when I decided to take psychology instead he threatened to disown me." He shrugged. "Wouldn't be the first time. Basically I'm an orphan with parents."

"Me too."

I had totally not planned on telling Sam about my mother—especially not so soon. But somehow it just kind of slipped out.

I had a basic rule for guys as far as my mother was concerned—never tell them the truth about her, and definitely never let them meet her. But Sam wasn't someone I was ever going to date. Already he was a friend, and that was different. And besides, there was something about him that kind of made him hard to lie to.

Sam had stopped walking and he was standing there looking at me like he was waiting for me to say something more.

I took a deep breath. "My mom is kind of . . . well . . . flashy. People think we're sisters sometimes. She loves that."

"How about your father?" Sam asked.

"Which one?"

"Birth dad?" His voice was surprisingly gentle.

"Mom says she doesn't have a clue who he was."

"Stepdad?"

"A few. Several. Depending on your definition."

It's not like it mattered, but at least he was asking.

Sam closed his eyes. Thick clouds were covering the stars. It was going to rain soon. I wrapped my arms tightly around my chest.

"How about we try live-in boyfriends that have lasted longer than six months?"

That narrowed it down. "Nine, and she was legally married to five of them."

"Rough."

"Yeah."

"See that's the difference between our world and theirs," Sam said, waving his arm in the direction we'd come. He'd started walking again and it took me a minute to catch up with what he was talking about. "People like Kevin or Lisa don't understand what real life is like. I bet you any money that Lisa still lives with her parents—a picture-perfect, happy little couple who have never so much as raised their voices in front of her.

"Don't get me wrong, I think Lisa is a really nice person. They're all nice—well mostly at least. But they don't have a clue what life is like outside their cozy, happy little church-life. And you can't talk to them about real life stuff because they just won't get it—won't want to get it."

"Even Nate?"

"I don't know," Sam said. "He might be different."

"You know him?" I asked.

"Only by reputation. Silverpoint isn't exactly brimming with gritty saints trying to save our town one drug-addicted heathen at a time, and my parents tried to give him some big financial grant, or name something after him, or something, last year. But of course there were strings attached and Nate refused to go along with the whole in-the-limelight, publicity-machine thing, so they dropped him and gave the money to someone who didn't mind smiling for the cameras and calling my parents miracle-makers."

Sam grinned. "Figure that took some nerve. Anyone who stands up to my parents has got to have some serious chutzpah. Doesn't seem like the kind of guy who likes to do things the easy way."

"And someone tried to kill him . . ." I said slowly.

Sam let out a long, low whistle under his breath. "Yeah. I was wondering when you'd bring that up again."

"Well, it's not the kind of thing that's all that easy to talk about."

"You don't have to—"

"No, it's OK. I want to."

Sam took my hand and led me down the beach to a little jut of land underneath the pier. It was like a little private sandy cove between the beach and the water. We sat under there with our backs leaned against a mossy support pillar.

"I don't know where to start," I said.

"Start wherever you want."

"I was praying."

"Interesting start."

I shrugged and took a deep breath. Then out spilled the story I'd gone over in my mind a thousand times.

Last summer I had visited Kat in Silverpoint for a few days at the end of August. It had been Monday night. My bus back home was leaving from Ashford at some ridiculously late time and so Kat was getting some sleep before having to drive me the hour-and-a-half trip to the station. I was standing on the tiny balcony of my funky little guest bedroom, praying.

Like I said before, I didn't know if anyone was listening. It was just that spending a week with Kat had sort of reminded me that some people actually do something with their lives, and if I was honest with myself I was desperately afraid I was going to end up alone, and useless, and like my mother.

It was one of those amazing still nights. The sky was awash in midnight blue and the water was rippling like velvet against the sand. I glanced up at the hills and a cross caught my eye—a huge, glowing cross just sitting up there in the blackness and for a moment I thought I had to be seeing things, so I dug Kat's binoculars out of the cupboard and took a better look.

It was a church, with a big illuminated cross spanning the front glass window. I was about to look away again when other lights caught me eye. There were two cars in the parking lot. One was a busted station wagon that was old-looking in a rundown, bad way. And a fantastic-looking red sports car that was old-looking in a very good way. And I wondered just how religious you had to be to be at church when it was almost midnight.

Two guys got out of the rundown car. One got out of the red one. They met in the middle of the parking lot and traded bags. And I was standing there, captivated, with my imagination running wild thinking it must be a drug deal, or a jewel heist or something.

Then the church doors broke open, Nate ran out of the church, and the guys high-tailed it back to their cars. The ugly-looking old car took off, but Nate made a beeline for the expensive-looking car, and braced his hands on the hood.

Of course I'd seen this all in gray shadows. I could barely see the guys and the cars had just been a dark gray lump and one that was even a darker shade of gray. But then the sporty car turned the headlights on full blast, and I could see the hood was red, and I could see Nate lit up in its glare. Nate blinked, squinted. Then he appeared to be yelling something at the driver. Nate looked angry. Livid. Furious.

He raised his hand. The car lurched forward, knocking Nate down. I was sure the car had gone over him. But it didn't even stop—it just drove away, leaving Nate lying on the pavement.

I screamed and dropped Kat's binoculars off the balcony.

CHAPTER THREE

I WAS doing a great job telling Sam the story—at first. I was being all serious, and factual, and pausing dramatically at all the right places.

But when I started telling Sam about seeing Nate lying there in the parking lot—and thinking he was dead—all of a sudden all the emotion that I thought I was doing such a good job hiding started bubbling up from underneath the surface, and the next thing I knew these big fat embarrassing tears were escaping under my eyelids. And I couldn't stop them—I just started crying.

Sam reached out and put his arm around my shoulder and pulled me against him in this really solid, brotherly way, and he didn't even pull away when I started blubbering all over his shirt. As weird as it sounds, having his arm around me made me cry even harder.

"You must think I'm an idiot!" I choked. "I just panicked! I mean, I thought Nate was dead and of course it turns out he's not."

"Hey," Sam said in a low voice, "it's OK, it's OK, Jo, breathe . . ." he squeezed my shoulder. "Did you wake up Kat?"

I nodded.

"And she helped you call the police?"

I nodded again, sniffing a little.

"It's OK," he said, pulling his arm tighter around me. "You did everything right."

I sat back and looked up at him.

"Really?"

"Of course really. Maybe even saved his life."

I wiped my arm across my eyes and sniffed hard in an undignified way. Then I pushed my hands through my hair, and he let go of me and sat back against the pillar.

"So," he said, "what do you want to do about it now? Would you like me to help you try and find out more about the accident?"

That was probably the last thing I expected him to say. But it was good because it got my brain thinking again and kicked me into logical planning mode and away from hysterical and panicky.

"Could you?" I said. "I mean, I know it sounds stupid. But I'd like to know if they ever caught the guy and if they did that he went to jail or something."

"No, that doesn't sound stupid," Sam said. "I get it."

And I realized he did. For a moment I was afraid I was going to start crying all over again, and maybe Sam realized that because he quickly said, "In a place the size of Silverpoint, it's hard to breathe, let alone be hit by a car, without someone noticing— especially if you've got a reputation like Nate does. And I thought I already knew every bit of gossip there was worth knowing. But don't worry. We'll find out everything we can. And I'll help you. I promise."

"You won't tell anyone though, will you?" I said quickly. "I don't want anyone to know. Not yet. I don't know how to explain it, but . . ."

"You want to be able to tell who you like, when you like, how you like, right?"

I could feel a smile spreading across my face.

"Exactly."

I couldn't begin to describe how great it was to just be sitting there with someone who got it—who got me—without me having to explain everything, or getting questioned like I would have been by my mom. It was pretty awesome actually.

But then I went and spoiled everything by reminding Sam, yet again, not to tell anyone. Only it sort of didn't come out that way and what I actually, accidentally said was, "Promise me you won't tell Kevin." It took me half a second to realize my mistake—the huge, invisible iceberg that had instantly materialized between us was a pretty big clue—and so I quickly added, "Or . . . or Patrick, or Lisa, or . . . or . . . your sister . . . or anyone else . . ." But something in the tone of Sam's sigh told me the damage had already been done and the next thing I knew we were both standing up and brushing the sand off our legs in loud, exaggerated motions.

"It makes sense that we shouldn't tell Kevin," I added defensively. "After all, he's like Nate's best friend, and could be really upset about it."

"Right," Sam said sardonically, "we wouldn't want to upset Kevin."

"What do you have against Kevin anyway?" I snapped, as another opportunity to drop the subject of Kevin whizzed past my nose.

Sam shrugged. "Nothing," he said unconvincingly. "I don't really know him, and he seems like a mind-numbingly boring guy . . ." OK, Sam really didn't say that. What Sam actually said was that Kevin seemed like a "harmless enough, decent guy." But I caught his meaning all the same.

"Yeah, well, I think you're wrong about him," I retorted loudly. "I think there's something guarded and edgy about Kevin. Maybe even dangerous. And maybe I'm being wise wanting to wait to tell Kevin until we're absolutely sure he can be trusted." Yeah, like that was going to work.

Sam laughed out loud. "You think there's something dangerous about God-boy?" he said, shaking his head in disbelief. "You've got to be kidding! You try telling Kevin about what it was like to see some maniac plow a car into his best friend and you'll see just how 'edgy' he is."

We were both walking back up the beach, and speeding up all the time, like we were racing to see who could get back to the road fastest.

"What is it with girls and always wanting to fall for some bad boy anyway?" Sam went on, huffing under the stress of talking while trying to pretend he wasn't trying to out-walk me. "Why don't girls ever just fall in love with guys who treat them the way they deserve to be treated?"

"I'm not the one who got his heart dumped all over the beach," I said with as much cool disdain as I could muster.

"Ouch." Sam clutched his chest and pretended to check for blood. "Perhaps I deserved that. Note to self—don't bug the pretty girl about matters of the heart. Stick to safe subjects like astrophysics and large sea mammals."

A smile was tugging at the side of my lips again.

"Fine. Look, I'm sorry, I'm probably the last person who should be dumping on anyone else's love-life," Sam said, sounding like he was trying to be conciliatory. "You guys are probably perfect for each other, and you'll have a wonderful romance and go riding off into the sunset together. Because hey, what do I know? You're not my type."

§ § §

I'm not his type? *I'm not his type?* What did Sam mean, I'm not his type? Why not? Because I don't have scary pink nails and scream at him in public? You don't have to want a guy to be offended by the fact he doesn't want you.

I have to admit, even though I pretended to ignore that little gem of his Sunday night, it was all I could think about Monday morning, which was stupid considering I had so many more important things to think about. Knowing Kat would be tired in the morning from her typically short night shift, I had big plans of getting up early, making her breakfast, cleaning the kitchen, and getting a solid start on looking for a job to reassure my cousin that I wasn't planning to live off her generosity forever. But I didn't wake up until almost eleven, and Kat had already gotten up, tidied up, and left to go grocery shopping. To make matters worse, my cousin had left a note for me in the kitchen: *Jo, we'll talk about the job situation when I get home. I have an idea. Kat.* Even the three smiley faces she put at the end of her note didn't make me feel any better.

Ignoring the shambles I'd left my résumé in the day before, I threw on one of my best casual outfits and set out to find someone, anyone, who was willing to hire me.

But if my self-esteem had been hurting a bit when I got up that morning, it was positively limping by the time I'd made it down to the waterfront. I stopped in restaurants, offices, and clothing stores. I plastered my best "you'll like me, I know you'll like me" smile on my face so many times that after an hour I really did feel ready to strangle the next person who said they could offer me something very part-time, alternative Tuesdays at midnight.

So when I got back home and Kat, who had beaten me there, started into her pitch about having had a brain wave about some potential work I could do, I was ready to tackle anything she could throw at me—well, almost anything.

Kat's two-story apartment sat on top of this dingy old store that had the windows plastered in fliers and looked like no one had used it in a million years. And speaking of a million years that's probably how long it would have taken me to guess that Kat actually owned it. While we were changing into old jeans and loose T-shirts—the right kind of outfits to enter the store that time forgot—Kat explained that she had fallen in love with the apartment when she first saw it, but the owner had only been interested in selling all three floors. The price was good, because apparently the place had been pretty much a pig sty, and so Kat had bought the whole building, planning to fix up the store to rent it.

Considering this was the preamble she gave me before I'd even seen the place, you can imagine what I was expecting by the time she managed to force the inside door at the bottom of her staircase open. Picture the dingiest convenience store you've ever seen. Then dump almost everything off the shelves onto the floor. Spray liberally with dirt, sand, and a few gallons of pop. Then leave for a thousand years. It didn't take a genius to figure out what my cousin's job suggestion was.

"I had some renovators in to take a look at it a few months ago," Kat was saying as we kicked our way through the dented cans and filthy newspapers. "They gave me this huge quote to clean the whole thing up. But when I took a better look at what they'd given me, it was all basic cleaning work; like getting rid of all the garbage, taking down the shelves, giving it a good clean, painting. There's a few weeks worth of work here, at least, and if you were willing to tackle it for me when you could, then you wouldn't have to worry about rent or food or anything. I'd consider us even."

I didn't know what Kat was expecting, but judging by the look on her face when I flung my arms around her and said I would be glad to do it, I think she was expecting me to put up more of a fight. It wasn't that I was a huge fan of cleaning or anything, but in one fell swoop Kat had saved me from having to look for a job, having to feel guilty about eating all her food, or spending the bit of money I had saved on rent. Besides, most importantly, it would feel good to help Kat for once.

I even jumped straight in and got started right away. After shuffling my way through the garbage a bit, I decided to start by cleaning off the front window, deciding a little light would make the rest of the job feel a whole lot cheerier. For some reason, people seem to think an empty store is the perfect place to glue up posters for garage sales, used CDs, lost dogs, and things for sale that were sold long ago. By the time Kat popped down a couple of hours later and told me that dinner was ready, I was thrilled to realize that over half the window had been scraped clean.

More importantly, I'd been far too busy working up a sweat to think anymore about Sam's stupid comment. Though I had spent some time making a list of reasons why I was 100 percent overwhelmingly and enthusiastically glad I wasn't Sam's type. I only had three, actually. One, I suspected he and Traci weren't quite as "over" as he liked to believe. Two, Kevin was a lot cuter and was probably way too much of a nice guy to ask me out if he thought Sam liked me. And three . . . um . . . I had a number three, I just managed to forget it by the time I fell exhausted into bed that night.

§ § §

I think Kat was shocked by the fact I was up and out of bed by eight the next morning, and, after a quick breakfast, was right back to scraping things off that window. But there was something really satisfying about tackling something that big and watching it come together a tiny bit at a time. For once I was doing something practical, where I could actually see results. And I really liked it.

By early Tuesday afternoon, I was ready to start on cleaning out the garbage. Finding Kat's small garbage bags weren't up to the job, I decided to walk down to the local supermarket where I not only loaded up on industrial strength garbage bags and rubber gloves, but also a large red plastic toy shovel, which I figured would be great for scooping up the worst of the mess.

For some unknown reason, by the time I was walking back up the hill I found myself thinking about Sam again. No, more like obsessing about why he had said I wasn't his type, and wondering if I should feel insulted by it. Was this his way of distancing himself because he felt all embarrassed for holding me while I cried? Or was he just a nice guy and wanted me to know I didn't have to worry he had some secret agenda at heart? Or was I really just not Sam's type? And what did Sam know about love anyway? The last person he had fallen in love with was certifiable.

"Hey! Jo! Can I give you a ride?"

I must have been deep in thought, because I didn't hear Kevin's truck until it had pulled up beside me, which was a feat in concentration considering it heaved like a mammoth steam engine. Kevin was leaning out the window. He looked even better in the daylight than he had in the darkened Pug. Tiny shivers went tap dancing down the back of my neck.

"Hi," my voice squeaked. What kind of opening was that? I shook my hair out and struggled to find a casual-sounding, normal voice.

"I was just running out to pick up some wood for my dad," Kevin said. His eyes were clear and bright like sunbeams on the water. "But I'm sure he won't mind if I go a few minutes out of my way. Where are you going?"

I gave him my address, hoping it would be on his way.

"Hop in." Kevin leaned over and pushed hard on the door. It swung open slowly with a long, plaintive whine. The floorboard was too high for any kind of graceful entrance, so I settled for dumping my bags in and pulling myself up by the seatbelt.

"Passenger belt is broken," Kevin said. "Nate usually ties it to the doorknob and prays. Maybe you should sit in the middle."

I obligingly slid over on the cracked leather seat. Kevin's hand knocked against mine as he moved to put the truck in gear.

"So . . ." Kevin glanced sideways at me, as the truck shook and rattled down the road.

I tightened my grasp on the edge of the seat and smiled weakly. "So."

Maybe it was my imagination, but Kevin seemed positively shy. It was no wonder Sam hadn't believed my idea about Kevin being dangerous. Besides, who ever heard of a bad boy driving around in a truck that shuddered like it was going to collapse the next time it went over a bump?

"Nate has a sweet pair of wheels," Kevin said, "it's a 1970s Camaro, but he only drags it out of the garage on special occasions, so he's always relying on me to take him places—like last Sunday. This is a total bag of bolts I know," Kevin added, patting the dashboard. "I used to have a really sweet bike, but . . . well . . . it kind of wasn't practical for work."

"What do you do?" I asked.

"I work for my dad. He runs a construction company." Kevin shrugged. "It's good, steady work, but it's only a temporary thing. When I've saved up enough money I'm planning on getting some training to do the kind of work Nate does."

Kevin started going on about how great Nate's youth work was. I kept thinking that this could be my chance to ask him about Nate's hit and run, but somehow I couldn't find a way to force the words out of my mouth.

"You and Nate seem pretty tight," I said finally.

Kevin ran his hand over his jaw. "Yeah, I guess you could say that."

We turned a corner and suddenly the huge golden light of Cornerstone's cross window seemed to dominate the sky.

"Now if you look closely you can see Cornerstone from here," Kevin said.

OK, so I was exaggerating a little about the cross dominating the sky. Cornerstone Church was just this small speck in the distance really, and if I held my hand up the right way I could block it with my thumb. I know; I tried. But it felt huge to me. It felt like this big, accusing signpost shouting, "You know that great guy beside you? You saw his friend, his *good* friend get plowed over by some evil maniac. Now if you were a nice, or kind, or caring person you'd ask how Nate was, or if he had any major injuries. But instead you won't bring it up because you're too afraid of saying anything that will make him stop liking you!"

Oh crud.

"Um, Kevin?"

"Yeah."

"Can I ask you something?"

"Yeah."

"Is Nate's work, you know with street kids and stuff, is it ever . . . um . . . dangerous?"

Kevin shrugged. "No, not really. I mean, every now and then some stupid kid half his size tries to take a swing at him or something. But Nate can handle it."

There was something kind of definitive, kind of final, in Kevin's tone of voice which made me think that he thought the subject was closed. But maybe I just had a lemming-instinct, or maybe it was that stupid twinkling little Cornerstone light, or maybe it was some sort of spiritual prompting—whatever it was, I just couldn't let it go.

"But, doesn't he work with, you know, criminals?"

Kevin laughed again.

"Sure some of the kids he deals with have had their problems—like they shoplifted something, or drank underage, or tried marijuana or something. But they're just normal guys who never got a break, not like hardened cri—"

"But, but wasn't he attacked last year or something?" I blurted out.

Wrong thing to say.

The conversation came to a screeching halt. Literally. Kevin hit the breaks so hard my knees banged against the dashboard. He turned and looked at me.

"What did you say?" Kevin asked flatly.

"I mean . . . I mean . . ." I took a deep breath and lied. "I just heard he'd been in the hospital for something. That's all."

"Oh, that," Kevin muttered. "Did Lisa tell you about that?"

He took his foot off the break and the truck started rolling again.

"Nate wasn't attacked," Kevin said lightly, coaxing the truck smoothly around the corner onto my street, "that was just some stupid accident."

"But—"

"Look, I really can't tell you anything about it," Kevin cut me off, "I didn't go to Cornerstone back then and it was before I really knew Nate."

He said it like it was no big deal, but I couldn't help thinking how strange it was that Kevin didn't even seem to want to know what had landed his friend in the hospital.

Kevin came to a gentle stop a couple doors down from Kat's and turned to face me on the seat. "Look, I'm sorry for stopping so hard back there." He gestured with his thumb back the way we had come. "There are hidden stop signs all over this town and the brakes on this old truck aren't what they used to be."

"Oh, no problem," I said, grinning weakly.

"You'll get used to it," Kevin added, then blushed. "Anyway, I'm feeling bad I had to run out so early on you Sunday night," he went on. "Nate needed me to help him take care of something and it couldn't wait. But maybe we could get together and talk some other time."

I smiled. "I'd like that."

A wave of relief swept over Kevin's face, and I suddenly realized just how nervous he'd been.

"You'll be at the Gathering Sunday?" he added hopefully.

I nodded.

"Great," Kevin said, "maybe we can talk more then. But right now, it looks like you've got company."

I looked where he was pointing. Sam's silver sports car was parked boldly in front of Kat's house, like a giant lump of tinfoil. Did he have no sense of timing? Sam was sitting on my front step. He was balancing an oversized book on his knees, which had the unfortunate side effect of making it look like he'd shrunk since the weekend.

"Sam isn't staying long," I said quickly, though I pretty much doubted that was true. "Do you want to come in for a drink?"

"Like to. But can't," Kevin said, shaking his head. "Dad's

waiting on the wood. But I promise I'll make it up to you." Kevin leaned out the window. "Hey Sam! How's it going?"

"Good." Sam stood. "Patrick told me more about that Gathering thing you mentioned and I was thinking I might drop by."

"Cool," Kevin grinned, "you should bring your friends." His eyes lingered on my face for a long moment. Then he leaned over me and shoved the door open. "I'll see you soon," he said, as I jumped down onto the street and grabbed my bags. I stood on the pavement and watched him drive away, wondering how long I could pretend I didn't know Sam was behind me.

"He drove you home?" Sam said the second Kevin's truck disappeared around the corner. "Now that's a cliché waiting to happen. Tell me, was the passenger seatbelt broken or were you two just huddling together for warmth?"

"Hi Sam," I said dryly.

"Hey, chill." Sam took a step back and raised his hands palm up in defense. "Honest, Jo, if Kevin had been thinking about coming in, I would have gotten right out of your way, instantly, I promise."

"And yet, you didn't."

"He was on his way somewhere," Sam protested. "Off to give Bibles to dying orphans or something."

"He was getting wood for his father," I said, feeling the hint of a smile thawing slightly.

"His Dad's with a construction company?" Sam asked.

"How would you know that? Been snooping into Kevin have you?"

"It was written on the side of the truck."

"Right."

My cleaning supplies had started to grow heavy; who knew how Sam was feeling with his gigantic superbook.

"Please don't be annoyed," Sam said. "I completely and honestly apologize for dropping by unannounced. I tried calling, but there was no one home. I brought you something."

"You brought me an encyclopedia?"

"No," Sam smiled, "something better."

Well, it's not every day a guy shows up at your front door with half a library in his arms, even if he is slightly infuriating. I forced the door to the store open and dropped my supplies in the corner. Sam walked in after me.

"Wow," he said, surveying the damage.

"Which do you see?" I asked. "Disaster or potential?"

"Potential."

"Good boy."

We picked our way through to the back of the store, and out into Kat's back yard. Sam dumped his megabook on the wooden steps while I headed up into the kitchen and came back with a tub of Kat's latest treat du jour—homemade coffee ice cream—and two spoons. Prying off the lid, I tossed Sam a spoon as I walked down to join him on the bottom step.

"So how's our prime suspect doing?" Sam asked. "Still dangerous and edgy?"

I dug out a spoonful of ice cream and pretended to flick it at him before sticking it in my mouth.

"Kevin's good," I said after a moment. "He doesn't know anything about Nate's accident last summer though. I mean, I didn't ask him outright. But I hinted pretty heavily, and he was clueless."

"I'm not surprised," Sam said nodding. "I asked Mandy about it, and she knew nothing about it either, which is kind of weird."

"Why? Are Mandy and Nate friends?"

"No, not really," Sam said, shaking his head. "I mean, they've met, but it's not like they're pals. But you don't understand how these churches—churches like Cornerstone anyway—operate. Lisa can't sneeze in the woods without half the church saying 'God bless you' on Sunday. Brian and Mandy bought this house near Bear Lake, which they're going to live in after they get married. Well, Brian was fixing it up and sprained his finger. It wasn't a big thing, but it appeared in the church prayer newsletter-thing, and he got prayed for during the service, and all these women showed up at the house with cakes and meals, and lots of people offered to help him finish the decorating."

"Wow."

"Yeah, I know. It's kind of a cool thing really. Anyway, so if half the town knew about Brian's sprained finger—you'd expect the near-death of everyone's favorite music leader and youth worker to be a pretty hot topic!"

Slowly, the implication was sinking in. "So, it couldn't just be a fluke and no one thought to mention it," I mused.

Sam snorted. "Or maybe Nate got amnesia. Or maybe he was replaced by a clone. Or maybe . . ."

"Or maybe it's a big secret," I interrupted. "But that wouldn't make any sense. Why would someone try to keep something like that a secret?" I dropped the ice-cream container beside Sam's book and ran both hands through my hair. "What's more likely: that Nate secretly got hit by a car and was left for dead with no one knowing, or that I just imagined the whole thing?"

Sam started to open his mouth, but I glared at him, and he shut it again.

"I was being rhetorical," I said dryly.

Sam arched his eyebrows. "And I was about to show you something interesting."

Sam grabbed the book and pulled it up onto his lap. "I got a new Web site job for the *Silverpoint Gazette* and they've asked me to put together an online archive of the best stories."

"And?"

"And," Sam said smugly, "look at this."

I followed his finger to where he was pointing and read, "A local man was critically injured in an apparent hit-and-run Monday night near Cornerstone Church. He is recovering at Saint Gregory's Hospital and is in stable condition." I scanned the date on the top of the page. "August twenty-eight. That could be Nate."

Sam nodded, "I thought so. No name though. And get this, it was a one-off story and they didn't write anything else about the accident, even though there were a lot of other crime stories they did write about: robberies, muggings, stolen cars. In fact, one article even quotes the chief of police saying an Ashford gang was trying to move into Silverpoint."

I could tell by the smug look on his face that he thought all this was leading somewhere really important, and to be honest I was starting to feel a little bit stupid because I didn't get it. Then again, it was beginning to sound a little bit too much cloak-and-dagger.

"So what?" I said. "So what if there were a million crimes last summer? What does that have to do with someone running over Nate?"

That seemed to take a little bit of the wind out of Sam's sails, but he rallied quickly. "So," he said, raising one finger in the air dramatically, "what if it wasn't one guy in one car who ran over Nate? Didn't you say that before he got hit you saw a few guys walking around with boxes and stuff? Maybe Nate interrupted a big drug deal. Or maybe he rescued one kid from a gang and a whole lot of other gang members came after him."

I rolled my eyes. "I liked your clone theory better," I said.

"Just take a look at the newspapers with me and keep an open mind, OK?" Sam pleaded.

"Fine."

It was fun actually—hanging out with Sam and going through the papers; reading small notices about various events Cornerstone had put on; the occasional blip about Nate's youth work project; and, to Sam's frustration, several large spreads about what heroes his parents were to various Silverpoint projects.

And we read about crime. So much crime that I started making a tally on the back of an envelope. Between May and August of last summer six people had lost their wallets or purses while swimming, the music store had been robbed, two kids had been mugged leaving a party, four houses had been broken into, three cars had been stolen and found again, and someone had burned down a cottage near Bear Lake.

I showed Sam my tally. He whistled.

"And here I thought nothing ever happened in Silverpoint," I said lightly.

But just when we thought it was beginning to look inter-esting, it all came to an end with a brief article in late October announcing there had been some gang bust and eight people had been arrested for theft, assault, drugs, and other equally criminal stuff. We scanned ahead a few more weeks after that, but all we could find were notices of fall fairs and pumpkin sales.

"So maybe you're right," I conceded. "Maybe there was a gang in Silverpoint for a while, and Nate somehow stumbled into the middle of it, and then later they all got arrested and carted off to jail. But it still doesn't explain why no one's talking about Nate's accident."

Sam nodded. "To be honest, my theory was that he'd seen them dealing in front of the church and tried to chase them away. But in that case he should have gotten a hero's welcome on Sunday morning."

"Yeah." I felt kind of flat. For a moment there, Sam had almost got me believing that we were onto something exciting, and the thought that I might never know what happened was kind of a letdown.

I sighed. "Is it all right if I hate not knowing?"

Sam smiled, and gave my shoulder a brotherly rub. "Absolutely."

Then I started feeling guilty about spending so much time just sitting around reading newspapers when I should have been cleaning up the store for Kat, so Sam offered to pitch in and help me shovel a few loads of incredibly gross stuff into the new garbage bags. Eventually Kat came home and made pizza. Sam hung around to watch a video, and then got talking to Kat about the courses he was going to be taking in September and the new cell phone store he was designing a Web site for, and what with one thing or another it was almost midnight by the time Sam left.

I walked him to the door.

"Thanks," I said, "this was fun."

"Yeah. It was great." Sam leaned up against the door frame. A lock of hair fell over his forehead and he smiled at me. "I've got a huge favor to ask you," he said.

"You need a kidney?"

"Worse," he said, and his eyes twinkled. "Traci sent my sister a text message, saying she's not sure whether she'll be able to attend the wedding or not."

"What?"

"Yeah, kind of a problem considering she was never invited in the first place."

"You think your scary ex-girlfriend is going to crash your sister's wedding?"

Sam shrugged. "Maybe."

"You miss Traci?"

"Sometimes."

"Just promise me you'll never get back with her."

"Yeah right," Sam said. I noticed he never actually promised. "Anyway, I need to find a date to my sister's wedding." He took a deep breath. "And I was wondering if you would go with me. As . . . as a friend obviously."

"I . . . umm . . . I'm not a big fan of weddings."

"Aw, come on, Jo," Sam pleaded. "I don't want to be there alone if Traci shows up, and I think you and I would have fun together. And I hate to have to pull this on you," he went on, "but you do owe me one. When you fell off the pier I could have left you all alone, floating in the ocean of your own humiliation."

"It was a lake."

Sam raised one eyebrow.

Yeah, he had a point.

"You're sure you want me to go with you to the wedding?" I asked.

Sam nodded. He said, "I can't go with a real date . . ."

"Thanks."

"You know what I mean," Sam said. "Even if I could find someone I was actually interested in between now and then, pompous family events with the optional psychotic ex-girlfriend episode is the kind of thing I normally save for the third date." He smiled at me wickedly, and I had to admit that it did sound kind of fun.

"Can you dance?" I asked.

Sam winked at me. "Guess."

I put up my last wall of resistance. "But what if Kevin gets the wrong impression?"

Sam snorted and stood up straight. "Then it's pistols at dawn," he said.

"Or," I said, "I could just tell him I'm not actually interested in you."

"Please," Sam said dryly, "I should have thought some things are obvious."

§ § §

I didn't know what to wear for the Gathering Sunday night, so I opted for a bright red strappy top with my favorite flowy skirt. Sam arrived to pick me up in faded jeans and an old green shirt that looked like it had been in a wrestling match recently. But as we got to the car he scooped a brown leather jacket off the passenger seat and tossed it into the back, which hinted that there might be a tiny bit of style hidden under all that scruff. Then again, maybe Traci had bought it for him. "How do I look?" I asked.

Sam paused, opened his mouth like he was trying to come up with something to say, and then finally came up with, "Fine."

I looked fine. Not quite the compliment I'd been looking for.

Sam shoved my door closed and walked back over to his side. "You know, we don't have to go to this church thing if you don't want," Sam said, as he started the car. "We could always just go out for coffee, or catch a movie . . ."

I've got to admit that for a moment I was tempted. "I don't know," I said. "I kind of told Kevin I was going to be there . . ."

"Oh right," Sam said, "Kevin."

The music coming from the Ugly Pug was so loud I could hear it as we walked across the parking lot. Muffled voices and solid rock riffs floated through the open doors.

Nate was up on stage wailing on a guitar. This time he and Lisa were joined by two more guitar players, a keyboard player, a saxophone, and an entire drum set. The lights were dimmed and the place was packed. About sixty young people and a few adult types were crammed into the pub. Most were standing and singing. Some were clapping. A couple of guys were even sitting on the floor. Some of the girls were standing on chairs, with their eyes closed and their fingers stretched up like they wanted to pull back the ceiling. Three other girls had linked hands and were dancing. It was like nothing I'd ever seen before.

Then I spotted Kevin standing over by the side wall. He looked toward me and smiled, casually pushing himself off from the wall. He started to walk toward us. I felt my face flush like my skin was on fire. This was crazy! I still barely knew anything about him, but there was something about this guy that just kept reeling me in.

"Hey Jo. Hi Sam. I'm glad you guys decided to come out," he said. "I saved you a couple of seats in the back."

Kevin stretched out his arm toward me, and I hooked my hand through it. Kevin flinched slightly, then relaxed, and pulled my arm tighter against him. Sam started to cough. I ignored him.

We squeezed through a row of metal chairs at the back. Kevin started singing and I tried to follow along with the words that appeared on an overhead screen.

"Can you believe this music?" Sam said in a stage whisper. "It's got serious kick. I thought they stopped writing religious music in the 1800s."

Nate finished the song with a fevered crescendo and stepped back up to the microphone. Wiping his glistening forehead with the back of his hand, Nate said, "Isn't it just incredible to think that there's a great, huge God who really knows you and cares about you personally?"

More like unbelievable actually.

"The next song is an old one, but it's one of the best," Nate continued. "The church was into retro even before retro was hip. And we're taking it back almost one hundred years."

Sam and I glanced at each other, and rolled our eyes simultaneously. I bit my lip to keep from giggling.

The music started back up again with a punchy drum roll. Nate snapped while he sang into the microphone.

"On the mount of crucifixion, fountains opened deep and wide. From the floodgates of God's mercy, flowed a vast and gracious tide . . ."

"Somehow I don't think they sang it this way back in the olden days," Sam said into my ear.

"Grace and love like mighty rivers flowed incessant from above. And heaven's peace and perfect justice, kissed a guilty world in love . . ."

It was like singing poetry. I glanced over at Kevin. His eyes were closed and his hands held out in front of him like he was trying to drink from a waterfall. He really seemed into it. And in a way, I could kind of see why he'd want to be. The idea of a God up there somewhere who watches over us and cares about every bit of our life was kind of amazing. But it was also kind of daunting. I mean, would I really want to have God involved in everything in my life? Seeing everything? Judging everything? I mean, maybe all this religion was good, but I didn't know if I could go for it as much as someone like Kevin could.

The singing stopped and someone took the words off the screen but Nate kept on strumming and singing quietly. Then other people started to pray out loud. It was like a whole make-your-own-church thing was going on. Kevin's eyes were still closed.

I glanced over at Sam. "Did they ever do this at your church?" I whispered.

Sam shook his head. "No, it was nothing like this."

The music stopped and people sat down again. Kevin turned and smiled at me. His face was shining like he had been running hard.

"You OK?" Kevin asked me.

I nodded. He grinned and squeezed my hand.

Lisa bounded up to center stage. She looked so cheery and confident it irritated me a little—must be nice to just be so up-beat, and confident, and perfect all the time!

Lisa slapped herself on the forehead and said, "Forgot my Bible. Can someone pass me one?"

Nate had put his guitar away and was now perched on a side stage speaker like a daddy longlegs. He said something that I couldn't make out, pulled a small tattered book out of his pocket, and tossed it to her. Lisa barely caught it, giggled, and said, "Thank you."

I leaned over to Sam to say something, but Sam put his hand to my lips and said, "Shush."

"A Bible reading from Philippians chapter two." Lisa read, "'Your attitude should be the same as that of Christ Jesus: Who, being in very nature God, did not consider equality with God something to be grasped, but made himself nothing, taking the very nature of a servant, being made in human likeness. And being found in appearance as a man, he humbled himself and became obedient to death—even death on a cross! Therefore God exalted him to the highest place and gave him the name that is above every name, that at the name of Jesus every knee should bow, in heaven and on earth and under the earth, and every tongue confess that Jesus Christ is Lord, to the glory of God the Father.

"'Therefore, my dear friends, as you have always obeyed—not only in my presence, but now much more in my absence—continue to work out your salvation with fear and trembling, for it is God who works in you to will and to act according to his good purpose.'"

Lisa handed the Bible back to Nate and sat down. Then Patrick took center stage. His brown beard was tinged pink in the stagelights. He didn't look much like a preacher. More like a father, a young father, the kind who would hold a baby in the night and sing to it.

"Work out your salvation," Patrick said, "work out faith. It's radical when you think about it. Here Paul, the writer, gives the whole message of Christianity in a nutshell. Jesus is God. Jesus became man. Jesus died. Jesus rose from the dead. There it is. Simple as that."

Sam leaned forward.

"But then, what does he say? Believe it? Accept it? Don't question it?" Patrick said. "No. He says, work it out for yourself. Examine it. Think about it. Argue about it. Decide whether it means anything to you or not.

"My youth group had a huge fight about this very issue. This guy in the group named Stephen loved to argue. He suggested we have weekly debates. 'One of us will argue the right side,' he said, 'and one of us will argue the wrong side. That way we will be prepared when non-Christians try to talk with us.'"

"Boy, I'd have loved to have met him," Sam said under his breath.

"So we divided up in pairs," Patrick continued. "We argued about Jesus and the crucifixion and drunkenness and teen sex and all sorts of issues. It was a lot of fun. Until the day we debated whether or not abortion was murder. The girl who was arguing that abortion was murder did a real pathetic job, didn't even quote a Bible reference, not that there weren't a lot she could have chosen. Psalm 139 is great for starters. But she just said something like 'it's wrong and we all know it's wrong and that's that!'

"The girl who was arguing the other side was a really quiet girl named Ronnie. She had done a lot of research. I mean a lot. She had even visited an abortion clinic and done interviews. She had looked up all types of Bible verses, including one in Ecclesiastes where Solomon says that no human being knows when an unborn baby gets a soul, and one in Exodus that says the punishment for killing a person is not the same as killing an unborn baby. Ronnie talked very slowly and very quietly, and you could tell people were listening. When she started talking about showing compassion to girls who had been raped, one of the other girls started to cry.

"Stephen was mad. He stood up and yelled at Ronnie, 'You shut up! We don't want to hear any more of that garbage! You can't be a Christian and believe that abortion's not murder!'

"It was like a bomb hit the group. Ronnie closed her Bible and looked up at Stephen with this really calm look on her face. She said, 'You said you wanted to debate, Stephen. You didn't tell me that one side wasn't allowed to have any good arguments.' Stephen got mad and walked out.

"I said, 'Ronnie, does this mean that you think abortion is OK?' She looked kind of sad and said, 'No Patrick, definitely, definitely not. But it does mean that I think some issues are more complicated than some people want to believe sometimes.'"

Patrick paused for a minute and took a drink from Nate's water bottle.

"We all come to God with different questions. Different problems. Different arguments. And that's OK. That's good. Every single person in this room has important questions. I want you to feel free to ask and challenge me on anything I say that you aren't sure you agree with. I am still working it out, with God's help. And I want the Gathering to be a place where we can work it out together."

Patrick opened the floor for questions after his talk. Someone asked if there were specific Bible references we were supposed to study each week. Thankfully the answer was no, but Patrick said he would try to put some notes up on Cornerstone's Web site. Someone else asked Patrick if he had seen this new controversial movie about angels and hell. Patrick said that he had—he'd enjoyed it and it had raised some interesting points of view about how people think about God. But, he added, other people had some valid reasons for not watching movies like that and it was important to respect those too.

I nudged Sam. "Ask him a question for me," I whispered.

"What?"

"Ask him a question for me."

"Why don't you ask it yourself?" Sam said out of the corner of his mouth.

"Just do this for me, please?"

Sam sighed. "OK."

"Ask him if he thinks that everything that happens in the world happens for a reason."

Sam grinned. "Good question."

Sam raised his hand. Patrick nodded to him. Sam stood.

"Hey Patrick, you know how you believe that God loves us and is watching out for us?" Sam said. "Well, do you think that everything that happens in the world—and everything that happens in our lives—happens for a reason then?"

On my other side, Kevin sat up suddenly like someone had just lit a firecracker under his seat. And Nate was leaning so far forward I was afraid he was going to fall off the speaker.

"Do I believe that everything happens for a reason?" Patrick repeated. "Well, the Bible says in Psalm 139 that God has planned out every single day of our lives before we were even born—Psalm 56 even says that he collects every tear we ever cry. And then in Ecclesiastes it says that there is a time and a season for everything—a time to be born, a time to die, a time to put things together, a time to tear things apart. And God also tells us in Romans 8 that he works everything together for our good if we love him.

"So, yes, I think everything that happens to us does happen for a reason. It may not be a reason we like. It may not be a reason

God decides to let us in on. But, ultimately, I believe God does have a reason—for everything."

Even Nate getting run over by a car? I wanted to ask.

And even me?

Chapter Four

THE LAST song started. Kevin leaned over, his cheek brushing against my hair as he whispered, "I've got to go take care of some stuff. I'm probably going to be a while. You OK on your own?"

"Yeah, no problem," I whispered back.

"Cool." Kevin was so close now I could feel his breath on my face.

"I hate to dash off like this," Kevin said. He ran his thumb along his smile, and it was all I could do not to stare at his lips. "Maybe we'll get more of a chance to talk next week."

"That'd be great." I could feel a blush spreading its way up my face. I watched as Kevin slowly peeled himself out of the chair and sauntered toward the back of the stage.

Oh, why did he have to be so heart-meltingly good looking? I really didn't think a guy like that would ever settle for a girl like me. And yet . . .

"You want to get going?" Sam said loudly, cutting into my thoughts. "Or are you going to hang around and wait for him?"

"No, it's OK," I replied, forcing my eyes back to Sam as Kevin disappeared into the crowd. "Let's get out of here."

Sam practically rushed me out the door.

"So what did you think?" he asked, as we walked to his car.

"It was weird," I said. "It kind of felt like a rock concert without a performer."

Sam seemed to chew on that one for a minute. "Interesting," he said finally.

I wasn't quite sure what I'd expected church to be like—not sure I'd ever really thought about it much. But I certainly hadn't expected it to be like that. Not so positive and upbeat anyway.

In fact there had been something about the whole night that had given me this weird, happy, uplifted feeling. I didn't know if I was ever going to be able to believe all that stuff Patrick had said about God planning my life, or counting my tears, or any of that. And I didn't suddenly feel that these people had all the answers—it really wasn't like that. But at the same time they kind of had something I wanted—and, though it may have only been for a second, something I thought I could even tap into. And there was something about the whole thing that almost—for a moment anyway—made me feel a little better about myself.

"You know," Sam said slowly, turning onto my street, "we don't have to go back next week if you don't want to. I mean, there's more to Silverpoint than the religion brigade . . ."

"But if I decided I wanted to go back would you go with me?" I asked.

"Of course," he grinned. "Us ungodly ones have to stick together."

I laughed and punched him hard in the arm. "Fine, we'll stick together. You really don't like religion do you?"

Sam shook his head. "Never been a big fan of letting someone else run my life."

"Not even God?"

Sam grinned at me. "Nope, not even God."

Sam came in when he dropped me off, and hung out with Kat and me in the kitchen for a while inventing new flavors for Kat's ice cream maker.

He popped by on Monday to borrow a movie, on Wednesday he brought his college course choices by to get our opinion, and then on Thursday went out with Kat and me to visit some new raccoon kits she'd rescued from someone's garage.

So on Friday afternoon, as I was working in the store, sorting garbage into different bags for glass, plastic, paper, and so-gucky-I-can't-tell-what-it's-supposed-to-be, I wasn't that surprised to hear someone knocking at the door.

"Sam, if you don't stop popping around here every five minutes I'm going to think you're stalking me—" I called, turning.

But the words froze in my throat. It was Kevin, his lanky form leaning in my doorway like someone had poured him there. He'd obviously come from work—his well-worn jeans were splattered with paint, with the bittersweet smell of sweat and smoke clinging to his white T-shirt. I felt my heart leap and clatter against my rib cage. I had to admit—Kevin looked good.

"Uh . . . hi!"

"Hi," Kevin said, staring down at his feet and looking slightly ill at ease. "Um, yeah, I'm sorry for dropping by unannounced. I . . . I hope this isn't a bad time."

"No, no this is good," I said, wiping my hands on my jeans self-consciously and wondering just how bad the damage was. "I'm not expecting anyone to drop by or anything. I mean, I am expecting Sam tomorrow because we're going to his sister Mandy's wedding . . . as friends obviously. But it's not like I'm doing anything today."

OK, I was still convinced by the look on Kevin's face that he thought I was waiting for Sam. He still wasn't saying much more than hello and he had this look on his face that guys get when they're afraid of stepping onto someone else's territory. But, after several false starts, and a few incoherent half-sentences on both our parts, I finally managed to string enough syllables together to communicate that Sam was just a friend, simply a friend, only a friend, absolutely 100 percent nothing but an f-r-i-e-n-d. So maybe I overemphasized it a little bit, but it's not like Sam would mind. And then we had one of those awkward moments you have with the opposite sex when you realize you've just spent the last fifteen minutes talking about some other guy.

But there's only so long you can stand there, feeling awkward, sending little nervous smiles back and forth, saying semi-useless things like "Well . . ." and "Yeah . . ." and hoping the other person will fill in the blank. So I offered to show Kevin around the store, and even though for a moment I was afraid I'd have to physically pry him from the door frame, he was quick to follow after me, and actually seemed kind of excited about my small, dingy space.

He knocked on walls and looked under things and said serious-sounding things about plaster, concrete, and reinforced shelves. I started to mutter something about it not being much to look at, but he cut me off.

"This place is great, really great—you'll be able to do a lot with this place. How long've you been working on fixing it up?"

"Few days," I said. "I know I've only done a little bit so far . . ."

Kevin nodded. "You've done a lot, I can tell."

"What do you mean you can tell?"

"Glue's pretty thick on the window—you'll need a good solvent for that but I think I might be able to give you something," he was walking as he talked, "and you can tell by the discoloration of the floor it's been pretty badly neglected for a long time." He put his hands on the counter and, pushing back, hopped up and sat on it. "I actually looked into buying this place once, long time ago," Kevin said. "No, actually that's not true—I never actually had a plan or anything. Just when I was younger I thought I wanted to set up my own business, selling music or something, I wasn't sure. And I remember walking by with my friends and looking in the window and saying that I was going to buy the place and do something with it. But that was a long time ago."

I think that was the most I'd ever heard him say in one go. "I thought you wanted to go to Bible college," I said.

"Oh, I do now," Kevin said, "I didn't then." He paused. "Actually I think it's kind of cool that you're working on cleaning up the place I used to dream about running." He smiled. "Feels good, doesn't it, being able to look around a room and go 'I did this today.'"

I smiled. "Yeah, it does. I've never really put it into words like that—and I know it probably wouldn't seem like much to someone like Sam who's going to university soon and has his own little Web-design thing going too—but there is something kind of cool about doing something practical with your hands."

"A sense of accomplishment," Kevin said.

"Yeah, that's it exactly."

His eyes caught mine and we smiled. And I know that connecting with someone over the fact a grimy room had a few less moldy magazines might not seem like much. But in that second I knew that Kevin understood how I felt, and that felt really, really great.

"When I was a kid my dad started building the family ranch-type house on a lot between Ashford and Silverpoint—and he hasn't stopped building on it since," Kevin said. "A few months ago, we converted the basement into a whole separate apartment for me to live in."

"You and your dad must be pretty close," I said.

"Yeah, we're pretty tight, but we haven't always been." For a second a sour look flickered across Kevin's face. But then he said cheerfully, "It's a really great place though, and I'm really blessed to have it. It has all these windows, so it's brighter than you'd expect. I should show you sometime."

"I'd like that."

"Cool."

Now the problem with flirting is it involves being kind of . . . well . . . subtle. You end up making these little half-statements and hoping the other person is able to read between the lines and catch on to what you are actually trying to say. So, as I went around showing Kevin the rest of the store—looking at the terrifyingly filthy toilet, and the small back room that looked like a hurricane had swept through it—I was having a really hard time telling if he was actually interested in me, or just naturally slightly incoherent. He was definitely sending me some signals, but spending time with Kevin was confusing more than anything else.

Kevin hung around for a while. After the grand tour he went back to sitting on the counter and rested his legs against the magazine rack. We chatted idly about Kat's plans for the store and I went back to sorting through the garbage. But there was just something about him being there that was making me so self-conscious. It was like every molecule in my body was totally aware of his eyes on me. And isn't there some science theory that everything acts differently when it's watched? So I was kind of relieved when he asked if he could pop out the back door to make a quick phone call. While he was gone I dashed upstairs into Kat's to quickly wash my hands and look at myself in the mirror. My hair looked all right—it had kind of been in a loose knot at the back of my neck, but half of it had fallen around my face accomplishing one of those messy-cute styles it takes ages to do on purpose. I wasn't wearing any makeup (drat!) but I didn't know how to fix that without it actually looking like I'd just run off and put makeup on while he was gone. So I settled on a small amount of hopefully subtle-looking lip gloss and then raced back downstairs before he could notice I was gone.

But Kevin still seemed to be out back. I was about to head out after him, when, out of the corner of my eye, I noticed something moving outside the front window. There were two guys standing on the sidewalk in front of the store. One was skinny, with stringy hair and a black hat advertising motor oil. The other was shorter and stockier with a bright red jacket.

And they were watching me. Staring right into the store—right at me—as if they were looking for something.

And no matter how hard I tried to tell myself that it was no big deal and that they were probably just curious about the shop, it didn't stop the sick, uneasy feeling spreading in the pit of my stomach.

I took a couple of steps back, willing my shaking legs to move, even as I could see the leaden eyes following me. I stumbled backward over one of the garbage bags, then turned and practically ran into the back room, where I plowed straight into Kevin's chest, knocking him back a couple of inches.

Kevin reached out and caught me by the shoulders.

"We've got to stop colliding like this," he said lightly, tracing his fingers slowly down my arms.

"Kevin," I hissed, "there are a couple of guys out front and they're watching the store."

He frowned. "Are you sure about that? They're probably just looking for an address or something."

I tossed my head vigorously. "No, no. They were looking right into the store. They were staring right at me!"

"I don't know, Jo," Kevin said slowly. "Silverpoint is a pretty safe town. It just . . . well . . ." He shook his head slowly like I'd just said something confusing. "It just doesn't make sense."

He didn't believe me. Kevin didn't believe me.

I couldn't help thinking that if Kevin didn't believe me about something as minor as a couple of guys watching me two seconds earlier, then how on earth would he ever believe I saw someone try to kill Nate last summer? At the very least he was sure to think I had a pretty overactive imagination. And if Nate didn't back me up, well then Kevin was sure to think I was some sort of hallucinating lunatic.

Then again, he did have a point. What reason could a couple of strangers possibly have for menacing me?

"I guess you're right," I heard myself saying, without really believing the words.

"Don't worry, babe," Kevin said, smiling reassuringly. "It's probably nothing." He slid his hands down my arms until his fingers brushed against mine setting off tiny little jolts of electricity through my palms. "But if you'd like, I'll go back out with you and we'll look."

Slowly I followed him back into the front room and up to the window. Motor-Oil-Guy and Red-Jacket were gone.

"See, no one's there," Kevin said with an awkwardly unnatural cheerfulness. "They were probably just window shopping."

I nodded again. What else could I do?

"But if you want to tell me what they looked like," he went on, "I'll keep my eye open in case . . ."

"No," I said quickly, "you're right. It's probably nothing."

"Anyway, I should go," Kevin said. "I hate to run, but I've got stuff I need to get done."

Oh right. Stuff. That age-old excuse for cutting a date short since the dawn of time.

One second it almost seemed like he was going to ask me out. The next he's suddenly got stuff he needs to run off and do. What was worse was I didn't know who I blamed more, him or me.

"But," Kevin went on, "it was really nice to see you. Really."

He leaned back against the counter and grinned at me. "Look, why don't we plan to get together and do something after the Gathering on Sunday? Have you ever been down to the park at the far end of the beach?"

I shook my head.

"Well you should," Kevin said. "It's kind of cool. Has all these water jets. How about we go do that? I'll even pick you up and give you a ride to the Gathering too. What do you say?"

What did I say?

"I mean, if you want to?" Kevin went on, "it's no problem—"

"Sure," I said cutting him off, "sounds great!"

Yes, yes, of course yes! You don't ask a girl you don't like for a walk along the beach. Well, maybe you did if you were Sam. But with Kevin it had to mean something. Maybe not everything. But definitely something.

§ § §

Saturday—Mandy's wedding day. Kat and I had found the perfect dress actually. It was simple and shimmery and pale green, and it kind of flowed off my shoulders and down to my ankles like a mossy waterfall. I'd even managed to find the perfect pair of flats to match. Not that it really mattered if I was towering over Sam. After all, it's not like it was a date or anything. But still.

After I got dressed, Kat wove a handful of tiny braids into my hair, pinning them up, and leaving the rest of my hair to fan out around my shoulders.

"You really look beautiful," Kat said.

"Really?" I spun around, in front of Kat's full-length mirror, and watched the silky fabric swirl around me.

"I don't ever remember your mother doing your hair when you were little," Kat said.

I shook my head. "She did sometimes, but not very often. Do you remember that dance I went to when I was fourteen, and I ran over to your place first so that your mom could do my hair?"

"I remember."

The truth was that I was feeling a little kinder toward my mother than usual. I'd gotten an e-mail from her Friday night, full of apologies for not getting in touch sooner and excuses why it was impossible to get online one second earlier. She'd had a computer virus—a life-altering, terrifying plague by the way she described it—and the most wonderful computer guy had come around to help her sort it out. The computer guy's name was Donny; he had blue eyes to die for and apparently he'd gotten her into instant messaging. In mother-speak, this was code for "Mac is out, Donny is in, and I feel guilty about not being in touch with my only child for three weeks." Well, at least it was better than nothing.

I wrote back and told her all about the store, and Kat, and my date with Kevin on Sunday night. Obviously I didn't tell her anything about Nate or the Gathering.

And I didn't mention Sam. I wasn't hiding Sam from my mom, really, I just didn't think she'd approve of my spending so much time with a guy I had no intention of dating.

Then again, I have to admit, I was still insanely nervous about my non-date with Sam and by the time I heard the doorbell ring, my stomach was doing so many flip-flops that I could barely open the door.

Sam was wearing a dark gray tuxedo, sporting a brand new haircut, and holding a corsage in his hands. And there was something about seeing him standing there on my doorstep that for a moment made my tongue forget how to form words. I don't know why, but something seemed different about him—something I couldn't put a finger on. He just looked so . . . well . . . un-Samish.

"For you," he said, holding out the flowers. "I hope you like roses and ivy. When I went to pick up the flowers for Mandy I thought you might like a corsage or something too."

Feeling suddenly shy, I nodded and held out my hand, as Sam gently slid the flowers onto my wrist. They matched his boutonniere.

"You got your hair cut."

"Yeah," Sam rubbed his hand over the back of his head, "I think I'd like it a bit longer on the top. What do you think?"

"I like it. It's a little less 'shaggy dog' and a bit more 'sister's wedding.'"

"Thanks."

"So how's Mandy doing?"

"A bit freaked," Sam said. "My mom's been driving her nuts but everyone at Cornerstone—especially Patrick—has been really great at helping her get everything sorted out."

We walked to the car. Sam opened the door for me, and held it while I slid into my seat.

"Kind of weird seeing you so dressed up," he said, without really looking at me, as he got in his side and put the car in gear.

"Yeah, well, I think this is the first time I've seen you out of blue jeans."

"Really?"

"Yeah."

"And?"

"And I think you're fishing for a compliment," I said. "But you look good."

"Thanks. You too."

As Sam drove through the wooded hills on the outskirts of Silverpoint toward Cornerstone Church, I told him about seeing Motor-Oil-Guy and Red-Jacket outside the shop window. To be honest, I was kind of hoping he would kind of help me laugh it off and agree with Kevin that it was nothing. But instead Sam's face hardened in a protective older-brother kind of way. He asked me if I had a cell phone—I didn't—and told me to call him if I ever suspected someone was watching me again. I accused him of overreacting and found myself trying to convince him they were just curious window-shoppers.

But Sam wouldn't be dissuaded.

He said, "Early this morning a bunch of us guys came over to the church to help set up the flowers and things for the wedding—Patrick, Brian, Nate, Simon-somebody, a couple I didn't know. We basically just provided the grunt work and one of Mandy's bridesmaids—Claire something—told us where to put things. Anyway, when Nate was lifting some flowers his shirt rode up a bit and I got a glimpse of the scar you mentioned."

"And?"

"And, it looks like he was in some nasty accident."

"So?" I said. "Still doesn't make it my problem." Sam frowned. "OK," I backtracked, "I phrased that badly. What I mean is, just because someone attacked Nate, or some gang went to prison, doesn't mean anyone can link that to me."

"Fair enough," Sam conceded. "But just be careful anyway. After all, since you did report it, your name and address has to be on file with someone somewhere. And if there was a gang—"

"Then someone might break into the store to steal the garbage bags and soggy newspapers?" I said.

A wide grin broke out across Sam's face. "OK, so maybe I'm being a little overprotective," he said, "but I would just hate it if anything happened to you."

"Don't worry," I said, "I'm fine." Still, it was nice to know he cared.

Cornerstone Church looked smaller up close than it did from a distance. It was still a magnificent building though, made of a golden-beige rock. The huge front windows were cascading shapes of blue, green, and yellow—almost like impressionistic paintings made of stained glass. It was all very peaceful and welcoming.

"I've got brother-of-the-bride duties to attend to," Sam said. "I'm going to be standing up front, but I'll try to find you someone to sit with. Will you be OK if I dash off for a minute?"

I nodded. Sam rushed down the aisle and disappeared through a door. He had barely been gone a second when the large wood doors behind me pushed open again and a short, irritated man in an expensive, dark suit marched into the front hall.

"The music group is late, Marjorie!" he barked. "I told you we should have gone with Robert's recommendation!"

Marjorie burst through the door a second later, her arms full of boxes. Her overpermed hair was unnaturally red. Her tailored suit glittered with hundreds of tiny sequins. Her painted face wrinkled into well-defined lines of frustration.

"Mandy never listens, Stan," Marjorie sighed like a broken kettle. "I thought you were going to handle it." She reshuffled the packages in her arms and looked at me in annoyance. I opened my mouth to ask if I could help, but the older woman turned away and hurried down the aisle.

Stan didn't even acknowledge my existence. He strode after Marjorie, casting a critical eye over every detail of the decorated church. I could hear his voice roaring long after the couple had disappeared through the doors.

"Tell the preacher not to waste our time with too much religious babble, I've got some major clients coming and I don't want to give them the wrong impression about Underwood and Ogilvie . . . Mandy, how in heaven's name do you . . . Samuel! Stop standing there like an idiot and do something useful . . ."

Those were Sam's parents? I have to admit I was totally shocked, and kind of angry too. What the heck was wrong with some people? I leaned my head back against the wall. How could someone as great as Sam have such nasty people for parents? I had only known his parents for all of three seconds and already I wanted to run back there, give Sam a huge hug, and tell him to never listen to another word either of his parents might say. It seemed totally unfair somehow that someone so amazing could have grown up with such odious people.

I was grateful for the distraction when four men in matching gray tuxedos came rushing out of the back room and began moving the candles around. None of them were Sam.

Guests began to arrive. I thought I recognized a few of them from the Gathering but I wasn't sure. Two of the men hurried to start showing people to their seats. I reluctantly started to join the end of the line when I heard a voice calling my name. It was Lisa, sticking her head out of a side door and waving. A friendly face in a sea of strangers. I smiled in relief.

"You're here for the wedding?" I asked.

"I'm helping my dad out by doing the sound, so I'll be up in the balcony," Lisa said. "You here with Mandy's brother Sam?"

I nodded. "Yeah, but he's busy doing ushery things."

"Well you're really welcome to sit with me," Lisa said. "I mean we'll be squeezed into a sound booth on folding chairs, but you'll have the best view in the house and won't have to sit in a pew."

"Sounds like fun," I said. I was never a big fan of weddings. I mean, by the time I was fourteen I had already been forced to sit through three long ceremonies, in three ugly, uncomfortable dresses, while my mother promised to spend the rest of her life with someone she was going to be hurling abuse at in a few months time. Then I would be hugged by a lot of strangers, who would ask me what I thought of my new daddy. And I would keep my mouth shut and wonder how adults could be so stupid.

"Hey Jo! Oh, hi Lisa!" Sam reappeared at my side. "I'm sorry to abandon you so long. And I hate to spring this on you but my mom is kind of insisting I proceed over to the reception hall with the bridesmaids right after the ceremony. Something to do with the photos. But as soon as I can I'll run back over and get you."

"Don't worry, I can show her where to go," Lisa chirped in quickly. "It only takes two minutes in a car, or like ten if you walk it, and since Jo and I are going to be sitting together it is really, really no problem!"

Sam took a long look at the short percolating girl. Then he turned to me.

"That all right with you?" he asked.

"Yup," I said. "I'm going to be sitting in the balcony with Lisa."

"Interesting," said Sam. "OK, have fun, and don't start throwing things at me during the boring parts."

"I'll try not to."

Sam started to dash off again, but I stopped him long enough to straighten his tie, and then I gave him a friendly pat on the shoulder and he ran off again.

The sound booth was up a winding flight of steps, on a small balcony at the back of the church.

"This place is so soundproof that we can talk through the whole service and no one will hear us," Lisa said, slipping into a chair behind a huge box of knobs and buttons. "I think they were planning this to be a proper balcony at some point, but the supports weren't right or something. See that sign on the wall— 'Maximum booth occupancy three people'? Well, that's because when I was like fourteen Nate decided to see how many of us could squeeze up at one go. We got like twenty-six teenagers crammed up here—all sitting on each other and piled on the floor and stuff. And when Patrick caught us I thought he was going to blow a gasket!"

OK, so I know I didn't know Nate really well, but he had never really struck me as a rabble-rouser. But before I even had a chance to think up a response Lisa had already changed the subject.

"Sam seems like a great guy," Lisa said.

"He is."

"And, you guys are . . . ?"

"Just friends." Like she even had to ask.

"Right." She paused for a moment. "And you and Kevin aren't . . ."

I shook my head. "No." Not yet anyway.

"Right," Lisa nodded cheerfully.

"And you aren't dating . . . um . . . anyone right now, at the moment, are you, Lisa?" I asked.

Lisa blushed a little and shook her head, her red and black hair flitting around her face like feathers. "Not at the moment," Lisa said. "I'd really like to though, but I'm waiting for God to give me the go-ahead. I kind of promised God I'd wait until I finished high school. And I graduated three weeks ago. So I'm kind of hoping God will bring the right guy along soon . . ."

Yup—just when I began to think Lisa seemed pretty cool, she had to say something to remind me she was from a whole different planet. But it didn't seem to bother her.

To be honest, I was really jealous of Lisa. She seemed so confident, and upbeat, and seriously, seriously happy. Sam was right, it was easy to be a happy little Christian when you had a picture-perfect life handed to you on a golden platter. But I felt deep down in my gut that no leap of faith—no matter how huge—was ever going to have me reborn as some joyful, secure, I-can-do-all-things person—any more than I was going to wake up the next morning with a great figure, funky highlighted hair, and fabulous legs that weren't ridiculously long and freakishly gangly.

Down below us, a women's quartet had started to play. Lisa sat back behind the big black box and moved dials up and down. The four young men who had been rushing around hurried back to the front of the church and stood in a solid gray line. The front doors opened and three more men in tuxedos came out—Patrick, Sam, and then Brian. The musical group started playing something beautiful and haunting, and everyone stood up from their seats in the pews. I stood up too, but when I noticed Lisa hadn't, I sat back down again.

"I wish we were singing," Lisa said. "Sunday mornings we have guitars and a keyboard and really good singing. It's not quite the same as the Gathering because we've got kids and adults and seniors and everybody together. But it's pretty amazing all the same."

Uh huh. "Have you always been really into church?" I asked.

Lisa laughed. "Well, yeah, my dad's the pastor," she said. But that didn't quite answer my question. Had Lisa ever wondered if there really was a God—and if there was, if that God actually liked her?

Somehow I doubted it. She had probably been born singing "Amazing Grace."

"Just to warn you though, when you see my dad, I don't look anything like him," Lisa went on. "I'm adopted."

OK—now that I did not see coming.

"My parents adopted me from mainland China when I was six months old. They had taken this trip to visit missionary friends who worked in an orphanage and rather than bringing back a little model of the Great Wall like most normal people, they decided to bring back an abandoned baby.

"They were there when I was found in a Dumpster behind a strip club, and apparently my mother stayed up half the night holding me and refused to go home without me. Of course there were a bunch of legal and immigration hoops they had to jump through, but my dad can be pretty determined about stuff sometimes."

Thankfully the wedding procession started then because I did not have a clue what to say. I mean, my mother may not like me very much most of the time, but at least she never actually threw me away.

Then again, what would it be like to know that someone had actually fought to have you?

We watched the procession of women walk toward the front, in flowing purple dresses and dyed purple shoes, with hundreds of tiny purple flowers in their hair, clutching bouquets of something green and purple.

Then came Mandy, resplendent in meters of white fabric and millions of tiny white beads that shimmered in the light. Over one arm draped a bouquet of long-stemmed white flowers, and with the other she held loosely onto Stan's arm. I knew people were going to say that she was a beautiful bride—and I don't know how to explain it, but it wasn't the dress, or the hair, or any of it that made her look beautiful. Mandy just looked so happy. Like she was absolutely thrilled to be there, and, as she stood up beside Brian, like she knew she was where she was meant to be.

A big black man in a long robe stepped up onto the stage, spread his arms wide, and announced that God was there with them.

"That's my dad," Lisa whispered, leaning forward with her elbows on the mixing board.

Pastor Wallace beamed and announced every word with joy and amazement, as though talking about Jesus and God's plan for marriage for the first time.

Then Patrick went up to the front of the church. "A reading from First Corinthians chapter thirteen," he said.

"'If I have the gift of prophecy and can fathom all mysteries and all knowledge, and if I have a faith that can move mountains, but have not love, I am nothing. If I give all I possess to the poor and surrender my body to the flames, but have not love, I gain nothing.'"

And the weirdest thing happened when Patrick started talking. I felt something. I actually felt something. It almost felt like he was looking right at me, like he was talking right to me, like every word coming out of his mouth was so important somehow that I suddenly wished I had a pen and could write it down.

"'Love is patient,'" Patrick read steadily. "'Love is kind.'"

But, love isn't patient, Patrick! I argued back inside my head. *And I don't think it's kind either.* Lots of selfish, horrible people are surrounded by people who like them.

"'It does not envy, it does not boast, it is not proud.'"

Oh really? So in other words if you are miserable you are supposed to just sit quietly and let people dump on you, and be thankful for whatever scraps God sends your way? *Well, maybe not everybody finds your perfect ideal love!* What about all the people that end up hurt, and broken, and alone? Where do they fit in?

"'It is not rude, it is not self-seeking, it is not easily angered . . .'"

Look at your perfect right-hand man Nate, Patrick! What happened to him, huh? Nate ran around doing good Christian deeds and his great reward was having some ungrateful jerk try to kill him.

"'. . . it keeps no record of wrongs. Love does not delight in evil but rejoices with the truth.'"

Did Nate forgive the guy who tried to kill him?

"'It always protects, always trusts, always hopes, always perseveres. Love never fails.'"

Don't you see how idealistic you're sounding? You church people want to convince us all that it's the right way to live—but what about the people like Sam and I that don't fit into your perfect world?

"'Now we see but a poor reflection as in a mirror; then we shall see face to face. Now I know in part . . .'"

What about those of us who aren't patient, and are rude, and don't think people are kind, or fair, or loving? How is this perfect love available for someone like me? And does it even work in the real world?

"'. . . then I shall know fully, even as I am fully known.'"

The service went on. Pastor Wallace preached a sermon about God having a plan for our lives. The vows were beautiful. It was probably the nicest wedding I'd ever been to. But it was Patrick's reading about love that stuck under my skin.

I hung out with Lisa in the balcony for a while after the service finished and watched the well-dressed mob filing slowly out of the church. The girl could talk—and I mean talk! She must have gone on about God so loving the world for at least fifteen minutes. But I didn't really mind. Because I'd decided that I kind of liked her. There was something about Lisa that made her seriously easy to hang out with; there were never any awkward silences and she didn't care if all you did was nod and make the occasional frivolous comment. And she wasn't at all self-absorbed—odd, I know, considering how much she liked to talk. But with Lisa it wasn't actually all about her—it was about God, or the latest gossip about some person from the Gathering I didn't even know, or how she hoped I was settling in well and enjoying life in Silverpoint.

But mostly, she talked about Nate. Nate was almost twenty. Nate was writing a new worship song. Nate led a Bible study for street kids. Nate was restoring a classic car. Nate was starting his second year of university in September. Nate invited all sorts of people to try church for the first time. Nate volunteered at a soup kitchen one night a week last year.

In other words—no matter how scary Nate had seemed to me, in Lisa's eyes Nate was wholly religious and wholly perfect. And Lisa wanted to go out with him so badly it hurt—not that she'd admit it.

"Sounds like a great guy," I offered tentatively.

"Oh he is!" Lisa chimed in enthusiastically.

"In fact . . ." I said slowly, "I'm surprised he's never gotten hurt . . ."

I felt guilty even as the words came out of my mouth. It's not like I was lying to her, I tried justifying it to myself—I mean, since when was it a crime to ask a question you already knew the answer to?

But at the same time, Lisa was being so nice to me and here I was trying to find out what she knew about Nate's accident, without being honest enough to come out and ask her. But it's not like there was any other way I was going to find out.

I held my breath, waiting for Lisa to give me the same brush-off that Kevin had given me, but instead Lisa nodded vigorously, her face the picture of sincerity. "Oh he did! It was horrible! I was overseas with my dad, and Patrick even called us at the hotel to let us know. I was positively sick with worry but Dad didn't want to go back early."

"What had happened to him?" I said, wincing for sounding so enthusiastic and not the least bit sympathetic. But thankfully Lisa didn't notice.

"I don't know," she said earnestly. "Nate hates to talk about it. I asked him about it a couple times but he totally stonewalled me. And all Dad would say was that there'd been an incident at the church, and that he didn't want me talking about it. Like they didn't trust me!"

They probably had a point there. As nice as Lisa might be she didn't exactly strike me as the kind of person you'd want to trust with your deepest secrets.

"I can't describe how bad Nate looked," Lisa went on. "He

looked positively sick. I mean, he had a couple of broken ribs—so he had to take it really easy. But it was like he was sick inside too or something. He just went all quiet and moody. And he was really angry for a while too. I was really afraid that . . . I don't know . . . that something really bad had happened to him . . ."

Lisa's face was lined with pain just remembering it.

"I know that Nate can be a little intimidating if you don't know him—"

A little?

". . . but he's really got a soft heart inside. He wrote a lot of songs while he was recovering—some of them pretty angry and he wouldn't let me hear all of them. But he also wrote this really great one called 'You Know All the Days of My Life' that we sing sometimes at the Gathering. I guess you're not used to talking about God, Jo, so I don't know if this'll make any sense to you. But sometimes when you go through difficult stuff it can make your faith stronger than it was before. And this seemed like a really, really hard thing he was going through."

Even as Lisa was talking I knew this was none of my business. This wasn't my life, or my pain, and if Nate had decided to keep this a secret then he probably didn't want us sitting around talking about it. But somehow I didn't try to change the subject.

"What got him out of it?" I asked.

"Kevin," Lisa said flatly. "I think it was Kevin that did it. I mean, obviously God did too. But Nate is really passionate about helping people find Jesus, and Kevin was like someone who was just beginning to get to know Jesus, so Kevin was totally like the kind of person Nate would reach out to. And next thing you knew, it seemed like wherever Nate was, Kevin was there too—helping him carry stuff, or set things up, or sometimes they'd go off and talk.

"In fact . . ." Lisa went on, dropping her voice as if she was afraid to get caught imparting state secrets, "don't tell anyone I said this, but just between you and me, I don't think Nate really liked Kevin when he first started coming."

OK, now I have to admit that surprised me. "But I thought Christians were supposed to love everybody," I said more than a little facetiously.

Lisa giggled. "Nate's more of a tough-love kind of guy," she said rolling her eyes conspiratorially. "But at first the two of them seriously did not get on. Kevin moped around like he wasn't happy to be here and Nate practically sat on him, like he was afraid Kevin was going to run off with a pew or something."

"Really?" I said. "But now they seem really close."

"They are now," Lisa agreed. "Now they go real deep. They're like spiritual brothers or something.

"But . . . at first . . ." she tossed her head grinning, "it was kind of like watching the head male of the lion pride circling around the new young stud who's just strutted onto his turf. Talk about tension!"

"What about tension?" a deep voice suddenly cut in and Lisa nearly hit the ceiling as Nate walked onto the balcony. My heart was pounding guiltily like I'd just been caught making faces at the teacher behind his back.

While I'd noticed Kevin was the kind of tall guy who seemed to underplay his size by slouching and sliding into the corner of a room, Nate seemed to do the opposite—filling the tiny balcony with his presence like some kind of mythological creature unfurling its wings.

"I . . . uh . . . hi . . . um . . ." For once Lisa was speechless, a pink glow of embarrassment spreading across her cheeks.

Nate searched her face, raised an eyebrow, and then glanced over at me.

"You're Jo, right? Kevin's friend," he said.

"Yeah. We met the other night at the Gathering."

"Right," Nate nodded. "Hi, I'm Nate." He raised a hand in casual greeting. Then he turned back to Lisa. "Your dad is looking for you," he said mildly. "He's locked out of his office again and apparently you have his spare keys?"

"Oh! Right!" Lisa slipped out of her chair. "It was really nice to see you, Jo!" she called over her shoulder, disappearing down the stairs. "Hope to see you again soon!" She was still talking as her voice faded into the distance.

"She was going to show me how to get to the reception," I said, half to myself.

"It's in the church hall. Come on, I'll show ya," Nate said. "Did Kevin tell you his dad Ken helped build it? His dad's company has done a lot of work around Cornerstone."

I followed him out, feeling more than a little nervous. I swear Nate was even more daunting up close than he was from a distance, and no matter how big of a softie Lisa might say the guy was, I figured you'd have to be either really stupid or really desperate to try and take him on—even with a car.

"Kevin tells me you're new in town," Nate said, as we walked out the front door into the parking lot. "How did you start coming to the Gathering?"

"Mandy's brother Sam invited me," I said.

"Yeah, I was talking to him earlier today," Nate said. "Interesting guy. Asked me if I'd converted any unsuspecting heathens recently." To my surprise Nate smiled a little. "I liked his question from Sunday—does God make things happen for a reason." He nodded. "Good question. It's one I've wrestled with."

He nodded again, without really looking at me, and for a moment his smile faded. It was like he was looking past me, to something lurking over my shoulder. Maybe if I knew nothing about Nate besides his wonderful worship-guy persona I wouldn't have thought anything of it. But to be actually standing with him, in the actual place I knew someone had tried to kill him, well it was more than a little bit creepy and part of me just wanted to run.

"Anyway," Nate said lightly, after what felt like a very long pause, "it's dead easy to find the reception hall from here. You just follow this road down and it's there on your right. Would you like me to walk you?"

I shook my head. "No, that's fine."

"OK," Nate said, "see you around."

He started to turn and walk back to the church when suddenly my brain started screaming at me that I didn't know when I would next get a chance to actually talk to the guy without an audience around and that if I didn't take the chance to say something to him then—

"Nate!"

"Yeah?"

He stopped, turning back to face me.

"I . . . uh . . . I . . . I was . . ."

But I couldn't force the words over my lips.

"I . . . I was wondering . . . I was just wondering . . ." I took a deep breath, and chickened out. "What does it mean to take a leap of faith?"

I smiled brightly, and tried to look really interested in his answer like that was the question I was meaning to ask all along. Nate gave me a long, hard look like he wasn't the slightest bit fooled and for a second I was afraid he was going to call me on it.

Then he said: "There's a proverb in the Bible that says we should trust God with our whole heart and not lean on . . . not rely on what we think we know. It's like that."

I was expecting him to say something more, but instead he just headed back inside the church, leaving me wondering.

CHAPTER FIVE

SAM WAS waiting for me outside the hall. When I saw him this huge wave of relief swept over me. I know it was just a little thing, but I hadn't been looking forward to walking into the reception alone. Sam looked kind of flushed—less polished than before—but still good. Who knew a tux and a haircut could make so much difference to a guy?

Sam rushed over and caught me by the hand. "I'm so sorry for ditching you for so long," he said excitedly, "but I've got something which I hope can help make up for it—I've talked to Mandy and you get to sit with me during the reception!"

Now, see, here I had been thinking I was going to be stuck at the back of the hall, sitting with some boring great aunt or something while Sam had all the fun sitting with the wedding party. So I was seriously, seriously happy to be sitting with him—if a bit surprised in an overwhelmed kind of way. And I felt even better when Sam added that Mandy and Brian had opted for round tables, instead of one of those long, intimidating head table things.

Sam offered me his arm. I took it. Then we walked up the steps and Sam pushed open the door. It was a long, wide hall, with a row of windows down the side. Lacy gauze and ivy cascaded down around the doorway. And on tall silver candlesticks, pale pink candles flickered from the sides. The ivory-draped tables were small, intimate, with maybe only six or eight people at each one. It looked like everyone else was already seated, and as we walked across the room to our table, I felt a flutter of butterflies settle into my stomach.

My arm stiffened. "You OK?" Sam asked, leaning his head close to mine.

"Feels like everyone is looking at me," I confessed.

Sam grinned. "Maybe they are," he whispered back, "that's a pretty cute dress."

Not quite the reassurance I had been expecting. I took another step and my foot unexpectedly slipped and skidded on the polished floor.

Without missing a beat, Sam pulled me closer to him, steadying me on his arm. Then he took my hand, and spun me around once on the floor, his hand holding mine tight as I spun on my toes—my long, green skirt swirling out around me like water. I gasped, then laughed, and punched him in the shoulder.

"Now they're looking at you!" he said.

I rolled my eyes and shook my head at him. "What's gotten into you?" I asked.

Sam shrugged, then tossed his arm around my shoulder. "I'm just happy," he said, "and I'm glad you're here."

When we got to the table, Mandy jumped up and hugged me, and told me she was glad I'd made it. Sam pulled my chair out for me, and even insisted on trying to push it in for me again while I was trying to sit down. He kind of got it caught on my skirt, and everyone laughed. Then Patrick tried to show him the right way to do it. And not to be outdone, Brian got up and tried to push Mandy's chair in for her again—which was quite the feat considering the miles of tulle she had streaming around her.

It was kind of hard to put my finger on what was so special about that night. I mean, dinner was amazing—chicken and pasta and vegetables all piled on platters in the middle of the table with everyone serving themselves. Mandy said she'd gotten the idea from a wedding she'd been to on her mission trip. And the speeches were short, and hopeful, and full of these great words about love, and faith, and happily-ever-afters.

And I don't think I'd ever seen Sam in such a great mood. It seemed like we were laughing every two minutes—over small things, nothing really. He'd lean toward me and say something silly. Or I'd just catch his eye and he'd smile . . .

Had Sam always been this much fun to be with?

Before long everyone else had moved away from the table, and Sam and I were alone again. I hadn't even noticed them go.

"Why don't we grab some cake and go outside?" Sam asked.

I nodded.

"I'll go make a run for dessert," he whispered. "Meet me by the door in five."

I saw him go over to where Mandy was talking with a group of people. Sam slipped his hand on her shoulder and said something into her ear. Mandy gave her brother a quick hug. Then she looked my way and gave a little wave. Sam ducked behind her to the dessert table, loaded a few things on a plate, then darted toward the door—waving at me to follow. Grabbing my bag I rushed over to join him.

"Quick," he said, "before my mother notices I'm going and tries to make me pose for a photograph with my great aunt Mavis."

"You don't even have a great aunt Mavis do you?"

Sam grinned. "Nope. But I'm not taking any chances!"

We slipped out back and sat down on a top step, the small plate of cake between us. Sam slid his jacket off and placed it around my shoulders. It felt good against my skin, and I wriggled into it.

"Cold?" he asked.

"Not anymore."

"I never thought it made sense that guys were expected to wear long sleeves and jackets, while women are expected to wear little strappy things," Sam said.

"Maybe it's just so they have an excuse to give us their jackets," I offered.

A wide smile spread across Sam's face. "Maybe," he said.

"So shall I tell you about my conversations with Lisa and Nate today?" I asked. "Or do you want to tell me how your brother-of-the-bride day went?"

Sam shrugged. "Neither really. It's been a day full of talking. I think I'd like to sit for a while and just enjoy the night."

The sun had set. The stars were out in full force. A light breeze rustled the top of the trees. We looked at each other and smiled again. Neither of us reached for any cake. I'm not sure how it had happened, but somewhere between the moment when Sam knocked on my door, and the second he put his coat around my shoulders, this whole day had somehow gone from feeling like a friendly non-date to a proper date-date.

I mean—there I was with Sam. *Sam!* My friend. You know, the guy who shows up at my house unannounced and talks about insane things. The guy I could probably hang out with on an indefinite basis. But not someone I ever thought about, you know, that way. Not until then.

Maybe it was the moonlight. Or maybe it was just because his sister had gotten married, and love was in the air or something . . .

I tried to cast a sideways glance at Sam, but he glanced back at the exact wrong moment. Our eyes met and for the longest time neither of us said anything—we just looked at each other, close enough to kiss, neither of us moving . . .

Maybe I was actually starting to fall for him. I don't know. But I do know a huge part of me was hoping that he was feeling that exact same way too.

"I kind of missed you a bit during all the chaos today," Sam said quietly. "When I asked you to come to the wedding, I was kind of thinking . . . hoping we could have more time together."

"It's OK. Hanging out with Lisa was fun."

"This is nice though."

"Yeah."

Sam was still looking at me, his green-gray eyes kind of locked into mine. I thought he was going to say something more, when all of a sudden this nasty, bright light shone right in our faces. I blinked and for a second I couldn't see anything. Then I realized it was a big, white taxi scrunching to a halt on the gravel in front of us.

The back door flung open. Traci jumped out. Sam leapt to his feet and ran down toward her—sending our cake cascading down the steps in front of me. And my heart crashing to the ground like a twenty-pound weight.

"Traci!"

"Sam—hi!"

"Hi. What are you doing here?"

"I was looking for you."

I could have told him that. I would have thought it was pretty darn obvious the only reason an ex-girlfriend would show up at her ex-boyfriend's sister's wedding in a pale yellow sheath dress, with her streaked blonde hair swept up into a sophisticated but funky-looking knot, is because she knows her ex-boyfriend will be there, and she knows she'll get his attention. And she sure as rain knew how to make an entrance too.

But no one was asking my opinion. No, I was just sitting there like a wallflower, while Sam and Traci did this big exaggerated rushing toward each other. And then—get this—Traci did a whole little theatrical fake tripping-thing over a microscopic stone, practically launching herself into Sam's arms.

"I'm so, so sorry," Traci said, "but this was the only way I could be sure of running into you."

Yeah right! Like I believed that.

"I really am *so* sorry for dropping by like this," Traci went on, "and please don't be mad Sammy. But you wouldn't return my phone calls and I really needed to talk to you!"

I was kind of hoping this would prompt a disdainful sniff from Sam—or something suitably Rhett Butlerish. But instead he actually patted the hand that was clutching his arm in a reassuring way and said, "Well, I'm here now."

What!

"Really?" Traci said, batting her eyelashes. "I just feel like I look a state!"

Oh boy, was she laying it on thick.

"No, you're fine," Sam said, "you look amazing."

And he was falling for it! Hook, line, and sinker!

Enough was freaking well enough. I stood up, feeling Sam's coat slide off my shoulders.

"Oh," Traci said, like she was pretending she'd just noticed me there for the first time. She turned to Sam, "Look, if you're in the middle of some . . . thing . . ."

Come on Sam, I tried vibing him, *this is your chance . . . I'm willing to forget the whole "you look amazing" nonsense if you'll just . . .*

"Oh? Jo?" Sam said, "She's just a friend. She's cool."

And that was my cue to make a dignified exit while I still had a waiting taxi in front of me.

"Thanks so much for tonight, Sam," I said, sweeping up his coat as I marched down the stairs, before dropping it unceremoniously in his arms like it was any old rag I'd picked up off the floor. "It was fun. But I've got to get going. Nice to meet you, Traci."

Oh—my exit was perfect. I gave Traci my best fake smile, before hopping right into the taxi and giving the driver my address so calmly you'd think I'd ordered it myself.

And when Sam got this panicked, conflicted look on his face and asked me to stay, I simply smiled and said I was sure he and Traci had a lot of things to talk about. Oh—and not to worry about giving me a lift tomorrow night, because I was going with Kevin. Sam started to say something more, but thankfully the taxi driver—who, being a woman, perhaps knew the importance of making a perfect exit—had already started rolling, leaving Sam to stand there behind me with half-spoken words falling out of his open mouth. I didn't look back.

The car started to roll down the mountain road. I slowly counted to thirty, and when I was sure they were far enough behind me, I leaned my head against the cool glass of the window beside me and stared out at the trees blurring by. It hurt. I hated to admit it, but there was a real, solid, aching pain in my gut—like in the moment I'd seen them standing there together, with that look of concern on his face, someone had come along and punched me in the gut.

I liked him. I did. I didn't know why I liked him—he was annoying, and demanding, and I knew there was this even hotter guy, who I had a real genuine date with the next day. So why on earth was I so . . . so . . . jealous? Why should I care that he was currently off with some other girl—someone he had history with, someone who had been part of his life for a long, long time . . .

Argh! I banged my head hard against the seat behind me. It had started raining a little—just a few little splotches—and even though feeling as if rain had come at just this moment for me was called pathetic fallacy for a reason, it made me feel a little bit better.

I'd been so stupid, sitting there all night, giving him little sideways glances. What did I think was going to happen? It's not like I wanted him to ask me out. And what if he did? It's not like I would have ever said yes—was it?

Well, I thought to myself, at least there's still Kevin—forcibly shoving any errant thoughts of Sam out of my mind. I had of course been attracted to Kevin first anyway—at least when my imagination wasn't going into overdrive. I mean, if they'd both asked me out at the same time, I would have picked Kevin over Sam for sure. Right?

And so what if what I had with Sam was just a friendship? Friendship was great. Friendship was good. Friendship was all I ever really wanted anyway . . .

It would have to be.

§ § §

No matter how badly a day ends, there's always a new one to follow right on after it, and I leapt, even bounded, out of bed on Sunday, fully determined to embrace a whole new outlook—

Hardly! In fact, I woke up Sunday morning with the memory of sitting next to Sam on those steps—wondering if he was thinking about kissing me—hitting me square between the eyes. I groaned and stuck my head back under my pillow. How could I have been such an idiot? I mean, the guy practically had "I just want to be friends" tattooed on his forehead. And there I'd been thinking that just because he was wearing a tux, and just because romance happened to be in the air, and just because he had been so great to me, and told me I looked cute . . . *Argh!*

I dragged myself out of bed. Then stood in a shower that was far too hot and made a mental list of all the reasons why I was happy it was Kevin, not Sam, who was picking me up that night.

For starters, Kevin was definitely much better looking than Sam: he was taller, his blue eyes twinkled when he smiled, his blond hair was just the right length to think about running your fingers through.

Sure Kevin hadn't believed those two guys were watching me through the store window—but who's to say he wasn't right? That just proved he was more grounded than Sam, not as gullible, and far less prone to crazy antics like jumping off the pier just because I . . .

I groaned and jerked the shower dial over to freezing. This was going to be a long day.

But when Kevin showed up at quarter after six, leaning casually up against my door frame, looking like a movie star, and smiling like he'd just won the lottery, I decided that I was definitely heading out with the right guy.

We arrived early for the Gathering, and I helped Lisa set up chairs, while Kevin and Nate assembled things on the stage. So, it wasn't exactly a date. But it was nice. Lisa was super-friendly, and Nate actually smiled in my direction. And as for Kevin, well . . . Kevin was such a sweetheart. A really nice, great guy. And it was high time I found one of those.

Kevin was working the sound during the Gathering and pulled up an extra chair beside his so that we could sit together behind the soundboard.

"So, you sat with Lisa at the wedding yesterday?" Kevin asked, as I settled into my seat beside him.

"Yeah," I smiled, "she's nice."

He grinned. "I heard you had a good gossip before the reception."

I felt a slow blush creep into my cheeks, which only deepened when he leaned his face close to mine and whispered, "Anything scandalous?"

Before I could work out a reply, Nate yelled for Kevin to turn something on, and they had one of those weird monosyllabic conversations across the room which techies seem to understand— "check one," "levels?" "check, check"—but which sounded like pure gibberish to me.

Out of the corner of my eye I saw Sam walk in. He looked my way and kind of gave me an offhand wave. But there weren't any other chairs anywhere near Kevin and I, and when I pretended to be overly interested in Kevin's sound check, Sam walked toward the front of the room and sat with Simon-somebody who I vaguely recognized from the wedding.

I glanced at Kevin sideways as he leaned forward and started moving dials up and down. This was my guy—I told myself. Well, maybe not my guy as such. Not yet anyway. But he really did seem to like me. And I really liked him too. I mean, he was polite, and kind, and incredibly cute, and when he glanced at me and smiled, well, a girl could get used to that kind of attention.

The music was great as usual. Patrick's talk was about the historical "proofs" that Jesus existed, and died, and rose from the dead, and all that. Patrick ended by saying that the greatest proof that Jesus was alive was right there in the room with them. It was written on human hearts. That the greatest testimony to Jesus was that people had felt him and had their lives changed by him. And that they could feel him now.

Maybe something had rubbed off on me from hanging out with Lisa, but it all sounded almost believable—in a totally unbelievable way. I mean, it was nice to think that there was this God somewhere who loved me, and had time for me, and wanted to be involved in my life.

But at the same time, it was all kind of like a fantasy too. Like when you get all swept up in a movie, then walk out the door and come down with a bang when you realize you can't fly, you haven't defeated the bad guy, and dreams don't all come true. Don't get me wrong, it was a wonderful kind of fantasy world Patrick was spinning, and part of me definitely wanted it to be true, but somehow getting from my world to Patrick's and Lisa's and Nate's world just seemed kind of, well, unbelievable.

And to Kevin's world—it must be Kevin's world too, I thought. Not that he'd ever really said as much.

Then Nate started playing this song called "You Know All the Days of My Life." I knew he'd written it, because of what Lisa had said. But he didn't tell anyone it was his song. He just started singing: "You were there when I was made. Fearfully. Wonderfully. You planned every day out for me. You see every tear. You hear every cry. You know all the days of my life."

And, I don't know how to explain it, but when I saw Nate standing there, singing how God knew, really, really knew everything that had ever happened to him, for a moment, it almost felt like, well, like God was talking to me. Like somewhere in my subconscious I could hear God saying, "I planned all the days of Nate's life. Even the day someone almost killed him. And it wasn't a mistake that you saw him get hit by that car. Because I planned all the days of your life too."

And inside my head I was yelling back, "Look, God, if you already know everything anyway then what on earth would you need me for?"

But God didn't answer.

"You OK?" Kevin whispered, squeezing my hand. I realized then I was shaking. "You're shivering. Do you want to borrow my jacket?"

I shook my head, and tried to ignore the words as Nate kept on singing: "God, you know everything I've ever done. And you know everything I hate about me. You see every scar. You know every fear. You know all the days of my life . . ."

I was kind of hoping to take Kevin up on his offer of a walk as soon as the music was over. But quickly sliding his long limbs out from under the soundboard Kevin said he needed to take care of something. Then he dashed off promising he would be back in five.

Lisa was still up on stage, talking to Nate about something. And so, left with seemingly nothing to do, I reluctantly wandered over to where Sam was still sitting and slumped into a seat beside him.

"So, where did your fair knight sprint off to?" Sam said. "Perchance abandoning the beautiful maiden to serve the king and slay the dragon?"

"Ha ha," I said dryly.

"Well, at least Kevin saved you a seat," Sam said lightly. "And let me guess, he's taking you off my hands for the rest of the evening too."

"As a matter of fact he is," I said.

"Ah well, *vive l'amour jeune* and all that good stuff," Sam said.

I wondered if that was supposed to be my cue to ask him how things had gone with Traci the night before, but I didn't want to give him the satisfaction. If he wanted to talk about the way he had totally overlooked and insulted me by running after the girl who seemed hell-bent on ruining his life, then the least I could do was wait patiently for him to bring up the subject.

"Well . . ."

"Hmmm . . ."

"So . . ."

I looked at Sam. Sam looked at me, and neither of us said anything for what felt like an eternity. Maybe two.

"Hey Jo."

Thankfully our mutual standoff of silence was eventually broken by Kevin's apologetic arrival.

"I am so, so sorry," Kevin moaned, "I know we were supposed to go out tonight. But some other volunteer hasn't shown up and Nate has asked me to stay and help pack up stuff."

Crud.

Crud. Crud. Crud. Crudity crudity crud.

"It's OK, Kevin," I said brightly, forcing my fake smile so wide I'm amazed my cheeks didn't start to crack. "I understand. We can always—"

"I'll do it," Sam interrupted, jumping up.

"What?"

"I'll do it," Sam repeated, "I'll go help Nate with packing up or whatever. You guys go out and have your date."

My jaw dropped so low I nearly swallowed my shoes. "Really?" I spluttered, before I could catch myself. "I mean . . . are you sure?"

"Of course I'm sure," Sam said loudly, practically pushing Kevin and me toward the door. "If I can rebuild a spam-ridden computer and design a functional multi-user Web-based interface, I am sure I can figure out how to stack a few chairs. And if not, I'm sure half the God-squad will be only too happy to point me in the right direction."

"That's really nice of you," Kevin spluttered, throwing Sam a slightly dazed smile. "Everything kind of gets stacked in the back. It's a real nightmare to fit everything in there. Are you sure you don't mind?"

"Nope! Don't mind," Sam said briskly. "And noooo," he grabbed Kevin by the shoulder and steered him away from the stage as if anticipating his next move, "don't worry about going to tell Nate that you're leaving. I'll go tell him."

"Well, thanks for this, man," Kevin said, "I owe you one."

"I know," Sam said, waving us off.

I swear I saw him smirking just before we disappeared through the door. But since I couldn't think of any rational reason to turn down his offer, I followed Kevin out to his truck, reminding myself that when you're as romantically challenged as I am you don't turn down the opportunity to go out with an unbelievably gorgeous guy, just because you suspect your best friend is laughing at you behind your back.

I hadn't been on a date—not a nice date anyway—for what felt like ages. And judging by the way Kevin kept stumbling over his words, I guessed that was pretty true for him too. The sky was this wicked shade of purply-black and the streetlights gave the trees this unreal silvery tinge.

We drove down by the waterfront, past the pier, under a bridge, and into a big, empty parking lot. Kevin opened my door and offered me a hand down.

We walked along the waterfront's boardwalk chatting aimlessly—about movies we liked and what music we listened to. Our fingers kept bumping against each other's, driving me crazy wondering if he was thinking about holding my hand. Every now and then we'd glance at each other, grin inanely, and then go back to talking about nothing in particular.

The boardwalk led through a wrought-iron gateway, into long wide paths of shadowy gray flowers and tiny phantom shrubs, to where a large white fountain lay dormant.

"I think this is my favorite spot in Silverpoint," Kevin said. "Sometimes I just come down here to think, get everything back in focus."

He put his foot up on the ledge of the fountain and stared down at the silent jets.

"I hope Nate doesn't mind that I ran out early tonight," Kevin said after a long pause.

"I'm sure he won't mind," I said quickly, hoping it was true.

"Yeah, I'm sure he won't," Kevin echoed, sounding about as confident as I felt.

"Sometimes I wish I was more like him, like Nate," Kevin went on, looking down at the water. "I think it's because he's known God since he was like two. But he's always so centered. So sure."

"Sure of what?"

"Life," Kevin said. "Rightness. God."

"And you believe Nate is right?" I said, without really thinking. "That he, and Patrick and everyone, really connects with a God . . . *the* God?" As the words came out I wished I could take them back.

Kevin turned and looked at me. His hand touched my arm, right below the shoulder. "Yeah. Of course. Totally," he said. "Haven't you ever felt that God loved you or known that God was there listening to you?"

I shook my head. "No, not really." Not that I knew for sure anyway.

"So you don't believe in God at all, not even a little bit?" Kevin persisted.

How do you answer a question like that?

"I wouldn't say that," I said. "It's not like that. I kind of do believe there could be a God up there somewhere. I just don't know what kind of God it is, or how much I really want to believe . . ."

I didn't know if I was making any sense. After all, this was the first real conversation Kevin and I had had about anything like this, and I didn't want to scare him off by babbling nonsense. But at least I was being honest.

"And you are really into it, um . . . Jesus . . . right?" I said.

"Yeah, at least I am now," Kevin said. "I remember what it was like when my dad started going to church though and I didn't believe any of it. It was rough, 'cause my dad pushed and pushed and really rode me hard until I finally had had enough . . .

"Look, it's a really long story," Kevin said abruptly. "I've got to work a full day tomorrow. I'll tell you some other time."

We walked back to his truck. Kevin was quiet again as he drove me back home, and we didn't really talk. At least not about anything worth remembering afterward. But he took my hand when he helped me down from the truck, and held it as he walked me to the door.

"Well, thanks for the walk," I said.

"No problem," Kevin grinned, "I'm sorry it was so short. And

I'm sorry too if I got a bit intense back there, I'm not always good at talking about what life was like before I knew God."

"It's OK," I said. "After two hours of sitting through the Gathering I guess it's pretty normal to be thinking about spiritual things."

"Right," Kevin nodded. "Anyway, I hope you don't think this is weird or anything, but my stepmom writes sort of reviews for the local paper and we're going to the new pizza place on Friday and I was wondering if um . . . you wanted to come with us."

Dinner? With his parents? Yeah, that was a little weird. Still, he was asking . . .

"Sure," I said.

"Cool, I'll see you Friday."

Kevin took a step back, and slowly let his hand slip out of mine. Then he waited as I went inside and closed the door behind me.

The hallway light wasn't on, which basically meant that I couldn't see a thing.

I reached forward and fumbled for the lights when I stepped on something—something soft, something which moved.

I jumped and gave a little screech when suddenly a shadow loomed up in front of me.

A man. Standing there in our tiny front hallway.

I shoved hard against him, meaning to turn again and run.

But he caught me by the wrist and somehow the momentum knocked us both over until the next thing we knew we were sprawled on the steps, with my one hand still caught in a death grip and the other one hitting at any part of him I could reach as if my life depended on it.

"Jo! Oomph . . . J-Jo! It's me! Sam!"

I was tempted to keep swinging.

"Sam?"

"Yeah!"

"Then let go of me!"

"Then stop hitting me!"

Slowly Sam released my hand, and I gave him another satis-fying jab in the direction of what I hoped to be his ribs. Then I sprung to my feet indignantly, only to trip over his leg and fall back down onto his lap again. Sam chuckled. This day was going downhill fast.

Pushing him away from me I stumbled onto my feet and snapped the light on with a satisfying click.

"What do you think you're doing sneaking around my house in the dark!"

Sam blinked in the unexpected brightness, squinting up like he was seeing three of me.

"I wasn't sneaking," he said indignantly, standing slowly. "Kat let me in. Then she went upstairs to bed and I was waiting in the living room. Then I remembered I had left something—something for you in fact—downstairs in my coat. Then when I was down here getting it, Kat turned off the staircase light upstairs obviously thinking I was still in the living room, and while I was searching for it I heard you at the door, and so I decided—"

"Why can't anything ever be simple with you, Sam?" I semi-shrieked. Sure I may not have been in hitting mode anymore, but my frustration level was not about to go back to normal yet.

"I don't know, Jo," Sam retorted, equally indignant, "why can't you walk two steps without tripping over—"

"Why are you in my house, Sam?"

"I was worried about you!"

"What, because I was out with Kevin? Because you're still punishing me for that stupid 'edgy and dangerous' remark?"

"No. Because . . . because I think I saw those guys you mentioned."

That sobered me up quick. "What? Where?"

Sam sat back down on the steps. "Well, I was staying late to help clean up right? And when I walked out to the parking lot there were these two guys walking between the cars like they were looking for something."

"And you're sure they were the same ones?" I replied, knowing the answer even before I asked it.

Sam nodded. "Tall guy with long, stringy hair and black base-ball cap? Heavy guy in a red football league jacket?"

"I didn't know it was football, but yeah, it sounds like them,"

I said, suddenly feeling tired. I sat down beside him. "What did you do?"

"I walked over to them and said hi."

Gutsy move. "And?" I asked, holding my breath for his response.

"And I asked them if they were there to hear a life-saving message from God . . ."

I giggled despite myself. "Seriously?"

"Yup," Sam grinned, "figured it was the quickest way to find out if they were just two more of our friendly neighborhood God-squad."

"And . . ."

"And, they swore at me, and one of them flipped me the finger, and then they left." Sam dug something out of his jeans pocket and held it up triumphantly. It was a tiny, silver cell phone. "I managed to get a picture of them though. I'm pretty sure they didn't see me take it either."

He flipped the phone open in my palm and I stared down at the small slightly fuzzy picture of Motor-Oil-Guy and Red-Jacket leaning against a car. I shuddered.

"When I saw them I reached into my pocket to get my car keys," Sam said demonstrating with his hands, "then I held the camera up against my side like this, and snapped a couple of quick pictures before approaching them. The first one didn't turn out, but I thought this one wasn't too bad," he added proudly. "I'm guessing by the look on your face that this is them."

"Oh yeah," I let out a slow breath. "Has anyone ever accused you of having a death wish?"

"Oh sure, all the time," Sam replied lightly, but I could hear the tension in his voice. "But I figure it wasn't me they were looking for . . ."

I didn't like the way he just left the sentence hanging. My head felt like it was filling with fuzz by the moment, and being crammed into the front hallway with Sam wasn't making it any easier. What was he implying? That they were looking for me? Why would a couple of total strangers be looking for me?

"And for some strange and paranoid reason you decided you

needed to rush over to warn me about this?" I said, a little harsher than I'd meant to. "What does this have to do with me? Yes, I saw someone run over Nate last summer. Yes, he apparently didn't gossip far and wide about it. And yes, Nate managed to get run over in the middle of what was apparently Silverpoint's only crime spree—"

"At the very end of it actually," Sam interjected.

I ignored him.

"But so what, Sam?" I shot back, "So what?"

Sam opened his mouth to say something more, but I was just beginning to pick up steam. "Why is this my problem, Sam?" I said again. "I'm not a police officer! I'm not a detective! I barely know Nate! I appreciate you care enough to come over in the middle of the night to share your paranoid rantings with me, but you simply can't convince me there's some big conspiracy that—"

"What did Lisa say when you asked her about the hit-and-run?" Sam leveled at me sharply.

And suddenly it felt like all the air had been let out of my tires. "Touché," I said wearily. "Yes, I asked her about it. She said Nate was badly hurt and wouldn't tell anyone about the accident."

"See?" Sam said triumphantly, as if Lisa's lack of available gossip proved some big, significant point. "So Nate has his reasons for trying to protect her and Kevin. And if no one's going to tell us what's going on then the least I can do is make sure that you're a little more protected."

"Here," Sam reached over and pushed the tiny phone into my hand. "Remember how I told you I was doing a Web site for a new cell phone store?" he asked. I didn't, but nodded anyway. "Well, they gave me a couple of phones as samples so that I could write reviews about them. They let me keep them." He turned it over in my hand, its blue buttons giving off an eerie glow. "See, it's got a tiny camera, and it sends text messages, and once you figure out how to use the keypad you can type short documents on it too."

OK, so it was a very, very cool phone, but I still didn't get it.

"You don't already have one of these, do you?" Sam asked, suddenly seeming less than confident for the first time that night.

I shook my head, feeling more than a little stunned.

"Then take it," Sam said. "Just in case . . ." His voice trailed off.

"You're serious?" I said, scanning his face. "You're giving me a phone?"

"Call it a loan if you want," Sam said shrugging, looking down at his feet. "I figure this way you can at least call for help if you need it."

"Thanks."

"Don't worry about it."

"I mean it," I said, punching Sam lightly in the arm. "Thank you."

Sam glanced up and grinned at me shyly. "Don't worry about it."

I smiled back. "I won't."

"Good."

A comfortable silence moved in and settled in the space between us. I leaned my head back against the step above me and looked up at the ceiling.

After a long minute Sam said, "Do you want to hear something completely insane? While I was packing up tonight Nate asked me if I'd be interested in taking the mic at his church one night. Says he was praying and God suggested he ask me."

"You're kidding!"

"Nope," Sam grinned. "Apparently Patrick is planning some big 'Come As You Are' event in September, and inviting different people to get up on stage and share where they're at in their spiritual journey. And for some reason Nate thinks I should volunteer!"

I sat up. "Seriously? What did you say?"

Sam laughed. "What do you think I said? You think I want to stand up in front of a bunch of church people and be the token heathen? Nah, they're nice and all, but that doesn't mean I'd ever want to be one of them."

I leaned back against the steps again.

"Sam?"

"Yeah?"

"Why don't you like Kevin?"

"Who said I don't like Kevin?"

I shrugged. "I don't know. You just seem kind of lukewarm about him."

Sam shrugged back. "Maybe he's just a lukewarm kind of guy." Sam leaned back on the stairs until his head was almost touching mine. "I just don't get why you like him. Are you guys going out on another date?"

"Yeah," I said, looking down at the steps we were sitting on, "we're going out to dinner with his parents on Friday."

"Just do me a favor, OK? Be careful."

I knew from the way he said it that he meant it really seriously. But still I kind of shrugged him off, and just said "sure" in a "yeah, but of course nothing's going to happen" kind of way.

But then Sam put his hand on the side of my face, with the tips of his fingers just brushing up against my hair, and he tilted my face so I was looking him straight in the eyes.

"Be careful," Sam said again, quietly.

"Why?" I said, my voice barely above a whisper.

"Because something doesn't feel right," Sam replied. "I don't know why, because he seems like a nice guy. But there's something about the idea of you going out with him that makes me uneasy. And I think he really, really likes you. You don't invite a girl to a family thing unless you seriously think something could happen between you."

Sam's voice trailed off, and a long, charged silence spread out between us, while the space between us seemed to shrink.

"Anyway, I got to run," Sam said, standing suddenly. "Enjoy the phone."

"Thanks, I will," I replied, scrambling up off the steps, "and thanks again for helping me out tonight."

"Any time," Sam grinned.

He slipped out the door and slammed it behind him. For a long moment I just stood there, staring at the wooden frame, wondering why my pulse was racing.

Chapter Six

I DECIDED on a floaty, patterned sundress for Friday, brushed my hair until it hung in a dark, glossy wave over my shoulders, and added just a touch of pink lip gloss to my lips. Then I checked the results in the mirror. Definitely "meet the parents" material. I looked cute, and friendly, and sweet and . . . nervous. Very, very, nervous.

I blamed Sam, and his whole "I don't trust Kevin, but I think he really, really likes you" speech. I mean, why had Sam told me that? Was he trying to turn me into a quivering pile of nerves?

Not that I cared much about the fact Sam wasn't thrilled to death about my dating Kevin. I mean, that had been obvious from the moment the two first laid eyes on each other and started sizing each other up like old-fashioned Western gunslingers.

No, it was the fact that Sam seemed to think Kevin really, really liked me. And I wasn't sure how I felt about that.

And of course it didn't help when I opened the front door and was suddenly reminded how unbelievably, overwhelmingly hot Kevin was. I don't mean normal, good-looking hot. Movie-star hot. Brad Pitt, Will Smith . . . name your poison, this guy was it. Black boots, jeans that were incredibly well broken-in, olive shirt, cross pendant on a heavy chain and . . . well . . . nervous.

It was written all over him—Kevin was even more nervous than I was. It was in the way he leaned over to kiss me, and then obviously thought better of it and ended up giving me this weird brother-type kiss on the cheek, which he obviously hadn't intended to do. It was in the way he told me about eighteen million times that he was sure his dad and Julia were going to love me, and I was going to love them. It was in the way he kept fidgeting—his leather thong bracelet had slipped down over his fingers and he fiddled with it as he drove. I don't think I'd ever seen a guy so nervous about going anywhere with me—and if his unease hadn't been adding to my whole scared-spitlessness it would have been kind of cute.

Dinner with Kevin's parents went pretty well, all things considered. We went to Michelangelo's, this small but kind of fancy Italian restaurant on the waterfront just off the boardwalk. It had fairy lights suspended from the ceiling, small tables with checked tablecloths, and big windows that looked out over the beach. Kevin's dad, Ken, and his stepmom, Julia, were there already. Ken looked like a construction worker, with broad shoulders and a full brown beard. He shook my hand firmly and called me "young lady." Julia was really flowery. Seriously, everything about her—her dress, her perfume, even the way she moved—made it easy to imagine she secretly enjoyed wandering around rose gardens in a big straw hat. And she smiled a lot—kind of like Lisa—and there was something about her I liked, though I wasn't sure why.

We sat down and everyone made polite conversation about stuff like travel and the weather. Julia asked me lots of friendly questions that were really easy to answer. Ken talked about what a great carpenter Kevin was turning out to be, and told me about different contracting jobs he'd worked on. Kevin never really stopped being nervous, but he relaxed a little and he was an absolute gentleman, doing all the right things like helping me with my chair and asking me if I wanted to share a dessert.

In fact everything was pretty much perfect until the dessert came. It had gotten kind of dark then and a waiter came around the room with a tray of amazing candles in wine bottles. You know, the kind where wax from countless candles has melted all over the green glass making all kinds of great shapes and casting weird shadows on the table. Well, I could tell right away that Ken didn't really like them. I mean, the moment he caught sight of that tray he kind of stiffened slightly, and then Julia and Kevin kind of shot each other an odd glance. And everything was slightly on edge until the waiter came by our table and Ken just smiled at him and said in a really friendly way, "No thanks, son, I don't want anything to block my view of the people I'm eating with." And then the waiter went away and everything went back to normal and that weird feeling was gone so quickly I wondered if I had just imagined it.

Kevin and I went for a walk alone by the beach after dinner. The sun was setting, and the sky was dark with low hanging clouds that hid the stars. The boardwalk's wooden planks were black with fallen rain and our feet left footprint outlines on the wood.

Kevin had seemed to be in a good mood when we left; almost relieved. But the further we walked, the deeper he seemed to be slipping inside himself, and by the time we reached the pier, I realized I hadn't heard him speak in almost fifteen minutes.

Kevin took my hand in his and gently led me over to a railing beside the water. He leaned his shoulder against a support, and stared out into the vast expanse of sky.

Then he said, "Do you think that if you like someone . . . like say, you want to get to know someone better . . . than you know them . . . do you think you can still keep secrets from them . . . or do you think it's better to let them know things right away?"

My brain froze, I mean it completely froze. And I said something completely useless like "I . . . ya . . . fum . . . da . . ." before I managed to get my mouth shut again. I tried to scramble backward in my memory to figure out if he had really said what I thought he'd just said: "Do you think that if you like someone . . . you can still keep secrets from them?"

What was he saying? What did he mean by that? Did he mean he really liked me? Did he mean he was keeping a secret? Nate's secret? Or did he think I was keeping a secret from him? Or . . . or . . .

Oh, why couldn't guys ever just say what they meant?

"My dad, Ken, used to be an alcoholic," Kevin said, his face set, his eyes a million miles away.

The subject change was abrupt and it took several moments for my brain to catch up.

"He and my mom both used to drink, but then she died when I was like eleven," Kevin said. "And then my dad started to drink a lot more. He was a mean drunk, which I guess explains some of why . . . well. Anyway, my school began to notice stuff that I was doing. And they sent a social worker person around and told him that if he didn't, you know, smarten up they'd take me away. And my dad yelled and said he didn't care. And I . . . well, I yelled and said I wanted to go . . ."

Kevin rubbed one hand hard across his eye. "But somehow my dad ended up at these parenting classes. They were held at Cornerstone and Lisa's dad, Pastor Wallace, helped lead them or something. And then Pastor Wallace needed someone to work on the new hall and he hired my dad. And, like, the next year, well, while he was still working on the church hall really, my dad started going to this alcohol anonymous group at Cornerstone. And eventually he stopped drinking."

Kevin stopped, rubbed his hand over his face again. And I just stood there, afraid to breathe. There was this awful pain in my chest like something inside me was cracking. He looked so sweet, so vulnerable, so beautiful, so hurt. I just wanted to throw my arms around him—do something to help take his pain away and let him know he wasn't alone. That I even understood, in a way. But instead I just walked over to him, and put my hand on the rail beside his. Kevin reached out and squeezed it.

"That's where my dad met Julia," Kevin said, "at church. They fell in love pretty quickly. I was about thirteen when they got married. Fourteen when the twins were born, my stepsisters Sherry and Terry, you've got to meet them, they're amazing.

"But anyway, I hated it at first. I know I should have been happy my dad had changed, but really I was just angry. Angry at Ken. Angry at Julia. Angry at God . . ."

"Did you believe in God then?" I found myself asking.

Kevin shook his head. "Hardly," he said. "I was an atheist, but then again my dad had been too. But suddenly I found myself hating this God I didn't even think I believed in.

"I don't know why I'm telling you all this," Kevin said suddenly, letting go of my hand, and pushing away from the railing. "I've probably scared you off now," he added, turning away from me. "I shouldn't have said anything. I don't know why I did. It's just that there's something about you. And now I know you're just going to think I'm some pathetic—"

"Kevin," I cried, "I'm not! I don't!" I grabbed hold of his arm and he kind of shrugged me off, but I didn't let go.

"Look at me," I said, and Kevin turned his head toward me, and for a moment I thought I was going to start crying. "Look, I get it," I said, my voice cracking, "OK? I get it."

I could tell by the impassive look on Kevin's face that he really didn't believe me. I wish I could say I was the kind of person who stopped and thought seriously about what Sam had said, and weighed up just how much I trusted Kevin and how much I wanted him to know about my life and my business.

But I wasn't like that. Standing there beside him, his face half-hidden in shadows, seeing him look so miserable, so vulnerable, well . . . it was kind of like I was seeing Kevin for the first time. I mean, I had always known he was really good-looking, and nice, and kind, and polite, and seemed to be a great guy, but . . . I had never realized that behind all that perfect outside there was . . . I don't know . . . someone like me.

"I get it," I said again, lowering my voice. "I've had to clean up after my mother when she was drunk, a lot of times. She'd go out on dates, or have guys over to the house, or have a party, and then I'd have to clean her up, and get her into bed, and clean up the house . . ."

Kevin's face softened. I could see his jaw muscles moving underneath the skin, like he was slowly trying to digest what I was telling him.

"My mom's not an alcoholic, at least I don't think she is. She's more like addicted to attention. From men. It's like she has to flirt with every guy she meets in order to feel good about herself or something. She's been married five times, and I don't know how many guys she's been with. She'd say it wasn't that many, because she was in a relationship with this one for six months, and that one for eighteen months. But it feels like a lot to me.

"The worst part was never knowing what you were going to get from day to day. Was the next guy she brought home going to be a monster? Was she going to be in a good mood or a bad mood when she walked through the door? You know, sometimes I hated whatever guy she was with so much I'd be literally praying that she'd break up with him, but then when she did she'd go into a foul mood and spend days sitting around on the couch crying about how no one loved or understood her. And no matter what you do for someone when they're drunk they never remember to thank you when they're sober."

"And drunks get this great amnesia," Kevin said, "which means no matter what actually happened, they're convinced they did everything right . . ."

". . . and anything that went wrong had to be your fault because it couldn't be theirs," I finished.

"Exactly!"

We smiled at each other.

"Of course my dad isn't like that anymore," Kevin said. "God has done amazing things in his life—in all our lives really. But in a way that almost makes it harder to talk about what happened. And I can't talk about this kind of thing with Nate or Lisa or any of them. They just don't get it. They're happy for me to talk about it, but I think it's like they feel sorry for me, and I feel like they're all normal, and I'm the only one who isn't."

"I know what that feels like," I said.

"You do, don't you?" Kevin said.

I nodded.

"Wow." Kevin put his hands on my shoulders and looked at me like he was in awe or something. Then he ran his hands slowly down my arms, and slid his hands into mine. "You're so beautiful Jo, you know that?"

Oh . . . ah . . . well . . .

Kevin pulled me close to him and wrapped his arms around me. My face pressed up against the cold, rough leather of his coat. "You're unbelievable," Kevin said, "I can't believe I found you. You're like nothing, like no one I've ever met before."

He ran his hand through my hair, wrapping a strand around his fingers. Then he traced a finger along the side of my face, touching me so gently it was like he was afraid I was about to break into pieces, or disappear.

Then, slowly, he let me go, and we started walking back toward the truck, with Kevin's hand holding mine.

"So, do you think you'd be willing to go out with a guy whose father is a recovering alcoholic?" he said.

I bit my bottom lip. "Maybe."

"Can I pick you up for the Gathering Sunday?"

"Yes."

We got back to Michelangelo's and Kevin told me he needed to pop inside for a moment to go to the bathroom or something. So I decided to use the bathroom too—and I'm happy to report that my makeup was still standing up under the pressure. But when I came out Kevin was nowhere to be seen (it's not like I had taken *that* long), so I wandered outside in case he was there. He wasn't. Yup, fifteen minutes after an unforgettable romantic moment and now here I was wondering if Kevin had run off somewhere.

So I went and sat on a wooden bench on Michelangelo's front porch and waited for him. It was definitely dark by now, so I wasn't quite sure if he'd see me. But what with the threat of rain and the water lapping against the shore, it was kind of romantic and atmospheric, and gave me time to mull over just how adorable Kevin was, and all the possibilities of what might happen between us.

I didn't notice the guys in the parking lot at first. I mean, I noticed there were a couple of guys—teenagers, I thought—walking between the cars, like they were looking for something or someone. But one was too short to be Kevin and the other was too broad, so I didn't really pay any attention to them. Then they started climbing into this ugly battered-looking station wagon and as a light came on inside the car I realized it was Motor-Oil-Guy and Red-Jacket—the same two creepy guys who had been loitering around outside my place and at the Gathering.

Now I know I had said, sworn practically, that I didn't believe anything Sam had said about me being in some form of potential danger—and I was absolutely certain I was no longer going to even be curious about why Nate was keeping his car accident secret from his closest friends. But for some reason I found myself fumbling in my bag for Sam's camera phone in a foolhardy and ill-conceived attempt to get a picture of the car as it drove away. There was a bright flash and a resounding click—resulting in a blurry picture of taillights with an only slightly legible license plate. In other words—a whole lot of nothing.

"There you are! What are you doing?"

Suddenly Kevin was at my shoulder. I turned.

"Nothing," I said quickly, guiltily sliding the phone back into my bag.

As we walked back to his truck I noticed something on his windshield. There was this piece of white paper stuck under his driver-side wiper. Before I could say anything, Kevin snatched it up, unfolded it, and scanned it quickly. Then he grimaced in disgust and crumpled it into his fist.

I started to ask him what it was, but before I could finish the first word, Kevin had pulled a lighter out of his pocket. With a quick flick he got a flame, then waved it back and forth over a corner of the note until it caught on fire. It flickered orange, turned black until it had burned down to Kevin's fingers, and then dropped as embers to the ground.

As he did it, uncertainty flickered in the back of my mind. Why didn't he just shove it in his pocket? Or toss it in the glove compartment? Or even just throw it on the ground like any normal person would?

"What did it say?" I asked.

"Nothing," Kevin said. He yanked my door open and walked over to his side of the truck.

Then why did you burn it? my brain yelled, but the words froze in my mouth. I mean, there I was on a gorgeous night, with a gorgeous guy, and I was going to obsess about his chosen method of waste disposal? Even if it was a little pyromaniac.

"It was just an advertisement, you know," Kevin said, as I climbed in, "one of those flyer things people leave on cars, selling things people aren't interested in buying."

"What was it selling?" I asked.

"Couldn't tell ya," Kevin said, looking down at the steering wheel. "Didn't really read it."

Kevin held my hand most of the drive home, his fingers gently tracing over mine. And I couldn't take my eyes off him. I know you're not supposed to call a guy "beautiful," but I don't think I can come up with any other word to describe how good Kevin looked to me that night. So intense, so fragile, so amazingly attractive, and yet also so broken in a way. It seemed like that journey home was lasting forever, and I didn't want it to end. Because what had happened between us was intense, and it kind of changed everything. But at the same time, I was afraid that the moment I stepped through my front door it was all going to be over.

We got back to Kat's. Kevin walked me to the door.

"I want to kiss you," he said.

I felt my heart catch and strain against my chest as it tried to keep beating.

"Can I kiss you?" Kevin asked softly. I nodded. Kevin cupped his hand underneath my chin and brought his face down to meet mine. I closed my eyes, and felt his lips hovering over mine so lightly I could barely even tell they were there. Then I felt him kiss me, gently at first, then—

I heard someone laughing.

Kevin stepped away. We looked up. Kat's living room window was open and wafting down was the loud, raucous, unmistakable sound of someone laughing—of Sam laughing. I was so not in the mood to see Sam right then.

Kevin still kissed me, but it was only a peck really. The sound of Sam had kind of drained all the electricity out of the night. After we said goodnight, I stomped upstairs to find Kat and Sam collapsed on the living room floor in laughter and Buddy barking at them wildly.

"Hi Jo!" Sam said looking up. "We didn't hear you come in." He was still laughing under his breath. "We've been having a contest to see how many pieces of popcorn we can bounce off Buddy's nose without him catching it. So far the score is Kat 28, Sam 6, Buddy 213."

I could feel every tension knot in my shoulders suddenly spring to life.

"Sam, I didn't know you were coming over."

"Neither did I," he said, grinning like an idiot. "My DVD recorder was on the blitz, and there was an old movie marathon on tonight, so I called Kat to see if she could record it for me, and she was watching it anyway so she suggested—"

"And you didn't know anyone else in the world who could

possibly know how to record off of a television so you just had to end up at my house?"

A little harsh maybe. But, I mean, come on, couldn't I get a break from this guy for even five minutes?

Sam looked at Kat. Kat looked at Sam. It was definitely a look with a capital L. Since when were Kat and Sam exchanging looks like that?

"Did you have a nice time?" Kat said mildly. She stood, picked up the popcorn bowl, and started to walk toward the kitchen.

"Yeah, it was nice," I said, which was almost a lie considering how "nice" was probably the last word I'd use to describe everything that had happened. But the last thing I wanted to do was talk to them about it right then.

"Jo, I—"

Sam jumped to his feet and started to say something, but I said, "Good night, Sam," marched straight into my room, and closed the door hard behind me. Then I laid down on my bed, dragged a pillow over my head, and tried to recapture as much of what happened between me and Kevin as I could before it faded entirely.

Below me I could hear Kat and Sam talking. Then I heard Sam leave. Kat came upstairs and I heard her turn the water on in the bathroom. After debating a few moments I wandered in and found her brushing her teeth at the sink.

"You and Sam aren't dating, are you?" I said, sitting down on the edge of the tub. "Because he's way too young for you."

Kat turned on me sharply. She looked at me like I'd just grown a second head and it was speaking Japanese.

"You're kidding, right?" She sounded more than a little irritated. "No, of course I'm not dating Sam."

She stared at me for a minute, like puzzling over what to say next. Then she turned back to the sink.

"He was lonely," she said simply. "His sister's still on her honeymoon and his . . . uh . . . love life has been a little rocky recently."

I snorted.

"Some people find me easy to talk to," she said pointedly.

I sighed. She was right. If I had an ex as manic as Traci, Kat would be my first choice of a person to talk to. And I knew I wasn't really being fair to her, but I just wasn't ready to talk to her, to anyone, about what had happened between Kevin and me yet.

So I gave her a hug goodnight, told her I loved her, and then crawled into bed and stared up at the ceiling. It had been a weird, weird few days. I know I had gone on and on about how good-looking I thought Kevin was. How attracted I was to him. But if I was honest I had never expected to like Kevin as much as I did right then—never, never expected him to like me back. And I wasn't quite sure what to make of it. Or even what I wanted to happen next.

§ § §

"So what do you think was on that piece of paper?"

It was Saturday afternoon. And for some reason, less than twenty-four hours after I had bitten Kat's head off for inviting Sam over, there he was sprawled across the filthy store floor with a tape measure in his mouth. I was standing beside him jotting down shelf measurements.

"It's just a shame you didn't get to see what it said before he burned it," Sam's voice was muffled behind three and a quarter inches of plastic. "But I guess snatching the flaming scrap of paper out of his hand and desperately stomping out the fire would have looked a little bit suspicious."

I rolled my eyes at him, "Yeah, just a little."

Sam chuckled.

I hadn't intended to invite Sam over, honestly. I'd just run into him when I was out shopping for a sledgehammer to knock down the last remains of the decrepit old shelves. And Sam just happened to know someone I could borrow one from, and offered to bring it over. And then I'd kind of put him to work helping me measure the length of the old boards before I bashed them into smithereens. It was good, in a way, because I felt bad about being so rude the night before and had hoped we'd be able to move past it. Turns out it was a lot easier than you'd think.

And of course I'd told him about what had happened the night before. Not about Kevin breaking down and telling me about his father—that still felt too intensely personal, even for telling

Sam—but I told him about seeing Motor-Oil-Guy and Red-Jacket, the suspicious note, and its fiery end.

"Maybe his pockets were already full of Bible notes and Kevin just has a twelve-year-old boy's obsession with burning things," Sam said. He stood up and wiped his dirty hands on his even dirtier jeans. "I wouldn't worry about that too much. I'm sure your new boyfriend is not a closet pyromaniac. Almost sure."

He flashed me a wicked grin and I stuck my tongue out at him.

"He's not my boyfriend," I said, pulling the tape measure out of his hands. "And he said it was nothing—just an advertising flyer. But even though it sounds stupid I can't help but wonder if maybe there was more to it than that. Like maybe Motor-Oil-Guy and Red-Jacket were trying to send me a message . . ."

"Like 'Hey pretty chick, I know you told the police we smashed into Nate McHolyMan and now we're coming for you'?" Sam suggested.

I flicked the tape measure at him, then dumped it on the counter.

"Something like that," I admitted, feeling more than a little foolish. "Sounds stupid though, right? Because if it was addressed to me then wouldn't Kevin have just handed it to me?"

I reached down and picked up the sledgehammer. Sam held up his hands in mock defense. I laughed.

"Not if it was something obscure," he went on. "Something like, 'You know what happened to Nate, well the same thing is going to happen to you unless you keep your mouth shut.' Then even if your God-boy was clueless he could have burned it trying to save Nate."

"No, then he would've taken it to show Nate," I reasoned. "Anyway, he said it was just an advertising flyer. Do you really think he would have lied to me?"

Sam shook his head. "Doubtful. So then logically either it was nothing, or something that he thought was nothing. Did you happen to see if there were flyers on any of the other cars?"

I shook my head and sighed. "No. But that doesn't mean there weren't." I swung the sledgehammer gently in my hand. Turns out it was a lot heavier than it looked. "Sorry the picture didn't turn out better."

Sam punched me gently on the arm. "You kidding? For an amateur sleuth taking a picture of a moving vehicle at night it isn't half bad. At least you didn't get your thumb in the shot." He took a long step back and slid behind the counter. "Now, don't forget I get a turn to smash things too when you're done," he said. "Oh, and don't forget to put on safety goggles."

I scowled, and forced the oversized, neon yellow, elasticized monstrosities down over my head. No girl ever looked her best in safety goggles.

So I started taking a few swings at the derelict wood which seemed to have melded itself onto the wall. How to hit one thing with another thing and break it might be a basic skill which most people pick up at about the age of two, but I've got to admit that getting the shelving off the wall was a lot harder than it looked and a few of my practice swings were a little off the mark. Sam's cowering behind the counter and wisecracking about my lack of demolition skill didn't help matters much. It's kind of hard to swing a heavy object accurately when you're laughing so hard you can hardly see straight.

Kat came downstairs to ask if Sam was staying for dinner, and that's when Sam dropped the bombshell that he already had plans—with Traci! Yup, that's right, Sam chose the exact moment when I was bashing wood into a satisfying spray of splinters to announce that he had a hot date with his psychotic, evil ex.

"She says she wants to talk," I heard Sam tell my cousin, "so we're just going to grab a quick dinner or something."

Crash! I raised my hands over my head and threw my weight into my swing, while pretending very hard not to have heard a word he just said.

"She, she says she wants to be friends . . ." Sam continued.

I swung for the shelves again and missed. Kat snorted.

"Traci knows we're never getting back together," Sam said. "I told her that I wasn't interested in her that way. And I know she understands."

Crack! I hit the corner of the shelf and knocked a good few inches off.

"Ha!" Kat said. "Of course Traci wants you back!"

"But she told me she's started dating someone else," Sam protested.

I paused, mid-swing.

"It doesn't matter if she's dating half the town!" Kat said. "That won't stop her from not wanting you to date anyone else."

"But it's not like that," Sam insisted. "All she wants to do is talk, and she said she thinks it would be great if I started dating someone else."

Kat snorted again. "I'm sure she did," Kat said, "but that doesn't mean you should believe her. If I were you, I wouldn't trust her as far as I could throw her . . ."

Hurray for Kat! Buoyed by my cousin's obvious brilliance I took another hearty swing at the shelves.

". . . especially if you want a chance of starting something with anyone else . . ."

My swing missed entirely, and the sledgehammer slipped out of my hands and flew across the room, where it dented the window frame and only missed taking out the entire window by a fraction of an inch.

Kat and Sam turned and stared at me.

"I think my turn's over," I said, in what I hoped was a light-hearted voice.

Neither of them smiled. Then Sam went over and picked up the hammer.

"So what do you think I should do about Traci, Jo?" he asked, not quite looking at me.

"You know what I think. I think Traci is a demented shrew who is going to make your life miserable if you give her half a chance and you should stay far, far away from her."

Sam's head jerked up like I'd just zapped him with an electric prod or something.

"But, hey," I added quickly, "your love life, your business!"

"Right . . ." Sam said uncertainly.

"Well, let me know if you change your mind about dinner," Kat said, choosing that moment to slip back upstairs.

Sam was still looking down at the sledgehammer. I yanked the goggles off and tossed them at him.

"Here," I said, "take a few whacks. It might make you feel better."

"Thanks."

"And don't go out with Traci tonight," I added impulsively. "Text her quickly and tell her you've come down with some horrible, disfiguring, fatal illness and then spend the evening hanging out with Kat and me."

Sam hesitated.

"Oh, come on," I cajoled. "You know you want to."

He grinned. "I'll think about it."

It was my turn to cower behind the counter, but it turned out that Sam was irritatingly good at smashing and bashing.

"So, do you think this thing between you and Kevin could be serious?" he said eventually, from inside the haze of flying wood.

"Maybe," I said noncommittally. "I like him."

Sam put the hammer down and started pulling at a piece of broken shelf, trying to wiggle it loose.

"Are you ever going to tell him that you saw Nate get run over by a car?" he asked casually, picking up the hammer again for another swing.

If I'd been a cat this would have been the moment all my fur stood dramatically on end. "No, I don't think I'm going to. And I don't want you to either."

Sam frowned, and I couldn't tell if he was confused or irritated, but I plowed on anyway, hoping I sounded more certain than I felt. "I mean, I know we joke about it, but the fact of the matter is that Nate, and Lisa, and Patrick, all of them seem like nice people. And if one day they decide to tell me all about it, then great. But when it all comes down to it, it's not really any of our business. And if Nate wants to hide the fact that someone tried to kill him, then who are we to try to mess with that?"

Sam dropped the sledgehammer so hard I was afraid he had dented the floor. "You don't get it, do you, Jo?" he said, turning on me. "They are not nice people. Not underneath," he said seriously. "Underneath all the smiles and happy songs they are completely delusional, Jo, and all they want to do is manipulate you into feeling bad enough to sign up for their religion."

Sam ran his hand through his hair, until it flopped out over the top of the goggles.

"I don't blame you for liking them, Jo," he said gently. "Heck, I kind of like them too. But you and I aren't out there pretending that we're better than everyone else. Nate is!"

A horrible uncertainty started to gnaw in the pit of my stomach.

"Nate walks around acting like he's better than the rest of us because he has this special inside connection with God," Sam continued earnestly, "but in the meantime he has this secret in his past he's apparently lying to Kevin and everyone about.

"And it's great that Lisa has decided you're her new best friend, but I guarantee you that the moment you and Kevin get serious she's going to be there shoving disapproval down your throat.

"You know what I'm thinking every time I'm sitting there in the Gathering listening to them go on about how much God loves them?" Sam asked. "I'm wishing that we really knew what had happened to Nate, because then we'd know exactly what kind of person he really is."

Sam's words hit me like a bullet in the chest. Of course I didn't believe everything that Patrick had said about Christianity, but I didn't want to disbelieve all of it either. To be completely honest I liked parts of what the people at the Gathering believed. I liked thinking there might be some cosmic power in the universe that liked me and had a plan for my life. I wanted to believe those parts. I just didn't want to believe it all. And now Sam was acting like I had to choose—like it was us or them—when deep inside I had kind of been hoping there'd be a way to find some comfortable middle ground.

"Then why do you go?" I asked him.

But I never got an answer to my question. Because before Sam could open his mouth there was a knock on the window, and in a display of cosmically bad timing we turned to see Kevin and Nate standing outside.

I turned and waved them in. Sam swore quietly.

"And now the God-squad arrives. Of course!" he spluttered.

"They probably spend all day just hiding around the corner waiting for a chance to pounce."

Kevin opened the door and made a beeline for me, throwing his arm around my shoulders.

"Hey babe, hope you don't mind us dropping in like this," Kevin said grinning. "Nate and I were just delivering a load of wood up the street and I thought I'd pop by and see how you were doing." He smelled so good—kind of sweet and smoky at the same time—and my heart skipped a little beat.

Acknowledging Sam with a little tilt of his head, Kevin said, "Hey man. Nice shades." Then, as Sam hurriedly yanked off his goggles, Kevin turned his attention back to me.

"You guys doing anything tonight?" Kevin went on. "Lisa has written this new play for Cornerstone, and they're having a dress rehearsal tonight, and she said it would be great to get an outsider's opinion of it."

I glanced over at Sam uncertainly. I mean what kind of friend would I be to agree to go to a Gathering thing barely a nanosecond after Sam had just derided them all as guilt-fuelled religion-junkies? But, at the same time, as I watched Sam stare murderously at the floor like he was hoping it would open up and swallow Kevin whole, this little rebellious thought flickered up in the back of my mind. I mean—who was Sam to tell me who I could and couldn't hang out with? Who was Sam to tell me that the guy I liked was dangerously delusional? Since when did Sam have all the answers anyway? Was I seriously going to let Sam run my love life?

"Sure," I said, looking up at Kevin, "sounds great."

"Cool!" Kevin beamed.

Out of the corner of my eye I was vaguely aware of Sam muttering something mutinous under his breath, and I was half afraid that he was going to start something with Kevin, but true to form Kevin picked that moment to excuse himself for a moment saying he had to go out back and make a phone call. So he took off, leaving me with a guy who looked ready to punch someone, and a convenient opponent who just happened to be leaning against the door frame.

Now Nate hadn't said anything up to this point. He'd just sort of arrived like a shadow behind Kevin, and was now standing in my doorway mildly minding his own business.

"Hey Nate!" Sam said, with a fairly friendly smile on his face. "Did I ever tell you I can list all sixty-six books of the Bible? I can spell them too, and even say them backward."

I didn't know what Sam was getting at with an opening like that, but I didn't like it. I stepped forward and put a warning hand on his arm, but he shrugged me off.

Nate raised an eyebrow, a slight smile curving up at the sides of his mouth. "Good for you, man," he said mildly. "I always forget to put an *e* in Zechariah."

"What I don't get," Sam went on like he hadn't heard him, "is why people like you are always trying so hard to push their religion like it's the one and only option. Why don't you tell people about all the different options out there instead of pushing your God like it's the only one that counts?"

Sam was still smiling as he said it. Nate was smiling too. But there was something else in the room I couldn't put my finger on, like the air around me was crackling with a hidden tension. Without even thinking, I slowly reached down and pushed the sledgehammer underneath the counter. But they were so deep into it, I don't know if they noticed.

"Have you ever tried—" Nate started.

"Tried what? Tried church?" Sam cut him off. "Sure, I tried church. My dad made me go to church every Sunday until I was like fifteen. But it's not like it made a difference to anything. It was interesting. But pretty pointless. I didn't spend the first fifteen years of my life having my dad run every stupid little detail of it, only to then want to turn over control to some big mystic invisible God and all his pointless rules."

"I don't blame you," Nate said, "I wouldn't either."

That seemed to knock Sam back a step.

"But have you ever tried talking to God about any of this?" Nate asked.

"You want me to try praying?" Sam snapped. "Fine." He snatched up the notepad I'd been using to record the shelf measurements, scribbled something down quickly, then tore off the page and stuffed it in his pocket.

"There!" he said triumphantly. "There, I've gone and asked your God for something. Now you tell your God that when he gives me what I asked for on this piece of paper, I'll start believing in him, and go to church every Sunday, and even follow all of his pointless rules."

Nate pushed himself up off the wall. "Sam? Why would you choose to believe in a God that was so weak you could manipulate him?"

I held my breath. But Sam merely chuckled.

"You just tell your God that if he wants me, he knows where to find me," Sam said, scooping his jacket up from the floor and heading for the door. "I've got a date. Bye Jo."

Feeling more than a little stunned I gave a little half-wave as Sam disappeared out the door. It was only then that I realized Kevin had reappeared behind me. I didn't know how long he'd been standing there. But before I could say anything, he gave me a little perfunctory kiss on the top of my head and said that they had to run but he'd be back to pick me up at eight.

And two minutes later I was standing all alone, in a pile of wood and splinters, suspecting that whatever Sam's argument with God was, I hadn't heard the end of it.

Chapter Seven

WHEN KEVIN came back to pick me up later that night there was this weird, though kind of nice, tension between us. It was the first time we'd been alone together since pouring our hearts out about our families the night before, and hearing Sam and Nate go at it had put an uneasy spin on the afternoon. So instead of talking about anything important we just spent the whole ride over discussing some science fiction show that had just been cancelled. And even though it was nice, compared to the amazing honesty we'd had on the beach it almost felt, well, wrong somehow.

When we arrived at the Ugly Pug, it was empty except for a few people who seemed to be hanging around the stage aimlessly waiting for their cue. The only lights on were the lights on stage, and the open space of the restaurant gaped dark and empty.

"Kevin! Finally!" Nate yelled. "Can I get you to give Si a hand lugging the monster onto the stage? Hey Patrick! Can we start again from your whole 'love' and 'sin' intro bit? Everybody, get into your places, we're going to run through the whole thing from the beginning."

With a slight squeeze on my shoulder, Kevin sprinted off toward the stage.

Feeling a bit lost and more than a little self-conscious, I sat back against the wall, blending into the shadows.

"God is love . . ." Patrick's voice echoed eerily in the room around me. "Jesus was blood and sweat and pain and nails. But Jesus is love.

"Now maybe that doesn't make sense to you right now. Maybe the only love you've ever known was flighty and unreliable. Maybe it's hard to get your head around how much God loves you, because at the same time this God seems to have such a problem with sin. After all, he doesn't even just let the stupid little ones go—but insists every little sin in our lives be eradicated."

Patrick paused for a moment as Lisa ran up to the microphone and whispered something in his ear. Then Patrick turned back to the mic.

"To be honest, I really don't like using the word sin because it's a word that has almost totally lost its meaning. Sin is damage—the damage we do to ourselves, the damage we do to other people, the damage we do to our world and to our relationship with God.

"We're all damaged goods."

The stage was empty now and I was beginning to feel more than a little foolish just sitting there alone. I scanned the room from side to side but I couldn't see Kevin. For a moment I wondered if he'd just left me all alone. For a second I thought about jumping up and running out. But Patrick's unrelenting words pinned me to the floor.

"Just for a second, imagine you have a big screen projected over your head constantly listing off everything you're really thinking and everything you're really feeling—and everything you've ever thought, and everything you've ever done and every secret thing that's going on inside you. I know I'd look pretty bad. Worse than bad actually.

"See, we blame God for hating sin. But, imagine that someone with your rap sheet showed up at your door asking a favor. And you could see all the bad things they'd thought about you. And you knew all the ways they'd hurt people you loved. What if everything they had done just added up to one, big, huge reason not to love them?

"See, that's the situation with Jesus. That's how strong and powerful and unflinching his love is. You just show up and say to Jesus 'See all this mess? This is the mess of me.' And Jesus goes, and takes your screen, and gives you a new, clean one. And every time you try to go back and remind yourself of just how bad you really are, you find Jesus has totally destroyed it. Because he carried it, and he suffered for it, and then he shattered it.

"That's how real Jesus' love is. It's not some random, make-you-feel-a-bit-good thing. It's a total destruction of everything horrible, and a whole new life."

Patrick pulled the microphone away from his mouth and

dropped it down to his side. The light around him dimmed until it faded to black.

A warm glow lit the corner of the stage, and grew until it spread down the side aisle.

Then I saw Kevin. He and Simon were dragging the pop machine from the hallway, through the pub and up onto the stage. They set it in the light, and then they disappeared into the shadows.

The play was about Jesus, and Nate played the man himself. Of course, Nate didn't look anything like the typical picture of Jesus—not that I'd ever been a fan of the pretty boy, fair-skinned, blue-eyed Jesus look; but still, it was kind of hard to imagine Jesus as black, bald, and beardless. But at least Nate/Jesus was wearing jeans and a cool flowing shirt—not a white bathrobe.

A few people I vaguely recognized were playing disciples. None of them were wearing bathrobes either. The disciples and Jesus had apparently been walking for a long time and were now in the middle of nowhere. I didn't really get how they got there or where they were going, but I figured that if no one was going to explain it to me, it probably didn't matter to the plot.

The guys had stopped outside a town by a gas station. Nate/Jesus decided to sit there and rest while everyone else went into town to get food. The disciples left and Lisa came on, dressed like my mother on a Saturday night.

Lisa stepped over Nate/Jesus, like she didn't even see him there. She dropped her coins into the machine, grabbed a drink, and pulled back the tab.

"Can I have a sip?" Nate/Jesus asked.

Lisa stopped in her tracks, the can halfway to her lips. She gave Nate/Jesus a dirty look.

"You're asking me for a drink?" she said with a perfect mixture of disdain and amusement, as if Lisa had been getting more then dressing tips from my mother. Lisa took a long, deliberate drink from the can and gave him a hard, mocking look. "Looked at yourself in the mirror recently? Since when do people like you talk to people like me? Let alone ask us for favors?"

She started to walk past him slowly. Nate/Jesus reached into his pocket. Lisa flinched and her body tensed like she was expecting to be attacked. But all Nate/Jesus pulled out was a small plastic cup. He held it up to reassure her. Lisa relaxed.

"If you knew who you were talking to, you would be the one asking me for a drink," Nate/Jesus said.

Lisa looked irritated, but she didn't leave. "Don't play games with me. If you already had a drink, then why'd you get in my space and ask me for one? As far as I can see, I'm the one holding the drink and you're the one with the empty, dinky cup."

Nate/Jesus wasn't fazed. "When you finish drinking your drink, you are going to eventually get thirsty again. But the stuff that I have been given by God isn't like that. I've got the kind of drink that seeps into the inmost empty parts of your heart and makes it whole again. I've got the kind of food that can fill up the gnawing emptiness that keeps you up at nights. I've got the real goods, the kind that will cure loneliness and fill you with real, lasting joy."

Lisa slumped against the side of the machine, her drink dangling loose in her fingers.

"That would be nice if it were true, now wouldn't it?" she said. "Are you telling me that you can give me that special drink of yours?"

Nate/Jesus said, "I can."

"Sure, what the hey." Lisa stepped forward and stuck her hand out.

"First, go get your husband," Nate/Jesus said.

I sat up. This was a weird twist.

Lisa stepped back defensively. "I'm not married."

"That's the truth," Nate said, pulling himself up so that he was standing beside her. "You aren't married. You are divorced though. You've been divorced five times. In fact the man you're currently sleeping with is married to someone else, and he's just one in a long string of husbands and boyfriends."

Lisa was shocked. But I was livid.

They had made a play about my mother.

All that stuff I had told Kevin yesterday, thinking I could trust him, and they turned around and made some stupid, demeaning, horrible play out of it! No wonder all those things that Patrick said had hit so hard. They'd been gunning for me.

Well, I wasn't going to fall for it.

I jumped out of my seat and headed toward the door. To be honest I didn't know where I was going—I just needed to get out of there. Kevin was heading back just as I was on my way out. I bumped into him hard with my shoulder—knocking him back a satisfying couple of inches. Then I looked him straight in the eyes, and said something very creative and invective, but completely unprintable, before dashing up the stairs. Kevin was hot on my heels.

Now there is no use trying to out-stride someone who is a good four inches taller than you unless you are willing to break into a serious sprint. So, when, by the time I got to the parking lot, it became pretty obvious that Kevin wasn't going to let up on following me, no matter how hard I pretended I was ignoring him, I spun around on my heels and blasted him with every barrel I had.

"Don't even bother. I know what you did and there is no way I'm ever going to forgive you for it!"

Kevin stopped and kind of jerked back like I'd just shot him in the chest. He looked sick—I mean, seriously like he was about to keel over. "How—"

"How did I find out?" I said, shaking my head in disbelief. "Do you think I'm stupid?"

"No, Jo," Kevin said, his voice shaking, his face ashen. "I've never thought . . ."

"Whose idea was it anyway?" I demanded.

"What idea?" Kevin seemed genuinely puzzled now.

"Was it your idea all along? Or was it Lisa's? Or Nate's?"

Kevin's face blanked. I mean completely blanked. Like I might as well have asked him where the crown jewels were hidden. "W . . . wha . . ."

"To make a play about my mother! You know, the slutty woman with five husbands? What? Were you sitting there making secret notes last night while I was busy baring my soul, then pretended to pop off to the bathroom so you could text them and tell them all about it?"

A light came on in Kevin's eyes. His lips slowly turned up at the corners. This odd, slightly amused look began to spread across his face.

Instinctively my hand shot up to slap him across the face. I know it was the completely wrong thing to do, but I wasn't really thinking.

But before I could even get close, Kevin grabbed my hand and held it in his—tightly.

"That play wasn't about your mother, Jo," he said evenly. "I agree there's a similarity of sorts. But it's not about her. And I didn't tell anyone about our conversation. Seriously. I swear."

"Then how do you explain it?" I demanded indignantly. "How did they know? Sam would never have told them."

"The story is from the Bible."

"Yeah right!"

"Honestly. Jesus talked to a lot of people while he was on earth," Kevin said. "He talked to thieves and prostitutes and politicians and priests and soldiers and fishermen and everything . . . I'm sorry this story sounded a little like your mother, but it's a coincidence. I swear."

He dropped my hand and pulled a small, tattered Bible out of his back pocket. "Look for yourself. It's right there in John chapter four. Of course it doesn't say anything about a pop machine—it's got a well. But it's essentially the same story. Honest."

He was telling the truth. I'm not sure how I knew it, but all of a sudden, standing there staring into those innocent blue eyes of his, it all seemed incredibly and overwhelmingly obvious— Kevin wasn't lying, and the whole play thing had just been some random, though not particularly nice, coincidence.

"You didn't tell them," I said, "and they didn't make a play about my mother . . ."

"Nope," Kevin shook his head. "I swear."

"Oh . . . OK . . . Sorry."

"Don't worry about it."

We stood there, just staring at each other for way too long. Then Kevin placed his arm around my shoulder, pulling me against his side.

"I can't believe after everything that happened between us last night that you thought, when I got home at midnight, that my first thought was—hey, why don't I call all my friends and tell them to scrap the play Nate and Lisa have been working on all week so we can throw together one about Jo instead," Kevin said, grinning at me. "I mean, you're cute and all, but still . . ."

I did smack him that time—but only lightly and on the arm in a sad yet flirty way. Kevin grinned wider.

But then his smile kind of faded. "Why don't you trust me?" he said.

"What do you mean?"

"About the play . . . you never thought it was Sam for a moment. But you thought me . . . that I . . ." his voice trailed off. "You just don't trust me."

"Kevin," I said, "I'm sorry . . . I guess—well, I don't really know you."

I saw instantly from the way his face fell that I'd just said the absolutely wrong thing, but it was true.

No, I didn't trust Kevin. How could I trust him? I barely even knew him. I mean, it's not like I was some happy, cheery, naive, Lisa-type person who believed every stranger was a potential new best friend.

But now here was Kevin, standing there beside me, with this wounded face, which he was trying hard to hide in a cool, manly way but failing miserably. I mean, Kevin, out of anybody, should understand why I didn't—why I couldn't—trust him.

And yet, Kevin was so sweet, so nice, and I just wished there was something I could do, something I could say to make him see that it wasn't personal, and I really did like him, and . . .

"Go out with me," Kevin said quickly, impulsively.

Excuse me? For a second I wasn't sure I had even heard him properly. But then Kevin turned me around so I was looking straight at him. "Please, go out with me, Jo," Kevin said again, earnestly. "You're beautiful. You're smart. You're different. You make me feel normal. I love spending time with you. I want to go out with you. Please."

I wasn't sure what to say. I wasn't even sure what I wanted to say!

But I let Kevin kiss me and it was an incredible, passionate, forget-your-own-name kind of kiss. And we sat together at the Gathering the next night. Then I let him come around on Monday and help me work in the store all afternoon. And Tuesday Kevin and I went to a movie. And Wednesday he called just to see how I was. And by Thursday morning it finally sunk in—I now had a boyfriend.

§ § §

Now the thing about dating relationships is that you always start off with this glorious, magical, madly-in-love stage where everything seems so wonderful and perfect that you forget to eat, and can hardly sleep, and everything else in your life fades into the background of this one, incredible, amazingly wonderful relationship. And no matter how great things start off that "everything you do is wonderful" phase is always temporary. Always. No matter what. And how long did it last with Kevin? About two and a half weeks.

Don't get me wrong—Kevin was a nice boyfriend. Really nice. Actually, really, really nice. Kevin was sweet and polite. He brought me flowers and held my hand every possible second he could. He came over and helped me in the store when he had a break in his work. Kevin told me I was gorgeous and beautiful, and the nicest person he'd ever met. And he was definitely, by far, the best-looking guy I had ever gone out with.

As boyfriends go, he rated an eight point five at least. Maybe even a nine when we were standing alone on the beach at night and I could tell he was thinking about kissing me.

But the funny thing is that despite that one intense night on the beach when Kevin had been pouring his heart out to me about his dad, when it came down to it, the whole day-to-day dating was kind of . . . well . . . normal.

Maybe it was because Kevin wasn't a big talker. We'd spend hours together walking on the beach, or scraping chewing gum off the store floor. And later as I was lying in my bed at night it was hard to remember anything particularly profound, or interesting, or memorable he'd said. Talking just wasn't him, I guess.

Kevin was also always going off places unexpectedly—working last minute jobs for his father, or popping off for a few minutes during our dates to check his messages; stuff like that. Kevin might have been nice, but he certainly wasn't reliable.

And that's probably why, after a few days of seeming to spend every second of my life either hanging out with Kevin, or thinking about seeing him, Sam somehow slipped back into my life.

It started one night at the Gathering when Kevin had disappeared to take care of something, and Sam had wandered over to ask how I was doing. We were still talking when Kevin came back, and when Kevin said he and Nate needed to go off somewhere, it was Sam who ended up giving me a ride home.

Sam came in to say hi to Kat, and then we all stayed up late watching old videos together. Kat finally kicked Sam out after midnight and told me to go to bed. After that, Sam would pop round sometimes on nights when Kevin was working, and we ended up e-mailing back and forth a lot.

I don't know why I found it so hard to ask him how his date with Traci had gone. I did overhear him telling Kat that he wasn't planning on seeing her again, and I could tell by the constant buzzing of his phone some nights that Traci was still trying to get in touch with him. So why did I have such a hard time asking Sam about her? There was just something, I don't know, that had kind of crept in between Sam and me. It was like this wall had been built up between us somehow and I didn't know what it was, or how to break through it. And Sam didn't ask me about my dates with Kevin either.

Kevin and I hung out with Sam a lot too—like just the three of us would go to a movie, or occasionally Kat would come too. Even though there was the odd time I'd be sitting between Kevin and Sam in the Gathering and suddenly have to remind myself of which one I was supposed to hold hands with, it's not like I really thought about Sam that way, not very often at least. I mean, why would I when I already had the best-looking guy in town?

I had been a little annoyed with Kevin too when, after he and I had been together for almost two weeks, I discovered that he had managed to not tell Nate or Lisa that we were even dating. And I hadn't even realized they didn't know, until I noticed we were getting some pretty weird looks from the two of them when we all hung out together.

Finally, Lisa just came out and asked me if something was going on between me and Kevin. And when I told her we were officially a couple now she just kind of went "Oh" like I'd poked her with a toothpick.

I don't think either of them were crazy about the relationship. But every time I brought it up to Kevin, he would just squeeze me around the shoulders, tell me not to be paranoid, and remind me that he decided who he liked, not his friends. But still I made a point of not being alone with Nate or Lisa in case they said anything to me, which they never did. Which was a shame really, because despite everything Sam had said, I had kind of hoped for a while that, after talking and everything at the wedding, Lisa and I would become friends. And dating Kevin had kind of changed all that.

Of course I'd been going to the Gathering for a few weeks now. You would think that by then I'd have learned how to tune it all out like so much white noise.

But instead it just felt like every Sunday they managed to get in more and more of these little jabs that got under my skin and bugged me for days afterward.

Nate and Lisa's songs were bad enough—I mean half the time I'd just be sitting there mouthing along with these simple rhyming lyrics about being loved forever and I'd find myself wanting to cry for no apparent reason. But Patrick's talks were the worst— especially the questions. He'd say something like . . .

"Do you ever feel like no one would ever really love you if they knew the real you?"

Or . . .

"Have you ever settled for second best because you felt you didn't deserve anything better?"

Or my personal favorite . . .

"Do you ever lie awake and wonder if you're just some random collection of atoms, or if there is a purpose, a reason, why you are alive on this earth?"

I tried talking to Kevin about it, but he didn't seem to get it. So instead I asked Sam. He said, yeah, Patrick did have this special gift for poking people's buttons. And whenever the floor was open for questions, Sam would be the first on his feet, throwing challenge after challenge at him, barely waiting for an answer before his mind was spinning ahead to his next question.

I wouldn't have been surprised if some of the God-squad had been secretly hoping that Sam would leave the Gathering and never come back. In fact, I once overheard Lisa mutter as much to Kevin when she thought I wasn't listening. But I was glad Sam was still coming because then, at least for a few moments, I felt like we were in it together.

To top things off I hadn't even seen Motor-Oil-Guy and Red-Jacket again since that date with Kevin's parents, so I was beginning to think that even if they had been trailing me for some bizarre and improbable reason, then they'd moved on. I mean, considering I rarely went anywhere without Kevin anymore I figured that seeing me firmly attached to the side of someone like him was probably enough to convince them to find some other random chick to pick on.

Anyway, overall, I spent the beginning of August stuck in a pretty comfortable rut. Nice boyfriend. Great best friend. Fun, mindless job. People to hang out with. Cousin to lean on. All in all, I had it pretty good.

But then, around the middle of August, and as if on cue, everything started to change.

It all started on a Monday morning when I was working by myself in the store. Kevin was supposed to have met me for lunch, but then he'd called at the last minute and told me something had come up and he was going to be late. So I was already feeling a little bit irritated and sorry for myself.

I hated it when Kevin was late, and it was already like the fourth time Kevin had changed plans on me. Even though his explanations were always totally understandable, and his apologies were always amazing, and he spent practically every moment we were actually in the same room together telling me how wonderful he thought I was . . . still . . . there was something about it that was beginning to get to me.

So there I was, stuck waiting for him to call, or text, or drop by and say something to fix how I was feeling. And the longer it took for him to do it, the more irritated I became.

The store's previous owners must have been really bad smokers because not only was the paint stained a disgusting yellow hue, there was a thick dark band of tobacco goop stuck along the edges of the window pane. It was a total pain to get off and the only way I'd found was to scrape at it with a chisel.

I was sitting on the floor, tediously scraping away, and something about the Gathering must have been rubbing off on me, because as I poked at the gunk I kind of started to pray.

I started off complaining to God about how Kevin wasn't turning out to be exactly the kind of boyfriend I'd hoped he'd be, but for some reason the words got turned around in my brain, and the next thing I knew I was asking myself why I was even dating Kevin. He was gorgeous, I told myself, and I liked hanging out with him. But still the question persisted—how much did I actually love him? And if I didn't love Kevin, shouldn't I let him go find someone who did?

But if I did break up with Kevin would I ever find anyone else who would want to be with me? And would I ever find anyone I wanted to be with, you know, *permanently*?

For that matter, when was I ever going to have anything in my life that *was* permanent? September was only a couple weeks away and people like Sam would be heading off to college then. The store was going to be finished soon, and once it was done how long would Kat continue to let me live with her?

But most of all, what I wanted to know was, well—was I ever going to become a person that I actually liked? Was I ever going to get up in the morning and look at myself in the mirror without being disappointed in what I saw? Was I ever going to be able to walk away from a conversation without worrying I had said the wrong thing? Was there actually some purpose, some thing, some reason for me being alive?

And that's when I heard the roar—the deep, masculine roar of a seriously hot muscle car. I looked up, and there it was—the "old in an expensive way" red car I had seen run over Nate last summer—parked right up close in front of my window.

I ducked back down below the window frame. Whoever had run over Nate must be back in town—and somehow they knew where I lived. Heart pounding into my throat, I crawled across the floor to the door and threw the lock across. The old store door was pretty battered, but hopefully if someone tried to force their way in it would hold them off for a while. Then I sneaked another peek out the window.

The car was stopped too far forward for me to see who was in the driver's seat. But I had a very clear view of the back. Inching my way up slowly, until my head was level with the back of the car, I pressed my face as hard as I could against the window and carefully slid Sam's phone up in front of me. The click seemed deafening, but I'd gotten it. A good, solid, clearish shot of the back of the car, with an easy-to-read license plate—JN832.

Then I sat back on my heels. Now what? My first thought was to call the police. But what would I tell them? That the car I suspected of being involved in an accident that no one apparently cared about was legally parked in front of my place? That my friend and I had seen a couple of creepy-looking guys hanging around recently and they'd made me nervous, and now I suspected whoever was in this car was in league with them? Maybe even the one calling the shots?

I was about to sneak upstairs and see if I could take a better picture out of the living room window, when I heard the deep purr of the engine starting up again, and I watched the car drive off.

It was only then that I realized I'd been gripping the phone so tightly my fingers hurt. Without even stopping to think, I dialed Sam's number. He was the one person who I knew would listen and understand. And he'd know what to do.

Sam's number was number one on my speed dial and it started ringing almost immediately. And then—

"Hello? Sammy's phone!"

To my shock a girl answered. I hung up instantly.

Why the heck was there a girl answering Sam's phone? And why was she calling him Sammy? And, could there be a chance—please, please, please, be some way, under the heavens—that that overly perky voice didn't belong to who I thought it belonged to?

I rang again.

"Hello? Sammy's phone! This is Traci. Who's this?"

Oh . . . oh . . . oh . . .

I cussed her out under my breath, calling her practically every bad name in the book. But somehow I managed to force a grin onto my face before actually opening my mouth. "Oh, hi Traci!" I said in a super-chipper, no-I'm-not-the-slightest-bit-bothered-that-Sam's-ex-is-answering-the-phone tone of voice. "This is Jo. Is Sam there?"

"Oh, hi Jo!" Traci enthused, like she'd been sitting by the phone all day in the hopes I would call. And like I didn't know Sam's phone had caller ID anyway. "It's so nice to talk to you! We met at . . . now where was it . . . Mandy's wedding, right? That was such a fun party, wasn't it?"

I was smiling so hard down the phone at her I was lucky my cheeks didn't explode under the pressure. "I think you're right!" I chirped. "Wow, I had almost forgotten that!" I hoped that God, if he was listening, would forgive me for lying. "Well, it's great to catch up, but unfortunately I've got to run. Is Sam there by any chance?"

"You want to talk to Sammy?" Traci said, as if the question confused her. "No, sadly he's busy at the moment, but I'd be happy to take a message for you!"

Yeah, I thought, *I'm sure you would . . .*

I dithered a little mentally over what message to give Traci, because, after all, there was no way in the world I could trust her. So I decided on something general which I hoped would catch Sam's attention.

I said, "Sam and I had been talking about this car that I saw last year that I'd been interested in. Anyway I found it and wondered if he wanted to see it. That's all."

"Okeydokey. I'll let him know. Byyyyeeeee!" And with that, Traci hung up.

I sat there like an idiot for a full thirteen minutes staring at my phone willing for Sam to call me back. He didn't.

Sam didn't call me back at all. Not Monday afternoon. Not Monday night. Not Tuesday even.

Kevin never did manage to show up on Monday, but he did

take me out for pizza on Tuesday. And I think I did a pretty good job of hiding the tendency of my mind to flit obsessively from "why was that car in front of the store?" to "why was Sam's evil ex answering his phone?" and back again.

Wednesday rolled around—and still no call from Sam. By Thursday, I was convinced that either Traci never gave him the message, or worse, she did and Sam decided not to call. Either way you looked at it, Traci was far too imbedded back into Sam's life for my liking.

Fortunately, I was too busy to give Sam a second thought . . . really.

To my surprise, on Friday night, Kevin took me out for a romantic dinner, with all the trimmings—candlelight, flowers, soft music, napkins folded into impossible little shapes. A girl could get used to being treated like that. It was a perfect date—like something out of a movie.

And as Kevin reached across the table to brush a strand of hair off my face, before running his hand along mine and curling my fingers into his, I had to admit that I could feel my insides just melting under all the attention.

Oh, I did like Kevin. I really, really liked him. And it was so easy to become addicted to the way he looked at me. What could possibly be wrong with that?

After a long, late, lingering goodbye at the door, I walked into the living room and found Kat sitting on the sofa waiting up for me—never a good sign.

"So, how was your date?" Kat asked.

"Fine," I said.

"Mmmmm," Kat replied.

So far, so good. But I knew there had to be more to it than that. So I curled up in my favorite chair, pulled my knees up to my chest, and wrapped an afghan around me. If I was going to be in for a lecture I might as well be comfortable.

"Things seem to be going pretty well between you and Kevin," Kat started, carefully, in her best now-I-don't-want-you-to-think-this-is-a-lecture voice. "And I'm glad about that—Kevin seems like a nice guy . . ."

And so it went, with Kat saying nice things about Kevin, and how well I had been doing with the store, and how nice it was to have me around, and on and on until I was getting kind of tired of hearing nice things and was really starting to dread whatever this heavy thing was she was going to hit me with.

Then it came—Kat was concerned that something was making me concerned, and she hoped I was OK.

I must admit, Kat's big-sisterly "I care about you" tactic worked pretty well. Especially as she started in with "I feel like I've barely seen you in the past few days . . ." then threw in a little "and when I have seen you, you've seemed distracted . . ." and then rounded it off with "I just want to make sure you're all right."

In fact, she was doing so well, I was really tempted to break down and tell my cousin just how conflicted I was. Until Kat made one, colossal, fatal mistake—she told me that Sam dropped by tonight just in case I was home, and mentioned to Kat he hadn't heard from me in ages either.

"Well I'm sorry if Sam thinks he can just drop by whenever he wants and expect me to be sitting here waiting for him!" I retorted kind of loudly—which wasn't quite fair considering it wasn't Kat's fault that Sam had Traci for an answering service. "It's not exactly my fault his nasty little on-again-off-again girlfriend Traci decided not to tell him I called, now is it?"

I could tell by the look of shock on Kat's face that Sam hadn't told her anything about Traci—and even though I wasn't completely off the hook, I could tell this little revelation had gone a long way to taking the wind out of whatever sails she'd been building up.

"Well, I didn't know that," Kat said, doing a pretty bad job of hiding her disgust at whatever Sam and Traci might be up to.

"I know!" I said, glad to have the opportunity to sound indignant and wronged. "No one was more surprised than me to discover that Traci was screening his calls. And I don't even think she gave him the message that I'd been trying to get in touch."

Kat nodded grimly. It was totally one of those us-girls-against-those-idiotic-men moments.

So from there it was easy to transition into a lot of reassuring things like "Thank you so much for your concern" and "I love you too." And I gave my cousin a huge hug and then we both went to bed.

But still, as I lay awake in bed that night I couldn't help but think I'd missed a good opportunity to talk to her about how confused I really was about Kevin. Only problem was, I really didn't know where to start.

CHAPTER EIGHT

KEVIN CALLED me first thing Saturday morning, told me he was going to take a load of wood to one of his dad's customers outside of Ashford, and asked me if I wanted to come. This was new. Setting aside the fact Kevin probably should have known better than to ask me anything first thing on a Saturday morning—I mean, it wasn't even eight-thirty yet—Kevin had never invited me to go along with him on a job. Never. I mean every now and then we'd drive past a house and Kevin would point to the porch, or the molding, or the whatchamacallit-woody-bit and tell me he'd worked on it. But nothing like this.

"Are you sure?" I mumbled. Probably not the best response, but hey, it was early and my brain hadn't started fully functioning yet.

"I'd really like it if you could come," Kevin said. "I . . . uh . . . I really need to talk to you about something."

That got me out of bed. He asked me to be ready in half an hour, and so after having the world's fastest shower, digging a red T-shirt and a faded pair of cropped jeans out of my laundry pile, and sliding into my most comfortable sandals, I managed to make it downstairs in thirty-six minutes flat—which has got to be some kind of record for me. But then Kevin showed up almost forty minutes late, leaving me plenty of time to alternate between decrying the uselessness of some guys, and worrying over what might be keeping him.

"Everything's gone wrong today," Kevin muttered, giving me a perfunctory kiss on the cheek. "I had meant to be here ages ago but everything just got out of hand and now I'm late and I'm in a pitiful mood. And I'm sorry."

"It's OK," I said. "It's all good."

Kevin smiled a little. "You're better than I deserve. I'll make it up to you, I promise. I know this really great restaurant just out-side Ashford and I'll take you there for dinner."

He helped me into the truck. But I grabbed his hand before he could close the door.

"You sure you're OK?" I asked.

"I'm fine," Kevin said, pulling away and heading around to the driver's side.

"It's just that Nate kind of showed up as I was getting ready to leave," Kevin explained, as he started the truck. "Dad had told me last night that he thought Nate should come along today and give me a hand. I'd told him it was fine, I wanted to do it on my own. But Dad must have called him because he showed up anyway. Dad said if I wanted to take you that was fine, but in that case we should go in his truck because it has a double cab. But as I tried to explain to them, I needed to talk to you about something alone and I didn't want an audience."

How's that for flattering meets daunting?

"Besides I already had all the wood loaded up in my truck and I wasn't about to waste the time moving it all over to my dad's. And so, well, we kind of got into it a bit."

Got into it? Got into what?

Kevin's knuckles were tight on the steering wheel. A flurry of questions ran through my head, but somehow I knew it wasn't going to be a good time to be asking questions he didn't seem to be in a hurry to answer, so instead I leaned back against the hard bench seat and stared at the trees whizzing past my window.

It was a chilly day, with a crisp breeze sneaking in through gaps around the window frame, reminding us that the summer was almost over. Despite Kevin's impassioned insistence that he needed to talk to me—about something important, alone—he didn't seem to be in any hurry to get started.

The drive took close to an hour and for most of it Kevin seemed content to grip the steering wheel in stony silence, as we listened to the sound of cars whizzing past on the highway and the best that AM radio had to offer. I did make one attempt to break the tension by telling him I was really sorry that he and his dad and Nate had had a disagreement and if there was anything

I could do to let me know. The edges of Kevin's jaw thawed a bit at that. But all he said was, "Thank you, Jo, but you just wouldn't understand."

Uh huh. I resisted the temptation to remind him that for me to actually understand something—anything—he kind of needed to talk to me about it in the first place.

The man who had ordered the load of wood had angry words for Kevin when we showed up. Apparently he thought Nate was coming as well, and didn't know how they were going to get all the wood to the second floor of his half-built summerhouse without an extra pair of hands. To add insult to injury it had kind of started raining—not real drops, more like pathetic little dribbly rain that seemed to come from all directions at once.

I rolled my sleeves up and threw myself totally into helping the best I could. But we had arrived there late to begin with, and even with the three of us working together, it still took over an hour for what the angry man had been promised would be a quick drop.

Even though the wood was insanely heavy and I ended up totally exhausted and filthy, I really did enjoy pitching in like that. There was something about working good and hard that helped push everything else out of my mind for a while. Because the way I saw it this "serious talk" of Kevin's could only be one of two things—either he wanted to stop dating me, or he wanted to take our relationship up a notch. And I didn't know which potential conversation I was dreading more.

We got back in the truck and Kevin pulled back onto the highway. The rain stopped as abruptly as it started. Figures. Kevin and I looked at each other and smiled.

"You're incredible, you know that?" Kevin said, reaching for my hand. "I'm so sorry everything's been so lousy today."

"It's all right," I said.

"No, it isn't, and you deserve better than I've been giving you recently." He sighed, and ran his fingers through his hair, making it all spike up on end. "How about we go for a walk around Bear Lake? It's not that far from here."

"Sounds great."

"Good." Kevin's face finally broke into a good and proper grin. "Let me just stop and pick up some gas and we'll head over."

Kevin squeezed my hand. I squeezed back. It was just great to see him happy again, with a real smile stretching all the way up to his eyes. Kevin cranked the radio up and we both sang along to some silly old song neither of us really knew the lyrics to. And it looked like the day was going to turn out OK after all.

We stopped at a big truck stop gas station on the highway, and as Kevin filled the tank I wandered around the back and through a parking lot to where the bathrooms were. Trying very hard not to look at anything that was scribbled on the walls or littered on the floor, I critically surveyed my face in the dingy mirror. Scraggly and mud-splattered—or "wholesome" as Sam would say—was certainly not my very best look. But there is only so much you can do without a hairbrush or makeup compact. So Kevin was going to have to take me as I came, mud and all.

I shoved the restroom door back open, then stopped abruptly. There was an ugly brown station wagon parked in front of the door with two familiar forms leaning against it smoking cigarettes— Motor-Oil-Guy and Red-Jacket. And unless I felt like hanging out in the filthy bathroom for a while, I was going to have to walk right past them.

Yeah, part of me was scared. But more than that—part of me was angry. What was wrong with these guys? What did they want with me? What had I ever done to them—except of course call 911 when I saw Nate get hit. But how would they ever have known it was me anyway? And why hassle me over it all this time later?

There were thousands and thousands of people living in Silverpoint and yet somehow these two creeps managed to show up outside my house, outside the Gathering, and even when I was out on a date. And not only did they now have whoever ran over Nate parking their red car in front of my place too—they were now following me even when I went out of town! I mean, there are eerie coincidences, and then there's just plain out-and-out stalking.

My heart was pounding so hard I thought it was going to

choke me, but what was I going to do? Hide in the bathroom and text for Kevin, or Sam, or some other guy to come and rescue me?

No. Forget it. I was tired of cowering and slinking and feeling scared when I hadn't done anything wrong. I was going to walk out there, head held high, and let them see that I wasn't afraid. But first, I was going to make sure I got a picture of them loitering out there, just in case. So quickly and quietly, I slid my phone in the gap between the door and the frame and clicked. I did it once again for good measure.

Then I shook my hair out, squared my shoulders, gritted my teeth, and started to walk back confidently, looking straight past them like they weren't even there, telling myself there was no way—absolutely no way—that I was going to let them see me sweat.

As I got closer Red-Jacket started cat-calling me. Just the usual kind of gross and demeaning stuff—a couple low whistles with a handful of "Hey baby, bring some of that our way!" which quickly turned into "Yeah baby, you keep walking!" as I passed them. And a smattering of derogatory terms and swear words thrown in for good measure.

I was working hard at not listening, not turning, not flinching, not reacting, not giving them the satisfaction, and just putting one foot down in front of the other. But then I heard the car doors slam and the spluttering of an engine behind me. I stiffened, waiting for them to drive past. But they didn't. Instead I just heard the guttural revs and growls of the car inching its way along behind my back. They were following me—at a snail's crawl.

Biting the insides of my mouth so hard I winced, I walked over to the side of the parking lot, giving them plenty of room to pass. They followed along behind me, laughing and yelling and calling abuse with every step I took.

"Hey baby!" I heard Red-Jacket call out. "Think you're all that do ya? Think we don't know how ya are? How ya think those"—muffled swearword—"legs of yours will look flattened under the wheels of my car?"

I know I should've kept ignoring him. I know I should've just kept walking forward and not given them the satisfaction. But something inside me snapped.

"Why don't you just leave me alone?" I screamed, spinning on my heels and turning on them. "What's wrong with you? What have I ever done to you?" My voice was verging on hysterical and I could feel tears building in the corner of my eyes.

"Sa . . . my friend and I know what you've been doing!" I cried, catching myself before I blurted out Sam's name, "We've seen you lurking around! And we want you to leave us alone! If you don't stop we'll . . . we'll . . . we'll . . ."

My voice cracked and threatened to give out on me. What would I do if they didn't stop following me around? Go to the police and try to file a restraining order on two total strangers whose names I didn't know? Go around looking over my shoulder every second of the day? And what if that didn't make them stop? Then what?

Motor-Oil-Guy started revving his engine, but it was the look on his face that scared me. It was furious and cold. It was the face of a guy who would hurt me without a moment's hesitation.

"You think we're"—swearword—"scared of you and that"—swearword—"guy?" he shouted. "You tell that"—swearword—"to watch his back because I'm going to kill him. And I'll"—swearword—"you up too!"

I ran.

Terrified.

I wove back and forth across the parking lot, then dove into the side door of the gas station convenience store. A half-empty beer can hit the door behind me even as I was shutting it. Then laughing, they drove off.

Feeling like I was walking through a thick wall of water, I stumbled through the store, out the front door, and over to where Kevin was parked on the far side of the parking lot. When he saw me coming he leaned over and opened the door for me, and I nearly slipped as I tried to climb into the truck. As Kevin reached for my hand and helped pull me in, I realized that my hands were literally shaking.

"You OK, babe?" Kevin asked, searching my face with his eyes.

"There . . . there . . . there were a couple of guys in the parking lot, hassling me," I said, "yelling horrible stuff. Then they . . . they

. . . started following me. They're . . . they're the same guys Sam and I saw before . . . and . . . they said . . . they . . ."

"Hey, hey, it's OK," Kevin slid across and wrapped his arms around me. I leaned my head against his chest and soaked in the solid warmth of his body. "I'm so, so sorry," he said, leaning his head against mine. "I didn't see them. Do you want me to go talk to them? Because if it'll help I'd be happy to—"

"No. No don't," I said, straightening back up again and running my hands through my hair. "It's . . ." I took a deep breath. "I think they've been following me. I don't know why but someone . . . someone's been following me . . ."

Kevin stiffened as he was about to start the engine, keys still in his hand. "Are you sure?" he said skeptically. "You think someone's been following you? Why on earth would you think someone's been following you?"

There was an edge to his voice and he was looking at me hard like he thought I was lying. He didn't believe me. I'd just been threatened and my boyfriend didn't believe me.

"I keep seeing these guys around town," I said earnestly. "This guy in a baseball hat and this other guy in an athletic jacket. And then there was this red car parked in front of the store yesterday and—"

"Lots of people have baseball caps and sports jackets," Kevin argued.

That's right—he was actually arguing with me. Not listening. Not comforting. But arguing. Like he thought I was some hysterical nut who didn't have a clue what she was saying.

"Lots of people have red cars too," Kevin was going on, "Julia has one, and so does Lisa's dad, and Nate—"

"No, this wasn't just any red car," I cut him off, desperately willing him to believe me, "it was—"

And just as the words were about to fly out over my tongue I gasped them back, as I realized what I was about to say. I'd been about to say, "the car that nearly killed Nate." Kevin still didn't know about the accident I'd seen, and I couldn't tell him. Not because I didn't want to. But because I knew that he wouldn't believe me. And there was no way I could be with a guy who wouldn't believe me about something like that. And where would that leave us?

"It was nothing," I said sullenly, staring down at my mud-specked sandals. "It was probably just some losers trying to get a cheap kick out of ruining someone else's day."

"You sure?" Kevin asked earnestly.

"Yeah," I muttered, "let's just go on to the lake. Please."

I sat there beside him, willing him to ask me more about what had happened and to tell me he'd believe me no matter how crazy it sounded. But instead Kevin just paused a long moment. Then he put the truck in gear.

We drove about another ten or fifteen minutes down the road, and then Kevin pulled over and parked on a little slip road by the side of the highway. He led me on a path through the woods. It was a good ten-minute walk, and so narrow we had to walk single file for much of it. But it was beautiful. The smell of the newly washed earth filled the air and made me wonder what kind of God decided to make the forest so beautiful.

Bear Lake was long and skinny, and as still as glass. Half a dozen tiny islands, some no more than a rock and a tree, reflected and shimmered on the mirrorlike surface.

"This is like the perfect place to come if you want to just be alone with someone and talk without any interruptions," Kevin said, turning to me. He put his hands on my waist, like he wanted to make sure I wasn't going to run away. Long, hanging leaves cast shifting shadows across his face. Kevin took a deep breath.

"I really like you, Jo," he started. "You're different, you know. Special. And you were right when you said it takes time to get to know someone. Because, you know what it's like, you get into this habit of walking around all your life with this wall around you. And you think that no one wants to really know you, but maybe it's just because you never meet anyone you think you could like enough to try . . ."

Kevin was actually dithering now. And to be totally honest I was having a hard time following what he was saying. He was going on about walls, and trust, and hiding away parts of our-selves. And I could tell he was being really serious, and really sincere, and trying to build up to something big. So, needless to say, I felt kind of guilty for the fact that my mind kept wandering.

"You know I love you," Kevin was saying, "and I do—you've got to believe me on that. But I haven't always been totally open with you about everything. And I was thinking that maybe it was time I was more honest about telling you, you know, things . . ."

Kevin took another deep breath. Like he was leaning out the door of an airplane, parachute on, knowing that once he took the plunge, and said whatever he was going to say, everything was going to change between us and there was no going back.

I squeezed his arm reassuringly, and braced myself for impact.

"And so . . . umm . . . well . . . um . . . you should know . . . um . . ."

"Yes?"

Then Kevin got this odd look on his face, like he'd suddenly realized the ground was just too many miles down, and he started desperately searching around for an escape hatch, or a panic button—some way to get away from this conversation, as far and as fast as his legs would carry him.

"What do you think of God, Jo?" Kevin spluttered.

"What?" I shrieked, feeling tempted to strangle him.

"How . . . how would you describe the way that God affects people's lives?"

"I wouldn't!"

I swear I had no idea where this new topic of conversation was coming from. I hoped it all made some kind of sense in his mind, because as far as my mind was concerned Kevin was quickly convincing me that I liked him better when he wasn't attempting to talk with me.

"Please Jo," Kevin said again, "I'm curious. I want to know what you think."

Somewhere in the distance I heard a booming crack, like the snap of a giant whip, or a clap of distant thunder.

"I think, I think believing in God makes people more confident," I said. "It's like they find it easier to take the stuff life throws at them. But maybe it's just that a certain type of people are more attracted to religion than other people. You know, people like Lisa who've got it all together. People who are more, I don't know, more secure, and happier, and well, just more perfect to begin with I guess."

"Perfect?" Kevin said, sounding kind of incredulous.

"Yeah, I guess," I said, squirming slightly. "I don't mean it as a bad thing! Honest! If anything I'm kind of jealous of you, and Lisa, and Nate, and Patrick . . ."

"For being more *perfect* than you?" Kevin said.

"Yeah, sort of."

Kevin laughed. I mean, seriously laughed, which kind of put me off because I hadn't thought I'd said anything funny. Kevin must have seen the look on my face, because he straightened up again pretty quickly.

"Knowing God is out there, and that God loves you, does make an amazing difference in your life," Kevin said, "it really, really does. But you have got to get over this idea that the group at the Gathering is this bunch of goody-godly perfect people. They're far from it. They are just a bunch of messed-up people who have had their lives put back together by God."

"Lisa is messed up?" I said sarcastically.

"Yes, I'm sure she is," Kevin said. "I know for sure I am, and Nate certainly has his less-than-saintly moments."

We started walking back to the truck, and Kevin apologized for never inviting me to go to Cornerstone with him on a Sunday morning—he really should have, he said, it was just that since the Gathering had been going full steam he usually skipped going to church Sunday mornings too. But he'd take me sometime soon, he said. "Because I really want you to know more about God, and I really should be doing more to help you than I have been."

I was only half listening to him. Mostly I was thinking about whether or not I was ready to believe that Lisa was messed up. "Damaged goods," that's what Patrick had said—because of sin everyone was damaged goods. But I just wasn't convinced. And as I picked my way around the trees, my feet crunching pinecones into the dirt, I caught myself thinking, *The day someone can convince me that Lisa is just as messed up as I am is the day I'll consider that her faith just might work for someone like me.*

When the trees cleared and the truck came into view, I could tell right away there was something wrong with it. At first I thought the light was playing tricks with my eyes because it looked like the corner of the windshield was frozen over with icicles. Then it hit me. It was broken. Someone had smashed in the windshield of Kevin's truck.

Kevin gave a shout and ran forward, yelling over his shoulder for me to stay back. There was glass everywhere. Kevin told me he was going to call the police, and that I should call someone to come pick me up. Before I could answer, he'd started walking down the road, his cell phone to his ear. Almost instinctively, I grabbed my phone and called Sam.

"Hello?"

"Sam?"

"Jo? Hi. Are you OK?"

The sound of Sam's voice was so insanely comforting that for a second I was tempted to collapse into tears. But instead I said, "I need you. Can you come pick me up? I'm at Bear Lake and someone has vandalized Kevin's truck . . ."

"I know where that is. You're not far from Mandy's. I'm on my way," Sam said. Just like that. Like there was never any question that he'd be there for me.

Kevin walked back slowly, like he had lead weights resting on his shoulders. This gnawing sense of guilt started to eat away at the inside of my stomach and for a moment I thought I was going to be sick. Had Motor-Oil-Guy and Red-Jacket done this? Was this my fault? My fault for yelling at them? Was this my fault for not being totally honest with Kevin about everything?

Kevin reached out and wrapped his arms around me. I was feeling so weak my knees almost buckled under the weight of trying to hold him up. He rested his lips on the top of my head.

"Talk to me," I said, "please."

But Kevin just stood there, holding me, kissing my hair. Then he reached for my face, pulling me up against him and kissing my eyes, my cheeks, my lips. Hungrily. And for a long time nothing existed but his lips, and his hands in my hair, the dirt under my feet and a chill in the breeze. Then Kevin pulled away. "Thank you," he whispered. Then he put his arm around my waist and we walked back to the truck.

"When Sam arrives I want you to leave with him, and I'll wait for the police with Nate," Kevin said.

"No, of course I won't," I replied automatically. "I'll stay with you until the police come."

"I'd really rather you left," Kevin said again, and that's when I realized he was serious.

"Well I'm not going! I'm staying!" I said. I couldn't believe what I was hearing. "There's no way I'm just going to leave you like this! You're my boyfriend and I'm sticking with you."

I tried to smile, but Kevin just kept shaking his head.

"Look, it's my truck," he said, "and it's a non-priority call for the police. It'll probably take them ages to get here, and then they're going to want to talk to me for a while and fill in paperwork, and then we'll need to get it towed and—"

"I want to stay and talk to the police too," I cut in. "Look, you might not think it's a big deal about those guys I saw hassling me at the truck stop but I want to—"

"And if you start going on to the police about that we'll be stuck out here all afternoon," Kevin cut me off sharply. "I will give them your number and tell them you want to speak to them, and they can call on you at home. No point us all standing out here at the side of the road—" "Kevin!" I practically shouted, stepping right in front of him so that he had to look at me. "Listen to me! Please! Something is going on! Something you don't know about!" Kevin gave me a piercing look. "Look, I know you don't want to believe me," I said, in a lower voice. "But I think I've accidentally stumbled into something criminal. I don't know how. But now I've got strangers threatening me, and I'm pretty sure that your friend Nate is somehow involved . . ."

I was going to tell him everything. I was going to tell him all about seeing someone try to kill Nate last year, and about how Sam had given me the camera, and how Motor-Oil-Guy and Red-Jacket kept following me.

But one glance at the look on Kevin's face and I knew he'd never hear me.

"No. No. You're just letting your imagination run away with you," he said firmly. He kept shaking his head like he was trying to shake my words away from him. "There is no way Nate could ever be involved in anything—"

"But Kevin!"

"No!" he yelled, his voice so harsh I took a step back. "Listen to me, Jo! There is no way Nate could ever be involved in anything illegal! Never! Ever! The only way Nate would ever come within a million-mile radius of something criminal is if he was fighting to shut it down!"

I started to speak but he practically shouted me down before I could say another word.

"You keep asking me about God, Jo. You want to know how I found God? It was Nate. OK, it was Nate and seeing what Jesus was able to make . . . able to help Nate do. Seeing how much Nate loved Jesus—that's what finally flipped the switch in my head."

I could hear the hurt and anguish pushing through his voice from somewhere deep inside him. I hadn't seen him like this since the night he told me about his dad, and seeing the pain on his face was breaking my heart so bad all I wanted to do was throw my arms around him and beg him to stop.

"That's how God saved my life, Jo," Kevin continued. "Before God, my world used to be more dark, and black, and miserable than you'll ever know, and if I didn't have God in it now I don't think I'd survive. So don't try to tell me that the guy who helped me find all that is a fake because I won't believe it. I can't."

"Then convince me I'm wrong, Kevin," I practically yelled back. "Convince me I'm wrong!"

Kevin stormed away from me, back toward the truck, punching the air in frustration. "I can't believe you still don't trust me!" he yelled.

"I still don't know you, Kevin!"

"How can you say that?" Kevin cried, turning back to face me.

"What?" I said. "Did you think that just by hanging out with you for three—four weeks, I'd somehow figure out what you think and how you feel by osmosis? It takes talking, Kevin. You know, communicating, to get to know someone."

"Well, I'm not Sam!" Kevin snapped back. "If you want someone like Sam then just go be with Sam! But things with me are kind of *complicated!*"

"And the rest of us are simple?"

"I didn't say that!"

"Then what were you trying to say?"

But before Kevin could answer, Sam pulled up beside us, barely stopping long enough to put the car into park before jumping out and rushing over to ask if we were both OK.

"We're fine, Sam, thanks," I said wearily. "Kevin has called Nate, he's on his way."

Sam nodded, "Yeah, Nate caught me on my cell phone a few minutes ago. Apparently he and Kevin's dad are both coming. Nate suggested that I take you back to Silverpoint, Jo, and he'd wait for the police with Kevin. But I told him we'd—"

"No, let's go, Sam," I said quickly before Kevin could cut in. "I think it'll be best."

Sam glanced inquisitively from my face, to Kevin's, and back again. Then said, "OK, but let's wait until Nate shows up at least."

But he'd barely gotten the words out of his mouth when Nate and Ken pulled up in Ken's white megatruck, and after a quick discussion it was confirmed that they would wait and I would head home with Sam. I didn't want to go, and I could tell Sam wanted to stay too, but by this point I was too tired to argue.

So I climbed into Sam's car, and just as we were getting ready to pull away Kevin rushed over and stuck his head in my open window.

"I love you, Jo," Kevin said in a low voice, just before giving me a kiss on the cheek, "I'll call you later." I nodded. And Sam and I left.

I don't know if Sam and I talked much as we drove away. Maybe he was talking and I wasn't listening. Somehow I find it hard to believe we drove twenty minutes without either of us speaking. But I was pretty shaken, so you never know. It was after we passed the turn for that angry client of Ken's that the dam burst and all of a sudden I just started to cry. Not big sobbing crying. Just little painful heaves like I wanted to cry, but didn't know how.

Sam pulled his car over to the side of the road. He undid our seatbelts and then he hugged me. He just hugged me—didn't say anything, didn't do anything—just held me against his chest. I closed my eyes and listened to his heartbeat, and I felt better, safer, happier, than I had in a long, long time.

"How did you get to be such a good friend?" I murmured. I tilted my head up to look at him, not realizing how close he was, and we nearly bumped noses. We both kind of laughed nervously and I sat back in my seat.

"I don't know," Sam said with a sort of forced offhandedness. "You're a pretty good friend too."

"No, I'm really not," I said.

Sam didn't respond. Instead he asked me if I had any idea why someone would have vandalized Kevin's truck. Then he started driving again while I filled him in about what had happened with Motor-Oil-Guy and Red-Jacket at the gas station, and how I'd seen the red car on Monday.

"They threatened to kill us, Sam. I don't know what you and I could have possibly done to—"

"Don't worry about it," Sam cut me off quickly, covering my hand with his, "OK? I don't want you worrying about it. They were probably just spouting a lot of hot air and had nothing to do with Kevin's windshield."

I could tell even as he said it that he didn't believe it. That he was just trying to reassure me. But I really appreciated hearing him say it anyway.

"But, but you do believe me, right?"

"Of course I do," Sam said firmly. "Always. No doubt about it." And despite everything that had happened, hearing him say it actually made me feel a little bit better.

The sun had come out again and was glaring down at us with that kind of intensity the sun seems to only get when its been hidden by clouds for too long. Sam reached past me, dug a pair of sunglasses out of the glove compartment, and put them on.

"Something weird is definitely going on with those guys," Sam said in that logical, we-can-work-it-out tone I loved so much. "You see these guys looking through your store window, I confront them at the Gathering, then you notice them loitering around a parking lot, maybe sticking a piece of paper on your . . . uh . . . boyfriend's truck. Then three weeks later the car that hit Nate shows up outside your door but drives off, and then the same two dirtbags threaten you just before Kevin's truck gets vandalized. So, how is all this connected? Yeah, you could definitely see a pattern there, but the biggest piece is missing. Why are they coming after you?"

"Exactly!" I said, "I just keep thinking it's all got to link back to whatever happened to Nate."

Sam shrugged. "It's entirely possible. But I don't know if it's probable. I mean, you were just the person who called the police. Shouldn't they be stalking Nate and trying to kill him? Besides, how would they possibly know you witnessed the accident?"

"I gave the police my name and address when I called."

Sam nodded, "But do you really think the local police are so corrupt as to give the details to some creepy losers with a seriously ugly car?"

I giggled despite myself. "But didn't you ask around a bit about it though?" I pointed out.

"Yeaaah," Sam said, "but so what? Who all did I speak to? My sister? Her husband? Kat knows too of course. But who besides that? No, there had to be some reason why they have something against you."

"Well, you did take their picture when you saw them outside the Gathering," I added. "And I took their picture twice, three times if you count my taking a picture of the red car."

Sam considered that one for a moment. "Yeah, I could see how that could get some guys riled, if they noticed you doing it." Sam nodded, slowly. "But it would be a leap definitely. Especially as this was after you saw them watching you in the store.

"It's just too bad you didn't notice what was on that paper they put on Kevin's truck," he went on. "Maybe that would have been the key to something. Maybe it was meant for someone else and they think you read it. Maybe they mistook you for someone else and were trying to sell you something illegal . . ."

"Maybe," I said noncommittally. "And Kevin says there's no way Nate could ever be involved in something illegal," I added.

Sam nodded thoughtfully. "You know," he said slowly, "to be totally honest, I kind of believe him on that."

Then Sam started talking about God for a while. While he'd never admit it to anyone else, he did kind of enjoy having some sort of spiritual dimension in his life. But he didn't want it to run his life. That was the problem with people like Nate, he said, they just wanted to take the whole faith-thing too far. And couldn't you just believe there was a God without having it take over your life?

I just sat back and listened. There was something so comfortable about hanging out with Sam. Everything with Kevin had been intense somehow. Whenever I hung out with Kevin—heck, whenever I thought about him—I felt like someone had reached inside my chest and set off a spray of sparklers. It was exciting, definitely. I mean, when he touched me sometimes I felt like I was going to jump clear out of my skin. But it was unsettling too. Almost painful.

Yet being curled up in a ball in the front of Sam's car felt, well . . . like I was coming home somehow. Without even thinking, I'd pushed my sandals off and tucked my feet up beside me. I was so deeply, insanely, unbelievably comfortable I could have fallen asleep.

Maybe I even did, because the next thing I knew we were well past the outskirts of Ashford, and Sam was suggesting we stop and get a bite to eat, and I suddenly realized how hungry I was. It was well after two, and I had barely had any breakfast, and absolutely no lunch.

So Sam took me to this burger van, right on the side of the highway. From the outside it looked like a complete grease bucket. But the food was unbelievably good. We sat there for ages on beat-up metal chairs, chomping away on huge meaty burgers with an enormous pile of greasy fries on the table between us. We talked about everything and anything, from our favorite cartoon to our worst childhood memory, and even after we had already eaten way too much neither of us seemed to be in a hurry to go anywhere.

But we eventually got back in the car and started going again, and Sam starting teasing me about the fact this was the first time he could remember going anywhere with me when I didn't check myself out in the sun-flap mirror as soon as my bottom hit the seat. So then of course, I couldn't look—not after he'd said something. But he could tell the desire to just take a quick peek was driving me nuts, so Sam started going on about how I had ketchup on my face and a fry in my hair, and finally it got the better of me so I yanked the sun-flap down and took a look. I looked fine. Not great, by any stretch of the imagination. But not so bad anyone was about to start throwing stones.

Sam laughed. "I don't know why you are so insecure," he said, shaking his head. "See, you look fine!"

I leaned over and pinched him.

"Yow!" he jumped. "What was that for?"

"For being a pest," I said, slumping back into my seat and pretending to sulk. "Why do you pick on me?"

"Because you make it so easy!" Sam said, his eyes twinkling at me. "I'll never get how someone as beautiful and loveable as you can be so incredibly convinced that they're so hideously unlovable."

I don't think Sam's words could have hit me harder if he'd tried. He was still looking over, grinning, like he hadn't said anything out of the ordinary. But in my world it was like someone had literally come over and punched me in the gut. *I'll never get how someone as beautiful and loveable as you can be so incredibly convinced that they're so hideously unlovable.* I could barely breathe, and when I opened my mouth, my words came out as a whisper.

"Did you just say what I think you did?"

Sam stopped smiling. "What?" he said, staring straight ahead.

I didn't respond, and when Sam finally spoke his words were so clipped he almost sounded bitter. "That I think you're beautiful? Or that I know you think nobody could ever love you?"

There was that feeling again—like I was drowning and couldn't breathe.

"Both," I whispered.

"Well, I do," Sam said, still staring ahead, "sorry."

I didn't want him to say sorry. I wanted him to tell me why he thought I was beautiful. I wanted him to tell me he really did think I was loveable. I wanted to ask Sam if he ever felt unlovable. I wanted to ask him if he knew how much I liked him, and respected him, and enjoyed being with him. And I wanted to ask him if he knew how much what he had just said meant to me.

But I didn't know how to say any of those things, because no matter how comfortable I felt around him, no matter how much I found him easier to spend time with than anyone else, it was still like there was this wall between us. This barrier I couldn't see, couldn't even define, that kept pushing us apart.

And sometimes, when I don't know how to say the right thing, I say the completely wrong thing.

"Why didn't you call me back on Monday?" The words sounded way more accusatory than I wanted.

"I didn't know you called Monday," Sam said flatly.

"Well I talked to Traci!"

That seemed to rattle him. "Why on earth were you talking to Traci?"

"Why was she answering your phone?"

Sam grimaced, like he had just tasted something foul.

"When was she answering my phone?"

"Monday," I snapped. "Like I just said, I called you Monday and Traci answered, and said she'd give you the message, but very obviously she didn't!"

"What time Monday?"

"I don't know what time Monday. I wasn't exactly looking at the clock. Why, didn't you see Traci on Monday, or did she just sneak in and answer your phone when you were in the shower?" Actually, I had a rough idea of what time it had been, but I wasn't about to help out. "So, when were you going to tell me that Traci was back in your life?"

"Well, I didn't think it was any of your business," Sam said.

"Fine," I snapped, "you're right. It is none of my business. If you want to ruin your life by dating some witch who treats you like garbage, go ahead and be my guest!"

"You know you really do like to sit up on your high horse and pass judgment on those below you, don't you?" Sam was nearly shouting now. "I'll have you know that Traci is a great, beautiful, interesting person. She makes me feel special, Jo. She wants me around! She calls me! She likes me! She needs me!"

"Well, then you're a complete and total idiot!" I shouted back. "Do you have any idea what a big deal you made about the fact that Traci is destructive and bad for you, and then she just snaps her fingers and you just prance along to whatever little tune she—"

"You don't have any freaking clue what you're taking about, do you?" Sam smacked the steering wheel hard with the heel of his hand. "You can be so, so stupid sometimes!"

I felt like he'd slapped me. "You think I'm stupid, Sam?" I said. "Fine! Well, it's good to finally know what you actually think of me. But I'm not the one stupid enough to be dating Traci!"

"Well, you're dating Kevin, aren't you!" Sam said, leveling it as an accusation.

"So what if I'm dating Kevin?" I shot back. "So what? He likes me! Kevin treats me like I matter!"

"Kevin treats you like a freaking china doll!" Sam shouted. "He tiptoes around you like he's terrified that one day he's going to break you!"

"Well, maybe that's because he loves me!"

"That's not love, Jo! That's *idolation*!"

"That's not even a word!"

"Well it should be! He treats you . . . he treats you . . ." Sam took a breath and shook his head hard in frustration. "It's like he doesn't even see you, Jo. It's like when he looks at you all he sees is this picture of you that he made up in his own mind and now he's afraid to do anything real because that might chase this illusion of the perfect Jo away."

"Well did you ever consider that I might like the way Kevin looks at me?" I cried. "That I might like the way he 'idolizes' me? It's certainly better than being around someone who keeps re-minding you of how pitiful they think you are."

"No. It's worse." Sam slammed his foot on the break so hard I was flung forward in my seat, and it was only then that I realized we had arrived back at Kat's place. Sam spun around in his seat to face me.

"It's worse, Jo. You want to know why? Because you are now so afraid of messing up this perfect little 'you' that Kevin's created that you're not even you anymore!

"You know what I thought when I met you? I thought, 'Wow, she's amazing. She cares about things more than anyone I ever met.' Heck, know how many people would care about seeing someone get hit by a car so much they would feel compelled, forced, to do something about it instead of just shoving it into the back of their mind like a normal person would? And yet, what did you end up doing about it? Nothing! You haven't done a flippin' thing because you're too afraid that if you do everyone's going to stop liking you.

"You are such a waste, Jo!" Sam exploded. "Here you are this amazing, incredible person, and you could do so much with your life. But instead you talk, and you whine, and you dither, and you date some guy you don't even love, and you putter away in your cousin's empty store with no plans for your future—and you don't do anything! You spend your life doing nothing because you're too scared to give anything that matters a chance."

"Drop dead, Sam."

Tears stung my eyes. I shoved my way out of the car and ran toward Kat's. Even as I heard Sam coming after me, begging me to wait and let him finish, or explain, or apologize, I slammed Kat's front door, then collapsed on the floor against it.

My heart was beating so hard in my chest it was deafening. I was too angry, too hurt, to even cry.

Outside I heard Sam sit down on the front step and slump against the other side of the door. I put my hand up, touching the wood, knowing that Sam was there, only three inches away. So close, I could almost touch him. And at the same time, a million miles away. I could almost hear him breathing.

"I need you, Jo," I heard Sam say finally. "I need you . . . I need you like I need a hole in my head." And for a long time after I could still hear him sitting there. And I didn't know why he didn't just get up and leave. But I didn't move either. And I didn't open the door.

CHAPTER NINE

IT WASN'T until the next morning that it suddenly hit me that I hadn't heard from Kevin. And what's worse, I hadn't called him. Never even thought to call him. Was I the world's worst girlfriend or what? So I called Kevin. And he didn't answer. So I texted him. And he didn't answer. Not a problem, I thought; he was probably at church or something. But when I called him after lunch there was still no answer, and that was when I began to get a little crazy.

I mean, normally—normally—I wasn't the type of girl to go nuts if her boyfriend didn't call her. Or didn't call her *back* to be more precise. But this was different. Because first of all something pretty major had happened the day before. And the broken windshield had only been part of it.

And the longer Kevin went without calling me back, the more upset, and paranoid, and worried, and freaked out I became. I oscillated between worrying something bad had happened to him, to freaking out that maybe he was avoiding me for some reason.

I'm sure on one level I knew it wasn't logical to get as panicked as I was getting. To be totally honest, I was so worked up that the whole "logical and rational" part of my brain had practically given up on me and gone on holiday. Then again, someone *had* smashed the windshield of my boyfriend's truck. Not to mention the two creepy guys threatening to run me over.

By the time seven-thirty at night rolled around, and Kevin hadn't even come to pick me up for the Gathering, I was nearing a panic attack. I thought of calling Sam, but realized that even on the remote off-chance that he was still speaking to me, Sam was probably at the Gathering already. So I walked there, and arrived really late.

I slipped into a seat in the back of the hall and started scanning the crowd for Kevin. I didn't see him and Simon was running the mixing board. I didn't see Sam either. I sat low in my seat, nervous energy bouncing through my knees, wishing Patrick would hurry up and finish.

And then Patrick started going on and on about the absolute worst thing I'd ever heard him talk about: crucifixion.

Of course, no one gets crucified anymore. There were pictures of crosses on churches sometimes, but crucifixion always looked kind of peaceful, and very unreal. But Patrick made it sound real. Too real. Painful and gross and mean and horrible and so unbelievably bad that I ended up slipping my hands underneath my hair and pushing my fingers in my ears. I thought I was going to be sick.

I didn't want to think about it. I didn't want to listen.

But Patrick kept going. Thorns. Nails. The hot, hot sun. Pulling up on the nails through your flesh just to be able to breathe . . .

I pushed my fingers in tighter, trying to block Patrick out. Then somehow all I could think about was the look on Nate's face as that evil maniac tried to kill him, of the look on Motor-Oil-Guy's face when he threatened to kill me, of Kevin's face when he saw what someone had done to the truck.

"When things stay hidden they can't be fixed," Patrick was saying, "and Jesus knows every single thing you are hiding. He knows all your secrets. He knows what you are ashamed of. He knows what you're scared of. And that's why he chose to go through all that and be crucified. It happened because of you. He did it for you."

No! He didn't, I argued back internally.

"Jesus did it for you," Patrick repeated.

No!

"He did it for you. He did it for you."

"But I didn't ask him to!" I shouted. And suddenly I realized I had said it out loud. And that I was standing up. The room froze. My words bounced off the walls and echoed through the crowded pub. Patrick put the microphone down by his side, and looked straight at me. Everyone turned and looked at me.

I had finally managed to find a way to top the whole tumble-off-the-pier disaster.

The whole roomful of people was staring at me. Watching me. Waiting.

The sick feeling in my stomach grew stronger. I wanted to turn and run but my legs seemed to have melted into the floor. Oh God. If ever there was a perfect moment for the ceiling to open up and some heavenly body to smite me.

"Yeah! I didn't ask him to either!" another voice yelled. People's faces swiveled forward and my heart started beating again. It was Sam.

From a few rows ahead of me, Sam had leapt to his feet and shouted: "You're talking like we should feel guilty Patrick. But I didn't kill Jesus! I never said: 'Hey Jesus, die a horrible death for me.'"

What in the name of everything imaginable was Sam doing?

I knew he'd mostly done it for me—that the whole reason Sam was dragging the spotlight onto himself and was willing to look like a total idiot was to save me the embarrassment of standing alone; but somehow I also knew Sam was deadly sincere about what he was saying.

"Sounds so ungrateful," Nate muttered under his breath, then winced as Patrick's microphone picked up his words and broadcast them around the room. I could tell Nate didn't intend anyone to hear him, but he was sitting on a speaker at the side of the stage, and so everyone could tell that he'd said it.

And it gave Sam the fuel to keep going.

"Yup, Nate, that's me! The ungrateful wretch!" Sam yelled back, calling him out. "Just because I refuse to feel guilty because someone decided to do me a favor I never said I wanted!"

Nate jumped to his feet. The audience unfroze. A low babble of voices spread over the room.

"You grateful to veterans, Sam?" Nate called back, in a kind of friendly but challenging way. "People who fought and died for the freedom you—"

"Bad analogy," Sam shouted. "Of course I'm thankful! But that's thousands of people dying for thousands of personal and patriotic reasons. Not some super-veteran with a bullet in his chest, going, 'Hey Lois! This one's for you!'"

The noise on the floor was growing. I was waiting for someone to start taking bets.

"Your mother," Nate began, "she went through labor to give you life—"

"Yeah! And do you let your mother run your life?"

Low blow. The murmuring grew to a small roar. Sam's comment seemed to have hit a mark. I was surprised Sam was getting so much ground support. But maybe he was just saying what a lot of us wished we had the courage to say.

Nate was still kind of smiling, but Sam wasn't. Sam's face was deadly, deadly serious. "Let's be honest," Sam continued, before Nate came back with anything. "You're not asking us to buy some pretty flowers on 'Jesus Day.' You're saying we should be so flippin' grateful we give Jesus our entire lives!"

"It's worth it," Nate argued.

"Says you," Sam shot back, "but maybe I don't believe it's worth everything I've got. Maybe I don't want to lose control of my life like that."

People were moving their chairs to get a better view of the action.

Sam turned and looked back, like he was looking for my face in the crowd. Then he turned back to Nate.

"Because that's what you're saying, Nate," Sam said. "You're saying it's personal!" His voice was beginning to break. "You're saying that when Jesus was dying he said 'Hey Jo Mackenzie! Hey Sam Underwood! Hey Nate whatever-your-name-is! I'm doing this for you!'"

"Yes," Nate yelled, "that's exactly what he did! And maybe you didn't ask him to do it. But he did it hoping that you would love him—"

"But how on earth can I love him—or even believe he exists, Nate? Stop being a drone and just think about it a minute," Sam said earnestly. "Haven't you seen what the world is like outside your pretty little doors? In the real world people get hurt—badly. They get their freaking hearts broken, Nate. And where is your God then?"

Sam looked so fierce—like he was really, really angry, though

I could tell that it wasn't with Nate. And I didn't know where all of this was coming from.

Patrick was still up at the microphone, but he wasn't moving. If anything, Patrick had gone so still, so dead calm, it was almost like he was daydreaming, or he'd fallen asleep on his feet with his eyes open.

"I mean, have you ever asked yourself why your God doesn't stop his own people from getting really badly hurt?" Sam shouted.

Nate wasn't smiling anymore. Not in the slightest. In fact, Nate looked about ready to punch someone, and I don't even know if that person was Sam, or God, or who. But I didn't think they made a knife strong enough to cut that kind of tension. And all of a sudden I really got what it meant to see someone's eyes "flashing like fire," because I could feel Nate's eyes burning through me, and all I was doing was just standing there. Sure, I had yelled out during Patrick's talk, but I don't think anyone was thinking about that right then.

If I could have had one of those freeze-the-world-moments, I'd like to think I would have reminded Sam that if Nate was hiding some huge, horrible secret about how someone tried to kill him, that maybe provoking him wasn't the smartest of ideas.

"Look, I admire the fact you want to defend your faith, Nate," Sam said. "I really do. But your God is undefendable. Did you know that my sister came back from her honeymoon on Friday and told me the hospital she helped set up three years ago now has even more dying children in it than it did when it was first built? More children hurt and dying just because this world is full of hideous, cruel, evil, self-centered people.

"And where was your God during slavery? Where was he during the Holocaust? Why does he let innocent people suffer? Why don't you ask your Jesus that?"

"I have," Nate said, through gritted teeth.

"I have, Sam," Nate said again, "I've asked God about racism and violence and pain. I have yelled at God, Sam. I have sworn at God. I have demanded that he answer me. Gotten down on my knees and cried out in anger. But I have also known when to shut up and listen for an answer."

The tension crackled like kindling. Sam met Nate's gaze full force. Nate didn't look away.

"Jesus can handle anything you want to throw at him, Sam," Nate added, "believe me—*anything*. So, if you aren't just blowing hot air around because you like the sound of your own voice, then I suggest you close your mouth for a minute, and listen. Because you might just find that Jesus wants to answer you."

"Then why don't you tell your Jesus that if he wants me to believe in him, then to come down and be man enough to talk to me one-on-one," Sam said, "because I need something more than some guy who died two thousand years ago. That won't cut it for me. I need more than that!"

"So do I," Patrick said. And there was something in his voice, this calm kind of authority, that signaled to Sam and Nate that their conversation was over, for now.

Lisa, looking kind of shaken, started in on a new song. Sam ran for the door. I didn't know whether to follow him or to stay and look for Kevin. For a long, agonizing moment I sat on the edge of my seat, torn between whether to leave or to stay. But then I found myself on my feet, running up the stairs, throwing open the door, and looking for Sam. But there was no one in the parking lot. So I rushed back inside to find Kevin.

The music had finished by then and people were standing, making it even harder to spot Kevin in the crowd. I went over to Simon who said he had seen Kevin earlier, taking care of some equipment. So I made a beeline for that space behind the stage where all the equipment was stored.

Instead of having a proper storage cupboard, the Gathering had a whole maze of stuff stacked in the back, behind the stage. Chairs, and crates, and books, and cables. It was kind of an off-limits area unless you were running something. I must have seen Kevin pop in and out of there a dozen times in the past. Heck, I'd practically run into him back there on the night I'd first been to the Pug—which now seemed like such a long, long time ago. If Kevin was stacking equipment, I knew that was where he'd be. And if he was avoiding me, well, it wasn't a half-bad place to hide.

I started to pick my way through the jungle of stacking crates and electrical wires. My jeans snagged on a speaker and I practically pulled a whole pile of something which looked like broken music stands down on my head. It wasn't until I was practically buried in the back of the deep, dark equipment jungle that I began to reevaluate my plan. OK, well, I began to realize it was pretty stupid actually. There I was clambering over boxes and battling cables when chances were that Kevin's phone battery had just died and he was standing over by the snack table looking out for me right now. Besides, I was now so deep in the thick of it all, I probably wouldn't have been able to see him if he was standing in the middle of the Pug holding a big sign that read, "Hey Jo, I'm over here!"

I turned to head back, accidentally missed my step, and smashed my shin against the corner of an equipment case. I pitched forward, landing hard on my hands and knees. *Ow ow ow ow ow* . . . I pulled myself into a sitting position. My palms stung. I had torn my jeans.

What was wrong with me? Why had I let myself get so worked up over this guy? Why hadn't I just casually shrugged Kevin off? When did a few simple dates turn into an excuse for all-out panicked lunacy?

It was all just becoming too difficult and Kevin wasn't worth it. OK, so Kevin was probably—no, definitely—more than worth it; but not to me, not in that way at least.

I was about to get up, dust myself off, and try to salvage the night the best I could, when I heard Lisa's voice saying my name. Suddenly all the random background babble of a restaurant full of people seemed to crystallize in one conversation happening just on the other side of the electrical heap.

Simon was telling Lisa that I was looking for Kevin. *Nice guy, I* thought.

And Lisa said, "He's just gone out with Nate to load some stuff into his truck . . ."

Great!

". . . but just between you and me, if you see Jo don't tell her where Kevin is . . ."

Excuse me?

I heard Lisa sigh. "Look Si, I don't want to be a gossip or anything. But you know how she and Kevin used to date?"

Used to?

"He kind of broke up with her yesterday, and she's not taking it very well . . ."

Hang on!

"Nate, Kevin, and I went out to the beach this afternoon, and Jo just kept calling him, and calling him, and calling him. And he got afraid she was going to do something crazy like just show up and start yelling at him on the beach. I think Jo is kind of . . . well . . . stalking Kevin."

Now, there are times when it's good to be rational. There are times when someone gets something so spectacularly wrong that all you can do is laugh it off. And there are times when you just need to take a deep breath, and think before you speak. But there is probably never a good time to leap out from behind a pile of storage crates with disheveled hair and wild eyes, screaming "He really likes me!" Especially if you want to persuade the person you're shouting at that you are not terrorizing the sweetest guy in church. But I was going on instinct here.

Lisa jumped so high that colliding with a passing jet plane wouldn't have been out of the question. But I could have cared less what she thought of me that very second. That would hit home later. Right then I just rushed past her and headed toward the door.

Lisa hurried after me, "Jo, wait! . . . Look, I'm sorry! We've all been there . . ."

Ha! I very much doubted that.

"Look Jo, nobody likes to be dumped. Heck, I don't—"

I spun on my heels. "I wasn't dumped!" I shouted.

Lisa was still dithering on about trusting God, and some people not being meant to be together, and how taking space can give you perspective. But thankfully my legs were twice as long as hers, and possibly her incessant prattle was slowing her down some too, because I'd almost lost her by the time I shoved out the back door and into the parking lot.

Kevin and Nate were leaning up against Kevin's truck, talking. They didn't see me at first. Just two best friends talking, hanging out. And for a moment it made me even angrier. Like they were just happy, going on with their lives and not giving a care about the stress and pain I might be going through.

"So, I see you got the windshield fixed."

Nate looked up first and his eyes met mine. It was a look of sympathy. My stomach lurched. Kevin leapt off the truck, and ran toward me.

"Jo, we need to talk."

Kevin tried to grab my arm. I pushed him off.

"You bet we need to talk! First you ignore me, and then I find out you've been telling people we've broken up!"

Kevin met my eyes briefly and I felt my heart twang like a broken guitar string. Then he looked away. "Look, I know I needed to call you," Kevin said, miserably. "And I didn't say we'd broken up, only that I was needing some space—"

"Space!" I said sarcastically. "Since when? Since you kissed me yesterday and told me you loved me? Sometime between then and now you suddenly realized you needed space from me and decided not to tell me?"

"I was going to—"

"When?"

This was good. I was angry—and as long as I was angry I was focused and I wasn't about to fall apart. But then Lisa came up behind me, still talking like she thought I'd been listening, and blurted out, "Look, Jo, maybe it would just be easier for every-body if you and Sam just stopped coming to the Gathering!"

Everyone froze. Nate looked absolutely sickened. Kevin looked like he was about to be sick. Lisa didn't seem to realize what she'd said at first, but thankfully she didn't open her mouth again right away.

And as for me, I was so stunned, so hurt, I felt like someone had just come over and whacked me on the head with a baseball bat.

So that was that. I was rejected. They didn't like me. They didn't want me. I didn't belong. Not there. Not anywhere. And somehow it hurt far more than just getting dumped by Kevin. I was being dumped by all of them.

Then I felt an arm around my shoulder. It was Sam. This

unbelievable wave of relief swept over me, and I virtually collapsed into his side. But he held me, firm.

"Are you OK, Jo?" Sam said, very, very calmly.

I shook my head. "No. Take me home, please."

Then everyone started talking at once—Lisa passionately trying to explain she didn't mean to say what she said, Nate trying to convince us that we were very welcome to stay and a valued part of the Gathering, and Kevin trying to convince me that we needed to go somewhere, just the two of us, and talk—their voices all blending together into one big buzz of white noise.

Without saying a word, Sam turned, taking me with him, and started to lead me toward his car.

"Jo! Wait! Please!" Kevin reached out and grabbed my arm again, but Sam spun me around defensively, so that he was standing between us.

"I think Jo needs some 'space' now, Kevin," Sam said.

We started to walk again, but then Sam stopped, and turned back.

"You know what, Nate? I actually wanted to believe in your God before this," Sam said. "Honestly I did. I was kind of hoping that if I just kept hammering at his door long enough he'd come out and talk to me. But you know what I can't get my head around? If you really believed in what you say you believe in, you'd act differently from the rest of us. You'd treat people better. Because your God isn't this nice little Sunday school story addition to normal life. It's more like a mind-blowing nuclear explosion that blows your entire heart and mind and life inside out. Or at least, it should be."

I think Lisa wanted to jump in and say something then, but Nate practically put his hand over her mouth and told her to let us go. Sam and I walked back to the car together.

"Thank you, Sam," I said.

"No problem," he said, his face set like stone, "that's what friends are for."

Sam had seen my run-in with Lisa and had followed me out. Then he'd stayed back, letting me have my space, while I argued with Kevin. Then he had stepped in when I needed him. In other words, he'd been nothing but a perfect friend. Even after everything.

I don't think I said much of anything on the way back to Kat's place. I was just too numb.

Sam pulled the car to a stop. Then he turned and looked at me.

"Look, don't let them get to you, OK?" He paused and looked down at the steering wheel.

Then he said, "You know all that stuff they talk about? Well, it can get to you after a while. Get under your skin, you know? And after a while, well, you can find yourself starting to believe it. But it doesn't work, OK?" He turned and looked at me fiercely. "It's not real. When it all comes down to it—it doesn't actually mean anything. It's . . . it's . . . ." Sam looked down again. "It's just words, Jo. Nothing but meaningless words."

Sam didn't suggest he come in, and I didn't ask him to either. Climbing up the stairs to the second floor of Kat's apartment I suddenly felt very, very tired, like someone had sucked all the air out of me and then squashed me flat.

More than feeling angry, or hurt, or deflated, or offended, there was this little sneering voice in the back of my mind telling me this was what I got for listening to anyone at the Gathering in the first place. After all, with a mother who was a champion liar and a first class promise-breaker, how could I expect some strangers in a church to be any different?

I found Kat upstairs in her bedroom, curled up in a chair. I slumped down onto a pillow near her feet and told her that I thought I was breaking up with Kevin. Kat gently tousled my hair, and told me she was sorry, and not to worry because I was going to be just fine and find somebody better. But her words just drifted past my ears like my head was wrapped in bubble-wrap.

Kat went to bed early. I brushed my teeth slowly. Then I changed into an oversized T-shirt and an old pair of faded shorts—normally my most comfortable pajamas. But I couldn't sleep. I tossed and turned in my bed for what felt like an hour and then gave up, grabbed a blanket, and headed down to the living room. Buddy came pattering down from his usual post at the end of Kat's bed, but after watching me pace up and down the living room for a bit, he gave up and went back upstairs. I wished I could explain how I felt. Put a name to all the emotions coursing through me, to somehow help it all make sense. But instead I felt both jittery and numb at the same time. And I couldn't sit still.

I heard a noise outside. With my fleecy blanket wrapped around me like a cloak, I walked over to the window, sat down on the ledge, and looked out.

It was Kevin. He was looking down, away from me, his face hidden in the shadows. I watched as he slipped a cigarette into his mouth and cupped his hand around it as he brushed the end with the flame from his lighter. He took a breath, tilted his head back, and exhaled with a sigh, the smoke curling up around his face. He looked tired, worn. Dark shadows outlined the hollows of his eyes. Dark stubble traced down the sides of his jaw. Had he looked this tired when I had seen him earlier? And if he had, would I have noticed?

I slid the window open. He looked up. "Jo?"

"Hi Kevin," I said. "I didn't know you smoked."

Kevin glanced at the cigarette in his hand, and then back up at me. "Yeah," he said ruefully, "I kind of didn't want you to know." He paused a moment, then put the cigarette back up to his lips again.

"How long have you been smoking?" I asked.

"Since I was twelve," Kevin said, shrugging.

"So, all those times you had to pop out to check your messages, or get a breath of fresh air . . ."

"I was really just grabbing a smoke and didn't want you to know."

"Ah."

In a way, I guess I should have felt glad to find out that all those times he disappeared he was actually just trying to hide a nicotine addiction from me. But instead I felt almost guilty for not noticing. After all, my mom had dated plenty of smokers—had I just not been paying close enough attention?

And it made me wonder what else I had missed about him.

"I know I really shouldn't smoke," Kevin said, shrugging again. "I pray about it sometimes, but Nate says that sometimes it takes time to change things about your life. I really am trying to quit though. And I'm down to only two or three a day."

"Good luck with that."

"Thanks."

I rested my head against the window for a while and watched him breathe in and out, in and out, until, finally, he dropped the butt on the pavement and ground it under his boot. Then he looked back up at me. And the silence between us stretched, and grew, until it was so deafening it nearly smothered me.

"Kevin?"

"Yeah."

"If you're going to break up with me, please just go ahead and do it. It's OK, really. I'd just rather know."

Kevin looked down at his feet again. "I don't know how to tell you this," he said. "I should have said something a long, long time ago, but I was just kind of hoping we could just keep going on as we were and somehow it would all work itself out." He kicked at the remains of his cigarette butt.

"I really do like you, Jo," he said so quietly I almost didn't hear him. "I . . . I . . . I've fallen in love with you. But it's not about what I want," he looked back up at me, "it's about who I want to be and what I want to do."

He groaned in frustration and shoved his hand hard over his head. "I don't know how to explain this to you. I'm not good at words and saying stuff. But, you know how I want to be a Christian? You know I want to be like Nate and have God be the biggest part of everything in my life? Well, somehow being with you has started taking me away from all that. And that's not your fault. It's mine.

"I've started screwing up things at work. I've started smoking more. I've been praying less. I've broken plans to be with Nate. And I've started . . . well . . . I've started having my head in a head space where I know it's not supposed to be.

"Please, please don't feel bad Jo," he quickly added, plaintively, "please believe me when I say that it's not you. You haven't done anything wrong. You've been nothing but amazing and I really, really wish I could just forget about everything else in my entire life and just be with you."

He sighed again, and rubbed the corner of his eye with his hand. "God knows I'm crazy about you. I really am. But I don't want to be this person again," he said, his voice cracking with emotion.

"It's OK, Kevin," I called down. "I know. I know. It's OK."

Kevin looked up at me. His lower lip was quivering. He looked so sad, so stressed, so utterly, incredibly miserable. And in the weirdest way, I realized he had never looked more handsome, more gorgeous. And for a second everything inside me was just crying out to dash down those stairs, throw my arms around him, and promise I would do anything it took to be with him again.

But instead, I forced myself to say "Good night, Kevin" and closed the curtain. I walked over to the sofa, curled up into a ball, and cried.

§ § §

I was standing at the back of Cornerstone Church. It was crowded. I could barely see the front. Pastor Wallace was talking about how real, permanent love is rooted in God. And I heard my own voice asking, "But how can you be sure?"

Then I heard yelling behind me. Shouting. Swearing. I ran outside. It was Kevin. He had Nate pinned down on the ground and he was hitting him, over and over and over again. I screamed at him to stop. I tried to grab his hand, but found I couldn't move. "You're killing him! You're killing him!" I screamed. Then Nate said, "It's OK, Jo. I know what I'm doing."

And I heard Buddy barking. And I woke up.

Oh great. It was almost three in the morning and there I was, wide awake. Buddy was still barking, doing this crazy circular chase thing of practically jumping on the couch on top of me, then dashing down toward the front door, then charging back over to me again. Psychotic mutt.

I stood up slowly, yawning. "Shhhhhh, Buddy, shhhhh! It's not time to play." But he wouldn't listen to me. So I followed him over to the stairs, and was about to head up to the bathroom, when I heard voices—male voices—talking outside, wafting up through the window I had stupidly forgotten to close.

I paused, hand on the banister.

Then there was a crash . . .

A bang . . .

A shout . . .

The smell of something burning . . .

The store was on fire.

Chapter Ten

I USED to wonder what I'd do in the face of a real, actual crisis. I used to lie awake and worry that I'd just stand there helpless like a deer caught in the headlights. But as soon as I smelled the smoke, something inside kicked me into slightly out-of-body overdrive.

I ran upstairs, screaming and yelling at Kat to get up. I barged into her room, jolting her awake and practically hitting her on the shoulder until she woke up enough to hear me. Grabbing her phone off the bedside table she scrambled after me, nearly tripping over Buddy on the landing.

Then we stumbled back downstairs, Buddy yelping at our heels. Thick, black smoke rose up the stairs to greet us from underneath the inside door to the shop. Eyes stinging, lungs on fire, we ran through the kitchen and out into the back yard. With shaking fingers, Kat dialed 911 and almost fainted with relief when she got through to someone almost instantly. Speaking with a voice so eerily calm it was almost frightening, Kat started walking away from me, her full attention locked on the 911 operator and a finger in her ear to block out the noise.

Instinctually I reached for my phone to call Sam, but as my fingers fumbled unsuccessfully in the pocket of my pajamas I realized I hadn't grabbed it. I was so used to it now that I felt naked without it. But I also hadn't thought to grab my wallet, or a blanket. For a second the need to talk to someone—anyone—was so strong I had to lock my knees to keep from running back in for my phone.

That was when panic hit. Without even thinking I fell down onto the grass and pushed my hands up against my eyes. "God, if you're there, help us, help us please . . ." I started babbling out a prayer. My shoulders were shaking. The words were pouring out over my lips as fast as I could form them, even as I was choking on tears and fear and the unrelenting smell of smoke.

Then I felt the comforting warmth of a leather jacket draping around my shoulders and the soothing brush of a breath on my cheek as a voice whispered, "It's OK babe, you're OK."

"Sam!"

Almost sobbing with relief I relaxed into the strong arms that held me, but the arms abruptly pulled away, even as I heard the reassuring wail of fire truck sirens. Jumping to my feet, I turned, and suddenly the yard seemed full of people. There were two fire trucks parked in front of the store and another one pulled up in the alley behind our back garden. There were police too, and all sorts of other random people who I guess couldn't sleep with all the noise or had just come out for the show. Firefighters were running around the side of the house and a couple were lugging a long hose through our garden and in the store's back door. To my surprise I saw Nate and his friend Simon by the back fence with a couple of other people I vaguely recognized from the Gathering. But I couldn't see Sam anywhere. A paramedic rushed up to me and tried handing me a warm, gray blanket, but I shrugged her off and instead slid my arms inside the leather jacket around my shoulders. That's when it hit me—it wasn't Sam's jacket. It was Kevin's.

Kat was walking back toward me now with a tall black man in a long, dark coat. He had such an air of authority about him that I just presumed he was with the firefighters or police. But then Kat said, "I've just been told we won't be able to get back into the apartment for a few days. But your friend's father has said we can stay with them," and that's when I saw it was Pastor Wallace.

"We have a guest room in our home where your cousin is more than welcome to stay," Lisa's father said kindly, looking me full in the eyes, "and Lisa has a futon in her apartment you could use."

It was only then I realized that Lisa was standing behind him. When I looked her way, she looked down at the ground.

In any other place and any other time in my life up to then I would have told them to forget it. I would have sworn at Lisa and called her a miserable, hateful witch—or worse—and that I'd rather spend the night in Kat's Jeep than ever go anywhere near her place.

But then one of the firefighters came over and told Kat that the fire was out, and after someone had gone through the place in the morning to make sure it was safe, they'd escort us in so that we could get a few of our things. And I saw the way Kat's shoulders sagged and her head dropped as she thanked him. And I hated myself for being the kind of person who was even thinking of telling someone I loved so much, and someone who had done so much for me, that I'd rather make her drive around looking for hotels just to make my life go a little easier.

"Her apartment is just over our garage, so you will be close by," Pastor Wallace explained, "and you are welcome to come to the main house for breakfast . . ."

So I nodded, even managed to look Pastor Wallace in the eyes and say thank you. But as we followed him to his car I refused to even look Lisa's direction, and kept my eyes firmly focused out the window as Pastor Wallace drove us there.

I didn't know what she was playing at. I didn't even know how she'd found out my place was on fire. But I wasn't about to thank her for coming, or even speak to her any more than I needed to.

With an unsteady hand, Lisa unlocked the door to her apartment and mumbled something quietly about the futon being in her study room beside the bathroom. I strode in past her, slamming the door of the room hard behind me and pushing the lock in place before she could try to follow me. Then I laid down on the futon and stared at the ceiling until eventually, around sunrise, I fell asleep.

§ § §

It was the sound of music that woke me. Something happy and uplifting was floating in through the crack under the door. And it took me a moment to remember where I was.

I was in the home of a girl who hated me, and who was probably that very minute waiting on the other side of the door to lecture me about what a bad and sinful person I was and how I should never have been dating her friend Kevin in the first place.

But what choice did I have? I slowly slid the lock back and opened the door.

Lisa was sitting at a table by the window in a little L-shaped living room putting on makeup. The window was open beside her and a gentle breeze was ruffling the frills on a funky pink and turquoise sundress she was wearing. And standing there in my old, faded pajamas, streaked with smoke and dirt and grass stains, I knew deep in my heart that this tiny little part of me hadn't wanted to like her ever since I'd first seen her bouncing and singing up on the pier in July. That even while we were being friendly at Sam's sister's wedding, there was still this little jealous voice in me that said that Lisa thought she was better than me. That a tiny part of me had even wanted to take her down a notch or two.

Lisa jumped up when she saw me. "There's . . . there're fresh towels in the bathroom," she said, "and I laid out some shampoo and soapy stuff, and there are some clothes on the hamper that I think should fit you. They . . . they belong to my sis . . ."

Her voice trailed off as she saw the look on my face. And then to my shock Lisa flew across the room and flung her arms around me.

"Oh Jo," she sobbed. "I'm so, so sorry about what I said last night."

Tears started welling up in Lisa's eyes and she didn't even try to wipe them away. "I didn't mean it. I really, really didn't mean it. I like you, Jo. I don't want you to leave the Gathering. I really don't. And I really am so, so, so sorry."

And I just stood there, too stunned to move. All I wanted was to yell at her. To hurt her. Better yet, to turn around and walk away without ever speaking to her again. To go on hating her forever.

Then I heard this little voice inside me say, "Do you think she doesn't know all that? Do you think that never crossed her mind that you'd laugh in her face when she invited you to stay? You think she didn't expect to get slapped when she tried to hug you?" And I was surprised to find tears pushing their way through the corners of my eyes.

Then Lisa let go and dropped down into a chair. She was full out crying now. Tears were pouring down her face, sending dark black mascara and bright blue eye shadow coursing down her cheeks in swirls and smudges, and landing in big splotches all over the front of her dress.

"I knew last night that I needed to say sorry," she went on in this little squeaky, teary voice, like she was trying to stop herself from crying but not succeeding very well. "And I told myself it would just have to wait. But then when I heard about the fire, I was so afraid that you were going to die before I had a chance to tell you I was wrong and that you were going to die thinking I hated you. And I'd never get another chance."

Despite myself I almost smiled. "Don't worry, it was just a little fire," I muttered, "and . . . and . . ." I took a deep breath. "And I know what it's like to say something, or do something, then just wish you could go back in time and take back everything you said . . . or did . . . or was," I said softly, adding to myself, *And the difference between you and me is that you think someone might actually give you that second chance. I don't think I've ever been gutsy enough to even ask.*

Lisa nodded. "I'm so bad at this," she said. She wiped her hand across her eyes and streaked her makeup even further across her face. I sat down on the couch and stared at her.

"I . . . I used to have this real problem with gossip and sniping at people," Lisa said. "I remember this one time another girl dismissed this idea I had about a Gathering thing, and everyone got all excited about her idea instead. And I said the nastiest, cruelest things to her and about her behind her back. And I froze her out, until she gave up and left altogether.

"Basically I almost never felt good about myself, and I found it so easy to be jealous of other girls who've got it more together than me. And I know the reason I was such a total witch to you is because basically I'm jealous of you."

See, now there was absolutely no way I saw that one coming. I swear, you could have knocked me over with a feather.

"You . . . are jealous of me?" I gasped.

Lisa nodded miserably.

"You've got to be kidding!" I exclaimed. "You have it all! You're petite, and cute, and have amazing clothes, and fantastic hair, and an incredible voice, and a great family, and Nate and everyone else at the Gathering would basically jump through any hoop you asked them to. Everyone loves you there. And your whole life is like filled up with God, and how much God loves you, and is there for you. Do you have any idea how much I would love to have even one ounce of all that?"

Lisa gave a funny little half-laugh. "Yeah, I have it all," she said ruefully. "I'm the 'perfect little pastor's daughter.' That's me. All my life people have been saying, 'Boy, did Pastor Wallace pick a good one when he adopted her!' Like if I was any less wonderful he'd send me back or something."

She stood up and grabbed for a Kleenex, but the box was empty. Not that it would have made much of a difference to Lisa's multicolored raccoon eyes at this point.

"You know, most of my life I have looked in the mirror and hated what I saw," Lisa said. "See, people expect you to have problems, Jo, because you didn't grow up in a church. People don't expect you to say and do the right thing all the time. But if I ever do something stupid, or let a swear word slip out, or get drunk, or find myself secretly hating someone—then I feel like I have let everybody down.

"That's not to say I don't believe in God and everything. I really, really do," she added passionately. "But I don't believe in God because 'that's what good Christian girls do.' I believe in God because I have to. I cling to God because I need him. Because I know what I'd be like without him. I'd be like . . . like the nasty little witch I was to you last night . . ."

Then Lisa sat down on the couch next to me.

"I used to wish my mother had just given me up for adoption," I said quietly. "I don't think she likes me very much . . ."

Lisa reached over and squeezed my hand. I squeezed it back.

"My mom was in Morocco when she found out she was pregnant with me. She'd been with this one guy for a while. Then had an affair with this other guy. But he only turned out to be a 'transitional' thing, and then she hooked up with some student who was traveling. She didn't know she was pregnant until it was too late for her to . . . you know . . . to do anything about it—especially not over there. So, she came home, moved in with my cousin Kat's family, and lived with them until I was like six weeks old. Then she took off without me and I stayed behind until I was almost two.

"Then Mom came back again, with her first husband Martin, and I moved in with them. Four years later he left her. Then there were a bunch of other men. Her life is so full of drama, you know, that there's no room for me."

Lisa didn't say anything, and for a minute I was afraid I had freaked her out with what I had said about my mom.

Then Lisa said quietly, "I know you probably won't believe me. Not after everything I said last night. But knowing God really does make all the difference in the world. Because no matter how stupid you are, or how messed up everything in your life is, you know that you're never really alone because he's there with you. And he doesn't give up on you, even when you've given up on yourself."

There was a knock behind me and Kat walked in.

I ran over and wrapped my arms around her. Lisa slipped back to the table and started cleaning the makeup off her face.

"The police want to talk to you now," Kat said, stroking my hair. "But I think it'll be OK if you want to go shower first."

I nodded.

"Did they say anything about your house?" I asked, pulling away.

"Oh, it's still there," Kat said, "but it sounds like the store's not in great shape."

"Have you called Sam?" I asked.

Kat shook her head. "I don't have his number."

Neither did I. It was programmed into the phone I'd managed to leave behind at the apartment.

Then Kat turned to Lisa, and to her credit didn't even blink at the multicolored makeup streaks running down her cheeks. "How on earth did you know that our place was on fire?" Kat asked.

Lisa shrugged, wiping a makeup pad over her eyes. "Would you believe anonymous phone call?" she said. "I was sleeping. And then the phone rang. And even before I was really awake to know what was going on this voice said, 'Jo's place is on fire. Pray for her.' Then hung up."

"What kind of voice was it?" I asked.

Lisa shrugged again. "I don't know. It was a guy I think. In fact," she added, "at first I wondered if I'd dreamed it. But you don't want to risk something like that, you know? So I ran and woke up my dad. Then I think I must have called half of the Gathering on our way there trying to get people to pray for you."

And what would I have done in her place? I wondered, as I dragged myself toward the shower.

§ § §

I met with the police in Lisa's parents' living room. There were two officers. One was a blonde woman not much older than Kat. The other was an older man with graying hair and the disconcerting habit of nodding impassively at everything I said. And I told them absolutely everything.

I told them about Motor-Oil-Guy and Red-Jacket, and Kevin's broken windshield, and Nate's accident, and the red sports car with the license plate JN832, and everything I remembered about the fire. I even arranged to send them all those pictures I'd taken when I got my phone back.

I wasn't sure how much sense I was making, or even if I was making any sense at all, but I made sure I didn't leave anything out. The police officers kept nodding and writing it all down. But they wouldn't tell me anything. Not even when I asked them if they knew who'd called Lisa.

The female officer was nice though and said reassuring things about how she appreciated my candidness and assured me that everything I told her would be kept in the strictest of confidence. The male one warned me that without a name it might take a while to find out who these guys were, but that they would trace the license plate, and there would be a cop car keeping an eye on my place until things were "settled," and that I should not go anywhere alone in the meantime, and that I should call 911 immediately if I saw anyone suspicious.

I had expected that getting all that off my chest to another human being would have made me feel better, but instead it just kind of made me feel uneasy and a little foolish for not going to the police sooner.

Then the gray-haired officer told me that we had been victims of an arson attack. No doubt about it. Someone had filled a bottle with gasoline, stuffed in some rags, lit it on fire, and thrown it straight through the store's front window. By the look of things, they had tossed a brick through first to make sure the window would break. He shook his head and said that any eight-year-old with Internet access could make a Molotov cocktail. The fire had burned a good patch of floor, gone up one wall, and turned half the ceiling black before the old sprinkler system finally kicked in and put out the fire.

However, if the store had still been filled with all those papers and garbage—especially the old paint—then the whole building could have gone up in flames. Maybe even the neighborhood.

When I was done talking to them, they escorted Kat and I back to the apartment to get out stuff, and I almost choked when I saw the ugly yellow and black police tape crisscrossed around the front.

Officer Gray-Hair held back the tape so that Kat and I could walk through the store.

"Be careful not to touch anything," he said, not unkindly.

Kat reached for my hand and squeezed it hard. The counter surface was charred and black. The floor tiles I'd worked so hard to scrub were peeled up harshly by the heat. The walls and ceiling were stained in black and gray. My washing bucket was twisted, my cleaning supplies melted freakishly into each other. There was broken glass everywhere. Dirty fire-extinguishing foam residue coated every surface. The stench of fire hung heavy in the air. I closed my eyes. Angry tears pushed their way from under my eyelids.

"Looks worse than it is," said Officer Gray-Hair. "Smoke damage is a pain. But don't worry, the building appears to still be structurally sound and I'm sure your insurance company can recommend some good people to clean it up."

Kat nodded. "Yeah, I've got to call them this afternoon."

"No Kat," I said, shaking my head to fight back a sob. "It's . . . it's my store. It's my work they destroyed. I . . . I want to help fix it."

Kat stopped and looked at me, in a way I've never seen her look at me before. Then she wiped her eyes and said, "OK, honey. Then you're in charge. I won't do anything without you."

Then we walked upstairs to pack some of our stuff.

§ § §

Kat wanted to pop into work, so I dropped her off, and then drove her Jeep back to Lisa's house. I hadn't called Sam yet. Kat was in a bit of a hurry, so I'd decided to wait until I got back to Lisa's.

It was the first time I had driven Kat's Jeep actually, and so while I was feeling more than a little pleased that she had offered to let me drive it, I was also concentrating hard on driving really, really carefully, which is why I didn't realize at first that I was being followed.

But when I started up the long, twisting road that led up to Cornerstone Church I was a little surprised to see that another car had pulled off behind me. After all, there wasn't much up that road beside the church, the hall, and a couple of houses. Even then I didn't think much of it, not until the car got a little bit closer and I could see that it was a red sports car. An old-in-a-good-way sports car. And then the panic hit.

I couldn't see the driver. The sun was glinting off the windshield and so all I could make out was a large, dark figure in sunglasses. But I could tell he was big. Scary big.

My first thought was of escape. Gripping the steering wheel so tightly my fingers ached, I mashed my foot down hard on the gas pedal. Kat's Jeep gave a lurch, then started to accelerate, leaving all previous concerns about road safety far behind in my wake. The red car did not match my speed increase, and with relief I watched as it became smaller and smaller in the rearview mirror until it disappeared from view.

My next thought was that I should probably call the police, but by this point I was going so fast that I was afraid to even take one hand off the steering wheel to dig my phone out of my bag.

Breaking hard I swerved into Pastor Wallace's driveway, hoping that the loud screeching noise wasn't a bad sign, then slammed myself to a stop just before running right up the tailpipe of Lisa's car. Only then did I remember to breathe.

Reaching down to the passenger side floor, I hauled up my knapsack and was just rooting through the bottom of the bag for my phone, when I heard the hard noise of a car door opening. I jerked up. The red car was parked right behind me. A hulking figure was stepping out. It was Nate.

And in that moment some of the confusing puzzle that had been swirling around my head suddenly clicked into focus. The red sports car was Nate's.

"That was some pretty wicked speed," Nate said casually, sauntering toward me, "though if you're going to challenge a guy to a drag race it's customary to pull up beside him and rev your engine a bit. Not that I've ever been challenged by anyone in a Jeep before."

I opened my mouth but no words came out.

"I hope you don't mind," Nate went on, "but I wanted to drop by to see how you were doing. I'm sorry to hear about your place getting torched. Did you just come back from seeing it?"

I nodded dumbly.

Nate nodded back, as if I'd just said something wise. "Well," he said, crossing his arms and leaning up against Kat's Jeep, "don't worry if you feel a bit numb for a while, or if you find you're having trouble sleeping or don't feel like yourself. Trauma affects people in different ways. It's normal and it'll pass."

I tried again, still no words.

"I hear Lisa spoke to you this morning," Nate went on, "and I just want to echo that I hope you're going to keep coming to the Gather—"

"Has anyone ever stolen your car and then run you over with it?" I blurted out, the ability to speak apparently returning before the ability to think through what I was saying.

It was crude, but effective, as Nate jumped up like he'd just been stung, turned to look at me face on, and demanded: "What on earth made you just say that?"

And you know what? I'm kind of ashamed to say that my first reaction was to try and bluff my way out of it. I guess it was a defense mechanism—or maybe I'd just gotten used to keeping secrets for too darn long—but I actually tried to pretend I was making some huge, funny joke and that Nate had just kind of misheard me.

But Nate just kept looking at me, with this we-both-know-you-meant-to-say-exactly-what-you-did stare. And he did have some pretty intense eyes when he wanted to use them. So eventually I told him—everything.

I told Nate about how I'd been praying on the balcony, and saw some kind of transaction going on, and then saw him rush out and get hit by his own car. I even told him about dropping Kat's binoculars over the balcony. I told him that I'd spent a year obsessing about what had happened to him and being convinced he was dead and then being totally confounded when it turned out he not only wasn't dead but that no one seemed to know about the accident. I told him about telling Sam everything, and wanting to do some secret sleuthing, but not really getting anywhere. I even told him about freaking out when I'd seen his car parked in front of the store a few days earlier.

And Nate just sat there, staring at me, and shaking his head in total disbelief, like I was sitting there trying to explain how I'd grown a second head or something.

Then finally he said, "Yes, I was parked outside your store last week. I was looking for Kevin, but just as I pulled up I got a text from him saying he'd meet me at the pub . . ."

"But, but what about the hit and run?" I burst in. "You do know what I'm talking about, right? I mean, you were in an accident, right? Please tell me you don't think I'm crazy!"

Nate raised a hand to silence me. Then, turning his back on me, he walked away a few paces and didn't say anything for a very, very long time.

But finally he turned around and said, "No Jo, it happened. Someone did steal my car last summer and run me over with it."

And in that second, something inside me exploded—this huge ball of tension that I was carrying around—and I thought I was going to start bawling again. But instead I held it in, and just stood there and listened as Nate filled in a few blanks. He and

Patrick had been in the church that night setting some stuff up. Patrick had been right behind him actually, and ran out a few minutes after the car had taken off, so no, he was never really alone for very long.

"The police and ambulance were pretty fast too. We'd known someone else had placed a call before Patrick got through, but we had no clue who. So, thanks for that."

Nate looked over at me and kind of smiled when he said that last bit, but then his face went really serious again, and he kind of rubbed his hand over his forehead and sighed. "I was in the hospital for like a week," he said. "I had three broken ribs and some internal bleeding. Wicked bruising too, of course. Some bad cuts and scrapes. Kind of black and blue for a while."

"Did they catch the guy?" I asked.

Nate nodded. "Yeah, absolutely they did."

"Did he go to jail?"

"Yup, he sure did," Nate told me. "But only for a few weeks. He pled guilty and got sixty days in jail—some of which were retroactive for the time he'd already served while he was waiting for his trial date. Then ten months probation." Nate rattled off the details in such a matter of fact way, that I found myself getting all emotional and indignant on his behalf.

"But that doesn't seem fair!"

"Nope, didn't seem fair to me either," Nate said slowly.

"But life's not fair," he added. "That's one thing Patrick likes to keep reminding me of—Jesus dying for my sins was hardly fair, so we should be the last ones to complain when people get more mercy than we think they deserve."

I wanted to know more. I wanted to know why they'd been gunning for him. I wanted to know how many people were involved. I wanted to know why Nate had kept it a secret. I wanted to know if he was afraid the guy would ever come after him again. I even wanted to know if this whole thing had affected his belief in a good God.

But Nate didn't seem to be in the mood to answer any more questions. Not that I didn't try asking them. But he had gone to staring straight in front of him like he was trying to figure out the answer to a really tricky dilemma, while all my rambling, and my neurotic need for answers just bounced off him like liquid against Teflon.

Finally, Nate unfroze.

"You told Sam everything," he said.

I nodded.

"Not anyone else?" he asked, looking at me kind of intently. "Not Kevin? Or anyone else?"

I shook my head. "My cousin Kat was there when I called the police, but she doesn't know it was about you."

Nate nodded, but it was like he wasn't really seeing me and was looking at something beyond me. He put the tips of his fingers together and kind of stared at them.

"I realize there's a lot of stuff you want to know," he said calmly, "and maybe in a way that you think you have the right to know . . ." He paused again.

"But there are reasons why I don't go around talking to people about that car accident. And I can't tell you everything you want to know . . ."

I must have looked like I was about to jump in because he kind of put his hand up like he was asking me to stop.

"Look Jo," he said. "Things are kind of complicated. And I can't explain to you why. But I promise you, I will talk to a couple of people, and make a pretty good case that, whether they like it or not, you are kind of involved and should have some answers . . ."

I really was about to jump in at that point, but Nate did his whole hand thing again.

"I've got to ask you to trust me here, Jo," he said. "I know you don't know me that well, but believe me, if there's some stuff I don't tell you it is genuinely because I think you are better off not knowing."

And with that he started to walk toward Pastor Wallace's house. Seriously, it was this whole I-have-spoken-and-let-that-be-enough moment.

But I wasn't going to let it go at that.

"But, who set my store on fire?" I blurted. "And who called Lisa to tell her? Why have people been following me?"

Nate stopped dead. He turned back.

"Who's been following you?" he demanded.

So I told him about seeing Motor-Oil-Guy and Red-Jacket outside the store, then in the parking lot, and Sam seeing them at the Gathering, and how they'd threatened me the day Kevin's truck got smashed. But I didn't tell him about trying to take their pictures—I didn't want him to think I was totally insane after all.

Whatever remained of Nate's smile was now completely and totally gone, and his face had gone deadly, deadly serious.

"What did they look like?" he asked. And as I did my best to describe them, he kept asking these little questions like, "Long nose?" "Thin cheeks?" which made me pretty darn sure he knew exactly who I was talking about. But when I asked him if he knew them he shook his head and said, "No, but I have an idea of who they could be. Have you ever seen them at the Gathering?"

I shook my head. "You thought you saw them there though, didn't you?" I asked.

Nate nodded. "Once," he said.

"Was that the Gathering open house night thing at the beginning of July?"

"Yeah," Nate said, looking kind of surprised. "How did you know that?"

I shrugged a little. "Oh, I just noticed you seemed phased at one point, like someone had walked in the room who you weren't sure belonged."

Nate gave me a little bit of a bigger smile then, and looked at me like he was even a little impressed.

"And you didn't tell anyone about seeing them hanging around the store, or the parking lot, or anywhere?" he said.

"Just the police officers. And Sam, of course."

Nate blew out a long breath again.

"OK," he said nodding, "OK."

This time I was smart enough to wait and see if he was going to start talking again.

"I honestly don't know why . . . or if . . . they had anything to do with your store being torched," Nate said, as we started walking to the house. "But I'm going to make a couple of calls when I get home. And I promise you, I'll tell you whatever I can."

And I believed him. But it's not like I expected to have Nate available to chat with me whenever I wanted, so as we were nearing the front porch I hit him with one more thing that had kind of been bugging me.

"You didn't like me dating Kevin, did you?"

Nate didn't stop walking this time, but he did give this big, exaggerated, guy-type sigh and mutter something about "women" under his breath.

"Look," he said, kind of firmly, slowing down enough for me to keep up with him. "It's nothing personal. Kevin is my brother. And . . . well . . . following Jesus is kind of hard sometimes. Life throws up all these distractions. And if you think your brother is slipping you give him a hand, or a swift kick, or whatever he needs, because he's family and that's what you do for your brother. But no, I never had any problem with you personally. You seemed nice."

He ran his hand over his jaw. "I'm not trying to stonewall you. We'll talk more later, I promise, I've just got to sort some things out first."

"Do you know who called Lisa to tell her the building was on fire?" I asked again.

He didn't answer me. But judging by the way his jaw tightened when I said it, I was almost positive that he did.

§ § §

I couldn't reach Sam. I tried at least six times and left as many messages, but he never called me back.

Nate wasn't the only person from the Gathering who dropped by to see how we were though. Over the course of the afternoon and evening there was this steady stream of people coming in and out to see if there was anything they could do to help. It was like constantly being at a house party. Several women from Cornerstone dropped by and brought with them enough frozen casseroles, chili, pies, and cakes to keep Kat and I well fed for months. Kat recognized a lot of them from animal rescue—or at least she'd met a lot of their pets before—but privately she told me she'd met more people in those four days than she had in three years living in Silverpoint.

Lisa buzzed around it all like a firefly. She knew everyone, hugged everyone, introduced me to everyone, and then told me six interesting things about them before they even managed to squeeze out a hello. She never brought up what we'd talked about that morning. But she smiled a lot. And hugged me, like she was convinced we were just going to be the best of friends from now on. And in a funny way, I kind of thought she was right.

I helped her make dinner for her folks and Kat, and then just as we were finishing dessert there was a firm knock on the door. A few moments later Pastor Wallace ushered Ken into the kitchen.

Turns out that when Kevin's dad had heard about the fire he'd taken it upon himself to source a new stronger front window for us and a full security system. He'd talked to suppliers. Gotten quotes. And was happy to get started as soon as the police gave the go ahead to get in. And when Kat tried to ask something about payment, Ken just shook his head and said people need to look out for each other, and he'd contact her insurance provider about covering the cost of the system, and that some people from the church had already donated some money to cover the deductible.

My cousin looked at me. "It's Jo's decision."

Ken looked at me seriously, like I was any other client. "And how do you feel about it?"

"It sounds amazing," I said honestly, "absolutely amazing."

Ken laughed. "I'm happy to help with what I can, and if you end up needing a quote for cleanup or decorating let me know and I can recommend some reliable suppliers," he said, eyes twinkling. "Now, before I go, Kevin's waiting outside at the truck, if you want to speak to him. But if you don't want to see him I can—"

"No, it's OK," I said quickly. "I'll go see him."

I slipped through the side door to the garage and up the stairs to Lisa's place, and grabbed Kevin's jacket. Then, slowly, I walked around to the front of the house. The sun was beginning to set and my heart leapt a little when I saw Kevin's lanky form leaning up against the truck.

"Hey Kev," I called.

"Hey."

I stopped a few feet away from the truck. Even after everything he still looked so good to me. Probably always would.

"Thanks for the jacket," I said, tossing it toward him. He caught it with one hand, and draped it over his shoulder.

"You OK?" he asked.

"Yeah, I'm fine."

"Are you coming to the Gathering this Sunday?"

I nodded. "Probably."

"Good." Kevin looked down at the ground and kicked at something with his foot. It was a cigarette butt. "I really am sorry for—"

"I know, Kevin," I said. Then I turned and walked back to the house.

I knew he was standing there, watching me go. But there was nothing left to say.

Chapter Eleven

WE MOVED back home on Thursday and on Friday morning I was just settling in to read a book Lisa lent me, when Ken appeared at the front door with two small curly-haired girls.

"These are my girls, Sherry and Terry," Ken said. "Your window has arrived and I've brought a few guys to help put it in. Would you mind watching the girls for a few minutes? Julia's visiting her mother, and Kevin's out on a job. I shouldn't be more than an hour."

OK, so I've never been the world's biggest fan of little kids. But Sherry and Terry were seriously cute, and seemed to have no compunction about making a new friend and giving that friend orders immediately.

They had brought a DVD—a cartoon movie about Jesus—and were insistent that we watch it. The girls had obviously seen the movie a dozen times before. They explained all the stories to me while they were happening, from the fact the loaves and fish really were going to be enough for everyone to eat, to how I shouldn't worry because the dead girl was going to come alive again. They hid their faces against my shoulders when the image of Jesus dying on the cross flickered across the screen. Then bounced and cheered when Jesus had risen from the dead.

I had always thought I knew the story of Jesus. I mean, everybody knows the basics about Jesus—don't they? But I'd never really seen it. Never really thought about it. Never really had a clue about how it all fit together. And as I sat there, the oddest thing happened; I started to feel a little, I don't know, emotional about it all. Especially the way Jesus treated people. He stopped a whole parade of people to talk to just one woman. He gently took the little girl's hand to help her up. He invited Mary to come and sit beside him. He asked John and his mother to take care of each other. He told Peter that he still loved him, even though he had completely messed up. Jesus loved people. And, as weird as it sounded, it kind of made me wish I could meet him.

The movie had just finished when Ken called upstairs to say that the window was in. I yelled back that if he and the guys wanted to head around back I'd make them some lemonade; then with the girls in tow, I went into the kitchen and got out some drinks while the girls helpfully tried to arrange some cakes on a plate. As the guys came round the corner, Terry and Sherry raced down toward them, squealing, and Ken scooped one up under each arm and carried them back upstairs. There were a couple of guys with him who I didn't really know. And for a few moments I was so busy making sure everyone had a glass, and that Sherry wasn't stealing all the cake, that I didn't realize Sam had shown up and was now just standing there in my yard, absentmindedly tossing a rag knot Buddy kept offering him.

"Where on earth have you been all week?" I said reproachfully, hurrying down the back steps. "Didn't you get my messages? I called you about a million times. Do you have any idea what I went through this week? Someone set my store on fire!"

Sam tugged the knot out of Buddy's mouth and hurled it down the side of the house.

"You think I don't know that?" Sam snapped defensively. "And you know how I found out about it? My sister! She calls me long distance from Bear Lake because apparently some person from her church who I've never met just called her to tell her about it. Because for some reason you didn't think it was as important to call me as it was to call the guy who just dumped you and all his friends—"

"I didn't call them, Sam! I wanted to call you but I didn't have my phone. Someone else called Lisa anonymously—"

But he wasn't listening.

"—so then I drive down here," he went on, "breaking every speed limit known to mankind, and what do I see? *Kevin* has got there ahead of me and you're practically melted into his arms! And then you choose to go stay with Lisa of all people and—"

Sam's phone started to ring, stopping him midsentence. He yanked it out of his pocket, scowled, then turned it off.

"That was Traci, wasn't it?" I said.

"So what if it was? Traci *needs* me."

He leveled the words like an accusation. And for a split second the words, "but I need you too, Sam," dashed to my lips.

But I bit them back at the last moment, leaving them hanging there unsaid as the space between us grew.

I couldn't tell Sam how much I needed him. I just couldn't. You just don't risk telling a guy something like that. Not when you don't know how he'll take it.

And all I could think of was how many times I'd heard my mother cry those very same words to man after man as he was kicking dust in her face and heading for the door. And how I'd promised myself that would never be me.

"Anyway," Sam said, looking down at his feet, "I just dropped by to tell you I am leaving."

"Leaving?" The words hit me in the gut like bricks.

"Yeah," Sam said, without really looking at me. "I've decided that commuting to college isn't really practical. So I'm going to move in with my sister and Brian, and start looking for a place to rent in Ashford. Maybe a dorm room will open up."

There was an edge to his voice as he said it, like he was reading off a script that he'd prepared.

"Anyway, I've got to be going," Sam said, "I . . . I'll see you around."

Then he started to walk away, and I was just standing there like an idiot not knowing what to say.

"Sam! Wait!" I yelled.

He turned back, this funny, anxious look flitting across his face.

My brain froze. I had no idea what to say next. And then an odd thought crossed my mind.

"On the day we met you told God that if you were ever tempted to go back to Traci that he should send someone to kick some sense into you," I said quickly. "Well, maybe . . . maybe that's what I'm here for. Maybe he wants me to remind you that if you give her another chance you'll be making a huge mistake."

But as the words came out of myself, they fell flat at my feet, and I realized what a stupid thing it was to say.

Sam snorted. "Believe me, Jo," he said, "if God is still up there listening to me, he stopped caring about what I want long ago."

He started to turn again, and again I got this weird feeling that there was something I ought to be saying. And even as I realized I was running the risk of sounding stupid, I found myself asking, "But did . . . did God ever answer your prayer?"

Sam frowned. "What prayer?"

"Remember a few weeks ago, Nate was challenging you about believing in God, and then you wrote one down on a piece of paper and told Nate you'd believe in God and follow him and everything if he gave you what you wanted."

Sam paused a moment, this little light going on in the back of his eyes.

"No," Sam said eventually with a hint of a sad, but real smile. "No, he didn't." He paused. "But you know what the funny thing is? I bet if God had given me what I asked for I wouldn't have listened to him anyway."

His mouth turned up at one end, and he gave a little laugh.

"I've realized something about myself since we started going to the Gathering," Sam said. "I didn't stop going to church because I stopped believing in God. I don't think I could have been so mad at someone I didn't believe in. I stopped because I didn't like God. He didn't play fair. He wasn't the kind of God I wanted him to be."

Sam started to walk away again, and I just stood there and watched him go. The pain in my chest was so overpowering that if I didn't know any better I would have thought my heart was breaking. Here all this time we'd been in this comfortable rut, and I'd never imagined one day he would just up and walk out of my life. And all of a sudden I wished I could go back in time and undo all those times I had the opportunity to hang out with him and instead chose to walk away and be with Kevin. Or when I had the chance to really talk with him about something that mattered and instead just prattled on about my own insecurities. Or undo all the time I wasted being annoyed with him for saying something I didn't like, or even hanging out with Traci.

I wished I had never taken for granted that this amazing friend was just going to be there in my life whenever, and however, I wanted him to be.

"Hey man, wait up!" this deep voice boomed out from behind me, and I turned to see Nate and Lisa appearing out my back door. Barely acknowledging me, Nate came bounding past me, catching up with Sam just as he was about to disappear out the gate. I stood there lost for a moment, and then I heard Lisa's voice calling me, so I headed back up and joined her on the porch.

"Hope you don't mind us popping in unannounced like this!" Lisa said cheerfully. She was clutching a bright pink glass of lemonade in one hand and nibbling up chocolate cake crumbs with the other. "Ken let us in. He told me to tell you that he's just taking the girls home and then he'll be back to do some sealing type of thing later tonight. Can I give you a hand cleaning up this mess?"

I nodded, only half hearing her. Sam and Nate were still down at the end of the garden. I couldn't make out what they were saying, but I could tell they were arguing. Nate kept gesturing with his hand like he was trying to make Sam look at some invisible thing right in front of his nose. And Sam was stomping around, waving both hands in front of his face like he was trying to bat that very thing away.

Setting her glass behind the sink, Lisa wrapped one of Kat's huge, flowered aprons around herself twice and started filling the sink, squirting in about three times the soap I'd usually use. Then her eyes followed to where I was looking.

I turned back, and started stacking the dirty dishes around the sink.

"Lisa?"

"Yeah?"

"Is all that following Jesus stuff good for your love life?"

She laughed. "No! I mean yes," Lisa said, flustered. "I mean, I like to think that knowing Jesus helps me in every area of my life even if, even if . . ."

She bit her fingers, then grimaced as she nearly swallowed a handful of bubbles.

"I made the decision, a long time ago, that I was going to wait for the right guy to ask me out, rather than just go out with some guy who didn't know God, or some guy who I didn't know deep in my heart would be right for me." She paused. "And so far the right guy hasn't asked me out. And I've been waiting a long time."

She glanced back toward the window. Sam and Nate had disappeared.

"They've probably gone out for coffee now," Lisa said, as if reading my mind, "and if Sam is ready to talk about God, they could be gone for hours. But Nate knows I can find my own way home."

Lisa plunged her arms back in the sink again, the bubbles rising up to her elbows.

"No," she said again, "following God is not good for my dating life. At least not at moments like this when I think I'm going to stay single for the next twenty years," Lisa added, laughing. "But I totally believe God is good for my love life."

"Aren't they the same thing?" I asked.

"I don't think so," Lisa said, shaking her head vigorously. "I think of it this way—if God really loves me, and really knows me, then why would he want me to go out with a guy who was only sort-of OK for me? Or even wrong for me? You think God wants me to let some random guy trash my heart just because I get impatient waiting for Mr. Right?"

Something odd that Sam had said that night when he'd picked me up from Kevin's smashed truck flickered in the back of my mind just then. I'd been so insanely happy to see him, and hanging out with him had been some of the most fun I'd had all week. And then, somehow, it had all fallen apart and somehow we'd gotten into this huge, stupid fight.

"I need you, Jo," he'd said, "I need you like I need a hole in my head." And after everything that's how he'd thought of me. Like a great big worthless headache.

"Lisa?"

"Yeah?"

"Why would anyone want a hole in their head?"

Lisa laughed. "They wouldn't."

Exactly. He wouldn't.

"Except . . ."

Huh?

Lisa crinkled her nose, like she was trying to figure out something tricky. "Except, when you think of it, we've all got holes in our heads right? Like our eyes which let us see, and our ears to hear, and our mouths to talk. Without those holes the world would be pretty dull, wouldn't it?"

"Sure," I said lightly, wondering why my stomach suddenly felt funny.

§ § §

I don't know how long Sam and Nate argued. I know they were still fighting, or talking, or something at nine o'clock that night because according to Lisa that's when Nate finally got around to texting Lisa to tell her he was going to miss music practice.

Then on Saturday, to my surprise, I got an e-mail from Sam.

To: jmac@ intermailbuzz.net
From: sam182@intermailbuzz.net
Subject: move

Hey Jo,

Found a place. Turned out Nate knew someone. You ever meet Simon Graeme-Nuttal? (How's that for a wicked name?) Si was at my sister's wedding.

Anyway, Si's just got a house in Ashford and he was looking for a roommate, and I move in tomorrow. He seems cool.

Don't laugh but Si belongs to this guys prayer group thing. Calls it his lonely heart's club band! (Too weird!) Anyway, I agreed to go with him sometime. Nate kind of talked me into it—said something about someone being there I needed to meet. Interesting.

Hope you won't be mad, but talked to Nate a bit about you. He said he'd find out who was harassing ya and keep an eye on you. I don't know what to think. He

IF ONLY YOU KNEW

wants me to do this event thing in Silverpoint in a few weeks. So if I'm in town then I'll give you a shout.

Sorry for, you know, being a jerk and stuff.

Take care,
Sam

I think I must have sat there at my computer and reread the e-mail a hundred times with my fingers frozen to the keyboard, trying to think of something to say back. I would probably have still been there an hour later if Kat hadn't come in and let me know that the police were outside taking down the crime-scene tape.

They left behind a big, neon yellow sign announcing that we'd been the victims of crime and to call a special number if you knew anything. And even though we wouldn't have a police car parked outside anymore, they would still have someone drive past at random intervals each day to show whatever nefarious bad guys that might be lurking that they were still keeping an eye on us.

Kat decided that we needed to go out for dinner somewhere fancy to celebrate. Just the two of us. Officer Blonde was still parked outside filling in forms, so Kat knocked on the window and told her we were going to Michelangelo's.

Of course the last time I had been there I'd seen Motor-Oil-Guy and Red-Jacket in the parking lot, so I had more than a few butterflies in my stomach as we pulled in. But the place was packed, and Kat stuck so close to my side you'd have thought someone had glued us together. So I figured we'd be safe.

We got this beautiful table by the window, and we'd both dressed up, because as Kat liked to say, even when you didn't have a man to dress up for it was important to look fantastic for yourself.

"I've been thinking," Kat said seriously, twirling some spaghetti around on her fork, "I've been really, really impressed with the way you pulled the store together. You've got a good creative eye, and you've got a really good sense of how to break a big project down into little manageable tasks. And, well, I've been thinking . . ." Kat took a deep breath, "I was wondering how you would like to go to Ashford College in the spring.

"They have a whole bunch of practical diplomas," Kat went on quickly, before I could even pick my jaw up from the table, "stuff like interior design, and retail management, and property restoration, and art design. Some even have apprenticeships attached. They're all very practical and you could apply to start in January. And I was thinking that if you wanted to go for it, I'd be willing to lend you the tuition. After all, I can pay you to clean up the store now out of the insurance money. And once it's done there's going to be rental income too, and I think at least some of that should be yours."

I was stunned. Shocked. Speechless. I must have sat there for a good ten minutes, just staring at my cousin, without a clue what to say.

Kat reached out and squeezed my hands.

"Jo, I've thought for a long time that you don't have enough faith in yourself, and if you put your mind to it, I'm sure there are a lot of fantastic things that you would be good at."

I practically flew across the table and gave Kat an enormous hug.

We had this huge, unhealthy, chocolaty dessert while Kat and I discussed all sorts of options, like whether I wanted to go to school part-time and keep living with her, or move to Ashford in January. Her cell phone went off just as she was paying the bill, and as the signal was pretty lousy inside Michelangelo's she headed outside to answer it.

There I was, sitting at the little table, staring outside the window thinking how great it was going to be to tell Sam that I was going to be joining him in Ashford soon, when all of a sudden I felt this weight on my shoulder, and this insidious voice whispered sweetly in my ear, "He's not in love with you, you know. He's in love with me."

I practically jumped out of my seat. There was this vicious little giggle behind me, and then, with a wave of perfume and golden hair, someone slipped into Kat's empty chair.

It was Traci.

She leaned forward, grinning at the dumbfounded expression on my face.

"Sam dropped by my place the other night," she said, stringing out the words with obvious delight. "He brought me a dozen roses, and a box of chocolates, and practically cried when he said how much he was going to miss me."

Unconsciously my hand slipped up to my neck, as if trying to dislodge the words that had frozen in my heart. She was lying—she had to be. Right? Sam wouldn't . . . He couldn't . . .

"I . . . I wanted to talk to you about Sammy for a long time," Traci went on, this impish, catlike smile spreading across her face. "I wanted to be sure you knew that he and I had gotten back together. Because I know you're in love with him. But you can't have him. He's mine."

It really was amazing how just a few little words like that could deliver a good, hard blow to my solar plexus. I shook my head like I was trying to stop her words from sinking in my ears.

"Oh, don't try to deny it," Traci went on. "It was written all over your face when I interrupted your little date last month. But if I were you, I'd start working really hard at forgetting that Sammy ever existed. Because he's never going to love you back, Jo. Never." Then she leaned forward, "Face it, Jo," she said, her voice nearing a whisper, "no one is every going to want to love an ugly, useless, pathetic waste of space like you."

Then before I could even try to find something, anything, to say in response, she slipped out of Kat's seat with her catlike grin, and wandered over to join a large table of girls.

Struggling to breathe, I stumbled out of Michelangelo's and stood, shaking, on the front porch, my heart hammering in my chest. Oh, how I hated her! I hated her beautiful blonde hair and gorgeous blue eyes. And I unbelievably, overwhelmingly, excruciatingly, painfully hated that wide grinning mouth that had probably kissed Sam thousands and thousands of times, and I never even got to kiss him once.

Kat found me outside.

"Are you OK?"

I shook my head.

"What was that all about? Who was that girl I saw you talking to?"

I gasped and found my voice again. "It was Traci, Sam's ex."

A dark look brushed over Kat's face.

"Don't let her get you riled," Kat said dismissively. "I wouldn't bother listening to anything she has to say."

I forced a smile on my face, and tossed my head like Traci was already forgotten.

But Traci's words continued to eat away at me deep inside until I thought I was going to be sick.

§ § §

Kat let me borrow her Jeep to go to the Gathering on Sunday night and Lisa had taken a week off from playing music so that she could sit with me. I did see Kevin, running around the stage. He looked up, blushed, and gave me this little "hey" wave. But he didn't come over.

I sang along with the songs on autopilot, barely seeing the words as they flickered on the screen. But some of them managed to slip through. So I sat there feeling miserable, and ugly, and useless deep inside while at the same time singing all these great reassuring things like: "You don't have to be strong. You don't have to belong. Because you are loved and by the one who matters most."

And you would have thought all those beautiful sentiments would have made me feel better. But they so didn't! They just made me feel worse—like I was more alone than ever.

Tears started welling up in my eyes. My voice squeaked to a halt. I didn't want to be alone. I wanted to believe I was loved. But I just didn't know how.

So, Patrick got up to speak, and I thought I was going to be lucky just to make it through to the end of the talk without keeling over or bursting into tears.

I don't know how to explain it—there was just this persistent gnawing in the pit of my stomach. And I couldn't tell you when it started, or how long it had been there, but somehow it felt like I had been sad forever and just hadn't realized it until that moment.

I was just so sick of feeling lost. Sick of feeling ugly, and worthless, and unlovable. Who was I kidding? Traci hadn't said anything that I hadn't thought myself a million times before. I hated who I was. And I was miserable. Completely miserable.

I looked up. The Gathering was over and Lisa was smiling at me with her usual don't-worry-the-world-is-secretly-a-beautiful-place smile.

"Are you OK, Jo?" Lisa asked.

"Nope, I'm not," I said, shaking my head a little. "In fact I am completely and totally miserable."

Lisa didn't even flinch, she just squeezed my shoulder and asked me if I wanted to pray about it. I was totally shaken. I don't tend to do brutal honesty all that often, and so was kind of surprised to hear the words coming out of my mouth. But I meant them, and it kind of felt good to tell someone. Even though it was kind of terrifying too.

A few minutes later I was sitting down with both Lisa and Patrick on faded packing crates in a little sheltered area behind the stage. And I told them all sorts of stuff—words just kept bubbling out of me like I didn't know where they were coming from or how to stop them. I told them I missed Sam so much more than I expected to and even though it had only been a couple days basically since I had seen him last it really did totally hurt like a punch in the gut that made you wince every time you took a deep breath in. I told them I wasn't surprised when Kevin broke up with me— but it was just another nail in the coffin of my whole conviction that I was never going to find anyone who actually loved me.

I told them that my mother tried to rid herself of me when I was tiny. That my mother had forgotten my ninth birthday. That when I was fourteen a guy I had fallen in love with told me the only way anyone would ever like me was if I had a bag over my head. That no one who had ever told me they loved me had actu-ally stuck by me—except maybe Kat—but that in a way I felt like that didn't count because she was just a nice person to everyone. That I still had no clue what I wanted to do with my life.

That I never, ever, really liked what I saw in the mirror and most of the time I just felt hideous. That I felt like nothing really good was ever going to happen to me, not lasting anyway, because sooner or later someone would always find out what an unlovable mess I really was on the inside. And then I kind of ran out of words, and just sat there, staring at the floor, wishing it would open up and swallow me whole.

Patrick reached over and gently put his arm around my shoulders in a really sturdy but gentle way. Lisa was squeezing my hand, and I squeezed it back, and was thankful when she didn't let go.

"Can we pray for you?" Patrick asked.

I nodded.

"Do you want to pray?" he asked.

I shook my head. "I don't really know how."

"OK," Patrick said gently, "how about Lisa and I say a quick prayer, and then you can add anything you want after that, if you want to."

"OK."

I closed my eyes tightly, tears pushing their way through my lids. Lisa prayed first. Her prayer was full of words like "precious," "loving," "redeemer," and "Lord." Her words were absolutely beautiful, like water streaming over pebbles, and even though I was afraid I'd never be able to pray like that, I loved listening to it. Then Patrick prayed. He addressed his prayer to his "Father in heaven" and his prayer was very solid and real. Like he thought Jesus was standing there beside him and Patrick could talk to Jesus man-to-man. Patrick thanked Jesus for loving me so much that he was willing to die for me, and asked God to give me a glimmer of how deeply Jesus loved me.

Then he stopped. And it felt like they were silent for absolutely ages. I didn't know what to say. I didn't know what to do. But even though part of me wanted to get up and run away, a huger part of me felt like I had this opportunity to maybe let God see I was there, and I needed someone to love me, and I didn't want to leave until I knew I had at least tried to talk to him, and see if he'd listen.

"Um . . . dear God. I don't know if you can hear me. But if you can, I want you to know that I'm really, really sad. And I feel really lost, and really alone," I whispered. "And if you are there, can you please talk to me. And tell me you're there and I'm not alone. Because I really would like to know you, but I don't know how."

I was really crying properly now. These huge tears were spilling out of my eyes and dripping down onto my lap. Lisa slipped a crumpled up tissue into my hand. But neither she nor Patrick left, in fact I think they were both kind of still praying under their breaths. And I just sat there, really knowing that despite everything else I might have done or said, I really did want God to touch me and help me sort out my life—if God was there and wanted to, that is.

And then, God answered me. It felt like someone was breathing on the top of my head, sending warm shivers through my arms. It felt like it did when Kevin had said he loved me, or when Sam had told me I was beautiful, only like a thousand times stronger and without that bit of nagging doubt that they may not actually mean it.

I don't know how to explain it, except to say that in that moment I really, truly, actually felt that God was there and God loved me. God loved me. Totally. God didn't look down on me, or pity me, or feel angry with me. God didn't even have this kind of general benign "I'm God so I love everything" kind of feeling for me. Jesus knew me. Jesus got me. Jesus loved me. It was so, so real. And I knew it, even deep inside.

This kicked my tears into overdrive. I was full out shaking and sobbing now, and when I looked up Lisa was crying too, and even Patrick had tears in his eyes.

"Did God speak to you?" he asked.

"Yeah," I said, sniffing. "I can't believe it. He did."

Then we all prayed some more, and talked a bit about what it meant to be a Christian and have Jesus as the center of your life. And Lisa wanted to start singing, which was kind of funny because Patrick and I didn't, and so she sang on her own. And I cried some more, but we laughed too. And we stayed there long after everyone else had gone. But that time, that feeling God for the first time, was awesome and special and amazing, and I never wanted it to end.

§ § §

When I woke the next morning, something felt different. It was like it was Christmas, or I had just fallen in love, or something. I just felt happy and excited and really, actually glad to be alive.

And that completely amazing feeling lasted for about all of forty-five minutes. But by the time I had finished showering and gotten dressed, a couple of my old fears, and doubts, and insecurities had started to poke and prod at me again, and squish this little fledgling, hopeful joy I had in my heart.

It started with looking at myself in the mirror, and realizing that while I did seem to like that person I saw a little bit more than I had yesterday, I still thought I was too tall. Then as I pulled my jean shorts on I realized they were dirty and I had forgotten to do my laundry again. And then it was the realization that I didn't know how Sam was going to react when I told him. All sorts of little niggling things like that.

Now, I don't want to make it sound like all I needed to do was look in the mirror and suddenly all the wonderfulness of the night before was gone. It wasn't like that at all. And it's not that it didn't make a huge, huge difference. It's just that, well . . . since God was supposed to be right there, in my everyday life, I had kind of hoped, well prayed, that he would have sent me a sign—something to let me know that things were going to be different now.

So I threw on some clothes, stuck my hair back without brushing it properly, and wandered down the stairs to the living room where, to my surprise, I caught a glimpse of a pair of boots—clunky, black boots—through my kitchen door. Big, worn boots with silver buckles. That didn't belong in my kitchen. I took a step closer.

They were attached to very long legs in tan khakis. Too long for Sam. Too big for Kevin. It was Nate. Sitting in my kitchen. Drinking my coffee. Reading my newspaper. Judging by the crumbs, he'd even helped himself to one of my muffins.

"Good morning," I said, my voice sounding a little louder than I'd planned. But to be fair, if I'd known I was going to walk into my kitchen and find Nate there I probably would have put on cleaner clothes, or maybe even some makeup. At the very least I would have brushed my hair. Then again, I might have just hidden in my room until he gave up and left.

Nate looked up. "Uh. Good morning," he said, "your . . . ah . . . cousin let me in on her way out."

Knowing Kat she probably made him breakfast too. Fortunately for Nate, there was still hot coffee in the pot and two more warm muffins in the basket.

"So this is how it works, is it?" I said, plopping down in my usual seat. "Lisa does the soft-sell in the evening and then you come over and hammer it in hard the next morning?"

At least Nate had the decency to look surprised.

"Excuse me?"

"I'm guessing Lisa filled you in on everything she said and now it's your turn," I said, a little surprised at the edge in my voice. "So, well, let's get on with it. I need to be a better person. I don't want to go to hell. Being a Christian is hard, hard work, blah di blah di blah . . ."

Nate looked seriously puzzled now. Downright confounded, which is no mean feat considering he was sitting in my kitchen after all.

"I have no clue what you're talking about," Nate said. "I didn't talk to Lisa last night. She texted me a couple of times this morning saying we needed to talk, but I haven't called her back yet."

"So, I'm supposing you spoke to Patrick then?"

"No," Nate said shaking his head. "I spoke to him for about five minutes after the Gathering, then I left as soon as it was finished, and went from there to see Pastor Wallace for like an hour, if it matters," he was talking really cautiously now, like he was trying to talk down someone holding a hostage. "Then I went home. Prayed. Went to sleep. Got up. Read my Bible. Prayed. Came here."

"So why are you here, then?" I asked.

"I . . . I'm not quite sure," Nate said. There was something in his voice I couldn't quite put a finger on. He took a sip of coffee. Kat has two kinds of mugs—those for guests and those for family. Nate was using a family mug. But to be fair, a guest one would have probably bothered me more. "So, what did I miss last night?" Nate asked.

"God," I said, trying to be smart.

Nate raised one eyebrow, but didn't say anything.

I sighed, decided I didn't much like the person I was turning into so far that morning, and when I opened my mouth again was pleased to find I sounded far less prickly.

"I prayed last night," I said, "with Lisa and Patrick. I told God I wanted to try believing in him, and following him."

I think I expected some form of big response from Nate. A bit of jumping for joy and table thumping, with a few hallelujahs thrown in for good measure. But instead, he took another sip of coffee.

"And?" he said.

"And I thought God spoke to me, OK? I thought I felt God. I thought that God was real and loved me and wanted to be in my life."

Again, no jumping or waving on Nate's part. "And now?"

"And now I feel foolish," I said honestly, slumping my head down into my hands. "I feel like I'm not so sure. Part of me feels like God is real and amazing and really has touched my life, and the other part of me keeps trying to tell the first part that I'm just an idiot."

This was the part of the show when I expected Nate to jump up and start laying into me—hammering home just how important it was that I believe in his God, and how I wasn't allowed to doubt it. Not now. Not ever.

But instead, he stood up, and went to pour himself another cup of coffee.

"Milk?"

"In the fridge."

"Thanks."

"What would you say right now if I told you I had decided that I was never, ever going to have anything to do with God ever again?" I demanded.

"I'd say, 'Why?'" Nate said, pouring himself two sugars.

"And if I told you it was because I was convinced there was no God?"

"I'd think you were lying to yourself," Nate said, sitting back down again, "but I wouldn't try to force you to believe anything you didn't want to." He looked so calm that part of me wanted to throw something at him.

"What if I don't want to believe in your God?"

"Then don't."

"What's the matter with you?" I snapped. "Aren't you going to try to talk me into it?"

"Nope."

"Well . . . well . . . well, why not?"

"Why should I? How silly would it be for me to try to force-feed you God's love, when he's just giving it away to you with free and reckless abandon?"

Nate sipped his coffee again, like he was just some friend who dropped by for coffee every Monday. "Sorry to ruin whatever conspiracy theory you have going on about how Christianity works, but the way I see it is it's my job to be a witness. You know, like someone who is ready to be called upon to tell people what I know about God, and what I've seen God do. Not to be some form of bully. But, you want to know about Jesus—I'm here to help you 100 percent." Up went the coffee cup to his mouth again.

This kind of took some of the wind out of my sails. But it was comforting too.

"Why are you here, Nate?"

"God told me to come," he said, sitting back down again. "I know it sounds crazy—hey, it was a new one for me too—but I was reading something in my Bible, and God said, 'Jo really needs to hear that this morning, so copy it down and go and give it to her.' So I came over."

"So God actually speaks to you?"

"Sometimes. Sometimes God seems 110 percent real. Other times it feels like he's a billion miles away."

"But God is real though?"

"Absolutely."

"And if I told God I want him to take my life and change it . . ."

Nate smiled now. I hadn't really seen him smile much, but it was a real, genuine smile that lit up his entire face. "Then God touched your life, Jo. He threw his arms around you and said 'I've missed you, and wanted you so much, and I'm so glad you're here now.' He adopted you. He changed your life instantly, and he's going to keep changing it until the day you die. And then you get to be a perfect person living in a perfect world, and you'll finally get to see him and really know how much he loves you." Nate raised his mug. "Welcome to the greatest adventure of your life!"

As Nate was speaking, that feeling of love from the night before rushed all over me again. I smiled back; I just couldn't help it.

"But if God is real, then why don't we feel him all the time?"

"Because we're messed up people, living in a messed up world."

"But one day we'll be perfect?"

"Yup. And until then, you're loved, and you're wanted, and you're never going to be alone," Nate said. "'Love always protects, always trusts, always hopes, always perseveres. Love never fails,' as the Bible says. 'Now we see but a poor reflection as in a mirror. Then we shall see face to face. Now I know in part; then I shall know fully, even as I am fully known.'"

"Patrick read that at Mandy and Brian's wedding."

"It's from the Bible," Nate said again. "Do you have a Bible?"

I shook my head. "I don't think so."

"Well, if I know Lisa she's probably out buying you one right now." Nate stood up. "I have got to go. But if you have any questions, or if there is anything I can help you with, just give me a call."

He placed his newspaper down on the table. It was folded over to a story on page six, and that's when I realized it was from last fall. "And take a look at this when you get the chance. There's a story on the top of the page I think you might be interested in."

Nate rinsed out his cup and set it next to the sink. He started toward the back door, then turned back. "Oh, I nearly forgot." He slid a piece of paper across the table to me. "I paraphrased."

I waited until he had gone, then opened it up.

It read: "Dear Jo, God says—Do not be afraid, for I have saved you. I have called you by name. You are mine. When you walk through the waters I will be with you. When you walk through the fire you will not be burned. Because, you are precious and honored in my sight, and I love you. (Isaiah 43:1–2, 4)

"For who can separate you from the love of Jesus? No one! I am convinced that neither death nor life, neither angels nor demons, neither the present nor the future, nor any powers, neither height nor depth, nor anything else in all creation, will be able to separate you from the love of God that is in Christ Jesus our Lord. (Romans 8:35, 38–39)"

Then I turned my attention to the year-old *Silverpoint Gazette* article dated October 26:

ASHFORD "GANG" FACES PRISON TIME

Eight young men, between the ages of fourteen and twenty-six, have been arrested and charged with a series of crimes including assault, theft, arson, issuing threats and drug related charges.

According to PC Max Hudson the gang is believed to be responsible for a series of burglaries in the Ashford, Silverpoint and Westin areas.

The arrests came after another seventeen-year-old youth, who cannot be identified for legal reasons, turned himself in to police and agreed to testify against others in the group in return for leniency. The youth, who is not believed to be a core member of the group, has pled guilty to assault with a weapon causing bodily harm. He has yet to be sentenced, but according to PC Hudson he is unlikely to serve further jail time.

§ § §

Nate was right about Lisa. She showed up later that afternoon with a Bible all ready for me. It was a beautiful brown leather thing, wrapped in tissue paper, and Lisa had already gone through and highlighted all her favorite Bible verses for me. She suggested I start with a book about Jesus, called Luke, and I had already read through most of it by the time I went to bed that night. It was pretty cool actually—it even had a few decent female characters.

Then I started on the other books about Jesus, and a couple of the Psalms. I never—ever, in a million years ever—expected to enjoy reading the Bible. But there was just something about it—about Jesus in particular—that made the words just jump off the page. I was surprised to discover how much I actually liked the Jesus I was reading about. I mean, the twins' movie Jesus had been nice. But the Jesus of the Bible—the one I felt close to when I prayed—he really blew my mind.

Of course now I'd instantly become Lisa's pet project, which sounds kind of scary, but considering the fact I'd now gone from having two guys in my life to being totally and utterly single, it was actually really nice to have someone around to hang out with. And it turned out Lisa was a lot more fun than I expected.

She took me to the morning service at Cornerstone the next Sunday—wouldn't take no for an answer even if I'd wanted to turn her down. It was different, but nice too. And, as weird as it sounds, I really started to enjoy the music, and the prayers, and hearing Pastor Wallace talk about God. It was like this new thirst had woken up inside me, and the more I fed it, the more I felt . . . well . . . satisfied and thirsty all at the same time.

Telling Kat hadn't been easy, but she kind of understood. She'd smiled at me and said, "Well, my mom always said that religion helps keep you grounded. Just don't go overboard."

And I realized that even though her "overboard" comment was exactly the kind of thing I'd have said before, I knew now why it wouldn't work. Because falling in love with God was like falling in love with a person, only bigger. There was no way to fall just a little bit in love. And what I loved about God was how "overboard" he went in loving me. No one had ever wanted to love me like that before.

I still missed Sam every second of every day. But, as weird as it sounds, on top of all the loneliness and heartache—which could sometimes feel pretty strong when I thought about him—a weird, supernatural peace was still there, holding me up.

I hadn't heard anything from Sam since I got that one e-mail. And I never e-mailed him back either.

At first I tried telling myself it was because I didn't know how I was going to explain to Sam that I'd decided to give my heart over to God and let him come into the mess of my life. And that I was afraid Sam wouldn't understand. But I knew that was only partially true.

Something about what had happened with Traci at the restaurant was holding me back. Maybe I was a little bit afraid that he really was in love with her—or at least liked her more than me.

But even that wasn't it. Because when I was completely and totally honest with myself, I knew I was scared of how much I missed Sam. I was scared of how much I thought of him, wanted to talk to him, and longed to just hang out with him again.

I'd never liked anyone in my whole life the way I liked Sam.

Traci had accused me of being in love with him. And I was afraid she might be right.

CHAPTER TWELVE

IT WAS the beginning of September, and as if on cue, a crisp, chilly breeze cut through the air signaling the end of summer. Lisa and I had gone down to the beach in the totally misguided hope that it might be warm enough for one last swim, when Lisa invited me to go for a hike around Bear Lake.

"I really want you to come," Lisa had told me. "I do it every year for the anniversary of when I was adopted and to remind myself that God has adopted me into his family too. Normally I just invite a couple of close friends, and we have a barbecue. And then at night, we light a campfire and we write out these letters to God telling him how sorry we are for all the stupid stuff we've done that year. And then we stick them in the fire to remember that he's totally wiped the slate clean and forgiven us."

Even though it had been a while since the fire, and the store was almost completely fixed up again, I still felt a little nervous about going out to Bear Lake. After all, that's where Kevin's truck had been vandalized and not far from where I'd last seen Motor-Oil-Guy and Red-Jacket.

But then Lisa said that Nate was going to be coming with us, which made me feel a tiny bit better. And the next time I saw Officer Gray-Hair circle past I flagged him down and asked him about it, and he seemed to think it was OK. So I told her that I would go. In fact, I was kind of looking forward to it.

But then, the night before, Lisa announced that Kevin was coming too—which kind of threw me for a loop. It's not like I hadn't seen Kevin around at the Gathering and stuff. In fact, when he found out I'd decided to get serious about following Jesus he'd come over and given me this super quick hug, before dashing off into the crowd again—which felt kind of good and kind of awkward at the same time. But being OK with smiling at a guy across a crowded room was a little different than going for a long walk in the woods with him. Although it's not like we were going to be alone together.

In fact, according to Lisa, it was Nate who was going to pick me up. Since I'd started hanging out with Lisa I tended to see Nate at least twice a week. We'd sit with him at church on Sunday morning and then go out for lunch. Or he'd drop by for this, that, or the other reason when I was hanging out at Lisa's. I'd prayed with Nate and Lisa a couple of times, and we went out to a movie once. But I hadn't properly talked with him—you know, about Motor-Oil-Guy and Red-Jacket, and the possibility of someone wanting to kill either of us—since that day after I gave God my heart.

So when Nate picked me up first that morning, before Lisa, because he said we needed to talk, to be totally honest my first thought was, "Well, I don't want to talk!"

For the first time in forever I was just beginning to feel happy about myself. And with the police keeping an eye on our place I had started to feel safe too. And I didn't want to ruin it by thinking about crimes, or accidents, or gangs, or threats. I mean, wasn't the fact I was trying to sort out how to follow God, and my feelings for Sam, enough for one girl to deal with?

But then Nate added, "It's about Kevin . . . I need to talk to you about Kevin," and slumped his arms against the steering wheel and looked at me head on.

"Kevin is planning on talking to you about something today," Nate said, "and before he does, I just want you to know that I'm behind him 100 percent."

Now of course I wanted to know what Nate was talking about. I mean, we weren't twelve anymore, so why the whole "my friend needs to talk to you" mysteriousness? But if I was tempted to make a joke about it, the look on Nate's face was so serious, that I didn't even dare smile.

"It's really hard for Kevin to say things sometimes," Nate said, "and being honest with people, especially when he cares about them, can be hard. And I'm not going to tell you how to react, or judge you if you decide to blow him off. But he needs to get something off his chest, and I think he's doing the exact right thing in this, so I hope . . . well . . . I hope you'll be able to give him a break and be kind."

Uh-huh . . . Great. So by the sound of things Kevin was going to drop a pretty big bombshell on me, and all Nate could tell me was to "be kind," as if I was planning on pointing and laughing or something.

"Just know, I'll be praying for you," Nate added, as he started toward Lisa's.

"Thanks," I said. I figured I could use all the prayer I could get.

So, we picked up Lisa, and then to my surprise we headed over to Cornerstone Church. Nate explained that we were going to meet Kevin there and all go to the lake in his dad's truck. But we were getting to the church early because Nate and Lisa were doing a couple of songs for an event that Patrick was running Sunday night and so they needed to pop in for a few moments to double check what songs he wanted.

I'd vaguely been aware that the whole "Come As You Are" event was coming up Sunday night, and I'd thought of going. Lisa had reminded me that the purpose of the event was to let all sorts of different people, who were in all different parts of their walk with God, get up and share about what God was doing in their life right then. It sounded really cool, and when we arrived at the church there was a mass of people there already practicing for it.

Anyway, just as we stepped into the big front entrance way of the church, before we got into the main sanctuary part, Nate put his hand on my shoulder.

"Everyone's busy running through what they're going to say tonight," Nate said. "It's kind of an interesting process some- times—even as you get up to speak, if you're open to God, some- times you can hear him speaking through you. Why don't you go up to the balcony and watch for a bit. I'll come let you know when Kevin gets here."

Nate gave me a little push on the back and next thing I knew I found myself heading up the small, twisty stairs to the balcony. I curled up in the same seat I'd been in for Mandy and Brian's wed- ding. Down below me I could see people wandering around and talking in little groups. There was a woman—who looked at least eighty—up on stage telling this great story about how God was helping her talk to her grandkids about him. And I just sat there, killing time, wondering what I was doing there.

Lisa had left a pad of paper up on the little wooden ledge that went around the balcony. At least I presumed it was Lisa because it was pink with big floaty balloons and had a little purple pen attached. And while I was listening to this random grandma talk about how she'd gotten up the courage to tell her six-foot-two, pot-smoking grandson that God loved him, I decided that I really had no good excuse for not telling Sam. So as I waited, I snatched up the pad and started to write.

My ideas came out really randomly at first. I wrote about how he'd been right when he'd accused me of thinking no one could love me. I wrote about what it was like to get up every morning and wonder if there was any point to my being alive. I wrote about crying out to God and hearing God answer me. I wrote about the Jesus from the girls' movie and the Jesus I was reading about in the Bible. I wrote about how I was beginning to fall in love with that Jesus. And how I was beginning to believe that Jesus loved me too.

And when I'd run out of words to say I set the pad of paper back on the ledge, sat back, closed my eyes, and asked God to help me know what I should say to Sam when I saw him again.

I was only vaguely aware that the grandma had finished and someone else had stepped up on stage. Then I heard a voice say, "Testing . . . hey hey . . . do I really have to use a microphone?" and I nearly fell out of my seat. It was Sam. He looked older somehow. Maybe it was the fact he had a new hair cut: shorter at the sides, messier on top, with that same shock of hair flopping over his forehead when he moved. Sam looked so, so good, it was almost painful somehow. I slid my feet onto the floor and leaned forward until I was sitting on the edge of the seat.

"I don't know where to start," he called over to Patrick, who I now saw was standing talking with Nate and Lisa at the side of the stage. "I'm really new to this kind of thing."

"Start anywhere you want," Patrick said. "Wherever God leads you."

Sam took a breath so deep that I almost felt it in my chest.

"I grew up hearing about God," Sam said, looking out around the mostly empty seats. "That God was a God of rules. And in a way that was bad because I always felt like I wasn't good enough—wasn't working hard enough, was too unlovable and 'sinful.' I did know that God supposedly loved me like a father did. But my father was big on rules too—and not big on hugs or that whole undeserved acceptance thing. And besides the only dad I remembered hearing about in the Bible was Abraham, who nearly killed his son because God told him to and he was supposed to do his duty. And it sounded like the kind of thing the kind of father I knew about would do."

Sam paused, ran his fingers through his hair.

"But a God of rules was OK with me. Because that meant when I did the right thing then God would bless me. That I could somehow earn God's acceptance. But it was working to do what you are supposed to do to get what you want to get. The idea of 'serving' never entered my mind. I'm not good at surrendering control of my life to anyone or anything. And I guess it's no surprise to tell you that I gave up believing in that God. He never worked for me anyway."

Sam stopped for a moment, stepped away from the microphone, and had a few words with Patrick. I was frozen in my seat, waiting to see if he was going to come back, wondering what I would do if he didn't. But then Sam stepped back up, and talked about the Gathering for a while. About the kind of loving God people there had told him about. A God who didn't demand his rights, but gave his rights up and laid down his life for people who didn't deserve him.

He talked about how Nate and Patrick had allowed him to ask question after question, and didn't judge him for not believing. He explained how when he found himself struggling with whether or not he was willing to trust his life to this God, that Nate had stayed with him for hours, just listening to him, and talking to him, and helping him through it.

"It's . . . it's funny the things that God does to get you to the point of being where you need to be to hear him and know him,"

Sam said. "For me, it was a girl. This crazy, amazing girl that I couldn't have but couldn't get out of my head. That's what finally drove me to trust God. Realizing I was in love with someone I couldn't be with."

I could feel myself shaking. I stared down at my hands and they were actually shaking, like I was afraid, or freezing cold. My heart stung as he talked about Traci. Actually stung as if Sam had reached into my chest and squeezed it.

"She drove me nuts," Sam said laughing. "And I couldn't stop myself from being in love with her, no matter how hard I tried to. I was out of my control. My own heart was out of my control. I even . . ."

He reached into his pocket, pulled out the crumpled sheet he had taken from my notepad at the store, and held it aloft.

"I even tried to make a deal with God! I told him that if he made this girl do what I wanted then I would believe in him. And you know what? God said no!"

On the floor I could hear people laughing. But not me. Hot, painful tears pushed their way out of my eyes and onto my cheeks.

Traci had been right. I was in love with him. Completely and totally in love with him. I don't know when I fell for him, and even though this was the first time I had really ever admitted it to myself, as I looked back on being his friend for so many weeks I couldn't think of one time when I hadn't loved him—even if I hadn't been willing to admit it to myself. When I saw him with Traci. When I smiled at him from underneath Kevin's arm. When he chatted with Kat about his college course selection. As he caught my eye across the room at the Gathering.

I was in love with Sam. I was so in love with Sam that seeing him down there, a million miles away, and not being able to put my arms around him was the most bittersweet torture imaginable.

"I was out of control," Sam was saying. "My own heart was out of control. And I hated that, because I kind of like being in control and I hate asking for help." He laughed.

"It got so bad that I made this snap decision to give up my apartment and go to Ashford. And the next thing I knew I found myself sitting in this Bible study where there were all these other guys like me, trying to convince me that the very God I didn't want to follow was the only one who could help me get over her."

Another laugh from the floor, and I think I heard Si's voice calling something about harder hearts prevailing.

"Yeah, Nate had ever so kindly tipped them off in advance," Sam grinned ruefully. "They asked me what she was like so I told them. I said she was too independent for her own good. I told them she wouldn't listen to me or let me help her. Time and time again she wouldn't say the words I wanted her to say. She wouldn't do the things I wanted her to do.

"I couldn't make her be the person I wanted her to be. I couldn't make her love me the way I wanted her to love me. That all I wanted to do was to love her. That all I could do was stand there and watch as she splintered my heart into a million tiny pieces. And you know what one of these guys said to me? He says, 'Sounds like how God feels about you!'

"That was the moment it kind of all went click for me. I had thought I was looking for a God who was going to answer all of my arguments, and my frustrations, and sort everything out to my satisfaction. I wanted a God that I could basically control who would do what I wanted him to do.

"And instead God was standing there going: 'I want to help you Sam! I want to love you! Turn your broken heart over to me before it kills you! Because I love you so much that I let it kill me!' There I'd been, feeling sorry for myself because the first girl I ever really loved had broken my heart, and suddenly I realized that I broke God's heart even more than she broke mine . . ."

I couldn't listen anymore. It was too deep. Too personal. Too painful. And it just felt wrong to sit there and eavesdrop as he poured out his heart like that. Yeah, I wanted to hear about him and God, and part of me desperately wanted to know how he felt about Traci. But not this way. Not like this. Not when he didn't know I was there.

I jumped up, knocking the silly pink pad of paper over the edge of the balcony where it skipped off the top of a pew before landing on the floor below. Behind me, I heard Sam stop talking midsentence. I turned. He was looking right up at me, squinting like he wasn't quite sure it was me. Sam's mouth opened slightly, and he reached out his hand, like he was silently asking whether I was there at all, but tearing my eyes away I dashed down the stairs and out of the church.

Bundling my jacket tightly around me, I kept running, through the parking lot, half fearing that Sam was going to run out after me. When I reached the end of the parking lot I stopped, took a deep breath, and tried to clear my head.

What was wrong with me? How could I have let this happen? How on earth could I have let myself fall in love with Sam? Sam! The sweetest, nicest, greatest, funniest, most incredible guy I'd ever known. The guy who had told me about a million times what a great "friend" I was! Oh, I was his friend all right. Just his friend. Only his friend. The friend, who even when all dressed up and looking her best, on a gorgeous, romantic, starlit summer night, was still unceremoniously dumped so that he could go running toward the girl who had broken his heart. The friend he'd over-looked so he could be with Traci.

"Oh God—why did you let this happen?"

I started to pray, like a drowning swimmer surfacing for air. Throwing my head down into my hands I told God everything—absolutely everything. How I loved Sam, and missed Sam, and wished he was back to being a big part of my life again. How I wanted Sam to be with me—not Traci.

And I begged God to bring me someone else to be in love with. Someone who would actually love me back. He didn't have to be a knight on a white stallion or anything. Just a nice guy who I knew liked me.

I was so deep in prayer I didn't realize that I wasn't alone until I heard a vehicle pull up beside me. I looked up. It was Kevin, leaning over the passenger side of his father's big, white truck, shoving the door open for me to climb in.

Kevin reached for my hand. Gratefully I took it and climbed in. "Hi Jo. What are you doing out here?" he asked, his blue eyes twinkling, a smile slipping across his lips.

"Just getting some air," I said. "Nate and Lisa are waiting for us in the church. We should get back up there."

But to my surprise Kevin didn't start the truck rolling. "It's OK. I texted Nate and he knows I'm here." To be honest, I was glad to have an excuse to not risk running into Sam; at the same time I still didn't get why he wasn't driving up to get them.

"It's really great to see you," Kevin went on, leaning on his steering wheel. "It feels like we never really see each other anymore."

Now I have to admit that confused me somewhat, because I had seen Kevin a few times in the past few days—at the Gathering, and once when he dropped stuff off with his dad. But just as I was trying to figure that one out, our conversation took a turn toward the even more bizarre . . .

Kevin said, "You're shaking. You must be freezing."

And I was about to say that actually it wasn't that cold at all. But then I looked at my hands and realized that I was still kind of shaking, which just goes to show how much hearing Sam like that had thrown me. But before I could say anything, Kevin reached for my hands and started rubbing them briskly as if to warm me up. And for a second I was too stunned to know what to do.

"There you are!" Lisa appeared, jumping into the back seat, dragging Nate behind her. Grateful for the distraction, I pulled my hands away from Kevin and quickly fastened my seatbelt, before jamming my hands into my pockets.

§ § §

We drove to Bear Lake. Lisa made one attempt to ask me if I'd heard what Sam had been talking about on stage, but I quickly shushed her and changed the topic to what college courses she thought I should take in the spring. A nice, safe topic of conversation.

My cell phone buzzed. It was Sam. But instead of answering it, I turned off my phone and tossed it into the glove compartment. Kevin gave me a funny, sideways look, but didn't say anything.

When we reached the lake, Kevin pulled the truck over at the side of the road, and I jumped out quickly before Kevin could try to open the door for me. The ground crackled underneath my feet, and I knew it was just a broken pinecone, but I couldn't help but remember the last time we were there, when someone had smashed in Kevin's windshield.

Lisa slung a big, ancient-looking camera around her neck in one of those old, hard, black cases. She and I walked on ahead and let the guys trail behind us. Then Nate led us round the lake to a shallow, rocky spot, where we could step-jump from rock to rock and clamber up onto one of the smaller islands, and Lisa left her camera on the shore. Kevin went over first and then there was a lot of hand-holding and arm-supporting as he and Nate helped Lisa and I across. I over-launched the last jump and practically flew into Kevin's arms. He gently helped me onto a rock and I could feel a flush rising to my face.

We wandered around on the island for a while, before Nate said that he and Lisa were heading back to the truck to grab some drinks and snacks. He announced it like a done deal, and Lisa— God bless her—suggested that maybe she and I should head back, while Nate and Kevin stayed to find us a place to sit, seemingly oblivious to the pained looks Kevin and Nate were shooting back and forth over her head. But finally, Nate and Lisa headed back through the woods—and I could hear her cheerfully chattering away as they disappeared into the trees. Then Kevin and I were alone. Completely alone. On an island. Surrounded by water. Oh no—this wasn't intimidating at all.

I glanced at Kevin. Kevin glanced at me. Then he smiled, nervously.

"OK, Kev, so you got me here. We're alone. Nate says you need to talk to me. What's up?"

See, that sounds like the kind of thing I'd just think in my head, while out loud I'd just stand there like a deer caught in headlights. But I actually said it for once. Took the moment in my hands instead of just waiting to see whatever said-guy threw my way. I don't know if it did anything for Kevin's nervousness level—in fact it probably made him feel more freaked—but for me, it felt great.

Kevin led me over to a flat rock by the water. We sat. We looked at each other again. And I waited for him to say something.

I could do this, I told myself. It was just Kevin. And after everything this guy and I had been through already, I could take it. Compared to the whole chaotic mess of realizing how I felt about Sam just while he was embarking on a new relationship phase with the former love of his life, there was no way whatever Kevin had to say—

"Jo. I'm in love with you. And I want to get back together."

Then again . . .

Kevin grabbed my hand, squeezing my fingers between his. "I've missed you, Jo," Kevin said earnestly. "I've missed you so, so much. I've thought about you every single day since we broke up . . ."

I thought I was about to pass out. It was so unreal, I kept wanting to pinch myself. And in a strange way, part of me was even tempted to burst out giggling.

"I know I didn't always let you in to what was really going on in my life. And I know I wasn't always completely honest with you about everything. But I've grown, Jo. Heck, I haven't had a cigarette in six days! And you've changed too and found Jesus and everything, and for once it feels like we're going in the same kind of direction.

"Please give me another chance. Because I think we have what it takes to make it. I mean, really make it. Like forever."

OK, so this was probably the most romantic moment of my life so far. The lake was gorgeous and there were trees everywhere and I could even hear birds chattering away in the distance. Or were they squirrels? I'd have to ask Kat later . . . What was wrong with me? Kevin was saying wonderful things. Romantic things, perfect things.

And yet somehow the whole thing sort of didn't work now somehow. If I had been back in high school Kevin would have definitely been someone I'd have gone out with. Someone I'd love to be with on a Saturday night date. But for something more permanent? Could Kevin really be part of God's plan for my life?

And then we heard the crash. The terrifying, bone-jarring sound of metal crushing, grating, against metal. And we heard Lisa scream.

Kevin was on his feet, running madly back toward the truck. He practically flew over the stepping stones, landing short in water up to his knees, and stumbling to shore.

"Jo!" he turned and yelled, looking back for me.

"Go!" I yelled back. "Don't worry about me! Just go!"

There were worse things in life then getting a bit bruised and a little muddy. As I scrambled to shore, I felt my foot snag on something, pitching me forward. It was Lisa's camera. I scooped it up without even thinking, and hugging it to my chest, I ran after Kevin, back through the woods. He was running a lot faster than me and I quickly lost sight of him. But I could hear voices. Shouting. Yelling. My lungs were bursting. I painfully gasped for air but forced myself to keep going. Then the trees parted. And I saw them.

An ugly, brown car was rammed into the side of Ken's truck. Kevin was half-standing, half-slumped against the driver's door. Blood on his face. Red-Jacket, fists raised, was threatening to kill him. Nate thrusting his way in between them, trying to talk Red-Jacket down. I couldn't see Lisa anywhere.

Red-Jacket was yelling, swearing, sounding almost hysterical, so it's no wonder no one seemed to notice me stumbling out of the woods, on the far side of the truck. Then I spotted Motor-Oil-Guy. He was fishing around in the back of the car, getting something out. It was a wooden bat. He started walking toward the guys, bat in hand.

For a second, I was literally paralyzed, petrified, unable to move. In terror, I heard my voice scream out the name of Jesus and suddenly I found myself hurling Lisa's camera toward him. It cleared the truck, and bounced ineffectually off the side of the brown car. Red-Jacket spun around to see what had happened. Nate pushed him sideways, virtually shoving Kevin into the truck and climbing in after him.

There was no way I was about to run around to the front of the truck, but the back was spun around in my direction. Sprinting toward it, I scrambled onto the open tailgate and ran across the crumpled back toward a tiny window in the back of the cab.

"Where's Jo?" Nate yelled.

I took a deep breath, forced the window open, and dove through head first. My belt got caught and for a terrifying second I had visions of Nate driving off with my tail end hanging out the back. But with a jerk, I fell through, and in one of those weird, world-frozen moments, promised God I was never going to complain about my lack of curves again. I landed on something soft that squeaked in surprise—it was Lisa. She had been ducking down in the back seat, cell phone pressed to her ear.

"Jo?"

"I'm here, Nate."

"Thank God."

Untangling my arms and legs, I slid into a seat and managed to get a seatbelt on as Nate got the engine to turn over. He threw the truck in reverse and pulled away. Just then Motor-Oil-Guy swung, taking out whatever remained of the front left taillight.

"Lisa!"

"Nate?"

"You get through to the police?"

"Yes!"

"Tell them we're heading south. Toward Ashford."

Lisa started jabbering away to the officer on the other end of the phone, Nate interrupting occasionally to give her directions, with calm, clear precision. The police were going to meet us at the gas station, Lisa told us. One would probably meet up with us while we were still en route. Nate told her not to hang up.

"I thought you were never supposed to leave the scene of an accident," Lisa said, to no one in particular.

No one responded. Presumably the rule doesn't apply if someone at the scene has a bat and is threatening to kill you.

"Jo!"

"Yes, Nate?"

"You OK?"

"Yeah. I'm OK."

"Lisa?"

"Yeah, Nate. I'm fine."

"Kevin?"

"Yeah, I'm fine," Kevin said, touching his lip gingerly. "I'm sure I'll feel it in the morning," he said with a half-hearted attempt at a smile. "But Josh doesn't have much of an upper-cut. And I think he only winded me some."

Hang on! Josh?

"Who on earth is Josh?" I shouted. Actually, I swore. But hopefully God understood how freaked I was. "You mean you know those guys?"

I had always suspected that Nate could be immensely tough if he needed to be. There was something about the cut of his jaw, something about the way the Gathering crowd would fall silent when Nate stepped up to the microphone, that always made me sense this guy could command a scary amount of authority if he needed to. But even I cringed when Nate spun round, fixed his eyes on Kevin, and yelled, "You still haven't told her yet!"

Kevin was shaking now. Visibly shaking.

Nate's eyes snapped up toward the rearview mirror and everyone else followed his gaze. For a split second my heart leapt, thinking it was the police. But it was them. Motor-Oil-Guy and Red-Jacket. And they were gaining on us.

"You need to tell her Kevin," Nate said. "Now."

"But, I don't think that—"

"Now!"

Nate snapped his attention back to the steering wheel and Kevin fixed his eyes on me.

"Last summer," Kevin said, "I stole Nate's car and then ran him over with it. I think I was trying to kill him."

And in that second everything piled in on me at once—betrayal, relief, disbelief, anger, pity. It was like every bad second of your life crammed into one tiny moment.

"I wanted to kill him," Kevin said again, "but thank God I didn't. I mean, thank God I didn't!"

I glanced over at Lisa, reached out to squeeze her hand; I think I was desperate to see that she was just as upset as I was. But she was so totally focused on the phone call—cell pressed to one ear and finger pressed into the other—that she kind of pushed me off.

"I really do like you, Jo," Kevin went on, his voice cracking with emotion, pleading to be heard. "Please believe me. I never lied to you about how I felt about you. Never!

"But my dad used to drink. A lot. And I used to drink too and use some drugs and stuff. Nothing all that bad. But some of the guys I kind of knew were into worse stuff. And we stole stuff sometimes, stupid little stuff. But then a couple of the guys I knew—Josh and Alan—got into some worse stuff with some other guys and that was around the time my dad was really getting into Cornerstone and pushing me to go too. And Dad told me he'd kick me out if I didn't go to Cornerstone, and so I went a couple of times, and I hated it. And Nate was there and he was bugging me, and saying he knew what I was doing and I needed to change my life around. And I hated him. I really did . . ."

Nate laid his hand on Kevin's shoulder for a nanosecond, in a comforting, brotherly way, before snapping it back to the wheel again.

"I wasn't really one of them—the guys, I mean—they kept pushing me to prove myself by like getting the keys of places Ken was working on. But Dad was too wise to me for me to ever do that. Anyway, I knew I could get hold of the Cornerstone keys. And they thought it would be the perfect place to meet up and do some 'business.' I even agreed to help them get into the church and get at the sound system and computers and stuff. So I tried to trick Nate into taking me up late, so I could 'accidentally' leave the door open.

"But everything went wrong. I was kind of drunk. And high. And Nate knew it. And then Patrick showed up and Nate told me to stay outside while he went in to talk to Patrick. And then the guys showed up. And Nate ran out. And I kind of panicked and thought if I just stole Nate's car, then I could just run away and . . . I just wanted to die, Jo!" Kevin choked. "I just hated myself and my life and everything and wanted to die! And when Nate tried to stop me I just ran him down and drove off.

"I didn't get far—"

I really was crying now. I was scared. I was angry. I hated Kevin. I loved Kevin. I felt sorry for Kevin. I thought I'd never forgive Kevin. I felt like Kevin was a total, total stranger to me, and I think that's what hurt most of all.

Someone pulled out of a side road in front of us, and Nate

swerved, hard, throwing me against the seatbelt. The other driver honked. I looked behind me. Motor-Oil-Guy fished his car out around the other driver and caught up to us in a second, getting so close to our bumper I thought he was going to crash into us.

Then they hit us. The truck jolted forward violently, sending us swerving across the oncoming lane.

"Hang on!" Nate yelled, wrestling with the steering wheel and yanking us back onto our side of the road.

Panicked, I scanned the roads ahead. Not another car in sight. Where were those police? Kevin was still talking but I didn't hear him. Grabbing Lisa's hand again I started to pray harder than I'd ever prayed before. Motor-Oil-Guy rammed his car into us again. We spun. Sideways. Off the highway. Into the woods.

CHAPTER THIRTEEN

I WAS swimming through a thick fog. Sam was sitting beside me. Brushing his hand over my hair. Leaning down until his cheek touched mine. Whispering something. To God. About me. I tried to open my eyes. Tried to tell him I was all right. But the gray fog was wrapping around me again. And Sam seemed so far away . . .

I woke up, stretched, and realized I didn't know where I was. There was sun filtering through gingham curtains. I was wearing a large, gray T-shirt I didn't recognize. It was cozy. Warm. I blinked and looked around. And to my surprise I saw a picture of Sam and his sister smiling down from the wall above my bed.

I could hear voices in the other room. Gingerly I stretched my limbs again. Everything seemed to ache. I lay back for a minute and let the fragments of the last few hours filter into place . . .

Kevin talking. The truck spinning. Hitting a tree. Throwing me against the seat. Then there were sirens. Lights. People. Mandy stepping out of an ambulance in her blue and white paramedic's uniform. Me asking her if she knew where Sam was. (I winced when I remembered that. I must have been in shock to say the least.) People in uniform talking to Kevin and Nate. Kevin getting into a police car. Pastor Wallace jumping out of a different car. Lisa running toward her father. Someone wrapping a blanket around me. Shining a light in my eyes. Asking me to move. Asking me what hurt. Telling me I was going to be all right. Trying to make me drink something sweet. Trying to stand, but my legs feeling like jelly. Mandy suggesting she take me back to her house, because it was closer and didn't have three flights of stairs. Mandy driving me to her house. Kat meeting me there. Lying down. Feeling like I could sleep for a million years.

I found my muddy jeans on the back of a chair and pulled them on. Then I walked into the kitchen where Kat, Nate, Mandy, and Brian were sitting around the kitchen table. Without saying a word Kat got up, walked over to me, and wrapped her arms around me, before leading me to a seat and pushing a cup of hot chocolate into my hands.

"Did I hear Sam?" I said.

"He came over while you were sleeping," Mandy said. "He even popped into your room for . . . a while, but you were pretty dead to the world." She paused, then added, "Sleeping like that can be a normal shock reaction."

"Where's Lisa?"

"At home, with her family," Nate said.

"She's fine," Mandy added quickly. "No injuries."

I looked at Nate expectantly.

"I'm fine," he added in a low voice, "just a little stiff. Kevin's OK too."

As if on cue, Mandy, Brian, and Kat all found reasons to wander out of the kitchen, leaving me alone with Nate. I held onto the mug tightly and looked down at the brown, swirling liquid. I took a sip, but didn't really taste it.

"Did Kevin get arrested?" I asked, without looking up.

"Today?" Nate said. "No he was taken down to the police station for questioning, but they let him go about half an hour ago."

I rubbed my head. Was it only today the accident had happened? It felt like weeks had passed. I glanced over at the clock. It was just past four in the afternoon.

"Was he arrested before?" I said. "Kevin. Was he arrested before, when he . . . when he ran over you?"

Nate didn't answer right away. I glanced up.

"Was he?"

Nate nodded. "He turned himself in. He was in jail for about eight weeks. Then he went on probation. Would have been up, probably still will be up, later next week in fact."

I nodded. What Nate was saying would sink in soon enough, but for now it was just words.

"Were those guys, Josh and his friend, were they arrested today?"

Nate's expression grew dark and his forehead got all wrinkly in a worried way, although I think he tried to hide it from me.

"They were arrested, but I'm afraid they're going to be let go again, at least until the police gather more information and some evidence. The good news is that they've been in jail before though, because of Kevin. Only got out at the end of June. That should count against them.

"The police interviewed me this afternoon, and will probably ask you some more questions tomorrow."

My head was still cloudy and what Nate was telling me wasn't really making sense. "What more information do the police need to gather? What more evidence do they need? They tried to kill us! What more do the police need to know?"

Nate sighed, and leaned forward on his elbows. "At the moment there are two different versions of events, and although I'm pretty sure that all the true facts will—"

"Two versions of events! How can there be two—"

"Alan and Josh, that's their names, said they had tried to park at Bear Lake, skidded on some oil or something, and accidentally hit the back of the white truck not knowing it belonged to Kevin's dad," Nate said in monotone. "They say Kevin showed up raving like a lunatic and they were 'deeply concerned' to see him because they were aware that as part of their own probation conditions they weren't allowed to socialize with former gang members—though why that didn't stop them hanging out with each other demands asking.

"Anyway, they say they got in their car and took off, that we chased them, cut in front of them and basically forced them to hit us by cutting them off," Nate added, sounding very tired. "Now there are four of us and two of them, which should definitely count for something, so I'm not that worried. The problem is, I suspect they've been stalking and threatening Kevin, and maybe you by association, since they got out of jail in June, ever since I saw them walk in the back of the Gathering almost two months ago. They're basically angry that his testimony sent them to jail. And maybe they knew the end of his probation was coming up and they wanted to scare him into doing something to break it. I don't know."

"But I don't understand!" I protested, my brain still reeling from everything that had happened earlier that day. "Why did they torch the store? Why were they after me?"

Nate gave this funny little smile. "Sometimes the best way to scare a guy is to go after, you know, the girl he . . . loves."

Oh.

I couldn't quite meet his eye.

"In fact, one of them called Kevin on his cell phone to gloat, or scare him, or something, when they set your store on fire. In case you haven't figured it out, Kevin was the one who called Lisa and begged her to pray for you. Called me too, which is how I made it there so fast."

"He told you that?" I asked, glancing up at Nate in surprise.

This time it was Nate who looked away. He shook his head. "He didn't need to.

"Anyway," Nate went on quickly, "what you tell the police is going to be incredibly important. Because if we could prove they'd violated their restraining order, they'd probably be looking at some serious jail time, but if we can't—"

"I have pictures!" I said suddenly. "I already sent them to the police. That should be all the evidence they need!"

I think Nate nearly passed out on the table in disbelief. "You have pictures?" he said, shaking his head. "Pictures?"

"Yeah I do," I said, nodding enthusiastically. "Not good ones, they're kind of blurry, but they have time and date stamps on them, which should hopefully back up my story somewhat. They're on my cell, which Sam gave me, which is in the glove compartment of the truck, and so we'll have to get it somehow. But it's something, at least."

Nate stood up, still shaking his head, and started walking around the kitchen. "You took pictures," he said again, this odd grin spreading across his face. "You took pictures."

"Not good ones," I said again, starting to feel a little self-conscious and standing up too.

"You have pictures," Nate said again with this funny laugh. "'Course," he laughed again. "Jo, you are unbelievable! This whole thing is unbelievable!"

To my shock, he reached out, grabbed me, and gave me a bone-crushing hug.

"You have no idea how paranoid everyone was about you,"

he said, letting go and starting to pace the kitchen again. "I mean, here Patrick and Pastor Wallace and Ken helped Kevin work out this whole plea-bargain with the authorities—I'll let him tell you all that—and all this time, in the back of their heads, they knew there was this random person out there who had seen God-knew-what and called the police. They were afraid you'd ruin everything. And instead, instead, you've probably saved Kevin's life."

Now I was shocked.

"I didn't really do . . ."

"Some of Kevin's former acquaintances got pretty light jail sentences," Nate said, "and for months we've been worried that when they got out they'd start bothering Kevin, or worse. But Kevin can be so pig-headed at times! So convinced that he can solve his own problems and so bad at telling people what they need to know to be able to help him, which is how he got himself in trouble to begin with.

"Do you realize what would have happened if it hadn't been for you, Jo? These guys would have come around, and hassled Kevin, and no one would have found out until it was probably too late. But instead, they must have followed Kevin to your store that day, seen you inside with him, and decided to try and frighten you—to take it out on the girlfriend—or maybe they thought Kevin was more involved in the store, I don't know. But the bottom line is they went after you, and you saw them, and even if no one believes Kevin—everyone is going to believe you!"

Everyone was going to believe me?

Everyone . . . was going to . . . believe . . . me?

Nate looked like he was about to hug me again, and while that was mostly a good idea, I was feeling kind of fragile. But instead, he did this odd jump thing and punched the air, then smiled at me again. It was the weirdest thing. I hadn't felt like I'd done anything special, hadn't really done much of anything at all, and now here was Nate—Nate!—grinning at me like I was some kind of hero.

"You really do love Kevin, don't you?" I said, the fact kind of dawning on me as I said it.

Nate paused, and sat down again. "Yeah, I do," he said. "He's like my brother."

"But he could have killed you," I said.

"I know."

Nate was still kind of smiling, though he seemed to have come out of his maniacally happy phase, and was looking at me like he was just telling me the coffee was ready or something simple like that.

"But . . . but that doesn't make sense!" I said.

Nate shook his head. "No, it doesn't."

He stood up again, seemingly full of nervous energy, and started to pace again.

"Does it help to tell you that I used to hate Kevin?" Nate said, looking at me seriously. "Before the accident he annoyed me and I kind of pitied him. After the accident I hated him. Absolutely hated him. And felt sorry for myself . . ."

"Well you had been hit by a car," I said.

"Yeah," Nate said with a small grin, and rubbed his hand over his head. "See, that night Kevin hit me, something in him kind of snapped and he decided he was ready to turn himself in, turn himself around. And Patrick, and Pastor Wallace, and Ken of course, were all there to help him. Pastor Wallace especially, who was on holiday at the time, called in every favor he could with politicians and police officers to help give Kevin a chance. They totally closed ranks around him. Supported him. Advocated for him. Opened doors for him. Kevin turned to God, honestly threw himself totally on God to help save him. And what those men did helping him get his life straight, and find a new life in God, is nothing short of miraculous. As I'm sure Kevin will tell you.

"But I felt betrayed. I mean, they said they were all there for me, but I felt like they were just using me, because they needed me to not press things in order to make things go smooth. I was the one wronged, Kevin was the criminal. But they rolled out the red carpet for him and just expected me to cope with it."

Nate rubbed his hand over his head again. "OK, that's not completely true. They did do a lot to support me, and to be fair it was my stubborn decision to not let anyone know about the accident. Made me feel more like a martyr. Then of course, by the time I realized what a stupid decision I'd made it felt like it was way too late for me to go back and change it.

"But I was angry, Jo. Because for the first time in my life I was face to face with one of the most awesome, important, incredible truths about God—he isn't fair, Jo. God is not fair. Kevin was a jerk, and God loved him. And I was angry, and resentful, and refusing to forgive, and God loved me too. And sometimes God puts us through a little bit of hell, to help us find a deeper side to his heaven."

Nate paused again, like he was hearing the story for the first time too. Then I realized, this was probably the first chance he'd had to talk about it.

"Thank you, Jo," he said suddenly, reaching for my hand and giving it a little squeeze before letting it go again. "You prayed for me, when I got hit, didn't you?" I nodded. "I felt so alone. So completely and totally alone. And to know that God appointed someone to stand there, see what happened to me, and then pray for me. That matters. A lot."

I wasn't sure what to say to that either, so instead I asked, "What happened with Kevin?"

"What do you mean?" Nate asked.

"Well, you don't hate him anymore, right? So what happened?"

"Kevin started coming to church things, and he honestly seemed desperate to make things right between us. And it was really hard for me to forgive him. And I prayed a lot. A lot! And slowly God changed my heart," Nate said. "It took a while, but I can honestly say that I really do love the guy. He is like a brother. He is probably the best friend I've had in a long time, maybe ever. And that's a miracle. A total miracle. One of a whole string of miracles that seem to be following Kevin's life around at the moment."

"And you stepped in to defend him yesterday. You might have even saved his life too."

Nate smiled a little. "I guess so."

Nate looked like he was getting ready to go. But there was one more thing I needed to know. One question Nate still hadn't answered for me.

"Kevin says he's in love with me," I blurted out.

Nate stopped. "I think he probably is."

"Do you think I should go out with him?" I asked.

"Do you?" Nate said. I kind of shrugged.

Nate walked over to where I was standing, and looked me straight in the eye. "When Kevin gave his life to God he became a new creature, a new creation. You know what that means? The old Kevin is gone. And neither you, nor me, need to treat him like the person he was before. Kevin really is a great guy, still kind of damaged, but a great guy. And he cares about you, and I think he'd treat you really well. And if he didn't I'd knock some sense into him.

"But this isn't about Kevin, Jo," Nate said. "It's about you. It's about you having the courage to know that you're never going to accept anything less than God's best for your life—whether you get to find that person right away, or whether you have to wait around a bit."

I bit my lip. I wasn't sure what I thought about that, and to be honest, I was still really, really afraid of ending up alone.

"Look, Jo," Nate said gently. "Sometimes God doesn't give you that thing you most long for, and sometimes he even takes your dreams away. But God never, never asks you to settle for second best. You see these trees?" He pointed out the window at the towering maples. "God's love for you will last even after they're gone. See the sky? God's love is infinitely higher than that. We may not know why God gives us what he gives us, or takes what he takes, but you can know, with 100 percent certainty, that whatever God has planned for your life will be so much more than you could dream or imagine. You can count on that."

§ § §

After Nate left, I asked Kat to take me home. I hugged Mandy about six times and told her I really appreciated everything she had done for me. But I wanted to have dinner in my own home, have a long soak in my own tub, and curl up in my own bed. Mandy gave me a sisterly kiss on the top of my head and asked me to call her later and tell her how I was feeling. I promised her I would and joined Kat at her Jeep.

When I got home there were three messages from Sam on the answering machine, but I didn't call him back. Sam called again while I was in the bath, but Kat was out getting us pizza so it just rang through to the machine again, while I lay back in the bath and listened to Sam's voice echoing down the hall. Call me—that was all he was asking. "Hi Jo. It's me, Sam. I hope you're OK. Call me when you get this." But I just couldn't.

Even though it was almost seven by this point, I put on a pair of fresh jeans and a sweatshirt before heading back downstairs. Normally, on a night like this, I would have changed straight into something comfortable and pajamalike. But I wasn't ready to wind down. Not yet.

The doorbell rang, and I went down to answer it. I opened the door to see a huge bouquet of pink and white roses, and it was such a magnificent display it took me a few seconds to realize that Kevin was standing behind them. I gave him a wan smile and took the flowers. He followed me into the living room.

So what happened between Kevin and I that night? Well, he told me he loved me, he told me he wanted me, he told me that he had never stopped being in love with me all the time we were apart and that he even hoped we had a future together. He cried. He swore that he'd always be 100 percent honest with me about everything from then on. He begged me to forgive him, and I told him I did.

I told Kevin that I did love him and I thought he was incredible looking, and that maybe at some point, when I was younger, that would have been enough for me.

"But I'm in love with someone else, Kevin. I'm sorry, but I am. And maybe I can't be with him, and maybe I'm not meant to be with him. But I can't be with you and be in love with him. It's not fair to you. And it's not right.

"And no, this isn't because of your past," I said earnestly, grabbing both of Kevin's hands in mine. "This isn't because of Nate, or jail, or your father, or the fact you used to drink or use drugs. And maybe you don't believe me about that right now. But I pray that you will one day. Because I think you are an incredible, strong, brave person. Not a perfect person—but an amazing one.

And I don't want you to think that the fact I can't be with you, won't be with you, doesn't mean I don't really like you. Because I do."

Kat came in with pizza. She set it down on the table, took a few pieces, and headed upstairs to her office. Kevin and I sat side by side and munched a bit. It was a weird, awkward silence, but in a way, it was a good and comfortable one too. I'd said what I needed to say, and there was something freeing in that.

"Finish the story for me, Kev," I said, "the story you started to tell me in the truck. You'd hit Nate with the car, you drove off. What made you turn around?"

Kevin smiled a little. "It's kind of funny."

"I'd like to hear it."

"OK," Kevin said.

"Basically I was running. I thought I'd killed Nate. I knew I'd totally blown things with my so-called 'friends,' not that I cared about them anyway. And I was a little high and more than a little drunk and that wasn't helping me either. All I wanted was to get as far away as fast as I could. Basically, I thought my life was over. I thought I'd gone beyond anyone's help.

"I didn't know where I was going. I was literally just driving down the highway with one hand and rummaging in Nate's glove compartment with the other, in case there was any money or anything I could use. A bunch of stuff fell out, including his Bible and cell phone, and for some reason I found seeing his Bible there really distracting. And I started arguing with it—like almost yelling at this book lying there beside me—saying 'God, if you're there—prove it! If you love me then do something to show me you're real! Send me a freakin' sign!'

"And then Nate's cell started to buzz. I'm serious—it actually started buzzing. And I picked it up and there was this ludicrous text message that literally said 'sign' at the top. Capital S, capital I, space, capital G, capital N. And it totally freaked me out."

"What on earth did it say?"

"It said, 'SI GN. Hey. Got your message. Try Romans 8:38–39.'"

"How on earth . . . ?"

"Have you met Si?" Kevin said, chuckling a little to himself.

"Graeme-Nuttal something?" I said. "Yeah, he's Sam's room-mate now."

"Yeah," Kevin said, grinning, "Si G.N. Nate had texted him earlier about some Bible study thing. But of course I didn't know that. In my altered state I thought this was a direct message to me from God, and maybe in a weird way it was, and so I pulled over and looked it up. You know, it's the verse that goes 'neither death nor life, neither angels nor demons, neither the present nor the future—'"

"'. . . nor anything else in all creation, will be able to separate us from the love of God that is in Christ Jesus our Lord,'" I finished. "Yeah, I know it."

"Yeah, well, my dad called on Nate's phone while I was reading it, and he told me that he loved me, and that Nate was fine, and that he wanted me to come home. And so I went. This leather bookmark had fallen out of the Bible while I was reading it, and I sort of took it with me. Not sure why, I guess I just needed to hold onto something solid to help me through it. Later Nate told me I could keep it." He held up his wrist and twisted the ends of the leather strap that encircled his wrist. "To help me, you know, remember that God had never given up on me."

Kevin told me about what it was like for him to see Nate in the hospital, and how terrifying it was to spend time in jail and then to talk to the police about his former friends and everything they'd been into together. Then watching the whole gang get sent to jail, and his former friends threatening to kill him when they got out. And I just sat there struggling to wrap my head around it all. It all sounded so hellish, and I couldn't believe he'd been brave enough to go through with it. But when I tried to tell him that, he just blew me off.

"I wasn't brave," Kevin practically spat out, "I was a coward—and I know it."

Kevin was quiet for a long moment, and then he said. "You want to know what the worst part of it all is? I have to live the rest of my life knowing that I was so self-centered, and so stupid, that I nearly killed Nate. And just when I was beginning to make peace with myself over that, now I have to live with the fact I nearly got you killed as well."

"No, Kevin," I protested, shaking my head, "you didn't—"

But he cut me off. "Yes I did, Jo," he said, pained. "You tried to tell me that Alan and Josh had been watching you. You practically begged me to listen to you and I wouldn't. I didn't want to listen. I didn't want to believe you. And then when Alan called that night and taunted me that he was torching your place—I just panicked, Jo.

"I did all the wrong things. I didn't call 911. I called Lisa and then hung up on her. And then I called Nate and made up this stupid lie about how I'd found out. And even though I ran over there as fast as I could, I took off again when the police showed up in case you saw them try to question me . . ."

Kevin was babbling so fast now he was practically gulping down air.

"I'm so sorry, Jo. You're such a sweet and truthful person, and I know you'd have never lied to me, and that made me feel like even more of a jerk for not being totally upfront—"

OK. This had to stop.

"Kevin," I said, practically clamping one hand over his mouth to get him to hear me, "Kevin! I saw you run over Nate with the car."

His eyes opened wide in disbelief.

"I was the one who called the police," I went on. "It was me. Of course I didn't know it was you. But I've known all along that someone ran over Nate . . ."

Gently he pushed my hand away.

"You never told me," he said quietly.

I shook my head.

"Did you tell Sam?"

I nodded.

Kevin looked down. "Oh."

"Nate knows too," I said gently. "I told him a while ago."

That seemed to take some of the wind out of Kevin's sails— OK, a lot of wind out of his sails. But he sat and listened as I told him how I'd seen the accident through Kat's binoculars, and had been confused about how he didn't seem to know anything about it. Nate had already told him about my little bit of camera espionage—though for some reason Kevin didn't think it was as funny as Nate had—and we talked about what the police had said to him and all the steps he thought would happen next: police interviews, a trial, maybe a new restraining order, stuff like that.

"Nate says your probation is up soon," I said.

"Yeah, two weeks Friday."

"We should have a party," I said, "get together with Nate and Lisa and Patrick, and anyone else you want, and go somewhere special."

"Seriously?" Kevin said. "You'd do that?"

"Seriously," I said. "Definitely."

I gave Kevin a long hug goodbye at the door, feeling the rough suede of his jacket up against my cheek one last time. And for one weird little moment, it was like we were locked in time. Not a couple anymore. But not "just friends" either. And I knew that no matter what Kevin was going to be to me in the future, that what we'd had, even though it had barely lasted that long at all, was actually incredibly special.

In a weird way, it was like our first real date all over again. Only better. Because this time I wasn't afraid, or uncertain, or caught up in a huge wave of emotions that threatened to take over. Because this time, for once, I kind of was starting to know what I wanted for my future. And I knew what part I wanted Kevin to play.

"I love you," Kevin whispered.

"I know," I said, pulling back and looking up into his fathomless blue eyes. "I love you too," I said. "Not in the way you want me to. But I do care about you, and I do think you're wonderful. And I know that there is some girl out there who will think you are the most incredible man in the world, and love you more than I ever could."

Kevin, to his credit, had gone into strong-man role now, smiling bravely and reassuring me that everything was going to be great, and that he really appreciated my friendship, and that he'd see me Sunday. And he smiled at me, and squared his shoulders, and walked out my door with a spring in his step and his head held high. And I knew we were going to be all right, and that in some way we'd make a friendship work. But I did watch him out the window, and as he turned the corner, I saw his shoulders slump and his head fall like someone had pulled a cork out of his back and let all the air out. And I prayed that God would help Kevin find a girl who would love him forever very, very soon.

After Kevin left, I decided to go for a walk. It was getting close to ten at night now, but I wasn't tired in the slightest. OK, that's not strictly true—I was actually exhausted! But I wasn't sleepy. It was more like that kind of fatigue you get at the end of a really good run. And I knew what I needed to do now. I just prayed that God was going to help me do it.

§ § §

I ended up at the beach. Deep, black water rolled gently back and forth along the long, dark stretch of sand, lit golden at the edges by little dots of lamplight. He was standing at the end of the pier. A lone silhouette, gray against the purple sky. I took a deep breath and walked out toward him.

"I didn't want to go back home until I'd had a chance to talk to you," Sam said. "But when you didn't answer my call, I decided that I'd just head down here and hope that, if you wanted to, you'd know where to find me." He was wearing his old, faded leather jacket, with the collar turned up against the wind. It was the first time we'd been alone in so long, and part of me was just aching to throw my arms around him. But instead I hung back against the railing.

"I've been talking to Kevin," Sam said.

"Me too."

"He's in love with you."

"I'm not in love with him."

"Oh."

Sam looked down at his feet. "I thought I saw you in the back of the hall this morning. I . . . I'm sorry that you had to hear it that way. I wanted to tell you myself, Jo. That's not how I wanted you to find out.

"But, I got your note," he added, to my embarrassment holding up the piece of bright pink paper with my scribbles on it.

I blushed. "That was kind of a rough draft."

"I loved it though," Sam said grinning. "So, despite all my best attempts, God finally broke his way in, eh?"

I smiled, "Yeah, but I hear he got to you too."

Sam gave a little laugh and looked down at his shoes. "Yeah," he said, "turns out God loves me after all. Who knew?"

We both smiled at each other for a moment.

Then, looking embarrassed, Sam looked down at his feet. He ran his fingers slowly through his hair, letting it fall back over his eyes.

"I . . . I wished you hadn't heard that other part, about, you know . . ."

"That's OK," I said quickly, "Traci told me."

"Traci?" Sam said, looking slightly disappointed at the thought. "I shouldn't have said anything to her and now . . ."

"It's OK, Sam," I said, stepping forward and putting my hand on his arm. "I mean, I was kind of shocked at first, I'll admit. I never expected you and Traci would be getting back together, but now that—"

"What?" Sam interjected, looking baffled. "Who said Traci and I were getting back together?"

"Traci did," I said innocently. "She said you guys were really serious, and you'd brought her roses and chocolate and . . ."

Then Sam started to laugh. I mean actually laugh at me!

"What the heck is so funny?" I demanded.

"Traci and I aren't going out," Sam said, still chuckling, "and I certainly never gave her chocolate. I haven't spoken to that girl once—not once—since that night you told me off about it."

"Then why would she tell me you were in love?" I shot back, still not quite ready to back down.

"Because she hates you," Sam wiped his eyes, "she knows I like you, so she hates you and was just trying to upset you."

Sam was still laughing a bit under his breath, but as for me, I was having one of those heart-spinning, unable-to-breathe moments.

"You like me?" I said.

Sam stopped laughing. "Yeah," he said seriously, "I like you, Jo. I always have. You were the girl I was talking about in church. Not Traci. You. Surely you've got to know that by now."

I felt like my heart was going to beat its way through my chest. Sam just stood there and stared at me like he was looking straight through all my masks and seeing me for the first time and couldn't believe his eyes. I'd never had anyone look at me like that before. I'd never felt a look so intensely. I'd never known it was possible to pack so much emotion, so much passion, into just one look. And it made me shiver. It made me gasp.

Then Sam stepped forward. He slid his hand along the side of my face, brushing his fingers against my neck and burying them in my hair. Then he leaned in to kiss me, teasing my face with his breath and then brushing his lips against my cheek, my forehead, my nose, and then—

"Sam, wait." I pressed my hands against his chest, pushing him away from me.

"What?" Sam practically shouted, with a funny grin on his face. "What, Jo? What now?"

He was still smiling at me—thank goodness—with this great, manic, lopsided grin like he wasn't sure whether to just go ahead and kiss me anyway, or maybe just toss me over the side of the pier.

"Talk to me, Sam," I said. "Tell me how you feel. Tell me what's going on here."

Sam gave this little laugh. "You're not sure what's going on here?" Sam repeated, shaking his head. "I thought I was about to kiss you, but if you're too confused I can always—"

"Sam!" I pushed him in the chest again. "That's not what I mean and you know it! I just . . ." I took a deep breath. "I just . . . I need you to tell me what you're thinking. I need to know how you feel. I've just been so wrong about this kind of thing in the past and I need to know . . ." My voice trailed off to a whisper, as I saw the look in his eyes.

"You want to know what I think of you?" Sam said, taking both my hands in both of his. "You want to know what I feel about you?"

I nodded.

"I think you're awesome," Sam told me. "I think you're incredible, and unbelievable, and completely and utterly crazy. You make me laugh. You make me smile. You are so unbelievably gorgeous. You make me feel like I'm a better man than I ever thought I was. You are like no one I've ever met before."

"And . . . and you like me?" I whispered.

Sam laughed and pulled me into his arms. "No, Jo—I don't 'like' you!" he shouted. "I love you! I adore you! I think of you a hundred times a day. I miss you when you're not around. And the more time I spend with you the deeper I'm falling in love with you. And I desperately want to kiss you right now. And if you would please give me a chance I'll do my best to spend the rest of my life trying to convince you just how incredible I think you are."

"So you do like me then?"

Sam nestled his face in my hair. "Just a bit," he said.

And then Sam kissed me. Or maybe I kissed him. I'm not sure it even matters. All I know is that somehow our lips found each other and in that instant everything else in the world disappeared and all I knew was that Sam's mouth was on mine.

But, no, sorry, the earth didn't suddenly shift dramatically, my knees didn't instantly turn to jelly, and the sky didn't break into a huge rainbow above our heads either. In fact, although it was an incredibly nice kiss, it certainly wasn't the world's greatest, and it took us a few tries to really get it right.

But it was Sam. And it was me.

And for once in my life I knew I had everything I really wanted right there in front of me. And I was really, incredibly, unbelievably happy.

If you liked

If Only You Knew,

try

The Last Place I Want to Be

by P. Buchanan

Excerpt from
The Last Place I Want to Be

My Disclaimer

My name is Amy MacArthur, and let me tell you right up front: If you want one of those books about some girl who owns a horse or who lived on the prairie a long time ago, stop reading this book now. You'll hate it.

If you're standing in some bookstore, flipping through the pages, looking for some girly story that will make you feel all warm and fuzzy, put this one back on the shelf.

Do it now.

I don't write mushy storybooks. I'm a reporter. All you'll get from me are the facts. I plan to be the next Ellen Goodman, journalist *extraordinaire*. So, if you're one of those readers always on the lookout for foreshadowing and symbolism and dramatic irony, this isn't the book for you. It's just some stuff about me, reported with journalistic accuracy.

Here's the truth about me: I don't always go around making people happy and helping lost puppies. I don't smile all the time and make my parents burst with pride. I'm not perky, and I don't have a lot of friends who come over to my house to talk about boys and do each other's hair. I don't always learn an important and valuable lesson from everything that happens to me. But I'm guessing *you* probably don't either.

It might be tempting to make myself look like one of those nice, sweet, cooperative Christian girls you're used to reading about in books like this. But, in fact, I'm not a Christian girl at all until the day after this story ends—and to be honest I'm not that sweet and cooperative even now.

Anyway, this book is about how my life completely unraveled, and how it slowly got knit back together again. It all started when my dad, a notorious workaholic, decided to quit his job as manager of the Glenfield Restaway Inn and buy a bed and breakfast out on the coast of northern California.

1
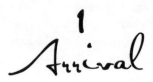
Arrival

The Saturday morning we moved away, there were no friends to see me off. The house was empty—we'd sold pretty much everything, and the movers had taken the rest. A big sign on the front lawn said our house was for sale. A smaller sign rode on top of that one; it said SOLD in uppercase red letters. None of our neighbors came to say good-bye.

Dad pulled the station wagon away from the curb, and I watched our house disappear behind us. It wasn't like in a movie. There was no sad music or tearful good-byes—and the lighting wasn't very good. We just drove away and left it all. It made my whole life up to that point seem so trivial.

⋆ ⋆ ⋆

Dear Dinah—

We've stopped at a hotel somewhere in Arizona. Everything here is Western, which I hate. Some of the guests even wear cowboy hats in the lobby. Most of them are here to see the Grand Canyon, which is only a few miles away.

I, of course, won't see the Grand Canyon. My dad only wants to hang around the hotel and talk shop with the people who run it, and then we'll sit in the car for a gazillion hours until we come to the next hotel where we have a reservation. This is my dad's idea of a vacation.

I think Dad's getting nervous about having his own B&B. After all, he bought it based on some photos and a few phone calls. What will happen if we open up our inn next May and no one comes? It would serve him right. Would they give him back his old job at the Glenfield Restaway?

Mom spends all her time sleeping. She hardly slept at all last week when we were getting ready to move, so I guess she's catching up now. If she isn't snoring in the car, she's sleeping in the hotel room until way after breakfast. I, on the other hand, haven't been getting much sleep.

I guess you can tell I'm still pretty ticked at my parents. Birch Point! Have you ever heard such a stupid name for a town? It sounds like some kind of pencil. And it's so small you have to drive fifteen miles up the coast just to find a McDonald's or Burger King. What am I going to do in a town like that? I'll wither and die. The closest newspaper office is probably all the way down in San Francisco.

Right now I know you're laying out the <u>Gazette</u>, with Miss Schwartz back at her desk grading papers. Has she read you any of the really funny sentences in the essays she's reading?

I hope it was hard to get this week's paper together without me. I hope you don't find me too easy to replace. Who would have thought I'd miss Glenfield Junior High—but I do. I hope <u>you</u> miss <u>me</u>. Do you?

—Amy

★　★　★

I woke up squinting. The sun was getting low in the sky, and it shone blindingly through the side window. I had that muddy taste in my mouth, so I must have been asleep a long while. It was our fourth day of driving.

I sat up and rearranged the sleeping bags so I could see out the window. When had we reached the ocean?

I rested my forehead against the cool glass and looked down at the rocky coast. It had been a couple of years since I'd seen the ocean, but it was hard to get too excited—I'd be looking at it every day from now on.

The road turned inland, and the ocean disappeared behind a grove of white-trunked trees. *Birches?* I leaned my head back and dozed off again.

When Mom and Dad woke me, the sun was setting.

"Almost there," Dad told me, excitedly. "We're almost home!"

Mom craned her neck to see past Dad to the ocean. "Look at that," she said. "Isn't it amazing? And it's practically our backyard now."

I looked out at the water, which glimmered golden in the sunlight. When we passed the sign on Highway 1 that said Birch Point 3 Miles, Mom cheered.

"Almost home," Dad repeated.

The sun sped along beside us as we crossed a long bridge over the mouth of a river. For a few seconds, I could see the wide, windswept cove far below and a small stretch of sandy beach along the riverbank. Would the ocean gradually become as uninteresting as the Adamses' house across the street from my bedroom window back home?

Home.

A huge sense of loss swept over me, like one of the cold waves below. I *had* no home. By now, some strangers were moving their strange furniture into my room. Maybe some other kid was right now looking down from my window on that familiar street. I'd never be in that room again.

When we got to the other side of the bridge, the ocean disappeared behind a grassy hillside, but I kept looking out the window, blinking back the tears. *I will not cry. I will not cry.*

We pulled off Highway 1 onto Front Street, directly into the setting sun. Dad, following directions someone had faxed to him, made a few turns on the narrow village streets. I watched the old buildings pass by, my arms folded. They looked shabby and cold, in need of a coat of paint and a good scrubbing. This wasn't the bustling, colorful town I dimly remembered.

"There's the Café Pelican," Mom chirped. She tapped the window as we passed the small restaurant. "Remember those great omelets?"

Like I'd remember an omelet from two years ago. All the little villages we'd visited on that summer vacation had blurred into one quaint, slightly fishy blur.

Dad parked in front of a little house with a white picket fence and a sign that read Mendocino Coast Real Estate. A light shone in a downstairs window. Grinning, Dad hopped out of the car, letting in a brief blast of cold air. He practically skipped up to the house. In a few minutes, he came out the door jingling a set of keys in front of his smiling face. He looked like he was about to break into song.

"Here goes," he said as he got back in the car. "We're almost there."

We retraced our path to the highway, crossed the bridge over Schoolhouse Creek again, and immediately pulled off onto an unmarked asphalt road.

The road listed to one side and was full of potholes, but that didn't dampen Dad's excitement. He drove slowly, and I sat in the middle of the back seat, stone-faced, arms crossed, bouncing from side to side. I was determined not to show the faintest trace of enthusiasm.

Up ahead, I saw a grove of trees. As we got closer, I glimpsed a steep, gabled roof among the treetops. This was it. I was about to see my new home. I suppressed every hint of curiosity. The road curved around the house and ended in a gravel parking lot on the far side. An ivy-covered stone wall surrounded the inn—tall enough that I could see only the house's highest windows.

Dad slowed the car, and Mom leaned across him to see the inn through his window. The gravel crunched and popped beneath our tires. Dad pulled up to the wall and shut off the engine. He sighed and leaned back in his seat, and then glanced over at Mom. She patted his knee. Dad had burned all his bridges behind him (and Mom's and mine while he was at it). Our house was sold. His old job was filled. Glenfield was a memory, and there was no road back—not even a bumpy one full of potholes.

I knew Dad would want to be the first one through the gate, so I got out of the car, pulled on my jacket, and walked across the gravel lot to look at the ocean. Now that I was closer, it didn't seem so much a cliff as a very steep hill. Down below, the waves foamed among the rocks.

I walked along the edge, past the front gate of the house, until I could see the village across the cove. Despite my homesickness and ears that ached in the cold wind, I had to admit Birch Point was beautiful—a cluster of old buildings and water towers in the golden light of sunset, and to the west the long, grassy headlands. I could see a little white church with its pointed spire, and the broad open door of the Birch Point Volunteer Fire Department. Lights were coming on in the windows and a few cars crept along Front Street toward the highway, their taillights clear as rubies. All these lights reflected in glimmering fingers across the water of the cove.

"Come on, Amy," Dad shouted. "It's freezing out here."

I meandered back to where Mom and Dad were waiting for me outside the gate, my cold hands dug deep in the pockets of my jacket. Time for our grand entrance.

The ivy on the walls was overgrown, and the tall iron gate tilted on its one remaining hinge. When Dad tried to push the gate open, it came off the hinge entirely and toppled with a heavy thud (I felt it through the soles of my shoes) onto the tall grass at the side of the path. I managed not to laugh.

Dad couldn't hide the look of alarm on his face. He'd bought this house based on a set of photographs and the inspector's reports, and now he was wondering if he'd been rash. He looked down at the gate, which had all but disappeared in the tall, wild grass. "It doesn't matter," he said. "I thought we'd tear down the wall anyway, so we'd have a better view of the ocean."

I followed Mom through the gap in the stone wall where the gate should have been. The house was three stories tall—Victorian with a broad front porch, four mismatched gables, and a round corner tower that had a cone roof and weathervane. The house needed a thorough painting, and the garden was a riot of weeds. I followed Mom and Dad up the brick path.

Dad climbed the steps to the wide front porch and patted one of the wood pillars. He looked up at the planks of the porch ceiling. Curling strips of paint exposed the gray wood beneath. "Those photos," I said. "How *old* were they?"

Dad looked pale and shaken now, but he was trying his best to hide it from Mom and me. I felt an unexpected pang of sympathy for him.

"We'll get this place fixed up in no time," Dad said with unsteady optimism. "We'll be ready to open in May. You'll see." He didn't look at either of us as he spoke. I wondered who he was trying to convince.

Dad pushed the front door open slowly, as if expecting bats to fly out. "The electricity and phone should be switched on already," he said, though neither Mom nor I had asked.

I followed the two of them into the house. Dad found a light switch in the dim hallway and flipped it up and down. "Maybe the bulb's just burned out," he said.

But the bulb wasn't the problem. None of the downstairs switches worked. There was no electricity.

Dad and Mom made their way down the gloomy front hallway, opening doors and trying switches as they went. I went through an entryway on my right into a large front room with a fireplace and two bay windows that let in enough evening light for me to see where I was going. Odd-shaped furniture loomed like angular ghosts beneath white sheets. Old oil paintings hung askew on their nails. The windows were streaked with dust. Everything smelled musty.

I passed through a wide threshold into the next room. Even larger than the last, this one ran down the side of the house. I recognized it as the dining room from one of the photos Dad had shown me when he broke the news that we were moving. The chairs all rested upside-down on the tabletops, with hammocks of spider webs sagging between the legs. The shades were pulled and it was too dark to see the wood paneling. The corner fireplace was just a black rectangular hole.

The next room was at the back corner of the house, through a pair of swinging steel doors—a kitchen larger than our two-car garage back home. There were a lot of stainless steel cupboards and counters, several sinks, and a huge island in the middle with an iron rack hanging above it for pots and pans. A round table was wedged in the corner—it looked like it had been dragged in from the dining room. Dad had been put in touch with a popular local chef who had moved from Birch Point down to San Francisco two years ago and was anxious to come back. This would be his new domain.

I noticed a phone hanging on the wall by the far door. I picked up the receiver and held it to my ear. When I heard the dial tone, I hung up. On the other side of the closed door, Mom and Dad were talking.

I pushed the door open and stuck my head into the other room—an office. Dad sat behind the desk, and Mom held back the curtains, looking out the window at the back of the house. "There's a phone in the kitchen here," I said. "It works."

While Dad called the electric company, I explored the rest of the house. There was just enough light to navigate the narrow hallways. The inn was old and run-down, but I had to admit it was intriguing. I found a couple of guest rooms on the ground floor, along with a pair of restrooms. It seemed strange to think that we now lived in a house that had a men's room and a ladies' room—complete with soap dispensers and hand dryers.

I climbed the staircase to the second floor. This was where most of the guests would stay. I passed down the long hallway, pushing open doors and looking in on rooms filled with stripped four-poster beds and more sheet-covered furniture. The ceiling corners were draped with cobwebs.

The third floor was where our family would live. It seemed smaller than the second floor, but it was a lot bigger than our upstairs back home. This, I decided, would be a good time to stake a claim on one of the four bedrooms. I left the largest bedroom at the back of the house for Mom and Dad. It had a small, built-in bathroom, two closets, and a fireplace— I knew I had no chance of getting that one.

The room I chose was smaller, but it had a little round sitting room in one corner, under the cone roof I had seen from outside. I peeked under the dusty sheets at a nightstand, a dresser, and an old rocking chair. I sat on the bed, and the springs groaned beneath me.

In the round room, I wiped away a small oval of dust from each window with my jacket sleeve. Through one oval, I could see the last glimmer of sunlight disappearing beneath the far rim of the ocean; through the other ovals, I could see the lights of Birch Point. On a dark finger of rock in the distance, out beyond the town, a sudden flash of light caught my eye, a lighthouse beacon slowly turning.

When I got back down to the first floor, the house was dark, and it took me a while to feel my way through the front room and back to the dining room.

Mom had lit a fire in the corner fireplace. She'd found some candles in a kitchen cupboard and placed them around the room so everything looked warm and cheery—almost as good as in the photo Dad had shown me. I pulled a chair off one of the tables (one of the few chairs that was spiderweb free) and set it in front of the fire, next to the bench Mom sat on. I leaned in toward the crackling flames.

Dad was on the phone in the kitchen, yelling at someone at the electric company. I was glad he was taking his frustrations out on whoever was on the other end of the phone, and not on me or Mom, like he sometimes did. When he finally came in from the kitchen, he looked worn and angry. "They'll be here first thing in the morning," he said. "But there's nothing they can do tonight. Should we go into town and find a hotel?"

Mom patted the bench beside her. "We're *in* a hotel," she reminded him. "We've got everything we need right here. It's just for one night."

Dad sighed and sat down next to her on the bench. She took his hand. In the firelight, he looked suddenly older. He stared silently into the flames.

"What are we going to do about dinner?" Dad said at last. "There's nothing here." I felt sorry for him. It was like he'd climbed out on a limb chasing the dream of owning his own hotel, and now he'd looked down and realized how far above the ground he was.

"We've got a phone," I pointed out. "Let's call for pizza."

"You think there's a place here that delivers pizza?" Dad asked. "This is a pretty small town."

That really hit me: Could we really be in a town so cut off from civilization that we couldn't get a pizza delivered to our door?

I stood up. "There's one way to find out," I said. I found the phone book on the kitchen counter where Dad had left it. I took it out to the dining room, set it on one of the tables, and flipped through it by candlelight.

Dad sat staring into the fire, his elbows on his knees, his face in his hands. Mom put her arm around him. "A roaring fire and candlelight," Mom said. "I'll bet this is what it was like for the original owners." It was clear she was trying to get Dad's mind off his worries. "Maybe this will help us appreciate the history of this wonderful house."

"Except they probably wouldn't be looking through a phone book for pizza," I pointed out. Someone had to keep their feet on the ground.

Mom laughed. Dad didn't.

"Here's one," I said. "Mama Frantoni's Italian Restaurant. They're right in town. It says they deliver."

I had just come out of the ladies' room in the hallway, carrying a candle, when I heard a knock on the door. When I opened it, the wind nearly blew out the candle. On the porch stood a girl about my age with long, curly, brunette hair. She was holding a pizza box and seemed pleased to see me.

"There *is* someone here," she said. "We weren't sure if it was a joke—and then I got out here and there were no lights. If I hadn't seen the car, I would have turned around and left."

"We just moved in," I told her. "There's no electricity. Come on in out of the wind."

The girl stepped into the hallway. I looked out the door and saw, through the gap in the stone wall, the dim shape of her car parked on the gravel. I closed the door. The girl brushed the hair from her face with one hand.

"Mom," I yelled into the other room. "Pizza's here. Who's paying?" There was an awkward silence while the delivery girl and I waited for Mom to find her checkbook. The candle dimly lit the hallway around us.

"Mama Frantoni said maybe it was a ghost calling for pizza," the girl said to break the silence. "She didn't want me to come out here on my own. But in the off-season money gets pretty tight; I didn't want her to miss a paying customer."

"I'm Amy MacArthur," I told her. I held out my hand.

She balanced the pizza box on one arm so we could shake hands. "I'm Billie Doyle."

"Billie Doyle," I repeated. "So Mama Frantoni isn't really your mama?" It was supposed to be a joke.

Billie smiled. "That's just what everyone calls her," she said. "But she *is* the closest thing to a mama I've ever had. My mom died when I was a baby."

As if on cue, Mom came out of the dining room with her checkbook and her own candle, and I felt suddenly awkward. Having my mom there made me feel like we were eating pizza in front of someone who might be starving, but Billie didn't seem to notice. I suppose she couldn't spend her life feeling deprived every time she saw someone else's mother.

Mom filled out the check, leaning on a sheet-covered table in the entryway, and Billie handed me the pizza. "Well, I'll probably be seeing you around," Billie told me when Mom disappeared into the dining room again.

"Did she remember the tip?" I whispered. This was the first girl I'd met here, and I wanted to make sure I got off on the right foot.

Billie looked down at the check and smiled again. "A good one," she said.

I opened the door for Billie and cupped my hand in front of the candle flame to keep it from going out. I watched her go down the porch steps to the front path. "It was nice meeting you," I shouted over the sound of the wind and waves.

"Welcome to Birch Point," she called back to me. "Or Birch *Pointless*, as we call it in the off season." She stepped through the gap in the wall and disappeared into the darkness.

Mom bowed her head in a silent prayer before she took her slice of pizza over near the fire. It was something she did at every meal, although neither Dad nor I joined her. It was like Sunday mornings when, lying awake in bed, I'd hear her drive off to church on her own, and I'd know that Dad and I were alone in the house for the next hour.

Mom had been going to church for a couple of years now, and she sometimes asked me to come along; but Sundays were my only day to lounge around in bed—and then there were all those Sunday morning news shows I needed to keep track of if I wanted to become a real journalist. I'd still be in my pajamas when Mom's car pulled back into the driveway at lunchtime.

✦ ✦ ✦

Dear Dinah—

We're here. We arrived on Tuesday night and found the electricity switched off, so we had to spend our first night using candles to find our way around. It was very—I'm not sure what word to use—suspenseful, maybe? Romantic?

The house is very run-down, especially in the cold light of day, but it's huge, and I think we can make it into a decent hotel. Since it's out on a point, it has views of the ocean from almost all the windows. I can look up from writing this letter in my little round office—yes, I have an office!—and see the ocean, and a lighthouse, and the village of Birch Point across the cove.

I guess as long as your back is to the inn, everything looks great!

I don't think Dad realized how much work this place would need before it was presentable. We spent the past several days dusting and cleaning and straightening things up. Dad went into town on Friday, trying to get the word out that he was hiring, but I don't think he had much luck. Today is Sunday, and everything is closed, so we pretty much just stayed home.

Tomorrow, we'll go out to the high school to get me registered. If all goes well, I'll start classes on Tuesday. Just think: I'll be a high schooler here!

How are things back home? I really miss you. I miss everything about Glenfield. Make sure you let me know everything that happens back there.

—Amy